Counter Ops

Book 2

A New Adult Dystopian Novel
by Jessica Scurlock

Cover design by Martin Scurlock
Edited by Emma O'Connell
First Edition
ISBN: 978-1-7348368-2-0 (hardback)
ISBN: 978-1-7348368-1-3 (paperback)
Printed in the United States of America
Visit my website at jessicascurlockbooks.com
Instagram: @jess_scurlockauthor

For my husband, Martin. Without you, I would have never had the courage to follow my dream.

To learn more about human trafficking and modern-day
slavery, visit www.hopeforjustice.org

National Human Trafficking Hotline:
1(888)373-7888

1. Affirmation

Nixon

"You know this is procedure," Piper says, pressing her palms against the scuffed wooden table.

Her skin is stretched taut over her already-prominent cheekbones, and her hands are skeletal. Whatever happened to our parents has obviously taken a toll on her, and worrying about me further must have contributed to her neglecting her health.

When I tried asking about Adam and Lacey, she couldn't provide a solid answer. After their house was ambushed, she was questioned by a detective and claimed she wasn't aware of their involvement with any resistance groups. Since then, she hasn't been allowed back to that house, and no one else has spoken of them.

With Adam being a well-respected doctor in the Northern Unity, there's a chance he and Lacey are out there somewhere, alive. I know the Black Hats tore their house apart after capturing me and Ivy, but I'm clinging to that tiny shred of hope that my adoptive parents were somehow able to get out unharmed. I refuse to accept—or even acknowledge—the other possibility.

"I know," I say, shifting in my chair. "But God, I hate reliving it. It was bad enough when I was actually there, and now it's all anyone wants to talk about."

We're in a safehouse in a rural northwestern city in the Green Zone. I'm supposed to stay here until the Commander figures out what to do with me. In the meantime, my second-in-command will be overseeing all tasks and missions I approve while I sit here and wait.

The majority of my members came to visit after I was saved from my execution this morning, and I've been told more will come over the course of the next few days. Overall, they seemed happy to see me and I was just as happy to see them, but there was an underlying tension—subtle but still there. Before any of them started asking me questions, I knew what they were all thinking, and the high from outrunning death and being reunited with my group quickly faded.

They're thinking the way I taught them to; I can't blame them for that. If I were in their position—if my leader had been captured and tortured and interrogated for over a month—I'd be cautious as well.

"They're worried about you, Nixon." Piper turns her head, exposing the bottom line of the tiny resistance tattoo behind her ear. "*I'm worried about you. Not just as another leader but as your sister.*"

It's well past curfew, and she'll be staying here with me tonight before heading back to the Blue Zone tomorrow.

I roll my eyes. "There's nothing to worry about. I've already answered your questions, and Eli can confirm what I've told you."

She pulls the chair out beside me, sits down, and brings one leg up, resting her chin on her knee. The action reminds me of when we lived together in the Blue Zone. We'd stay up late, sitting outside or at the kitchen table, and talk for hours after our parents went to bed. Any time Piper was about to admit to something or bring up a subject that was difficult for either of us, she'd sit that exact same way. I picked up on it a year after I moved in, when she admitted to me that she'd been secretly seeing a girl in our dad's resistance group.

"I'm not talking about what you did or didn't tell them," she says, gathering her long black hair in her hands and sweeping it over one shoulder. "I'm talking about *you*. Are you okay?" Her dark eyes are full of concern and pity, momentarily flitting to the gash across the heel of my palm where I was cut free from the stake.

I turn my face away from hers. I can't stand it when she looks at me like that. It's the same way she always looked at me after I lost my biological parents. It's endearing that our bond has stayed strong over the years—even after I moved zones—but right now, I don't want her viewing me as her injured little brother. I'm a leader, same as her.

"Carter said the broken ribs and fingers are already beginning to heal," I say. "As long as the lacerations are kept clean, they'll be fine, and the bruises will go away over time."

"That's not what I meant," Piper says.

Curling my fingers, I tap my knuckles against the wood and face her. "I'm fine. Nothing to worry about."

"Nixon…"

"I'm *fine*. Are we done here?"

She studies me for a moment, running her fingers through her hair. Whatever's on her mind, she's debating whether or not she should voice it. When she finally speaks, the sisterly tone is replaced with an authoritative one.

"Why did Ivy try to save you?"

"What?"

"I'm not repeating myself."

Leaning forward, I rest my head against my fist. The adrenaline from earlier has long since worn off, and all I want to do is sleep. We've already discussed that failed mission and the auction, but I know she won't let me go to bed if I don't give her something.

"Eli gave her—"

"I know what Eli did, but *why*? From what I understand, you two didn't get along very well." Her eyes take on an accusatory sharpness.

I know exactly why Ivy attempted to save me, but that's not something I'm willing to share. Piper may be my sister—in a legal sense—but she's also one of the four leaders, meaning she has direct contact with the Commander and is required to report everything to him. This isn't something he can know about.

If he knew what went on between Ivy and me, I'd lose my position for sure, maybe be kicked out of the resistance all together. Not much happened really—a couple of kisses, and we slept in the same bed twice. That's as far as it went, and it was all consensual. I made sure of that. But it could still be viewed as me trying to take advantage of her, given the state she was in at the time of her rescue.

"I don't know," I say. "To return the favor, I guess."

She laughs, sliding her leg down. "I expected you to do better than that."

"I don't know what you're—"

"Damn it, Nixon, stop!" Slamming her hand on the table, she abruptly stands, pushing the chair backward. "Eli already told me what happened before the auction."

I keep my face straight despite the panic that shoots through me. "Eli wasn't there."

"No, but he heard it from the guards who had to pull you two apart!" She walks toward the small living room, grabbing a handful of black hair at the top of her scalp. "How could you be so *stupid?*"

Propping both elbows on the table, I hold my face in my hands, wishing for just one goddamn moment of peace. "God, Piper, I'm *exhausted*. Can we not do this now? You've already asked your questions."

"No! We are doing this now, because *somebody* seems to have forgotten how to do his job!" Her shoes thump against the laminate floor, pausing beside me. I can feel her hovering over me, anticipating some sort of reaction. When I don't give her one, she lets out a frustrated sigh and drums her fingers against the table. "It's against the rules for a reason. You know how everything went to shit with Jazmine and me."

Jazmine was not only Piper's secret girlfriend, but her squad leader. As soon as Adam found out, he relieved Jazmine of her position, demoting her back to an entry-level medic, and moved Piper to a new squad. A no-contact order was implemented, and breaking that order was grounds for immediate termination.

At the time, Piper was consumed by the thought of being with Jazmine and lost sight of her job in the resistance. But her former squad leader didn't feel the same way, and I was there to pick up the pieces after reality finally set in for my sister.

"It's not the same," I say, looking up at her. She looks just like Lacey when she's angry—her nostrils flare and her wide, dark eyes turn deadly—but has a shorter temper like Adam. "Ivy's not in the resistance."

"No, but she was your mission—not to mention your second-in-command's sister, who asked you to protect her, not fuck her."

"We didn't fuck. We just…" With a sigh, I lean back, suppressing a groan as the chair rubs against the wounds on my back. Piper can think whatever she wants. No matter how much I deny it, she won't let go of this idea she already has. She's stubborn; that's a quality we both share. "What do you want me to say? That I'm sorry?"

"Just tell me why. Out of all the girls in this shithole country, why *her*? You're smarter than that. And it's not like you ever cared that much about having a relationship with anyone."

After joining the resistance at sixteen, I closed myself off from the rest of the world. Anyone who wasn't with the resistance couldn't be trusted. With my biological parents gone, I stitched together my own makeshift family from my comrades and Piper's parents, who had taken me in a couple of years prior. My bond with those around me was strong, but with every person I lost to the Society, I recoiled, becoming a shell of a person who was too afraid to get close to anyone else.

Stepping up as leader of the Green Zone three years later made my detachment worse. No longer was I side-by-side with other members; I was above them and responsible for their lives. I formed friendships with nearly all my members, but still tucked away the deepest parts of myself until I almost forgot they were there. Liam, my second-in-command, was the person I got closest to after moving from the Blue Zone, and that was only because we'd become friends before he joined the resistance. But I still hid most of myself from him, too, and his joining put a strain on our friendship.

Meeting his sister, Ivy, was never something I'd planned. I met her briefly a couple of times before all of this happened—once when Liam asked me for a ride and she was with him, and again when I went into the only flower shop that was open after the Green Zone's first raid and she happened to be working there. Then her mother sold her for the Elite Auction and the Black Hats came for her. Liam came to my house, begging for my help in getting her back, and to my surprise, the Commander approved the mission.

Twenty-four hours later, Ivy and I were stuck with each other.

"I don't know," I say. "It just happened."

Ivy didn't strike me as anything special the first time I met her. Or the second time. Or even when I left my entire group behind to rescue her from the Black Hats and lie low in the Blue Zone. But I watched her grow in our short time together. She learned to trust me and the rest of the resistance while opening her eyes to the corruption that is the Enlightened Society.

Soon, I found myself trusting her, too. I opened up to her in a way I hadn't done with anyone in a long time, and it turned into something more than I'd expected. At first I just shared small bits about myself to make her more comfortable. She was scared, and I was essentially a stranger to her. In her mind, I was the enemy, and if I wanted her to go along with the mission, I had to show her I wasn't a threat.

But… the more I opened up, the closer I felt to her. After her initial distrust, she was kind and gentle. She was eager to learn more about the resistance and me as a person. Whenever I doubted myself, even if I didn't vocalize it, she was there to comfort me and build me back up. When I spoke, she listened without judgment. She was the support I'd needed but had never been able to find in anyone else.

"So, what, you love her now?" Piper sneers.

"No," I say. "I don't know… I *care* about her—more than I should, I know, but it's not like I can help it."

She returns to her seat beside me, crossing her legs and folding her hands in her lap. I'm about to be lectured. But she doesn't launch into some rehearsed speech or criticize me any further. She just watches me, studying me as if I'm someone new, as if we haven't known each other most of our lives.

"You know it would've never worked out, right?" she finally says. Her voice has taken on an empathetic tone, but her eyes remain accusatory.

"You don't know that," I say.

Deep down, though, I do know she's right. I made a promise to Ivy that I would make things work, that we could be together after she made it to the Commander's camp outside the Northern Unity. I'm always thinking ahead, planning out my every move, but if I'm honest with myself that was one of the rare occasions where I was just hoping things would fall into place. More than anything, I wanted to be able to stay with her, which was why I convinced the Commander to allow me to escort her and Liam outside the walls—to buy a little more time with her. I told myself I'd figure it out from there.

Why does Piper care so much, anyway? She's a leader of the resistance, sure, but her relationship with Jazmine was strictly against the rules; she has no right to lecture me on what I should and shouldn't be doing. If I didn't know her as well as I do, I'd think she's hiding something. But she's my sister. I know she just wants me to be safe and not get into trouble with the Commander.

"That's not important right now," I say. "We need to focus on getting her out of there, wherever she is."

Piper shakes her head. "You know that's not possible."

"So we just let the Society win? That's what the resistance does now?"

"It's always been like this. We can't retrieve victims after they've been purchased or taken to re-education."

"We need to try!"

"The Commander won't approve of it. Even if he did, we don't know what Ivy is like now. I mean, come on, it's been over a month. You think living amongst the Elites hasn't changed her?"

"Are you suggesting she ratted us out?"

She shrugs. "I wouldn't doubt it. You told us that she threatened to turn you in multiple times."

"That was at the beginning. She was scared. She thought she was being kidnapped, but she changed."

"She spent her entire life trusting the Society. I seriously doubt the couple weeks you two spent together had that much of an impact."

Her words sting, but I refuse to accept them as truth. She only met Ivy once, when Kase, one of her rogue members, was brought to Adam and Lacey's and I was tasked with interrogating him. The interaction between her and Ivy was brief, mainly because Piper and I were bickering.

I know Ivy would never go back to how she thought before we met. Once that veil of ignorance is lifted, it's impossible to buy in to the Society's bullshit again, no matter how hard you try.

"You're wrong," I say, "and I'll prove that to you."

"Good luck with that, because we're not going after her."

"You don't have jurisdiction over my group now that I'm back. I'll put a team together. I know Liam will be more than willing to go."

She stands, tucking the chair in, and averts her eyes. "Don't march your members to their deaths just because you have a crush on this girl." She starts out of the kitchen, pausing halfway to the living room. "Eli and I haven't told anyone else, by the way, but I suggest you at least come clean to Liam."

2. Dancing With Your Ghost

Ivy

I've dreamed of him every night.

As that dreadful day grew closer, the dreams became more gruesome. Even when I'm awake, they haunt me.

Thick crowds of mindless people, cheering for his capture, demanding that his blood be spilled. Men, women, children. They're all the same—zombies blind to the truth of the Society, just as I was. Their method of murder is different every time—beheading, firing squad, hanging—but it's always the most brutal ones that take form.

I'm in the crowd, too, with tears streaming down my face as the zombies shove me toward the front. I always try to scream, to protest, but my mouth is sewn shut and my throat feels as though it's full of cement. And he's always the same: bloody, bruised, and angry. He's so angry, and although he doesn't say it, I sense his anger is directed toward me. The arms that once held me are bound behind him. Those beautiful eyes that were so warm once they thawed are frozen again, lifeless. The smile—the *real* smile I only saw a handful of times—is a permanent scowl. The warmth that once radiated from him is replaced with a frigid hatred. And when I reach the front, inches from him, I'm handed whatever weapon has been selected to take his life.

That's when I wake up, whimpering and crying and soaked in a cold sweat, wishing I were dead instead.

I dab underneath my eyes with a wad of tissues, careful not to mess up any more of my makeup. The tears came out of nowhere, smearing the mascara the maid applied just a couple of hours earlier.

Yesterday was difficult enough. I somehow managed to maintain my composure around Wyatt and his family when they returned from their trip to the Green Zone. After spending a few hours with them, they gave me permission to retire early for the evening, and everything came out as soon as I was buried under the covers. Sleep came in short fragments, interrupted by more sobs and the nightmares that had finally manifested.

Today is just as bad—worse, even. Shards of glass seem to rip into my heart, relentlessly slicing away at what's left, determined to bleed me dry. In the spotless mirror, my eyes are red and swollen. No amount of makeup can hide that.

I know the execution was broadcast, but I wasn't allowed to watch. I haven't been allowed to watch any news coverage since agreeing to comply with the Everetts, probably because they think it will send me spiraling out of control again. Wyatt and his parents attended the barbaric show, but of course, they didn't say anything about it when they got home. I'm still tempted to ask about it. I need to know what he looked like—if he was afraid, or if he wore that impenetrable mask up until his final moment. I need to know if anyone he knew was there with him—Liam, Piper, any of his members. Someone had to be. But asking those questions or anything else about him would result in a punishment. I learned that the hard way during my first couple of weeks here.

Lowering the tissue from my face, I ball it up in my hand but can't bring myself to move any more. All I can do is gaze at my ghostly reflection while millions of questions circulate in my mangled mind.

Did he think of me? Was he angry with me? Did he suffer?

Two arms circle my waist and a kiss is planted on my cheek. "How are you feeling?" Wyatt asks, tucking a strand of blonde hair behind my ear. The smell of his cologne overwhelms me, and I feel as though I'm absorbing the smell from his touch.

"I'm fine," I say, forcing a smile that I pray looks believable.

He spins me around and plants another kiss in the center of my forehead before pulling me into him, pressing my head to his chest. "I know yesterday was upsetting for you." His low voice reverberates in my skull. There's a hint of something that sounds like it should be sympathy, and I'm automatically uneasy.

I tried not to show how broken I was yesterday, but I know he heard my sobs when he silently crawled into bed beside me. He didn't offer any sort of comfort—no reassuring words or even a single touch. He just turned over and drifted off to sleep. This morning, I know I've been quiet. I hardly touched my food at breakfast.

Sinking my teeth into my bottom lip, I nod, swallowing back the fresh tears that threaten to spill over, and ready myself for whatever punishment he's prepared for me. But it doesn't come. Instead, he slides a hand up my back, making soft, circular motions. I tense beneath his touch, but I'm quick to soften my body.

Wyatt's normally cold and detached, but there are times like this where he resembles a real person. It's only a matter of time, though, before something makes him flip and the relentless monster comes out again. These moments almost make me forget about who he truly is, and temporarily snuff my ever-growing fear of him.

"Let's get out of the house," he says. "Maybe that will take your mind off things."

Pulling back slightly, I look up at him. His dark brown curls brush the edges of his jaw, and his face is freshly shaven. "Really?"

I'm rarely allowed to leave the property, and never without someone else accompanying me. Usually I'd jump at the chance to go outside—it was something I always loved back home—but with him, there's nothing enjoyable about it. He'll watch my every move, monitor who I talk to and who talks to me, and won't let me wander farther than a few feet away from him.

"Unless you'd rather stay in," he says. "But I'd at least like to take you out for lunch."

He makes it sound like I actually have a say, but I know all too well that if I turn down his offer, I'll end up paying for it one way or another.

"I'd like that," I say with another smile that comes a little easier. "Thank you."

"Change into something warm," he says. "I'll be waiting for you downstairs." He brings my hand to his mouth, and his lips brush my knuckle below the sparkling diamond engagement ring. Then he exits the bathroom, and moments later, I hear the gentle click of the bedroom door closing.

I drop the crumpled tissue that's still in my hand into the trashcan by the sink and eye the cabinet beneath it. Temptation crawls over me, urging me to inspect the materials hidden under there for the hundredth time.

I could do it now, I think, though I know it would be idiotic and I would potentially get myself killed in the process. And keeping Wyatt waiting for too long will bring out his vicious temper. Days like this don't come often, and I don't want to mess it up.

Not wasting any more time, I head into the massive bedroom and slip out of the nightgown I've stayed in all morning. My maid has already laid out an outfit for me on the bed—a ribbed, cream-colored cashmere pullover and a pair of black high-waisted jeans with four gold buttons down the center. I quickly dress myself, still not used to having someone micromanage my wardrobe and the fact that they had all of this ready for me before I even arrived.

I still shudder when I think about the file Wyatt said he read on me. Before I was brought here, he already knew almost everything about me; six weeks later, I can't say the same for him. For someone who loves to talk, mainly about himself, he hasn't told me much other than how powerful he and his family are and how much money they have to throw around.

Once I'm dressed, I slip on the pair of black velvet high-heeled boots that were placed beside the bed and exit the room. The bright, empty hallway opens up before me. It's a short walk to the curved balcony and swooping marble grand staircase. I know the mansion is full of servants at this time of day, yet it's dead silent as I descend the stairs. The resounding click of my heels against the glossy black marble is all I can hear. Afternoon light floods the circular foyer of the main level, dousing the open space with an angelic white hue.

Faint murmurs reach my ears as I descend the final few steps, and I follow them, hoping one of those voices belongs to Wyatt, or at least someone who can direct me to him. If I'm unable to find him in a timely manner, he'll accuse me of avoiding him, which will spark another violent argument.

I pass through the grand dining room—the long, black table already set, as always—and take a left through one of the arched doorways into the catering kitchen, where one of the chefs dices vegetables at the white marble island. His attention shifts to me when I enter, but only briefly.

The voices get closer as I cross through the casual dining room. A girl's high-pitched giggle cuts through the air just before I round the corner at the far end of the room and stop in the archway to the family room. With one arm propped on the mantle of the fireplace, Wyatt stands a mere foot away from a young brunette maid in a freshly ironed black dress. From her side profile, I vaguely recognize her as one of the new girls hired within the past week. She giggles again, twirling a brown curl around her dainty finger.

For a split second, I hope this new girl interests him enough to call off the wedding completely so he can marry her instead, but I immediately hate myself for thinking such a thing. This girl doesn't deserve to endure the monster that is Wyatt.

Wyatt's eyes pan to me. He winks at me with a mocking smirk, then leans in closer to the maid. With a hand on her arm, he whispers something in her ear, and she nods before exiting the room, brushing past me with her head down.

"Ready?" Wyatt asks as he approaches me. Not waiting for an answer, he places a hand on the small of my back and guides me toward the front of the house, back the way I came. We pass through the foyer and living room and pause in the back stair hall, where he opens the door to the four-car garage.

He leads me down the small staircase to the far end of the garage, where a metallic blue sports car awaits us. Opening the only door on the passenger side, he kisses my cheek, and I quickly get in and buckle my seatbelt. The door slams shut (did he do that on purpose, out of anger, or was it an accident?) and he walks around the front of the vehicle to slide behind the wheel. He opens the garage door and pushes the red button beside the steering wheel. The engine purrs to life and he backs out into the cobblestone driveway, looping around the front yard toward the iron gates at the entrance.

Crossing my legs, I keep my eyes locked on my window, resisting the urge to scrunch up against the door. The gated community glows in the afternoon sun. Front yards are speckled with busy landscapers preparing the properties for spring. I peek at Wyatt, who has both hands on the steering wheel, apparently completely relaxed. His harsh features are softer than normal and his posture is looser. Attending the execution yesterday was probably the highlight of his life, especially since he somehow knows how close I had gotten to Nixon.

I expected more from Wyatt when he came back—for him to describe every detail of how the terrorist was killed, or at the very least express how happy he is that Nixon's dead. He didn't say much, though, and he was unusually quiet and tense. When I asked if everything was okay, he just shot me a deadly glare.

I'm glad I haven't been tortured with the brutal details yet. Without knowing them, I can tell myself his death was quick and painless, though I know that's not the Enlightened Society's preferred method. Still, it doesn't change the fact that he's gone.

Another wave of tears threatens to overcome me. I swallow the lump in my throat and dig my manicured nails into my palms until the stinging is impossible to ignore. Not only am I not allowed to speak of Nixon, but I can't cry over him either. I learned that quickly. The second time Wyatt hit me was on my ninth day here, when he and his father were making arrangements for their journey to the Green Zone. Everything was still so fresh; just the mention of my old home, already knowing what was going to take place there, made me break down.

Even though I'm punished for it, I know Wyatt gets some sort of sick satisfaction from seeing me mourn the person I care about. Every time I've cried over him or Liam or my old life in general, there has always been a trace of a smile on Wyatt's lips as he repeats the same phrase I've heard over and over again: *"This is what's best for you."*

Nixon's face at the auction forces itself to the front of my mind, making it more difficult to keep the tears at bay. His pained expression and apologetic eyes consume my thoughts, along with the last thing he said to me: *"Promise me you'll be strong. No matter what happens."*

I've *tried* to stay strong through everything—Wyatt's abuse, his unwanted advances, being forced into the Society, being ripped away from everything I ever loved—but it's so damn hard. I don't know how much longer I can do this. Each day is a nightmare that I keep praying I'll wake up from.

I made the choice to cooperate with the Everetts. I chose to go along with their scheme, because I thought I could gather information useful to the resistance. But I'm not resistance material—that's been made abundantly clear. How Liam and Nixon were able to do it, I don't know, but I'm quickly nearing my breaking point.

Wyatt removes a hand from the steering wheel and rests it on my knee. I sink my nails deeper into my palms.

"Only four more days," he says with a smile in his voice. His hand slides up, stopping at the middle of my thigh. "Are you excited?"

"Of course I am," I say, turning to him. Not looking at him when he speaks to me is another thing I've been punished for a few times.

Only four more days until I'm bound to him forever, as if the tracker in my arm and receipts from my purchase weren't enough. After we're married, he'll be officially initiated into the Enlightened Society in front of his parents and the other twelve families. Wyatt will enter as a Level Ten and work his way up just as his father has, but unlike his father, who's content with his ranking, Wyatt wants to become a Level One like President Hoffman. He wants to hold complete power over the Northern Unity with the other ranking numbers alongside him, advising him in everything he does for our country. As long as he's at the very top, he'll be happy, and even happier if our future children rule after him.

Carrying on his bloodline is something he often talks about. He says it's crucial for humanity, especially since he's an only child. As soon as we're married, we're expected to start trying for a baby, which is something I'd never given any thought to. Not with him or anyone else. Children are something I've simply never wanted—but now at nineteen and as someone who will be joining the Enlightened Society, it's my duty.

Wyatt's hand inches farther up my leg, and I stop him by setting mine on top, threading our fingers together. He chuckles at my silent protest, giving my leg a squeeze but not exploring any more.

"You can't put up a fight much longer," he says.

"I know," I say. "I just want to wait."

I've used that excuse dozens of times since being moved to the main mansion. Mr. and Mrs. Everett approve of my decision, saying they're pleased Wyatt has found a woman who respects tradition. Waiting until marriage for anything remotely sexual isn't something I care about, but the white lie has worked in my favor so far. The less Wyatt's hands are on me, the better, and if everything works out the way I've planned, he'll never get what he wants.

He rolls his eyes but smiles, though I can't tell if it's genuine or not—much like the rest of him. "You're lucky my parents hold the same beliefs. Otherwise…" He squeezes my leg again, and it takes every ounce of energy not to slap him away.

"I want it to be special," I say, internally cringing. Leaning across the center console, I kiss his cheek.

The action sends a lightning bolt of guilt throughout me. This isn't the man I want to be with—to be marrying or kissing or touching—but I'm doing it to survive. I pull back, turning my face away from him, and squeeze my eyes shut, willing the tears away.

Pulling into the moderately crowded parking lot of a two-story upscale steakhouse, Wyatt wordlessly shuts off the ignition and exits the vehicle. I unbuckle my seatbelt but wait for him to come to my side and open the door. Another thing I quickly learned from living with him is to never do anything without explicit permission. Once my door is open, Wyatt pulls me out by my arm and grabs my hand as we climb the concrete stairs to the entrance.

Guests sit in the waiting area of the restaurant, not paying us any attention when we enter. The smell of various combinations of foods makes my stomach clench. Eating is the last thing I want to do right now, and I wish I'd refused to leave the house. Indistinct chatter circulates throughout the building. My head is already throbbing from my fits of sobbing last night and this morning, and this only makes it worse.

The woman at the hostess stand greets us with a warm smile, and when Wyatt gives his name she immediately grabs two menus and leads us deeper into the restaurant, skipping over everyone who's been waiting for a table. She stops at a circular booth where a server is finishing resetting the table with water glasses and cutlery. When he sees us, he removes two of the glasses and rolled-up silverware sets and steps aside for me and Wyatt to sit. The hostess sets the menus down in front of us, whispers something in the server's ear before introducing him, and disappears. Our server fills the two crystal glasses with water and begins listing off today's specials, but I'm not paying attention.

We're seated in a secluded corner of the dimly lit dining room. I scan the other guests and passing wait staff. Every time I've been allowed out in public, I've made a habit of doing this in hopes of spotting a familiar face, someone I can go to for help. As usual, no one stands out. The few guests I can see at their tables look like all the other Elites in this zone, and the employees that pass by pay us no mind, save for our server in front of us.

Forks clank against plates in between soft murmurs. I strain to pick up bits and pieces of the multiple hushed conversations, but don't make out anything valuable to me—a man talks to his colleague about an increase in sales, a woman asks her husband about their vacation this summer, and the nauseating couple closest to us constantly touch one another with virtually no space between them.

"Is that okay with you, Ivy?" Wyatt's arm wraps around my shoulders, pulling me closer to him.

"Hm?" I look from him to the server, who has a pen and small black book in hand. "Uh, yeah, sounds good."

The server smiles, making a final note, and snaps his book shut. "I'll get that started right away for you, Mr. Everett. Let me know if you need anything else."

"Everything okay?" Wyatt asks me once we're left alone. I shift in the booth beside him and his arm tightens around my shoulders. His leg is pressed against me, and he places his free hand over mine, running a thumb over the engagement ring.

"Great," I say, turning my face to him. "Thank you for bringing me out here. This is exactly what I needed." I dig my nails into my palm again, then lean in to kiss him on the cheek. At the last minute, he turns his face, mashing his lips against mine and sliding his hand up one side of my face.

My nails go deeper into my skin. The guilt and disgust are ice in my gut. I hold my breath as its chill twists throughout me until Wyatt pulls back with a seductive smile.

He gives my hand a squeeze that makes my body tense and leans back. I lean into his side, and a bolt of pain rips through my frostbitten heart.

"If you're lying to me…" he begins in a low voice.

"I'm not," I interrupt.

I can't tell him that being near him makes me angry and sick and dirty. Even though he already knows there was something between me and Nixon, I can't admit that he's the main thing I've thought about since the auction. He can't know that now, more than ever, I have a burning hatred for the Enlightened Society and every person who took part in yesterday's vile event. He may have his suspicions still, but I'm not going to confirm them.

The first time Wyatt hit me—when I defended Nixon—flashes before my eyes, and his words echo in my head. *I forgot, you're that rebel boy's whore.*

"It's still just a bit weird being in this setting, surrounded by people like… this."

"You'll get used to it," he says.

I hope I don't have to.

"Is everything ready for the wedding?" I ask, desperately wanting to steer the conversation in another direction. Mrs. Everett has done nearly all of the planning with Wyatt, only asking for my input on small things such as centerpieces and caterers. Things like the guest list, my dress, and the rehearsal dinner were never run by me.

Wyatt nods, his eyes locked on a young waitress at another table diagonal from us. "My mother has some dresses she wants you to choose from for the rehearsal dinner, and you need to prepare for your speech."

The speech I'm expected to give is something I've been trying not to think about, but with only four days until the wedding and three until the rehearsal, Wyatt and his parents continue to bother me about practicing it. Not only do I have to speak in front of a group of Elites and Society members, but I'm also required to continue my studies on the entire history of our country and government. As someone marrying into one of the thirteen families of the Enlightened Society, I need to know everything about the inner workings so I can push the same narrative and agenda to the rest of the citizens as they do.

"I'll do it as soon as we get back home," I say. I know Mrs. Everett has already drafted the speech for me, and whatever dress I choose, I won't have the final say.

The waitress leaves the table she's been at, and my attention gravitates back to the young couple, who look to be around Wyatt's age. They've been all over each other since we got here. The woman laughs, covering her mouth with her hand, and the light of the table-top lamp catches the sparkling diamonds of her engagement ring and wedding band. Her husband leans in close, whispering something in her ear while sweeping her black hair back. When he pulls away, his eyes flick to me then Wyatt, and he offers a smile and subtle wave. Wyatt responds with a nod and smile of his own.

"Who's that?" I ask.

"Nolan," Wyatt says. "He's a good friend and Level Nine member." One rank above entry level.

"What does he do?"

"He's an executive for his father's armament manufacturing company." When he turns to me, he rolls his eyes at my confusion. "They produce weapons and ammunition for the military."

"And does he participate in the auction, too?"

The woman he's with doesn't seem to have been forced into the marriage. She looks as happy and shallow as any other Elite I've seen in this zone. She laughs again—a light, carefree giggle.

Wyatt studies me, looking defensive. "Why are you asking?" The way his callous green eyes harden makes me paranoid he already knows everything, as though he can see into the depths of my mind.

I ignore the unreasonable suspicion. There's no way he knows anything—I've been careful and conscious of every word I've said over these past six weeks.

"Just curious," I say with a smile. "I've never met your friends and you don't talk much about them. I thought since I'll be your wife soon, you could let me in a little more." For extra emphasis, I slide my hand up his chest and rest my head on his shoulder.

Before Wyatt can respond, our server reappears, carrying a black tray with two plates. Keeping the same customer-service smile painted on his unblemished face, he sets our plates in front of us. "Your veal with braised asparagus, Mr. Everett, and a roasted beet and goat cheese salad for your lovely wife. Is there anything else I can get you two?"

"I think we're fine," Wyatt says. "Thank you."

Unfolding my silverware, I place the cloth napkin in my lap and take a quick bite of vinaigrette-saturated spinach as Wyatt watches me from the corner of his eye. He cuts into the veal, his leg still pressed to mine. The knife scrapes the plate, sending a chill up my spine, and again, I wonder if it's intentionally done out of anger.

We eat in silence, and I block out the sounds around us. I'm not hungry but force myself to eat. The sooner we finish, the sooner we can go back to the mansion, where I'll bury myself underneath the covers and allow the overwhelming anguish to suffocate me.

How is it fair that I'm here, living this indulgent life, while the person who risked everything to protect me was killed—slaughtered for pure amusement? I didn't choose to be here, and if it had been possible, I would've escaped already. How the hell do they truly expect me to accept all of this?

The Society knows they tore me away from everything I care about—somehow knows what I felt—feel?—for the Green Zone's *terrorist*. I was purchased as if I were an object and have been treated as such the entire time I've been here. Yet I'm supposed to follow their orders, play their games, and participate in their perverse activities as if none of that happened.

"To answer your question," Wyatt says, wiping his mouth with his napkin, "yes, Nolan takes part in the auction from time to time."

I push an almond sliver around on my plate, shoving it under a piece of oily spinach. "And what does he do with them?"

I've heard plenty of tales about the men, women, and children victimized by the Society, mostly from Wyatt or his parents or the servants, who have all insisted I'm lucky to have been chosen by this family. Anything can happen after someone's purchased, from forced marriages and domestic servitude to organ harvesting and even murder. Crime may have been nearly eradicated since the Enlightened Society took over, but that doesn't mean those dark urges completely vanished. Those with money and power just found a loophole.

Wyatt chuckles. "Whatever he wants, and soon, you'll be able to partake in the fun."

I look up from my salad. "What?"

He takes a bite of asparagus and says, "I've already signed us up for the next auction. You'll get to see what it's like from the other side."

My stomach tightens, immediately threatening to force out what I just ate.

No. I refuse.

Despite everything I know is expected of me, taking part in the auction again was never something that crossed my mind. I could never buy another human being for my own satisfaction. People aren't things we can own. No one has the right to take someone away from their friends and loved ones. No one deserves to be forced into this horrific modern-day slavery.

With a shaky hand, I stab a beet but can't bring myself to eat it. The air in the dining room suddenly feels too thick, impossible to inhale. Voices and laughter are amplified, ringing in my ears and making my head throb. The smell of mine and Wyatt's food is revolting, and his leg against mine makes my skin crawl.

I have to get away from him—away from here. But surrounded by Elites, I have nowhere to go. Everyone knows who Wyatt is and what power his family holds. If I tried to get out, someone would recognize me and return me to him, and I'd be punished.

I just need to breathe, I tell myself. Just a few minutes away from him to gather my thoughts and calm myself. That will be enough for now.

Setting my fork down, I say, "I'll be right back."

Wyatt grabs my wrist before I can move. "Where are you going?"

"I have to use the bathroom." Thankfully, my voice doesn't match the trembling of my hands.

He studies me for a moment, but lets go. "Be quick."

"I will."

I slide out of the round booth, bumping my knee against the table. Once I'm on my feet, I start toward the lit hallway at the back of the dining room, keeping a casual pace even though I'm desperate to make it there as quickly as possible. As I walk, I feel Wyatt's eyes on me, probably questioning whether he should've allowed me to leave his side. Most of the other guests pay me no mind as I maneuver around tables and busy wait staff. But Nolan does. His wife remains oblivious beside him, but his gaze locks with mine for a moment, and I can sense the same wickedness as Wyatt within him.

I avert my eyes, focusing solely on the hallway just a few feet ahead. When I push open the door to the women's restroom, I suck in a long breath, the lingering aroma of chemicals burning my nose. But at least I can breathe.

Only one of eight stalls is closed. Not completely alone like I want to be, but it's good enough. Although the claustrophobic feeling has somewhat let up in here, the thought of locking myself in a tight bathroom stall threatens to bring it back.

I walk to the row of sinks decorated with fake rose petals and simplistic bouquets and turn on the hot water. I wait for steam to rise before running it over my hands. The stinging grounds me, momentarily pulling me out of my thoughts. I pump the foamy soap from the dispenser on the wall and take my time lathering my hands, which are already turning a bright pink, before rinsing.

I mindlessly scrub, feeling the divots in my palms where my nails have left their marks. As I run my thumb over one of them, I remind myself that this is temporary. I won't be in the Red Zone forever, and even if I am, it won't be with Wyatt. This wedding will not happen.

The hinges of the closed stall squeal as it's opened, and from the mirror, I see a uniformed woman step out. She stops at the sink beside me, tossing her black apron onto the counter, and rolls up her long sleeves before turning on the water. Keeping my head down, I brace myself for any questions she may ask. If she's anything like the other citizens of this zone I've met—Elite or not—she'll rattle off all the same questions about me marrying into the Everett family and becoming a part of the Society.

But she doesn't. She doesn't even look at me. She just washes her hands and dries them off with a paper towel from the stack beside her when she's done. When she reaches over to toss it in the built-in trash can to her right, I spot something on the inside of her wrist that makes my heart race.

Three black lines.

She steps back and unbuttons her shirt, revealing a black tank top, before grabbing her apron and turning toward the door. Quickly shutting off the water, I wipe my hands on my pants and say, "Excuse me." I turn around and she freezes, barely glancing me over without a single hint of recognition. "I need your help."

"Sorry, love," she says, "I'm off the clock."

She steps forward, but I jump in front of her.

"No, wait." I look over my shoulder at the door and speak barely above a whisper when I turn back to her. "That mark on your wrist… You're part of the resistance."

Her dark eyes narrow. "I don't know what you're talking about." She tries to go around me, but I block her again and she clutches her apron close to her chest, concealing the tattoo. "Ma'am, I really need to go, so if you could please—"

"Listen, please." I swallow down the anxiety bubbling up inside of me, unsure of what I should even say to her. She's part of the resistance. She has to be. Nixon had that same tattoo and so did Eli, the Red Zone's resistance leader. Whether or not she knows who I am, that makes her someone I can trust. "My name is Olivia Clearson. I was purchased from the Elite Auction six weeks ago by Carson Everett in order to marry his son, Wyatt."

The woman's eyes click to the door behind me and she takes a step back.

I pull my left sleeve up past my elbow, revealing the scar on my inner forearm, and hold it out to her. "This is where my tracker is. Please, I need help."

She shakes her head, disbelief still in her eyes. "I'm sorry, love, but I—"

"I know Eli," I interrupt, and her focus is back on me. "I met him before the auction. I'm from the Green Zone, and I was part of a mission carried out by their leader, Nixon. His second-in-command, Liam, is my brother."

Her gaze drifts from my face to the door, then to my arm. "You said you're with the Everetts?"

I nod.

She keeps the apron pressed to her chest, but her face softens. "Can you give me a location?"

Before I can answer, the door bursts open and I jump, yanking my sleeve down and spinning around.

Wyatt. He looks from me to the woman, nostrils flaring.

"What's taking you so long?" he asks. His tone is pleasant despite the anger in those monstrous eyes.

"Nothing," I say, walking toward him. "I bumped into her and was just apologizing."

He reaches out and grabs my wrist, jerking me toward him. "You should learn to be more careful." An obvious warning coats his words, which he conceals with a smile. He looks at the woman, who hasn't moved from her spot near the sinks, and says, "I apologize if she caused you any trouble."

Wyatt drags me out of the bathroom and into the dining room. Guests look up at us as I stumble behind him, and his fingers press into my wrist. I scan the restaurant behind me for the woman, but I can't see her anywhere.

It was stupid of me to talk to her. I know better. But I need help, and she's the first person I've encountered who isn't a member of or in some way connected to the Society. Whatever discipline I receive, it's worth it if that interaction saves me from this man.

I wish I could have told that woman more, like what Wyatt does to me or the things I've learned about the Society. But she at least knows my name and who I'm with. I can only hope that's enough.

"Where are we going?" I ask once we pass our table.

"Home," Wyatt mumbles. "It's clear you haven't learned your lesson."

3. Sirens

Ivy

I pace the bedroom with my arms wrapped around my torso. Four elegant gowns lie across the white cashmere comforter, but I'm too anxious to try them on like I'm supposed to.

I've been up here for an hour now, wondering what method of punishment awaits me. Wyatt didn't speak to me once we were out of the restaurant. He drove in silence; I knew better than to say anything. When we got back here, he ordered me to go upstairs while he spoke with his father. His mother came up shortly after to bring me the dresses for the rehearsal dinner, and since then I haven't seen anyone.

I don't know what's worse—when Wyatt punishes me or when he doesn't do anything at all. At least when he lashes out, he gets it out of his system and I'm not left to fear what's coming. When he doesn't react immediately, he has more time to let that rage fester until it explodes, and I'm always on the receiving end, even if the original issue was no fault of mine. There's no doubt in my mind that something worse than a slap across the face or being locked up for days at a time is coming.

Maybe this time he'll give up on his attempts of disciplining me himself and send me to re-education. I remember being told I wasn't exempt from that. Or maybe he'll ship me back to the facility I was kept at before the auction and demand a refund or another girl. I won't be able to go back home; they'd more than likely put me through Transitional Adaptation and sign me up for the next auction. But at least then I'd be with a leader of the resistance—Eli.

Nixon told me before that Eli can't get too close to anyone taken to that facility without getting caught, but surely he could do something to get me out, like staging another diversion while some of his members slipped in.

I eye the gowns again, stopping beside the bed to run a hand over the silky pink one with the plunging neckline. Everyone I've met here—the Everetts, the servants, higher-ranking Society members—has tried to tell me how grateful I should be that I'm here, that anyone would love to have this opportunity. And maybe some people would, if this arrangement were voluntary. But I was sold to the government by my mother and auctioned off to a psychopath who only wants me as his toy. There's nothing to be grateful for. Maybe the fact that I'm not dead, but there have been plenty of times I wish I was.

For six weeks, I've begged whatever higher power that's forsaken me for a way out. Every time someone has come to the mansion, I've hoped it was a member of the resistance here to save me. But it never is. Four fully functioning resistance cells in this country, and not a single person has attempted to free me from this prison.

After the first week, I began the early stages of planning my own escape, but now that the time is fast approaching, whatever confidence I had is dissipating. I'm not sure it will even work, and if it does, I have no idea where I expect to go. It's a half-baked scheme at best and was only supposed to be a last resort. There was always a part of me that believed the resistance would come for me, especially since my brother is the Green Zone's second-in-command. A tiny shred of that hope remains after speaking with the woman at the restaurant, but with only a few days left, I don't expect anything to come from it.

Crouching beside the king-sized bed, I move two of the shoeboxes that peek out from underneath and reach into the dark space. My fingers graze nylon, and I pull out the blue drawstring backpack. I open the bag, revealing the fifteen or so loose papers inside. Five weeks' worth of planning and stealing documents, and this is all I've been able to come up with. Between now and the wedding, I should have at least one more opportunity to hunt for more information useful to the resistance—if I'm able to make it out of here, that is. I need to make my final search count.

I don't know where I even got the idea of stealing documents. If Wyatt found out, he'd be livid; I'd be lucky to only receive a new collection of bruises. Still, now the execution has taken place, I'm determined to gather as much information on the Society as possible. Nixon would probably have told me it's too dangerous, but if it can help in any way, I don't care.

There's a knock on the door, and I shove the bag back underneath the bed, sliding the boxes in front of it.

"Come in," I call as I stand up. I'm busy studying the gowns when Wyatt enters. He crosses the massive room without saying anything and stops beside me, surveying the clothing.

"Your mom thinks I should go with the pink one," I say.

He gives the dresses a disapproving look and says, "Come with me," as he takes my hand and leads me through one of the doors at the far end of the room.

The walk-in closet opens up before us, its size close to that of our bedroom. Dazzling spotlights showcase the countless articles of clothing that hang on the other side of glass doors. The curtains of the full-size window are parted, and sunlight bounces off the limestone floor. Releasing my hand, Wyatt walks along one of the walls, carefully inspecting the cases of dresses in all different colors and styles.

For what feels like the hundredth time, I take in the extensive collection of clothes and shoes, still not accustomed to the idea that this is all mine. Wyatt has a closet of his own this size, and I'm sure his parents do, too. The surrealness of it all hasn't let up. We didn't have anything like this in the Green Zone. We weren't poor, but we weren't wealthy either. The Enlightened Society keeps everyone comfortable—comfortable homes, comfortable jobs, comfortable wages—but nothing more. Anything more than that is a luxury reserved for the Elites of the Red Zone.

While Wyatt continues his search, I migrate to the window, drawn once again to the outside world. I wasn't allowed to go outside until my third week here. It's not the same, though. I'm not free like I was back home when I'd roam the streets after curfew. I'm constantly supervised, constantly followed, despite the tracker embedded beneath my skin.

"This one," Wyatt says, and I spin around. He's holding up a short black dress woven with fine metallic fibers, six large, gold buttons vertically sewn onto either side of the front.

It's not something I'd normally wear in this life or my old one, but I know not to argue, especially after this afternoon. So I walk toward him, tentatively run a finger over one of the buttons, and say, "It's perfect."

He removes the dress from the hanger and hands it to me. "Try it on."

"Here?" I ask when he doesn't make any attempt to leave. He's never seen me nude or even close to it before, though he's tried plenty of times. I've at least won those battles for my last shred of privacy.

His glare hardens and he nods.

I swallow hard, resisting the urge to squirm. "I just… you know how I feel."

"It's only four days away; it's not like it matters."

I hold his gaze, silently refusing to give in and preparing for him to lash out again. After a few moments, he rolls his eyes and turns his back to me. Seeing that it's as much privacy as I'm going to get, I quickly pull off my shirt and pants and slide into the dress. I shiver as the cold chain-link straps touch my shoulders and back. The fabric hugs my chest and hips, showing off more of my body than I'd like.

I clear my throat as a signal for him to turn around, and he guides me to the full-length gold-bordered mirror that's perched in the far corner near the window. Positioned behind me, he zips up the back of the dress and gazes at my reflection. Whether he's admiring or criticizing me, I can't tell.

Sweeping my hair to the side, he presses his lips to the side of my neck, sending an electric shock through me, and I keep my eyes on our reflection. It's like staring into the face of a stranger. I don't know who I am anymore. Maybe I never did. The past month and a half has been agonizing—a constant cycle of breaking and rebuilding. How many more of those cycles do I have to repeat before I finally feel whole again?

Another kiss at the base of my neck near my shoulder. He slides his hand up my arm, gripping my bicep and turning me to face him. "You know this is what's best for you." A crease forms between his dark brows.

"Yes," I say.

This is what's best for you.

It's been chanted countless times every day since arriving here, like a spell they've been trying to cast on me—as if I wasn't already tied to them. Since I was late to the auction and unable to attend Transitional Adaptation, though, they've had to take extra precautions to make sure I'm not *defective*, corrupted by the terrorist I spent so much time with.

"He's dead," Wyatt says, echoing my thoughts. "He died not giving a shit about you." His face remains composed but his grip tightens on my arm, and I refrain from jerking away.

"I know," I say, his words digging at the fresh wounds. My heart wrenches, and although I try to convince myself that can't be true, it doesn't soften the blow.

I honestly don't know what I believe. At first I was firm in what I thought was true and what wasn't, but the longer I've been here, the less sure I've become. Wyatt has this way of getting in my head, somehow twisting my thoughts to coincide with his version of events. Most of the time, I'm able to collect myself and pull myself out of that bottomless pit of doubt. Other times, I'm left to fall, battling conflicting thoughts. Unable to trust myself or what I thought was true.

Wyatt runs a finger along my jaw, stopping at my chin and tilting my head up so I'm looking him directly in the eye. "But *I* care about you. I *chose* you."

"I know." Mustering a smile, I lift my hand to his face and cup his cheek. The gesture, which usually relaxes his tense shoulders and coaxes out a semblance of a smile, does nothing this time. "I'm happy to be marrying you. We're going to do amazing things together."

With a smirk, he draws me in closer, and his lips brush mine. Just before it turns into a full kiss, he whispers, "What were you talking to that girl about?"

"I told you—I was apologizing for bumping—"

He grabs my face, and his other hand tightens around my arm "Don't you *dare* lie to me!"

"Wyatt, you're hurting me," I whimper.

"You know the rules," he growls.

"I'm sorry."

Squeezing my face between his fingers, he slides his other hand down to my wrist. "What did you tell her?"

I desperately search for something to say that will sound believable. My heart lodges itself in my throat and my breathing becomes shallow. His fingers tighten around my wrist, and when I don't respond, he bends it backward. Pain shoots up my arm, making my eyes water and my knees buckle.

"Answer me!" he yells over my yelps. "What the hell did you tell her?"

"Nothing!" I cry. "She just asked if I was okay—she said I looked upset. Please, stop!"

"I never want you to mention that bastard terrorist again, and if I see you shed one more tear over him, I'll make sure you regret it. Got it?" He pushes my wrist back farther, and another wave of pain radiates upward.

"Yes, yes—Wyatt, *please!*"

He lets go, shoving me backward, and draws in a deep breath. His face returns to its usual callous expression as he watches me cradle my throbbing wrist.

"Get changed. I'm taking you out tonight."

4. Crashing Down

Nixon

I can't move.

I'm lying on my back. My limbs are stiff and my eyes are glued shut while my pulse violently hammers. I try to focus on the weight of the blanket over my body, the sweat-soaked sheets sticking to my skin, the whoosh of the ceiling fan, but nothing helps.

Safehouse—I'm at the safehouse. Piper left early this morning, and Liam took her place. He should be somewhere outside my room.

Still, I can't bring myself to move, can't stop the nightmare's remnants from flashing through my head. Although it was only a dream, I felt it all as though it was happening again.

Fingers knotted in my hair, forcing my head back down before I can gasp for air. The icy water fills my nose and mouth as I involuntarily suck in a breath, burning my throat and lungs. And when I'm brought back up, more questions are yelled—faceless men demanding answers about the Green Zone's Police Chief, other members of the resistance, the hijacked plane, who I work for. I don't give them anything, and the process repeats until they tire of their game. Then I'm thrown to the floor, a boot collides with my side, and I'm left alone until a guard comes to drag me back to my cell.

I bite down on the inside of my lip until the pain pushes away the images of my captivity. Focusing on the metallic taste, and again on the blankets and fan, I'm finally able to open my eyes, blinking away the residue of sleep.

The digital clock on the nightstand tells me it's well into the afternoon, but the blackout curtains on the window across the room block nearly all the sunlight. With a deep breath that's thankfully not full of water, I force myself to move. My fingers curl first, then my toes. I focus on my breathing and heart, willing both to slow to a normal pace as I ground myself in the present, in reality. Finally getting feeling back in my arms, I raise a hand to my face and wipe away the sweat coating my forehead before sitting up.

I wince at the wounds on my back, sure some of the fresher ones have broken open again. While I was in captivity, the constant pumping of my adrenaline and anxiety kept me alert and made it easy to ignore how weak I'd become. Now, it all hits me at once. Despite having slept for sixteen hours, I'm exhausted. Drained. I've lost weight over the past six weeks, yet my body feels a hundred pounds heavier.

Reaching toward the nightstand, I click on the table lamp, squinting in the sudden light. I kick the blankets off myself and swing my legs over the side of the bed. The room tilts and I hunch forward, gripping the nightstand to steady myself. Blood rushes to my head, pulsing behind my eyes. After a few deep breaths, I move forward with slow, shaky steps, my legs wobbling under my weight.

When I open the door, two of my members on the couch look up from the notepads in their laps. In the eat-in kitchen across the small living room, Liam and one of my scouts turn around, and all four sets of eyes are on me. Everyone from Liam's squad. I knew more of my members would be coming by, but I thought I'd at least have twenty-four hours with just Liam and me. I was too tired to talk with him when he came to relieve Piper, and we have a lot to discuss.

"There's our fearless leader!" the scout, Sebastien, says with a smile. "Did we wake you?"

"Uh, no," I say, stepping into the living room. "What's going on?" I nod toward Isaiah and Jonah on the couch as I make my way to the open bathroom beside my room. I open the medicine cabinet directly by the door, grab the single bottle of ibuprofen and shake two capsules into my hand.

"Shuffling the rotation of safehouses," Isaiah, the logistics expert of this squad, says. "Lancaster is a hot zone. We also got word of a military bunker twenty miles south of here; we'll have a team of scouts out there in the next forty-eight hours."

When I exit the bathroom, Liam approaches with a bottle of water.

"Thanks," I say, taking it from him and swallowing the pills with it. "What do we know about this bunker?"

"Five miles from an army outpost," Isaiah says, checking his notes. "Allegedly used to stockpile weapons."

"And the safehouses—have we cleared everyone out of the ones in Lancaster?"

"Almost," Jonah, the medic, says. "We have a few injured members who are being cared for. I was there this morning. Most should be cleared soon, but there are a few who are… critical."

Guilt settles in my stomach. "Why critical?"

Jonah looks to his comrade beside him, then to Liam. "After yesterday's mission—"

"Jesus fucking Christ," I interrupt, dragging a hand down my face. My palm comes away streaked with blood, and the sting of my mouth confirms it's from my split lower lip. "How many did we lose?"

An unsettling silence hangs in the atmosphere, and though I know it means we lost some people, my mind tries to tell me it's not true. It can't be. Elizabeth has been the only casualty in the Green

Zone since I took over. That was enough to send me spiraling into an unrelenting abyss of anger—at the Society *and* myself—and guilt.

Guilt seems to be the only thing I feel anymore. I knew I was responsible for every single person in my group, but I never expected it to be like this. Maybe I should have. I've lost people before, but this is an entirely new level. When I took this position, I made a promise to myself that no one would lose their life. It was foolish and unrealistic, but I still stood by that. Even now, I'll sacrifice myself before anyone on my team gets hurt.

"Two," Liam says. "Maverick and Drew."

Two scouts—Squads Four and Eleven. I grip the water bottle in my hand, the crackling of the plastic echoing throughout the room. Regret crushes me, weighing on my chest and stealing my breath. I close my eyes, willing the storm of conflicting emotions to dissolve. They don't.

Two lives were lost in order to save mine. More are injured. Meanwhile, the girl I was supposed to protect has been auctioned off to some sadistic Elite in the Red Zone, and I have no idea what's happening to her.

"Why the hell would you allow two people to die?" I ask, opening my eyes.

"We tried our best," Liam says. "There were bodyguards for the Elites who attended in the crowd. We didn't account for—"

"You should have accounted for them!" I yell.

Jonah's eyes drop back to his notepad. Isaiah shifts on the couch but keeps his head up.

Seb steps into the living room. "We can't protect everyone," he says. "The mission was to save you."

"If it had been one of you tied to that stake, I would've made sure no one was killed," I fire back. My glare shifts to Liam, beside me. "And what the hell did you think you were doing, conducting a mission on your own? You were still my second-in-command; you had no right!"

"You're my leader," Liam says. "I wasn't going to let you die. And Eli and the Commander approved it."

"Everyone knew the risks," Isaiah says. "When Liam told us the plan, he gave us the chance to opt out, and no one did."

Of course no one opted out. We look after each other, no matter what—but I never wanted anyone to die for me. Maverick has a wife and six-year-old son who will never see him again, and Drew, only a few days shy of eighteen, left behind a brother and his parents. What's worse is that none of them know the work either of the men did, and we can't tell them. They'll be left to wonder why the people they love more than anything have been taken from them.

"When's the memorial?" I ask, loosening my grip on the bottle.

"We're working on that," Liam says. He leaves my side and holds out his hand for Isaiah to pass him the notepad. "Surveillance is heavy though; we may have to hold off until things cool down."

"For what it's worth," Isaiah says, "we captured one of the bodyguards. He's being monitored at a safehouse fifteen miles east."

"Has he been questioned?" I ask, crossing over to the kitchen and sitting at the same table Piper and I were at last night. Angling the chair so I can still see everyone, I slide the manila folder Liam brought toward me and mindlessly flip through the stack of papers, unable to focus enough to actually read any of them.

"Not yet. They've kept him sedated until they receive orders from you."

"Checked for trackers?"

"Yes, sir. Nothing found."

Every part of me wants to drive to that safehouse right now and make that bastard pay for what his people did to my members. But he could have valuable information, and it's already been made clear that I'm not to leave this location. Plus Liam is supposed to stay here with me, even though I know the house is being guarded around the clock.

The two of us always conduct interrogations together unless another zone is involved—then it's up to me and the other leader. This time, though, I'll have to improvise.

I turn my body completely toward the four men, resting my arm over the back of the chair. "Seb, when's your next shift at TCG?"

"Tomorrow afternoon," he says.

"You and Isaiah head out to that safehouse. Get whatever information you can out of that guy, including what family he works for and their occupations in the Society. And Liam…" He looks up from Isaiah's notes. "Any word on your sister?"

Grief flashes in his brown eyes. "No."

"Then I want to know if this family in question has acquired anyone from the most recent auction. If they have, make sure you get a name and any details surrounding the reason for purchase. Do whatever it takes to get answers."

"Yes, sir," Seb and Isaiah say—Seb using a lighthearted sarcastic tone, as usual. He claps a hand on my shoulder in passing and says, "Good to have you back. Liam isn't nearly as fun to harass."

"Yeah, yeah, I missed you, too," I say, smiling in spite of myself and brushing him off. "Go do your job."

He offers a loose, smart-ass salute before motioning for Isaiah to follow him outside. On the way out, Isaiah repeats a similar 'happy you're back' line.

"Jonah, you can head out, too," I say. "Unless you and Liam have work to do."

"I think we've covered everything," Liam says, collecting the second notepad from the medic. "He can take a look at your injuries, though."

"Piper already did," I say. Not much can be done anyway.

"If you need anything," Jonah says, standing up, "let one of us know. Not just for pain management, but your mental state, too. We can get you some medication to help you cope with everything that's happened."

"I appreciate it, but I'm fine. Just keep us updated on the wounded members. I don't want any more deaths."

"Yes, sir," he says with a nod. "Glad you're okay."

And Liam and I are left alone.

Turning toward the table, I rest my head against my fist and try forcing myself to focus on the documents in front of me. Exhaustion creeps over me once more. My eyes are unbearably heavy, and I stifle a yawn when Liam takes a seat next to me.

"How are you holding up, man?" I ask.

This is the first time I've actually been alone with him since getting here. When he showed up early this morning, I was in and out of sleep and only got up long enough to say goodbye to my sister. Just from looking at him, I can tell these past weeks have taken their toll. Worry lines have formed on his forehead and dark rings rest under his eyes. His leg subtly bounces—a nervous habit of his I've picked up on over the years—but he sits tall, shoulders back and chest out.

"I'm alright," he says. "Been trying to stay busy. Addison was able to get those documents from her father. I know she's not part of the resistance, really, but—"

"No, these are great. Thanks." I flip through a few of the pages—all documents with the current Police Chief's signature. "But how are you after what happened yesterday?"

Piper and Eli were sharing the role of the Green Zone's leader in my absence while Liam remained second-in-command, but yesterday's mission was ultimately put into action and overseen by him. Maverick's and Drew's deaths are Liam's first casualties. He may not have witnessed everything firsthand, since he was in charge of getting me away from the chaos, but it's enough to weigh on anyone.

Liam shrugs, leaning back in his chair, but I can see the pain he's masking. "I wish I could've been there with them—like, if I'd put someone else in charge of freeing you, I could've done something, or at least been with them when they…"

"It's best you didn't see anything," I say.

Liam's never had to watch someone die; I've made sure he's never been put in a position like that. Only a fraction of my members have taken someone's life. Killing is a last resort—a matter of survival—and even then, it's difficult to process. I always make sure they have the support they need when wading through the mental turmoil that follows.

"I'm sorry. We should have accounted for—"

"Don't. Like Seb said, we can't save everyone."

"But I know how much you care about everyone—and I do, too. And after Elizabeth—"

"Liam, seriously." I turn my full attention on him. Elizabeth is the last person I want to discuss right now. The first person lost under my leadership, her death hit differently from the handful of comrades I lost while in the Blue Zone. It made me question why the Commander promoted me and my ability to lead my own zone. "You did your best; that's all I ask of you. We have one of the bodyguards in custody. That's a plus."

"And you think he knows something about Ivy?"

"Or something about the auction that can tie us to her. When I was in the Red Zone, Eli said she was supposed to be marrying her buyer's son, so we know she's at least alive." Unless they changed their plans. Anything goes once a victim is in their buyer's custody.

"I tried hacking their system to get a list of the victims and buyers and was able to see their employees and schedules. But I couldn't dig any further without giving up my anonymity."

"There's no way to get around their security?"

He runs a hand over his dark beard and glances at the folder in front of me. "Not unless I was in one of their facilities and got access to the server that hosts all their files. Red's group could do that if someone had the clearance. The thing is, no one gets that close."

"And the Commander doesn't give us permission to interfere once someone's sold." I sit back, letting out a frustrated sigh. "Damn it."

Interfering could lead to most, if not all, of us getting caught—and since we're viewed as a terrorist organization, the Society wouldn't just send us to re-education. We'd all be dead. But I can't let Ivy stay there. I can't let her be forced to marry some sadistic Elite who views her as property. Maybe part of it has to do with my feelings toward her, but it's also why I joined the resistance. The whole point of our organization is to help people any way we can.

"I'll try talking to him," I say. "One way or another, we'll get her out of there. I promise you that."

5. Me, Myself, and Hyde

Ivy

"What are we doing here?" I ask when Wyatt parks the car in front of the cast stone mansion. The lights lining the walkway cut through the night, illuminating the elegant home. Past its beauty, though, there's an eerie presence to it as it looms over us atop the raised ground.

We've arrived in another gated community—a fifteen-minute drive from the Everetts' home. After the incident with Wyatt, he let me get changed and left me upstairs for three more hours. Then his mother and I went over the final details for the wedding. The entire process has been expedited for the wedding to take place ten days earlier than they had originally planned, and because of Carson Everett's Level Three ranking, no one argued. The higher-ups of the Enlightened Society always get what they want.

"You said you wanted to meet some of my friends," Wyatt says, "so here we are." He turns in his seat to face me, taking both of my hands in his. "But first some rules. No talk of the terrorists, no wandering the house unless you're accompanied by someone, and no speaking of your old life unless you're asked directly, and even then you're to keep it short. Understood?" A wedge of orangish light from outside slices diagonally across his face, punctuating the sternness of his words.

"Yes," I say.

"Good girl." The corner of his mouth that isn't shrouded in darkness twitches upward, and he brings my hand to his lips before exiting the vehicle. Circling the car, he opens my door and offers me his hand, and like every other time, I obediently take it.

Together, we stroll up the stone walkway. Our stretched shadows dance across the front of the mansion as we climb the fourteen stairs leading up to the enclosed front door. With each step, dread crawls further up my body and envelops my mind.

I didn't think my mention of Wyatt's friends would compel him to let me meet any of them, and it's not like I actually wanted to; the fewer people I meet like him, the better. That can't be the only reason we're here. Wyatt doesn't do anything unless it benefits him in some way.

I don't know what he'll gain from bringing me here. Maybe it's his way of convincing me that being part of the Society isn't that bad, by allowing me to interact with other Elites and see the lavish lifestyles they live. Or maybe he thinks if he gives in this one time to something he believes I want, it will be a distraction from what took place yesterday and I'll behave better.

Wyatt knocks on the wooden door and mutters, "Be on your best behavior," while squeezing my hand tighter, making the diamond on my ring dig into my middle finger.

The door swings open before I can respond, revealing the man from the restaurant. Nolan. His short, ash-brown hair is parted to one side, making his already-harsh features more rigid, and the grin that spreads across his face hardly does anything to soften them.

"Finally!" he says, stepping aside for us to enter. "I've been try-ing to get you over here for weeks."

"I know. I've been busy," Wyatt says, glancing at me.

"Ah, yes, your soon-to-be wife," Nolan says, shutting the front door. He leans back against it, folding his arms over his chest as his marble-gray eyes travel up and down my body, making me shiver. His grin has faded into a mocking smirk. "I've heard a lot about you, Ivy. Let's hope you don't turn out like the others."

My heart stops. The others?

Wyatt chuckles. "I have a good feeling about her." Pulling me close to his side, he squeezes his arm around my shoulders. To his friend, it may look like a gesture of endearment, but I'm familiar with the warning behind it.

I smile uncomfortably as he kisses the top of my head. There were more girls before me. What happened to them? Were they rebel-lious like me? Or did they not fit the criteria he pushed on them? If they were victims of the auction like I was, he didn't allow them to walk away freely. They would've been sent to re-education… or worse.

Wyatt's abusive, manipulative, and controlling, but would he really go as far as killing a person—or people? I never assumed he was capable of that, though I should have. Maybe a part of me has become too complacent. I've let my guard down.

His father made it clear when I arrived here that they don't have much time left for Wyatt to marry. He needs to marry in order to be initiated into the Society, and I know his family is embarrassed it's taken him so long. He won't kill me—not yet. After I'm forced to carry a few of his kids, maybe.

"Well," Nolan says, pushing himself off the door, "let's get your fiancée settled, and I can finally show you what I've been inviting you over for. Consider it your wedding present." He winks as he passes us, taking the lead down the brightly lit tiled hall. "Hope you don't mind, it's a bit used." He glances back at Wyatt. "But it's not like you have to keep it."

Framed paintings of different landscapes—from rainforests to rocky beaches—decorate the beige walls, and the wall-mounted light fixtures cast a warm glow throughout the house. We pass the two archways on either side of the narrow foyer, striding toward the U-shaped staircase where the hall opens up. Just past a second, shorter corridor to the right, Nolan leads us into a large alcove.

The single glass-paneled door and bay windows look out toward the dark, dense treeline to the side of the house. Logs crackle in the fireplace between two built-in bookshelves. The sweet scent of vanilla wafts through the open space of the living room, dredging up a memory of home that I force away before it fully surfaces.

Snuggled under a blanket in the corner of the gray sectional is a woman with her eyes glued to her phone. Her black hair is pulled up into a high ponytail and the makeup she was wearing at the restaurant has been removed, making her appear a bit younger than I originally thought.

Nolan stops behind the sectional. Placing a hand under her chin, he tilts her head back and smiles as he leans down to kiss her. "We have visitors." Looking up at Wyatt and me as we circle the couch, he says, "Ivy, this is my wife, Bridgett."

Bridgett offers a smile—the most genuine one I've seen from an Elite—and locks her phone, setting it aside and sitting up straight. "Nice to meet you, Ivy. And always good to see you, Wyatt."

"And you, Bridgett," Wyatt says in the cordial tone I've heard him use plenty of times before. "How are you feeling?"

Bridgett groans, but the smile doesn't leave her face. "Exhausted, constantly, but at least the nausea has finally gone away."

"It will all be worth it," Nolan says, reaching a hand under the blanket and rubbing her stomach.

She kisses his arm and lightly nudges his hand away. "Go. You two have fun. Ivy and I will be up here."

"Behave," Wyatt whispers in my ear before following Nolan out of the living room.

Only after their footsteps fade do I finally take a seat on the far end of the sectional, crossing my legs and folding my hands in my lap. The anxiety of being around Wyatt—always watching me, always monitoring everything I say and do—wanes, but this woman brings on a new sense of unease. She knows Wyatt and is married to his best friend. Whatever I say to her, she'll likely report it back to one of them. And the fact that Wyatt actually brought me here himself makes me that much more nervous, like he's trying to trick me into opening up to this woman about my hatred for him and his family and the Society.

"So," Bridgett says, straightening out her legs and crossing one ankle over the other, "how are you liking the Red Zone?" The blanket slips off her abdomen, exposing her swollen stomach.

"It's different from what I'm used to," I say, "but I like it."

"You're from the Green Zone, right?" She leans over, grabbing the mug from the glass coffee table and bringing it to her lips. When she lowers the mug, I catch the purplish scar on her inner forearm, just below the bend.

"Yeah." I quickly redirect my eyes to hers. "What about you?"

"Yellow Zone. I know, I know—the zone with executions at least once a week, but it wasn't *that* bad."

Everyone in the Northern Unity knows about the regular executions and stricter curfew there. Before I was taken from my home, President Hoffman visited the Green Zone after the first raid that followed the incident of the hijacked airplane. She assured us the *terrorists* would be found and dealt with accordingly, but she swore our zone wouldn't embrace the Yellow Zone's form of punishment. We never did—until yesterday.

Hoffman went back on her promise. What's stopping her from making that a permanent method of dealing with the resistance there, too? The thought terrifies me. My brother is still there, and although he's careful, that may be his fate if he makes one false move.

"But you like it more here?" I ask.

"Oh, definitely," Bridgett says. "Nolan has given me the life I've always dreamed of."

I've had to repeat a similar line to the Everetts' acquaintances. Has she been forced to say that, too, or does she genuinely think that?

"And what about your family?" I ask. "Have you had any contact with them since moving here?"

Her smile falters ever so slightly, and she slides a hand across her belly. "My parents were at the wedding and I called them when we found out I was pregnant, but other than that, not really." Dropping her eyes to her bump, she shrugs. "We have our own lives though, you know? But Nolan promises we'll go visit once the baby's here."

I nod, my gaze drifting back to her scar. "You must be excited—about the baby, I mean. How far along are you?"

"Six months tomorrow, and I'm already ready for him to be here." She laughs to herself. "It's such a weird thing, growing another person inside of you. Have you and Wyatt started trying yet?"

A shiver climbs up my spine at the idea of Wyatt ever touching me like that, let alone carrying his child. "No, we're… waiting until after the wedding."

Bridgett raises her eyebrows. "Really? That's not like him. I mean, having kids is something he's always talked about since I've known him."

"How long have you known him exactly?"

"Just since meeting Nolan—four years, maybe."

"So you were purchased four years ago?" When her friendly expression is replaced with a skeptical one, I add, "I noticed your arm. I have a tracker, too."

"Oh, right." That perfect smile returns. The more she does it, the more unsettling it becomes. "Yes, four years ago. Nolan and I have been married for three. And honestly, I couldn't imagine it any other way."

"It's not… weird to you? Relocating and having your spouse chosen for you?"

"At first it was. They kind of prepared me for it with Transitional Adaptation, but it still took some getting used to." She picks up the mug again, taking a small sip and resting it in her lap with her hands clamped around it. "You're still pretty new, though, so I get it if you're nervous—everyone is their first few months. New place, new people, new responsibilities; it's a bit of a culture shock."

That's one way of putting it.

I scan her exposed arms and neck for some kind of mark—bruises, welts, or anything else—but her skin is blemish-free, save for the incision site. Maybe her husband treats her better than Wyatt does me. Under my own long sleeves, my upper arm is still sore from where Wyatt grabbed me earlier. Bruises from my first weeks here have disappeared, but the memories of how I received them are fresh.

"But like I said," Bridgett continues, "I have the life I've always wanted, and I'm thankful Nolan chose me. If it weren't for him, I probably would've never been able to have children." Twisting the string of the tea bag around her finger, she lifts it out of the mug before dunking it back in. "He was so generous, paying for the fertility treatments, and he's constantly looking after me, making sure I have everything I could ever want. But you probably know what that's like. You're so lucky to have been chosen by Wyatt."

"Yeah. Definitely lucky." Uncrossing my legs, I plant both feet on the floor and glance around the room, pausing on the entrance and listening for any footsteps or voices. "Since being with Nolan, have you ever attended an auction?"

Bridgett shakes her head. "That's kind of Nolan and Wyatt's thing—they go at least once a year together."

"And you're okay with that?"

She briefly looks away from me, taking a sudden interest in the paper at the end of the tea bag's string as she turns it over between two fingers. "He devotes so much time to me and his work, he deserves some for himself. Besides, it's all for the benefit of our country, just like our participation."

All of my focus zeroes in on her. "What do you mean?"

How did my *participation* in the auction benefit this country at all? The only person who reaped any reward other than Wyatt was my mother. After she sold me to the Society, she used that filthy money to buy herself a house in the Red Zone like she'd always wanted. I was torn away from everything I love, and my brother was left without a family.

Bridgett waves a hand in the air. "Nothing. Forget I said anything."

In my search for information on the Society and how they work, the Elite Auction is something I've especially kept an eye out for. But I've yet to find anything about it, and with only a few days until the wedding, I'm running out of time. It doesn't help that I rarely have any alone time to snoop either. Had I not been dragged here, I probably would've been able to have a look around tonight while I was supposed to be studying.

I remind myself Bridgett isn't someone I can trust, so I don't push the subject. We sit in awkward silence. So many questions burn inside me that I can't ask without raising suspicion, and for once, I wish I was at the Everetts'. At least there I could be doing something useful.

"So," I say, dragging the word out, "have you met any other people like... us?"

"A few," Bridgett says, quickly taking another sip of tea, "but I tend to spend more time with Elites."

"Did you ever meet Wyatt's other fiancées?" When that skeptical look returns, I add, "Nolan said something about them."

She rolls her eyes but smiles. "I love him, but he doesn't know how to keep his mouth shut. Yes, I met a couple."

Intrigued, I unconsciously lean forward. "What were they like? What—what happened to them?"

Bridgett shrugs. "They didn't work out, and Wyatt didn't seem that happy when he was with them anyway. But you... He's talked a lot about you. I'm happy he's finally found 'the one.'"

"Yeah, he's great." I bite down on my tongue to keep from saying anything else and search for another subject to move on to.

Bridgett opens her mouth but immediately closes it, her gaze shifting behind me. A hand lands on my shoulder right as I turn my head to find Wyatt.

"Sorry to interrupt," he says. The faint smell of sweat clings to him, mostly concealed by his cologne. His hair is disheveled, a few curls dangling over his face, and his nails are caked with a flaky, reddish-brown substance. "Do you mind if I steal her from you for a minute?"

"Not at all," Bridgett says, plastering the smile back on her face.

Wyatt slides his hand from my shoulder, and I reluctantly stand, preparing myself for whatever's to come. Paranoia of him hearing me talk about the auction anchors itself in my gut, and I immediately sift through several excuses as to why the subject was brought up. Bridgett and I are the same in a way, both living similar lives. I can tell him she's someone I feel comfortable with, since she understands—that it was a way to bond. And I followed his rules. My old life wasn't brought up, aside from what zone I came from. That should be good enough.

With a hand on my back, Wyatt guides me out of the alcove and toward a staircase that leads to the lower level. The heels of my boots clack against the polished wooden steps, echoing off the walls and vaulted ceiling.

"Where are we going?" I ask.

"I want to show you something," Wyatt says. No underlying tone of anger or accusation, and when I steal a glance, he appears completely calm. Still, the paranoia continues to burrow itself deeper.

The stairs make a sharp left once we're beneath the wide window along the back wall, and on the ground floor, a bright, vast room opens up before us. A small sitting area makes up the back corner beneath the stairs, complete with a fireplace and built-in bookshelves like the living room. On the wall beside it is an entrance to a small, dark kitchen, and directly across from the stairs is an archway that opens up into a rec room. Three white doors are spaced out along the wall to our right, but the rest of the bright room is completely empty—only vacant hardwood glaring under the spotlights.

Wyatt directs me through the center door and down a hallway with several doors on either wall and a set of double white doors at the very end. Our footsteps are muffled by the carpet, but another sound replaces them, making my stomach drop. Suppressed sobs fill the otherwise silent hall, interrupted briefly by a thud before continuing.

The farther we walk, the more amplified the cries become, twisting their way into my ears and coiling around my brain. I look to Wyatt for some indication as to what's going on, but his expression remains unreadable. My paranoia is replaced with full-blown panic, and every fiber of my being screams at me to run. Forget about the consequences, just run. But Wyatt continues guiding me forward, un-bothered by the sobs that are becoming more and more desperate and the muffled man's voice that joins in with the hideous chorus.

"What are you showing me?" I ask, my voice quivering.

A smile finds its way to Wyatt's lips, and he slides his hand up, clasping it over the back of my neck. "Something I should've shown you a while ago."

We stop in front of the double doors where the crying is loud-est. Wyatt faces me, twirling a strand of my blonde hair around his finger before tucking it behind my ear. "I love you."

"I love you, too," I say, hating myself for it just as much as all the other times.

Pressing down on one of the handles, he pushes the door open and pulls me into the dim bedroom with him. Nolan spins around as we enter, adjusting one of the sleeves bunched up unevenly around his elbows, and the same wickedness I saw in him at the restaurant flashes in his eyes. Puffy pink trails wind up his forearms. *Are those from… someone's nails?* The cries have ceased, leaving a chilling silence. A musky odor hangs in the air, mixed with sweat and something stale.

Without a word, Nolan steps aside, and I gasp, bringing my hands to my mouth. All the oxygen is sucked from my lungs and the rushing of my blood roars in my ears. My knees buckle underneath me. The room spins, my vision tunneling, only focusing on one thing.

A woman kneels in the center of the room with her arms bound to her sides. She's only wearing underwear and a stained tank-top, leaving the cuts and bruises speckling her arms and legs on full display. She lifts her head slowly, peering at mine and Wyatt's shoes from underneath her short, matted hair before meeting my gaze.

Tears well in my eyes and a scream claws at my throat, desper-ate to escape but coming out as a sob muffled by my trembling hands. Blood spills from her nose, pouring over her duct-taped mouth and chin and trickling down her throat. Whimpering into the duct tape, her fearful eyes dart between me and Wyatt.

"This," Wyatt says, stepping in front of me so I can only see the woman's face over his shoulder, "is the wedding gift Nolan got us." Al-though he's standing only a couple of feet in front of me, his voice is distant, drowned out by the woman's whimpers and unintelligible pleas.

Not *our* wedding gift. His. I want no part in this. The disgust is overwhelming. With each forced breath, the rancid air fills my lungs, making me want to vomit. I make myself lower my hands, clasping one over the other at my chest.

My eyes travel around the room, searching for anything else to focus on—the lamp on one of the nightstands; the tangled, blood-stained sheets on the bed; the claw marks on the black headboard. But my gaze finds its way back to the woman, and no matter how hard I try—no matter how badly I want to—I can't look away.

"What do you say to him, Ivy?" Wyatt says.

The exit is clear. I could run. But I can't move. Every muscle is stiff with terror.

"Ivy," Wyatt repeats impatiently.

"Th-thank you," I stammer through my uneven breaths.

Wyatt pushes my face to the right, forcing me to look at his friend beside the bed. "Look at him when you speak to him!"

"Thank you," I force out, reaching my fingers under the collar of my shirt and digging them into my skin.

Nolan smiles, taking a seat on the edge of the bed. "My pleasure. Don't worry, we've already had our fun with her, but I think your fiancé had something in mind for you."

My stomach tightens. Acid creeps up the back of my throat. Burning. All of me is burning, yet the room has taken on a frigid chill.

Wyatt pulls me forward by my arm, and when my legs don't move, he jerks hard. I stumble toward the woman, reflexively reaching out to the monster beside me to steady myself. An arm's length from her, I can make out a trail of blood on her inner thighs. Sweat clings to her pale skin. Her swollen eyes search mine, silently begging me not to do whatever it is I'm here for.

A drawer opens somewhere in the room, and Wyatt steps away to retrieve something from Nolan. When he reappears in front of me, he holds the object behind his back, and the woman lets out an ago-nized scream. Fresh crimson spits from her nose and she struggles vi-olently against her restraints. Nolan's quick to intervene, slamming his foot into her stomach, and she folds forward, letting out a strangled moan.

I lurch toward her, but Wyatt blocks my path and shoves me back. Fear and adrenaline pump through me. I push back against him, swiping at his arm, face, and chest, desperate to get to her as Nolan digs his heel into her side and another groan makes it past the tape.

"*Stop!*" I cry. Hot tears streak my face. "Leave her alone!"

Wyatt grabs the back of my neck, jerking me toward him, and produces a knife, holding the long blade to my throat.

"Calm down," he sneers, "or you'll end up just like her." He studies my face, my uncontrollable tears, and chuckles. "You have no idea how lucky you are, do you?" Keeping one hand on my neck, he turns and points the knife at the woman crumpled on the floor. "That could have been you—sold to someone just for them to take advantage of you and dispose of you when they were finished. Do you understand that now?"

Gulping, I nod.

"After all I've done for you, you're still an ungrateful little bitch."

"I'm sorry," I say, gasping for air. My breaths come in shuddering hiccups, and my vision is blurred. "I... I'll be better."

"Then prove it." He forces me toward their victim.

The spinning of the room accelerates. My legs shake, barely holding me up. That stale smell becomes stronger, and I can finally see the source. Bile, fresh and brownish-yellow, stains the woman's tank top, mixed with more blood. I gag.

Nolan grabs a fistful of her hair, jerking her upright with her head back. Her chest heaves and she thrashes against him, screaming and sobbing. Wyatt grips my wrist and forces the hilt of the knife into my hand, closing my fingers around it.

Leaning in close, he whispers, "You're going to do to her what was done to your precious terrorist."

I shake my head, heart pounding furiously. "No, please. I'm sorry. I'll be better—I promise!"

My hand is guided toward the woman. The tip of the blade traces her jaw and stops at the bulging vein in her neck. Wyatt releases me, and my hand trembles.

"I'll do anything—anything! Just *please* don't make me do this!"

"She's not even a citizen," Wyatt says over the woman's cries. "No one will miss her."

"I can't!"

"*Now!*"

"*I can't!*" I scream, pulling the knife away, but Wyatt seizes my wrist again, shoving the blade against her skin, pressing it harder.

Nolan rips the tape from her mouth, and her tormented scream tears through me, burrowing into my skull. My own cries crescendo and I squeeze my eyes shut while trying to fight back against Wyatt's force on my wrist.

"Please don't do this!" the woman begs, her raspy voice sending chills throughout my body. "Please! I have children—two babies!"

"Shut up!" Nolan yells, followed by the sound of flesh against flesh and more sobbing.

"Do it, Ivy!" Wyatt demands. "Prove to me that you're a good girl."

My body convulses. The wails get louder. My legs give out. Images of Nixon with a knife to his throat and crimson soaking his body flash in my mind.

I'm not like them. I'm not a murderer.

My knees hit the hardwood floor with a thud. The knife remains in my hand, my arm suspended. More cries. More yelling, screaming, demanding.

Can't breathe.

The woman's bloodied face pops into my head, then morphs into Nixon's and back again. I squeeze my eyes tighter. Wyatt twists my wrist. There should be pain, but I'm numb to it.

Can't breathe. I need to breathe.

Wyatt relinquishes his grip on me, and my arm falls to my side. The knife clatters to the floor. The woman's cries quiet but don't stop completely. I open my eyes and lift my head. No new markings on her neck.

Nolan's glare shifts from me to Wyatt, and I look up at him beside me. Bending down, he picks up the knife and jerks me up by my arm. He propels me toward the door, throwing it open and shoving me into the hallway.

"Go upstairs to Bridgett," he growls. "We're leaving as soon as I'm done down here." Then he slams the door and I'm frozen in place.

Shallow breaths return, but nowhere near enough to ease the building pressure in my head. Tears still pour from my eyes and the burning sensation courses throughout my body. The air is lighter out here, but the odors from that room linger.

Only when the woman's wails and pleas return do my legs function again. I back away from the room, keeping my eyes glued to the door and my arms wrapped around my torso. Halfway down the hall, I force myself to turn around and stagger toward the opening.

With my hand gripping the banister and my foot on the first step, a final excruciating scream shreds through the lower level. It pierces my brain, replacing the burning with a biting cold.

6. Slaves to the System

Ivy

I take my first long gulp of air when I reach the top step and use the banister to pull myself up onto the main floor. The tears and shaking won't stop. Her screams still carve into my mind, stabbing at my ears and consuming all other thoughts.

Bridgett looks up when I stumble into the living room, wearing the same awful smile that quickly fades. Setting her phone aside, she pushes the blanket off and stands.

"Ivy?" She takes a step toward me. "You're okay. Calm down."

Gasping for air, I shake my head and back away from her. My fingers find the spot on my throat where the knife was pressed. "You knew."

"Ivy—"

"You knew what they were doing to her and you didn't stop it!" I twist my fingers in my hair at the top of my head. "She was one of us. How could you let them do that?"

"It's for the good of the country."

"Bullshit!" I whirl around, still forcing my fingers through my hair, tempted to rip it out. Tempted to claw at my skin until it's raw and I feel nothing but the burning. Nausea bubbles in my stomach.

That woman is dead. They tortured her, ripped her away from her children, and for what? To get off by preying on the weak—the ones who don't have the money or power to fight back?

I couldn't stop them. I didn't even try. I'm alive. She's not. Why the fuck am I still alive? It should've been me. It should've been me in the Green Zone. It should've been me in that bedroom. But instead I'm left with that woman's bloodied face seared into my mind. And I'm expected to go along with it.

"This is how the Enlightened Society provides for their citizens," Bridgett says, her tone even, indifferent. "The Elite Auction—it's how they give back to everyone else. All they ask for in return is a few participants—"

"That's fucking crazy!" I spin around, dropping my arms and clenching my fists. "They kidnap innocent people and do whatever they want to them! Are you seriously *that* brainwashed?"

"I know it's hard to understand," Bridgett says, stopping at the end of the sectional. "It was scary for me at first, too, and maybe it was too soon for Wyatt to show you that. But this is how it works. You're one of us."

I'm not. I'll never be one of them. Through Wyatt's methods of breaking me down, I've clung to that promise I made to myself. It's hard enough to separate the truth from the lies and remember who I really am, but that's one boundary I'll never cross.

"And it's not always like that." Bridgett takes a tentative step toward me, eyeing my fists at my sides. "They should have eased you into it, okay? But you proved to Wyatt you're strong and can handle it—that's good. And that girl... she's one of the ones who've been passed off to dozens of different people. Nolan and Wyatt did her a favor by ending her suffering."

All I can do is gawk at her. She's going to be a mother, and she really supports all of this? What if it was *her* child who was trafficked and tortured? I can't find any words to say to her. Any questions I ask won't get a real answer—just more rehearsed propaganda—and reasoning with her is futile. She's completely brainwashed. Would I be the same way, had I attended Transitional Adaptation, or am I less willing to give in because I spent time with resistance members prior to being captured?

"Ivy," Wyatt calls, making me jump, but I don't turn around or respond. Bridgett and I continue staring at each other. Her brows are slightly raised and pulled together and her eyes are wide.

"Just do as he says," she whispers, "and everything will be fine."

Nothing is fine. Nothing will ever be *fine*.

Wyatt's mix of sweat and cologne hits me before his hand grasps mine, and it takes everything in me not to jerk myself from his grip. My sobs haven't stopped, and my hand continues to tremble in his. Nolan isn't anywhere in sight. He's probably downstairs cleaning up their mess, and thinking of that makes the stomach acid return to my throat.

Bridgett and Wyatt exchange goodbyes, which I'm not paying attention to. She says something that I'm fairly certain is directed toward me, but I can't concentrate. All I can focus on, other than the horrid images in my head, is how badly I want Wyatt to stop touching me. The feeling of his smooth skin against mine makes the bile creep further up my throat, and when he tightens his fingers between mine, my stomach coils up.

I couldn't do it. I couldn't do what he wanted, and I'm going to be punished for it.

He pulls me out of the living room, and I have to force my legs to move. Through the hall, he keeps a tight grip on my hand and his gaze locked on the door ahead. Still no trace of Nolan. Bridgett doesn't follow us out. I try to take deep breaths, to make the tears stop. A whimper sits in the back of my throat, but I don't let it escape. I don't need to give him another reason to punish me.

Wyatt carefully closes the door behind us and drags me down the steps, the heels of my boots scraping against them on the way down. The cold air rushes down my throat and stabs at my lungs as they greedily welcome it. Between the stairs and the car, I inhale several more times, drawing in as many deep breaths as I can.

Wyatt opens the door and forces me inside, and I jump when it slams shut. Within seconds, he's in the driver's seat beside me and starting the engine, but the vehicle doesn't move. I keep my gaze forward, focusing on the hazy black sky through the windshield. Wyatt thumps a finger against the steering wheel, and I can feel his eyes on me, studying me. I stay completely still.

No more tears. No fidgeting. Slow breaths.

"I'm disappointed in you, Ivy," he finally says. "And here I thought you'd finally learned your place." He shifts and leans toward me, slinging an arm over the back of my seat. "Didn't you like finally getting to meet more people like us—like you?"

"Yes," I whisper.

Bridgett and I are nothing alike. She accepts all of this—whatever it really is. She's blind, just like I used to be. Ignorant. But unlike her, learning about the evil that is the Enlightened Society and the Elite Auction was enough to open my eyes. It's not something I can ignore now, especially since I'm trapped in it.

"And now you know how much worse it could have been for you," Wyatt says. "But you still disobeyed me."

I stay quiet. Apologizing won't change anything. This is the second time in less than twenty-four hours I've disobeyed him. He can do whatever he wants to me, but I refuse to take someone else's life—especially that way. Between the resistance and the Society, I've been surrounded by death for the past few months. The resistance, however, only kills when it's a last resort to protect themselves. The Society doesn't have a reason; they don't need one. They hold all the power and can get away with it.

"I brought you here to teach you a lesson," Wyatt continues, poking a finger through the gap underneath my headrest and running it up and down my neck.

"I know," I say. "I'm lucky to have been chosen by you."

He chuckles. "Not just that." Sliding his arm from my seat, he places a hand on my cheek and steers my face toward his. "You may not have taken part in the auction directly, but you've been contributing to it your whole life."

"What are you talking about?" I ask, genuinely curious.

My father? Does he know about my father and the role he allegedly played in the auction? He must know—he knows everything about me and the life I came from. But what my father did had nothing to do with me. Liam and I grew up only knowing him to be the Green Zone's Police Chief. I never knew he worked the auction until Nixon brought it up, but even he wasn't completely sure what his exact role was.

"I never even knew about the auction until I was taken," I say.

Wyatt clicks his tongue and smiles. "Your terrorist never told you?" He removes his hand and straightens himself in his seat, buckling his seatbelt before looping the car around the circular driveway. "Not that you should believe much of anything he said, but considering you were sold to the Enlightened Society, he should've at least told you why."

"My mom wanted the money to get into the Red Zone."

That's all Nixon told me, and it turned out to be true. She sold me when the Red Zone's residency program was open for entries, and when Nixon and I were hiding in the Blue Zone, I saw the news segment where she was announced as a winner.

"How do you think the Northern Unity became what it is today?" Wyatt asks. "Jobs and housing for everyone, no hunger, unlimited healthcare… the government assistance you received after your father left you? The Enlightened Society provides all of it—we make sure every citizen is taken care of. But how?"

I keep my eyes on him as he drives, racking my brain for some sort of answer, something I learned in school about the structure of our country. When the government of the Old World was eradicated and the Society rose to power after the Second Civil War, the military budget was cut and troops were pulled out of warzones around the world. The hundreds of billions of dollars saved were redistributed to other things the Society perceived as high priority, like the wellbeing of its citizens.

"The Elite Auction," Wyatt says. "That's how you and everyone else have been able to live your comfortable, carefree lives. *That's* how we take care of everyone—the money we spend on the participants. All you've ever had is because of the auction."

7. All Eyes On You

Nixon

My eyes dart across the neglected property, zeroing in on the front corner of the house. Twenty paces away, I'm crouched in the dense treeline with my pistol ready. It's two hours until sunrise, and my eyes have somewhat acclimated to the dark after turning off my flashlight a few yards back. I adjust the earpiece of my radio, which has been silent since I got out here. The two scouts on lookout at either end of the deserted road are to contact me if they get any company, but so far, everything has been clear.

I run my hand along the right side of my tactical belt, feeling the two remaining attached magazines. Plenty left in case I run into anyone else. Two men are down in the woods, so there should be two more close by.

One more sweep of the yard and I rise to my feet. Get in, get Liam, and get out without being caught. That's my objective.

Pressing the push-to-talk button on the small device clipped to my shirt, I say, "Any contact out there, guys?"

Luke's voice comes through. "Negative."

"All clear," Theo follows.

"Alright," I say. "I have eyes on the house and I'm moving in. Stay in position."

Semi-crouched with my gun in front of me, I sprint to the side of the house and press my back against the weathered siding closest to the front corner. No one follows. I peer through the window beside me, unable to make out anything on the other side. Without a floor plan or even a general idea of this house's layout, I'm going in completely blind.

Clicking on the flashlight mounted to my gun, I step onto a nearby cinder block and do a quick scan of the interior through the window. Chipped countertops are coated in dust and dirt. Open cupboards reveal broken, bare shelves, and a split dining table lies on its side, surrounded by dead leaves. To the left, a door.

I switch off the light and holster my gun. Shoving my gloved fingers under the lip of the window, I push up, cursing under my breath when it groans in protest and jams a fourth of the way up. I take a deep breath before trying again, but it doesn't budge.

The snap of a twig somewhere to my right causes me to spin around, drawing my gun in the process. It doesn't come again, and I can't make out anything toward the front of the barren property. I inch forward, staying close to the house, and pause at the corner. The moon provides little light past the clouds that have begun to form. Trees are still, skeletal figures against the night.

The creak of a plank of wood echoes in the dark, followed by the scuffing of boots and crunch of gravel. Crouching, I move farther up and peer around the building. A shadowy figure moves toward me, approximately six feet away, but his head is turned, focusing on the far end of the driveway, then the treeline ahead. I raise my gun, aim, and fire without a second thought—the resounding crack muffled by the suppressor. The figure grunts, and I turn back toward the partially opened window just as he crumples to the ground.

Three down, one to go.

I stand, holstering my gun again, and step back onto the cinder block. Gritting my teeth, I press the heels of my hands against the underside of the window's lip and push up. It groans again, scraping in its track as I struggle against it, but it finally moves. With just enough space made for me to fit through, I step down and search the ground beneath me.

I grab the first decently sized rock I see and toss it through the gap. It ricochets inside, sending several resounding thumps through the air before the silence returns. Pulling my gun out, I flatten myself against the wall and put some space between myself and the point of entry.

I wait.

I count twenty-two seconds until the footsteps come. Five more seconds and I can tell they're close to the window by the crunch of dead leaves. A beam of light shines outside momentarily before frantically moving throughout the room. As expected, my target turns around and the footsteps fade. He should be checking the opposite side of the house.

Once the thumping of boots against the floor completely vanishes, I step onto the cinder block and hoist myself up onto the ledge. I slowly wriggle through the space, wincing as the raised metal digs into my abdomen. My hands make contact with the floor a few feet below, and face down, I carefully slide my legs off the windowsill one at a time. Stepping over the clusters of leaves, I crouch behind the toppled table.

I wait a few moments before continuing, listening for any movement or voices. Nothing comes. Standing, I step around the table and move forward. Against the wall beside the doorway, I peer into the next room, squinting through the dark as I quickly survey the space. What must have been a living room is absent of any furniture, and the only light source comes from the small window at the top of the front door. I round the corner.

A dull pain radiates up my left side as I inhale deeply, and I bite back a groan. Carter told me to take it easy, and I know I'll get shit from the next medic I see for doing this. The faster I locate Liam, the faster we can get back to the safehouse and I can force myself to rest.

Ignoring the ache in my ribs and putting as little weight as possible into each movement, I move toward the other side of the room where another doorway opens up. The next room is a dead end—some sort of den with two busted windows. I continue down the hall to my left, feeling along the wall as I go. Everything becomes increasingly darker, to the point where I can't see anything in front of me.

My hand glides over a raised surface, and I pause, feeling around until my fingers bump the doorknob. Turning it, I crack the door and reach into my pocket, pulling out a familiar, slender tube. I grip it in my hand, pressing it into my palm with my thumb until I hear the muffled snap. Just as the neon green glow begins to form, I toss it through the cracked door, and within seconds, the tiny bathroom is illuminated. It's empty.

I repeat the ritual with the next door on the same wall, only to find a room full of cobwebs and empty cans. The third door on the opposite wall leads to a shallow closet. At the end of the now partially illuminated hall, I have two doors left before it branches off to the right, and I'm down to three glowsticks. I glance behind me, checking one more time for any sign of another person, but I'm alone.

I approach the last door to my left, turn the knob, and nudge it open with my foot as I reach into my pocket. The bluish-white hue of an LED lantern engulfs the room. Peeking inside, I spot Liam sitting in a chair with his back to me and hands cuffed behind him.

The pain in my ribs grows, making my breath catch, and I reflexively grab my side, leaning forward to ease the ache. I push the door farther open with my shoulder and tighten my grip on my gun. Liam turns his head as I step inside, but I don't have a chance to see his full face.

An arm wraps around my neck, the crook of the elbow pressing into my throat, and a hand grasps at mine, wrenching my weapon from my grip. My heart pounds, and everything around me fades—Liam, the empty room, my gun that clatters to the floor. Images from the

Red Zone flash before my eyes. All that fills my mind is being dragged away for another round of torture and interrogations.

I slam my elbow into my attacker's stomach. He grunts, stumbling back and loosening his grip, and I reach for his bicep while securing his wrist with my other hand. In one swift motion, I throw my torso forward with all my weight, careening to the right, and as soon as my attacker thuds against the floor, I'm on top of him. Unsheathing my combat knife, I press the edge of the blade to his throat while digging my knee into his ribs.

He coughs and wraps a hand around my wrist. "Alright, you got me."

My heart races. It thunders in my ears. His face is a blur, distorted by shadows and the visions invading my head. When he tries to push my hand away, I instinctively press the knife deeper.

"Nixon," a second, urgent voice says. There's the clanking of metal and an audible click, followed by a chair scraping against the wood floor. Liam. "What the hell are you doing? Let him go."

His words pull me out of my head. I squeeze my eyes shut, willing away the remnants of the flashbacks, and jerk my knife away when I reopen them. Seb lies under my weight, his face contorted with fear and shock. Sliding off him, I offer my hand and help him stand.

"It's just a training session, dude," he says once we're on our feet. "You don't actually have to kill me." He runs a gloved hand along his throat where the blade was.

"Sorry," I say, sheathing my knife. "You alright?"

"Yeah, fine, but damn—what *was* that?"

"Good work, Seb," Liam interrupts, walking toward us with the cuffs and a key in his hand. "Radio your team and meet up with Luke. We'll be right behind you."

Seb looks between me and his squad leader, his gaze lingering on me longer than I'm comfortable with. He wants me to answer his question, but doesn't argue. Pressing the button on the device clipped to his shirt, he turns toward the door and says, "We're heading out, guys. I'll meet you outside."

"Hold on," I say just before he steps out into the hall. "What did you find out from that bodyguard?"

When he finished the interrogation, I immediately called him and the other scouts for this training session. I was anxious to get back to doing my job and regaining my strength, and since Seb has a shift at TCG this afternoon, I wanted to do this as soon as possible.

"He worked for the Astor family," Seb says. "Isaiah will bring you the brief later today." Then he's consumed by the darkness, and his footsteps fade down the hall.

I start toward the exit but stop myself. Part of me wants to follow him, to ensure he's okay and apologize again. Doing so would open up a new conversation I don't want to have, though, especially not with him. Seb and I are friends, but we've never been that close. The last thing I need is my members thinking I'm no longer able to do my job.

I pick up my gun, reminded of the pain in my ribs when I bend over. The dull ache turns into a burning throb, and I grab my side, taking shallow breaths until it subsides.

"You okay?" Liam asks.

Wincing, I force myself to stand up straight. "Fine. Just need to rest."

He shoves the handcuffs and key in his pocket and looks me over, paying extra attention to the hand on my side. "I told you it was too soon for this. You need to take it easy for a little while."

"I've been stagnant for weeks. I just need to get my body used to this again."

"That's not what I meant." He looks past me at the door, as if expecting Seb or one of the other scouts to come in, and runs a hand over his dark beard. He may have prevented Seb from prying anything out of me, but that doesn't mean he won't. "I've never seen you lose it like that in training."

"I didn't 'lose it.' I zoned out for a second, that's it."

"You had a knife to his throat."

"It was nothing. Leave it alone."

"It's okay if you're not ready yet—we'd all understand. You've been through a lot, and I'm only bringing it up because I'm concerned."

"There's nothing to be concerned about." I click on my light and motion for him to turn off the lantern. He does, and we're left with the single beam to guide us.

"If you need to talk about whatever you're going through, I'm here."

"I appreciate that," I say, turning back to the door and stepping out into the hall. I switch out my magazines, exchanging the chalk rounds for my live ones. "Let's get back to the safehouse."

8. The Shift

Nixon

Rain pelts against the window across from me, falling in sync with the rapid clicking of Liam's keyboard. After a few hours of sleep, my body is even more sore than it was when I woke up yesterday. The pain in my ribs is no longer constant, but makes itself known any time I move too quickly or attempt to stand straight. My arms feel like lead and the wounds on my back burn from my shower.

I force myself to focus on the papers laid out in front of me—reports of increased military activity in the Green Zone; forged identification papers Seb was able to pull together for a few other squads; a debriefing of a failed mission that was revived by Liam's squad, where they succeeded in transporting weapons outside of the Northern Unity. Then there are the documents Addison was able to swipe from her father, but none of them are really anything I care about at the moment—only reports of local crime and resistance activity. Nothing about the Elite Auction, which means the current Police Chief must not have been selected to work it like the last one—Benjamin Clearson, Liam and Ivy's missing father, whose role in the auction is still unknown.

"How's it going?" I ask without looking up.

Liam lets out an exasperated sigh and shifts in his chair. "I've been able to crack about… eighty percent of the encryptions. Whoever created this simulation is good."

"That would be Nadia."

He's been working on the same exercise for a couple of hours now—hundreds of files I had Nadia send over so he could get more practice. He's already good at what he does, but I need him to be faster and as familiar as possible with decrypting time-sensitive files that have an expiration.

"I know you've been busy in my absence," I say, "but we need to get our numbers up. Our decryption rate has dropped to seventy percent, and we can't rely on Nadia's help forever; she has enough going on in her zone."

"Yeah, I know, and I'm glad things are starting to feel a little normal again. But is there some other reason you're having me do this?"

"No."

"Really? It wouldn't have to do with tracking down Ivy?"

"No," I lie, finally looking at him. "But if improving your skills helps us do that, then I'm all for it."

"I've already told you I can't do that without being in one of their facilities. Even if I could, what then? We can't infiltrate another zone."

"I don't know, okay? But she's your sister, and I owe it to you to get her back."

Liam shakes his head, his fingers continuing to fly across his keyboard. "You don't owe me anything. I mean, I appreciate it and I want her back, but this is out of your hands."

"I'm not going back on my promise."

"What, are you going to go against the Commander?"

I don't say anything. Instead, I focus on the rain streaking the window and the watery gray clouds consuming the sky.

The thought of going against orders has crossed my mind. I even entertained a few vague plans after this morning's training. It would be stupid and I'd likely be kicked out of the resistance entirely, but if overstepping the Commander means Ivy's safe, I'm willing to try anything and deal with the repercussions later.

"Wouldn't it be worth it?" I ask eventually.

The typing stops, and Liam hesitates before saying in a hushed voice, "What if she's not even there anymore?"

"Don't think like that."

"Haven't you thought that, too? We know what they do to their victims."

"Eli told me she was purchased to be married. They haven't killed her."

That was three days ago; things can't have changed that quickly. But that doesn't mean she's completely safe either. Ivy wasn't able to attend Transitional Adaptation, so her buyer has probably used his own techniques to break her down. Every day since we were separated, I've thought of her and hoped she was okay, or at least as much as she can be. When I was tied to the stake, awaiting my death, I was hoping the resistance would put something in place to get her out and let her know how sorry I was.

Now that I'm free, though, I'm going to be the one to do that.

Still, Eli told me the same thing as Liam: they don't have a location on Ivy, and they may never have one. Everything pertaining to the auction is kept hidden. Even our most skilled hackers have never been able to get past their security, and no one has the clearance to get close. Unless a victim escapes on their own, which is incredibly rare, no one comes back from being sold.

"Have you talked to your mom since Ivy was taken?" I ask. I know Liam moved in with his girlfriend following Ivy's kidnapping, and not long after that, their mother was accepted into the Red Zone through the residency program. I wish I'd thought to ask earlier, but it's not like I had the chance while in captivity.

"No," Liam says flatly.

"You should get in contact with her, see what she knows."

He lets out a sardonic laugh, glancing up from his screen. "You can't be serious."

"She's the last person you want to talk to, I get it, but she might know where Ivy is."

He shuts his laptop, pushes it aside and leans back in his chair. "And what makes you think she'll tell me anything? Or that she even knows?"

"Your mom may be a shitty person, but she should at least reassure you that your sister's okay. Ivy had a private buyer, meaning the check was made out to your mom directly from them, so she should be able to give you a name."

He crosses his arms over his chest and drops his gaze to his closed laptop. Under the corner of the table, I catch him subtly bouncing his leg. This is asking a lot of him, and I don't blame him at all for never wanting to speak to his mother after what she did. But this could also be our key to freeing Ivy.

"Addison's dad conducted your mom's exit interview before she left the Green Zone," I say, "and he has her new address and phone number on file. All you have to do is get that from him and call her—you don't even have to see her."

"I'm not supposed to leave you alone."

"I don't need to be watched." It comes out harsher than I meant, but he doesn't flinch.

"I'm just following orders."

Of course he is. But who gave those orders? Eli? Piper? The Commander? And why? After being in the resistance for this long, why do they need to keep an eye on me? I didn't give up any information when I was in the Red Zone, and Eli can attest to that. I'm lying low like I was told, not putting my group in danger. My wounds are healing, and I'm catching up on what I missed. There's no reason for me to have a babysitter.

"When I'm here, you follow *my* orders." I stand up, pushing my chair in. "Contact your mom and report back to me."

"Are we going to talk about what happened this morning?" Liam asks.

"There's nothing to talk about."

"Again, you had a knife to Seb's throat."

"I told you, I zoned out for a minute."

"That's completely unlike you."

"Yeah, well, I've been pretty unlike myself lately, but I'm fine. It won't happen again."

"If you need to talk—"

"I don't. Do you have your burner on you?"

"Uh, yeah." He shoves his hand in his pocket and pulls out the small, black flip phone. "Why?"

Taking it from him, I turn and walk to my room. "Calling Eli."

I shut the bedroom door behind me, both thankful to have a small amount of privacy and fearful of what the solitude might bring. Being around Liam gives me some sense of normalcy, a way to slip back into a time that doesn't exist anymore. Talking about missions and the different squads feels natural, and for a fraction of a second, I'm able to be here in the present.

I have no idea how long I'm expected to stay here or if I'll ever be able to go back to leading my group the way I used to. That alone eats at me. I was never a leader who called the shots from the sidelines or stood idly by. I always made the effort to be part of as many missions as possible, to be there for anyone who needed me. Now I can't do any of that, and I'm being babysat by my second-in-command as if I'm unable to look after myself.

I step away from the door to pace back and forth, turning the phone over in my hands while I try to go over what I'm going to say. Aside from when my sister was here, I haven't spoken to any of the other leaders since being back in the Green Zone, nor have I really cared to. Whatever's happening in the other zones isn't my priority right now, even though we ultimately all work together. My failed mission is the main thing I care about, and only once I get some sort of closure there can I move forward.

Flipping open the phone, I go into Liam's contacts, assuming he has Eli's number saved, since he's been reporting to him in my absence. I scroll down until I find *RL* and select it. My thumb hovers over the green call button, and I debate whether or not I should do this. Doubt clouds my mind, fueled by Liam's assumption that his sister may be dead. If that's the case, I'm not sure I want to hear it.

I press the button before I can talk myself out of it and hold the phone to my ear. It rings several times, making me think he won't answer. I hold my breath, waiting and pacing.

On the sixth ring, Eli picks up and says, "What can I do for you, Liam?"

"Eli," I say with an exhalation, "it's me."

There's a beat of silence, and when he speaks again, his voice is low, hesitant. "Are you safe?"

"Yeah, just me and Liam here." And the hidden scouts who are watching this place around the clock.

"Everything okay?"

"Fine—everything's fine. I was calling to see how things are in your zone."

The sound of a door closing comes from his end, followed by the scraping of a chair. "Quiet. Not much activity here." Which is how it usually is after the auctions, but following my escape I expected there to be more, especially if Elites attended my execution. "I imagine you have your hands full over there, though."

"Yeah, not much I can do about it either."

"Lying low is what's best for you right now."

"I know." Given the circumstances, this *is* what's best. Showing my face anywhere will get me arrested along with anyone I'm with, but that doesn't make this any easier. Being out there with my members, being by their side on missions or collecting intel… that's what I've dedicated my life to these past few years. Making a difference while keeping as many safe as I can is what I live for. Here, I'm useless. "Any idea how long I'll be here?"

"As of right now, we're taking it one day at a time. Either the Commander or I will inform you if anything changes."

If. I already suspected I'd be kept here until things cooled down; I knew I'd have to adjust to a new normal and accepted that nothing would be exactly as it was before. But I at least thought I'd be able to get back in the field sooner rather than later. Because of my capture, my group has only been carrying out a small fraction of the missions they normally do, and without an active leader, they've been limited on what they can accomplish.

"Why are you really calling, Nixon?" Eli asks. "Would it have anything to do with your second-in-command's sister?"

I stop pacing. "Have you heard anything?"

In the few moments of tense silence, I prepare myself for the worst. As long as I know she's alive, I can live with that and go from there.

"We're investigating," Eli says. "I'm working closely with the Commander to figure something out while we follow up on a potential lead."

"You have a lead?" Excitement creeps into my words, despite my effort to hold it back.

"I said *potential*. As of right now, I don't have anything substantial to share."

"You have to have something if you're launching an investigation. What can you tell me?"

He sighs. "Nixon—"

"Eli, please. She was my mission and is Liam's sister. Anything I can pass along to him is useful."

I can almost hear him internally debating whether or not he should tell me. Sharing any details before they're substantiated would get our hopes up, only to tear them back down if this lead is false. But if the Commander is involved, it has to be solid. Eli wouldn't waste his time otherwise—not when it comes to something as important as a victim of the auction.

"Allegedly," Eli finally says, "a young woman approached my second-in-command at a local restaurant upon seeing her tattoo, claiming to be Olivia Clearson."

"What else did this woman say? Who was she with?"

"That's classified, and unfortunately I can't discuss it any further with you at this time."

"That's bullshit! We have a right to know."

"When we find out more, you'll be the first ones notified. We need to be cautious about this. If she does happen to be Ivy, there's always the chance she's flipped. Are you prepared for that?"

"Yes," I mutter. After what happened with Kase, a member from the Blue Zone and my former friend, the resistance will take extra precautions with Ivy. But she's not the same as him. I learned the hard way that I don't always know people as well as I think I do, but if Ivy had told the Society anything, they would've already made arrests. She knows who Eli is and where he works. She knows me and Piper, and she vaguely knows who Seb is.

"I know you… care about her, but you can't let your emotions cloud your judgment. You're a leader first."

"Yeah, I got it. Thanks. Keep me updated."

"And, Nixon." His tone takes on a cautionary edge, so subtle that I might not have picked up on it if I hadn't known him for years. "Whatever that was between the two of you, be sure to bury it. The Commander wouldn't be too pleased if he were to find out."

I curl and uncurl my fingers, forcing back the futile urge to argue with him. He already knows. No point in trying to deny whatever he heard from those guards at the auction. But I'm not going to admit to it either.

"You have nothing to worry about," I say, and I end the call.

The flip phone displays the call log on the screen, and I'm about to exit it when I notice the most recent contact before Eli: *BL*. Four calls within the past forty-eight hours, with the most recent being an outgoing at 8:03 a.m. today. What reason did Liam have to call Piper this morning?

A quick knock on the door makes me shut the phone and spin around as Liam steps halfway into the room.

"Isaiah's here to brief us," he says. His gaze drops to the phone in my hand. "Any news from Eli?"

"Potential lead," I tell him as I pass the phone over and follow him out of the bedroom, "but he wouldn't give any details."

"How confident is he in this lead?"

"Couldn't tell, but he has the Commander involved, so that has to count for something."

Isaiah hands Liam three stapled sheets when we approach him in the kitchen and looks over the handwritten notes on his legal pad.

"What do you have for us, Isaiah?" I ask, stopping beside the table.

The logistics expert flips the pad back to the first page and looks up at me. "Nicholas Fuller—works for a company that dispatches security for the thirteen families as well as the auction. For the past three weeks, his occupation has been with the Astor family in McLean, who he's worked for frequently, specifically Level Nine Society member Nolan Astor and his wife, Bridgett. Mr. Fuller attended the execution with Nolan while his wife stayed behind. In the past six months, he's worked for several different families—Astor, Freeman, Oswald, and Collins.

"Asked about Olivia Clearson, he claimed he'd never met her nor did he know which family had purchased her. He did mention that Nolan had purchased a victim within the past week from another family, but the description given didn't match Olivia's."

"What are Mr. and Mrs. Astor's occupations?" I ask, glancing at the report Liam's reading.

"Nolan is an executive for an armament manufacturer," Isaiah says. "Bridgett doesn't have an occupation. She was a victim of the auction four years ago."

"It says here that the Astor family is in close contact with the Everetts and Russells," Liam says, pointing to a paragraph at the bottom of the second page. "Any more info on them?"

"No, sir," Isaiah says. "The guard claims he's never worked for those two families specifically. A few members of those families would visit the property, but he isn't necessarily familiar with any of them."

Not the information I was hoping for, but it should be enough to get us moving in the right direction. Either way, having names of specific Society members is an advantage for us.

Liam hands the report over to me. "Ivy was sold to a private buyer. How familiar is he with that side of the auction?"

"We, uh, didn't ask," Isaiah says. "But he's just a guard; he's not going to have as much to offer us as an actual Society member or even law enforcement."

"Let him rest and then go back for more. I want to know about this Nolan guy, potential private buyers, and details on what his role was in the auction." Liam looks at me for approval. "What do you think?"

"Yeah," I say, "squeeze as much out of him as you can."

"And when we're finished with him?" Isaiah asks.

"Kill him."

9. Sleep In the Fire

Ivy

Carson Everett's study is the only place I'm truly allowed to be alone. Most evenings, I don't mind being in here. I pretend I'm not a prisoner in this mansion while I sift through all the information left at my disposal. Shelves are packed with books and binders, overflowing with the history of the Enlightened Society, and as someone marrying into the organization, I'm expected to absorb as much as possible to understand their cause and the role I'm expected to play.

As much as I hate doing it, it does make it easier to gather information for the resistance. I flip through the book that's on the executive desk in front of me, the worn pages crinkling under my touch. The ticking of the grandfather clock across from me is amplified, tugging at what little focus I have. It's a quarter past ten and we're supposed to be up early tomorrow to go over the final touches of the wedding and rehearsal dinner, but I have to wait for Wyatt to come get me.

I skim over the section about re-education, having already made copies and tucked them away for my own viewing outside of these four walls. Skipping through the next few pages of the same topic, I search for something I might have missed, but it's all the same stuff I've read before.

Re-education is the Northern Unity's alternative to the Old World's prison system, which proved to be useless. Criminals are taken to re-education centers, where they endure some degree of questioning. Questioning can last anywhere from a day to weeks, depending on the severity of the crime. After all possible information is extracted from the offender, they undergo a surgery where a chip is placed at the base of their brain. The AI chip constantly monitors the person's mood and thought process, periodically emitting electrical pulses to ensure submission. It's still not a perfect fix, but it's proven to be more effective than the ancient prison system. For those who are defective, where the chip doesn't work as it should, the Society chooses another method of re-education, such as extensive forced labor or flooding the criminal's senses with pro-Society propaganda. In most cases, though, the chip is a quick, flawless fix.

Slamming the hardcover closed with a satisfying thud, I stand from the leather chair and return the book to its place on the shelf behind me. I scan the room for my next read, wishing I could just curl up in bed and drift to sleep without Wyatt beside me. I know this is important, but it's so mind-numbing; every detail seems to bleed into the others. This is too much to absorb for one person, and I don't have any help. Mr. and Mrs. Everett want me to learn on my own. Wyatt has popped in a few times for short study sessions before, but I won't be getting that tonight.

None of the gold text etched into the cracked black spines interests me. *The History of the Enlightened Society: Volume XI. Re-Education: The Solution for Modern Crime. The Rise of the Enlightened Society. Black Hats: Covert Defense Against Domestic Terrorism.*

Selecting a book without paying attention to the title, I plop it on the desk but remain standing, continuing to scan the shelves. I've made notes on the most important stuff, like the information on re-education, but what I've really been curious about, I have yet to come across: The Elite Auction. It was already at the top of my list of secrets to uncover, but after what Wyatt told me about it, I'm even more intrigued… and terrified.

Wyatt *has* to be lying about the auction and how the money generated from it provides us with what we have. It has to be another way for him to scare me into submission after I refused to murder that woman. Our government couldn't have built their entire empire from trafficking people. There's no doubt they take part in the disgusting practice, but it can't possibly be the source of the Northern Unity's wealth.

Yet as much as I want to deny it, a small part of me knows it's true. Nixon did tell me that the Enlightened Society started the auction. I never knew why or how before, but he told me that much.

I walk along the massive bookshelves, squinting at the titles, but nothing indicates anything about the auction or even Transitional Adaptation—something that has yet to be explained to me. Finding anything on one topic might lead me to the other, and I can hopefully add to my stash of stolen secrets.

I turn back to the desk, drop into the chair and swivel around, opening the book in front of me to a random page. I glance over the black text but don't retain much of what it says.

'*The Second Civil War resulted in nearly 8,000,000 casualties, making it the deadliest war in American history… The United States government was at its breaking point but refused to relinquish its 250 years' worth of power… Politicians who vowed to protect the people turned against them… Secrets were valued over human lives.*'

The woman from Nolan's mansion flashes in my mind—bloody and beaten and utterly terrified—and I squeeze my eyes shut, willing it away like I've had to do all day. The image eventually retreats to the back of my thoughts, but not before morphing into Nixon's face once more and then being replaced by Wyatt's rage-filled expression.

Opening my eyes, I lean back in the chair. My thumb finds the inside of my forearm, grazing the section of flesh that was sliced open and stitched back together while I was unconscious. The scar is mostly flush with the skin surrounding it, but when I press down, I can feel the tracker—approximately the size of a quarter—that's embedded there. It moves around a bit when I make circular motions, but I know it's not going anywhere. It's intended to remain there for the rest of my life.

I glance at the door, which is cracked open. No one has passed by in over an hour. Mr. and Mrs. Everett went down to the bottom level to unwind in the hot tub, and the servants have left for the night. My gaze drops back to the open book and then the desk drawers to my right. If I'm going to find what I need, it will be somewhere in there, and Mr. Everett keeps them unlocked.

Pushing myself away from the desk, I find the knob of one of the drawers, keeping my eyes locked on the door, and pull it open, flinching when it squeaks on the track. With only a couple days until the wedding and tomorrow being the rehearsal dinner, this is likely my last chance to 'study'. Parties here last well into the night, and even when the Everetts announce that the festivities are wrapping up, there are usually still at least fifty or so stragglers for a couple more hours.

I pull an unmarked folder from the drawer and transfer it to my lap, thumbing through the stack of papers inside. I've blindly selected files on the Black Hats. Most of what's typed out I already know, but I comb through it just in case. My heart skips when I spot a report at the very back that's dated December of last year. Location: Green Zone. Not exactly what I was hoping to find, but any new material is useful, so I slip the three pages from the folder and stash them under the back cover of the book on the desk.

Checking the door again, I trade the folder for another. Nothing significant. The third is just as useless: receipts and contracts for every business involved in the wedding. After searching four more dead-end files, I peek outside through the French doors to my left. It's unlikely anyone would come in that way, but there's a prickly feeling creeping up my neck, and with every document I pull out, it grows stronger.

Not finding anything valuable, I move to the drawer on the bottom. It opens with ease, revealing more stuffed, unmarked folders, and I select one at random, not expecting to find much. The first page is a receipt with signatures I can't make out and a payment for half a million dollars. The second page is similar but with a payment double the previous amount.

When I turn to the third document, I suck in a breath that feels like shards of glass cutting into my chest.

A fairly recent picture of myself stares back at me, eyes glowing and smile bright. The photo's been cropped to focus on me—I can tell that the arm thrown over my shoulders belongs to my best friend, Addison. The pages following contain all kinds of information on me, from school transcripts and employment to medical records and even things I never knew about myself, such as my ancestry, traced back long before the fall of the Old World.

This is how the Everetts knew so much about me before they ever met me.

I slam it shut, heart drumming rapidly, and return it to its designated place. Information about myself isn't of any use to me, but if that's here, I have to be close to what I'm looking for. With trembling fingers, I flip through the folders in the drawer, on high alert for any details that will steer me in the right direction. The prickly feeling turns into full-blown shivers of paranoia. I check both doors again. Still alone, but I swear I see some sort of movement from outside.

Plucking another folder from the drawer, I set it in my lap, and my stomach drops at the bright red words stamped on the front: TOP SECRET. This folder is lighter than the rest, holding maybe ten papers at the most. I do another sweep of the room, settling on the French doors a few moments longer, then open the folder.

The first page is blank, but the second confirms I've found exactly what I wanted. *Inside the Elite Auction.* I remove the stack of papers and replace them with some other random documents from another file before returning it to the drawer. Nudging the drawer shut with my foot, I swipe the three papers from underneath the book on the desk and combine them with the new stack, folding them in half.

There's a light knock on the study door just as I stuff the papers into the waistband of my pants. I look up from the book I was pretending to be paying attention to and see Wyatt standing in the doorway. Propping one shoulder against the door frame, he smiles, his glassy eyes scrunching up at the corners.

"Hey there," I say, straightening up. "Did your friend leave already?"

He nods, pushing himself from the frame and stumbling into the room. "What are you up to?" he asks. His words are slightly slurred.

The smell of liquor engulfs my senses as he leans against the front of the desk, and for a moment, a memory rises from the grave I've dug for my old life. The last—and only—time I smelled such an odor was when Liam and I went to our aunt's house after she and our mother had a falling out. Illegal possession and consumption of alcohol was the original reason Naomi was taken to re-education, thanks to the tip to law enforcement from my mother. I later found out that Naomi's reason for re-education and eventual transfer to a psych ward ran much deeper.

Alcohol and other substances are still illegal throughout the Northern Unity, but the Elites feel that certain laws don't apply to them. As long as their secrets never get out, they can do as they please without any repercussions.

"Final study session," I say, tapping a finger against the book. "I'm nervous about this speech."

Wyatt covers my hand with his, his skin absent of calluses and blemishes. "You'll be fine," he says, giving my hand a small tug. I obediently stand and round the desk, where he pulls me into him. "I'll be up there with you the whole time."

He draws me in closer, snaking his arms around my waist, and I force myself not to tense as his hand glides only centimeters above the papers on my hip. His kisses become hungry, aggressive, and his lips make a trail from my mouth to my jaw and down my neck. When I try to put some distance between us, his arms tighten around me.

"What's wrong?" he says into my neck. His breath is hot against my skin, and the smell of alcohol masks his cologne. "Do you not love me?"

"Of course I do," I say, taking his face in my hands and angling it so he's looking at me. Standing on my toes, I give him a peck on the lips and smile. "I'm nervous. That's all."

Something flickers across his face that almost makes him appear to be a normal person. That's one of the many things I hate about him—he's *not* normal. Not because of his social status or his impending initiation into the Enlightened Society; he truly doesn't seem human. One minute, he's lively and somewhat pleasant to be around, and the next, he's cold and vicious.

"Everything's going to be fine. It's just one speech—five minutes at the most."

I take a deep breath. "I know. It's just…"

"Is it the wedding?" He recoils, suddenly looking as if I've offended him.

"No, no!" I reach for his hand, but he pulls it away. "That's not it. I promise." I reach for him again, securing his hand this time. "I'm nervous, not just about the speech but how many people will be there. Especially since the President will be attending."

"You've attended large parties before."

I have. Fundraisers, conferences, 'small' get-togethers (consisting of at least a hundred of the Everetts' *closest* friends)—but for the majority of those functions, I stood quietly by Wyatt's side as he spoke to nearly every guest.

The Everetts' friends and colleagues know how I was acquired—not all of them, but most. I've overheard Mrs. Everett gossiping with a flock of her pretentious friends about how I was *infected* by the terrorists, as if they were a virus. But in the same string of drunken words, she went on to boast about how they've helped me come to my senses and how excited she is that I'm marrying her son.

"I know," I say, "but not anything where the attention was solely on us."

He studies me as though trying to decide whether he believes me. He raises his hand and I instinctively flinch, expecting my face to be met with his palm, but he simply brushes a lock of hair from my face.

"It'll be fun; you have nothing to worry about." Stepping forward, he gives me one more kiss and says, "Let's get to sleep. We have a long day tomorrow."

I return the book on the desk to its shelf, and he takes me by the hand, leading me out of the study. We pass through the grand dining room, which is already prepped as always, and enter the enormous, overly bright entry room to the mansion. I can't help staring at the front door as we pass it and take one of the swooping staircases up to the next floor.

The memory of the night I first came here invades my mind in short, sporadic clips. Mr. Everett welcomed me late that night, after my botched attempt to escape my fate. I saw Wyatt for the first time, informally, from the upstairs window of the guesthouse as he made his way back to the main mansion. I cried alone in the dark under the heavy covers that offered no comfort, desperate for some sense of normalcy, desperate for the Green Zone's head terrorist to be beside me.

I've never told anyone of my thoughts from my first weeks here, when I was locked away from the rest of the world. They all knew I was upset—one maid even attempted to sympathize with my situation—but they don't know what I felt, what I wanted more than anything. They don't know about the fire that raged inside me, made up of grief, anger, and trauma—all because of them. I swallowed that fire down, promised myself I'd use it to my advantage when the time was right. Soon I'll let it burn, let it consume everything in sight. Whether it's for the right reasons… I don't know anymore.

We enter our bedroom, and Wyatt immediately disappears into the bathroom. Only after I hear the shower start do I pull the folded papers from my waistband and crouch beside the bed, retrieving the small drawstring backpack again. I slip the new stack of papers inside with the rest I've smuggled from Mr. Everett's office. I'm sure there are plenty of other gems around here I could add to my stash, but I've run out of time.

Closing the bag, I return it to its temporary hiding place and go into my closet in search of something to wear to bed. Every article of clothing offered to me here is elegant and elaborate. They want me to look the part I'm playing.

I open one of the glass doors and run my hand along one of the black, silky nightgowns. As a kid, this would've been a dream come true. I can imagine myself at elementary-school age, prancing around the mansion in dresses of silk stitched with lace, allowing my imagination to take me to countless different worlds. Now that I'm living a life that would appeal to a younger me, I miss the simplicity I grew up with. I miss the normal clothes, the normal, not-so-wealthy friends, normal conversations.

And intimacy.

I long for the familiarity of my family, the closeness of my best friend, and the connection between me and—

"You sure you're okay?" Wyatt asks from the doorway.

"I'm fine," I say, pulling the nightgown from its hanger.

As I pass by him, he grabs my wrist, bringing me to a halt. I don't react or look at him; I just fix my eyes on the silky gown draped over my arm.

"If you're lying to me—" he begins in a gruff voice, tightening his grip.

"I'm not. I promise." I turn to him, plant a kiss on his cheek, and wait for him to let go. He doesn't, though. His cold, callous eyes sweep over my face as if trying to detect a lie. I hold my composure, even offer a smile and say, "I love you."

Another moment of hesitation, he finally lets go of me, parroting the words back, and I escape to the bathroom. Locking the door behind me, I toss the nightgown on the marble countertop and start the shower. I'm thankful to have a little bit of privacy in here, unlike the guesthouse I was kept in with its see-through bathroom walls.

As the water heats up, I crouch in front of the cabinet below the sink and open the door on the left. I pull out the stacked rolls of toilet paper, makeup bags, bottles of lotion, and various hair-care products, revealing the fully equipped first-aid kit. Unlatching the box, I open it and scan its contents, making sure everything is in place. I run my finger down the blade of the medical scissors, taking comfort in the glinting stainless steel and the freedom they'll offer soon. With that comfort comes an uneasiness as my brain flips through every possible thing that could go wrong, but I push that away. Whatever dilemmas I face, I'll deal with them then. Worrying now won't solve anything.

Closing the box, I push it to the very back of the cupboard and return the rest of the contents, stacking everything in front of the first-aid kit exactly as it was before. Standing, I pull off my clothes and toss them on top of Wyatt's, knowing the maid will gather them in the morning. I bathe quickly, afraid of Wyatt being alone in our room for too long. I haven't given him any reason to snoop, but he doesn't usually act with reason either. I never feel clean after my showers here anyway, despite the outrageously priced soaps and lotions that have been purchased for me. Every day I've spent here, I've felt dirtier, like a thick layer of grime has grown on every inch of my skin. It's a filth I'm not sure will ever leave me, even after I'm out of this mansion. If I get out.

Wyatt is already in bed when I emerge from the bathroom. His eyes flick up from his phone to me, a bluish hue cast on his face. All the lights are off, save for the lamp on his nightstand. As I make my way to the other side of the bed, I glance down, making sure the bag is concealed. My breath catches in my throat when I notice that one of the shoeboxes has been moved. Or did I forget to push it back in its place? I discreetly nudge the box over, hiding the backpack, as I crawl under the covers beside Wyatt. The light goes out.

I lie on my side with my back to him. Seconds later, I hear the click of his phone locking and the rustling of sheets as he gets comfortable. His arm finds its way around me, pulling me back against him. His heat penetrates my thin nightgown, but it brings no comfort. It doesn't wrap around me like a blanket or warm me from the inside like I tried to tell myself it should. I've faked many things since arriving here—some so well I've almost begun to believe my own lies—but this is one thing that can't be feigned.

Wyatt buries his face in the crook of my neck, showering me with kisses once more as his hand cups one of my breasts. I attempt to shake him off, to which he responds with a chuckle and "I know, I know. Not yet."

We lie there in silence, his heart beating against my back. It's all so faint and insincere compared to what I once knew in a life that feels lightyears behind me. Despite my silent protest, Wyatt's hand remains on my chest. His touch is like acid, burning me through the sheer silk, and I internally recoil, folding up inside myself. I want him off me. Knowing it's him who's touching me like this nauseates me. But resisting any more will result in something much worse.

"I remember the first time I saw you," he whispers. "I didn't take you as one who would sneak out past curfew."

His words take me by surprise. I only met him on my second day here, the afternoon after I caught him lurking outside. The doors to my temporary home were locked from the outside and the windows were reinforced; there was no possible way for me to sneak outside. Even if I had, I wouldn't have been able to get very far with the tracker in my arm.

Back in the Green Zone, though, I did slip out occasionally, after my father left. It started out as me searching for him, but I soon found that I enjoyed wandering the streets at night when no one else was around. I knew it was illegal—re-education awaited me, had I been spotted by one of the officers who patrolled our city—but that added to the experience. It was exhilarating and calming and terrifying all at once. I was always careful, always aware of my surroundings. I stuck to areas I was familiar with and never ventured too far from home. I wasn't a professional by any means—that's my brother's forte—but I was never seen. That was what mattered.

Except…

I choose my next words carefully. I don't want to give him too much information and incriminate myself, but I can't lie to him either. That will only get me in trouble. But I'm curious…

"I don't recall ever seeing you before I came here."

"Oh, you did, but I wasn't your main focus that night."

"What are you talking about?"

He lets the silence stretch before he continues, either for dramatic effect or to let me figure it out on my own. I know what he's referring to—at least I think I do—but I don't say it. Can't say it. I don't even want to think about it. There's no way it could've been him.

"That night in the alley," he finally says.

There's an obvious smile in his voice, and I can feel his lips lift against my skin. My heart pounds furiously, and I know he can feel it against his hand.

He squeezes my breast, and with his lips to my ear, he whispers, "The night I killed that rebel bitch."

My stomach bottoms out. It takes every ounce of my energy to keep from tearing myself away from him, to keep from showing any sort of emotion.

That man, that *murderer*, was him?

Elizabeth was the resistance member who was killed one night I'd decided to sneak out. After learning about her murder, Nixon and his comrades were sure it was at the hands of the Black Hats. I was there by complete coincidence when it happened. It haunted me for weeks, and now I'm in bed with her murderer.

"I saw you before you hid," Wyatt continues. He moves his hand up and traces my jaw with a finger. "I knew you were there the whole time. You were so scared. I almost took you with me that night. That was when I knew I wanted you. Nothing was official in terms of your place in the auction, but my father was able to work around that, since your mother had already inquired."

"I don't understand," I whisper, knowing if I speak any louder my voice will crack. "You're not a Black Hat."

"Unfortunately, no. My father would never approve of it. But I like to help them out from time to time—without his knowledge, of course." He drapes his arm over me again, tucking his hand underneath my side. "You're lucky I was there to protect you."

An array of emotions crashes over me: A current that pulls me under, drowning me in the memories I've tried so hard to forget. Heat radiates from behind my eyes, and I squeeze them shut to keep the tears from erupting.

I won't cry. Not yet. Not here. He knows about my time of unwillingly being tangled up with the resistance and what came from it. This is his final attempt to break me before I'm bound to him forever, to sever the thread that ties me to the terrorists.

So I give in one last time, knowing tomorrow I'll be free. Placing my hand on his forearm, I give it a light squeeze and say, "Thank you… for saving me."

10. Let You Down

Nixon

I've been sitting against the wall for the past hour, staring at the radio that's been completely quiet. I don't know what I'm expecting to hear from it, but I haven't been able to bring myself to leave my room in case any important information comes through.

After another nightmare, I've decided to keep myself closed off. Unlike the first one, I wasn't able to shake it off. It started out the same, being tortured by pawns of the Society and questioned about my group, but then I was teleported back to the auction. It felt more real than the last one—if that's even possible—and the entire time, all I could focus on was Ivy. Her tear-streaked face and pleading eyes were the center of my attention, and her desperate screams echoed in my ears long after I woke up.

We haven't heard back from Eli yet, and although it's been less than twenty-four hours, I'm anxious. He was right in saying we need to be cautious moving forward with this potential lead; there's always the chance that Ivy flipped, whether I want to believe it or not. But that's not the reason he's holding back on what he knows. We've shared details about our missions plenty of times before, whether we had hard evidence or not.

Eli doesn't want to let me in on what's going on because he knows what happened between Ivy and me. He doesn't want me to act impulsively and drag a squad out to the Red Zone to save her. But she was *my* mission. She may be in Eli's jurisdiction right now, but she's still my responsibility.

"It probably isn't healthy to lock yourself away like this."

I turn to see Liam standing in the doorway.

"You know you can talk to me, Nixon." Just as I can tell when something's bothering him, he can do the same with me.

"What makes you think I need to talk?"

He doesn't answer, and I know he's debating whether he should touch the subject. He's thinking what everyone else is: *Is he okay? Is he still capable?* It's nice to know I have a team who cares about my well-being, but I don't need them questioning my ability to continue doing my job. If, for whatever reason, I couldn't, Liam would step up to take my place and would do so well. But I'm here. I can do it. If I doubted myself, I would step down in order to protect my group.

What makes it all worse is the guilt that eats at me because Ivy is still out there somewhere. I know this stuff takes time, but I have to at least know she's okay—or as okay as she can be with her buyer. I constantly find myself worrying about her, thinking about how scared she must have been over the last six weeks, wondering if she hates me for not keeping her safe like I promised, and looking at her brother right now doesn't help. Especially since I'm harboring a secret from him.

Liam steps into the room, stopping to sit against the wall beside the door. "I know you've been through a lot," he begins, pulling at his fingers to pop his knuckles. It's a nervous habit I've seen a few times, but never when speaking to me. He shakes his head, as if trying to erase what he just said. "I know you didn't tell them anything, and we all trust you."

"But?"

"You're not one to open up easily, and I get that, but after everything… If you're depressed or have, I don't know, PTSD…" He hesitates for a few moments before his gaze finally meets mine. "I'm not doubting you by any means, okay? You're just as strong as you were before you were captured, if not stronger, but you're my friend and I'm concerned."

"I'm fine. Seriously."

"Everyone has a breaking point. You're no exception."

I tilt my head back against the wall, closing my eyes. The majority of the past few days has been spent sleeping and regaining my strength, but no matter how much I rest, the fatigue doesn't let up. My mind never wants to fully shut off. It's stuck in survival mode, alert and expecting the enemy to return. For the most part, I know I'm safe here. Liam is staying with me, and a squad is guarding the safehouse. But I also don't want anything to happen to them while they're protecting me.

My brain replays everything when I try to sleep, and it's worse at night. The demons live in the darkness. They come for me when I'm on the border of unconsciousness, when I'm most vulnerable. As childish as it may be, I've been tempted to sleep with the light on to ward off the terrors that lurk in the night.

Liam has been sleeping in the room beside mine, and as much as I know he wouldn't mind me waking him up to talk, I haven't been able to bring myself to do it. Not when one of the things I see when I close my eyes is his sister being dragged off the stage at the auction, and definitely not after what happened with Seb during our training.

"Do you blame me for what happened to her?" I ask.

The question hangs in the air too long for comfort, and the longer the silence drags on, the more sure I am of what his answer is.

"No," he finally says.

"You're lying."

"I'm not. It wasn't your—"

"It was my fault. You trusted me with her."

"But you didn't lead the Black Hats there. You were outnumbered when they attacked. Maybe if Addison and I had stayed—"

"You would've gotten yourselves killed." I sit up, opening my eyes. "You did exactly what I expected of you. If you'd stayed behind, I wouldn't be alive right now. *I'm* the leader and it was *my* mission. Never blame yourself for what happened, got it?"

"Isn't that exactly what you're doing?"

"Don't get smart with me. It's different."

"It's different? She's my *sister*!"

"I didn't mean it like that." Now is the perfect opportunity to tell him the truth while we're on the subject. But I don't want to deal with the argument I know will follow—not yet. "I was ultimately responsible for her, and I got both of us caught. I don't know, I guess I just feel guilty that I'm here and she's out there somewhere."

"You can't think like that. It's Kase's fault you two were captured, not yours."

"Kase?" I can't have heard him correctly. When I was captured, I did have a feeling Kase had played some role in it all. Piper, Adam, and I assumed he'd already told the Black Hats Ivy was with me, since we were originally supposed to stay at a safehouse with his squad. But after his miraculous escape and my questioning of him, Piper was supposed to take care of him. "What does Kase have to do with this?"

Liam's eyes widen. "Shit. Piper didn't tell you?"

"Tell me what?" I push myself to my feet, and a pins-and-needles sensation crawls up my legs from sitting in the same position for so long. "Answer me. What did Piper not tell me?"

"This really isn't my place. I'm not a leader."

"As *your* leader, I am ordering you to tell me!"

Kase wanted out of the resistance. At the time, I sympathized with him, but I still couldn't understand why he would want out after three of his comrades had been murdered in his safehouse. I went through hell, probably worse than anything he could've imagined, but I never sold anyone out. Everything the Society's done to me and those I care about has made me want to fight even more, not walk away.

"What—did she let him go?" I demand.

Liam stands, shoving his hands in his pockets. "Yeah."

I clench my fists. Resentment flares within me. Blood rushes to my head, and I'm blind to everything else. "And she told you this?"

"No, Eli did. He contacted me after she told him and the Commander."

"God damn it," I mutter, looking at the radio on the dresser. I should call Piper and scream at her for what she's done. She betrayed us—not just me and Ivy, but the entire resistance. But even the thought of speaking to her disgusts me. Not only did she contribute to the capture of Ivy and me, but she potentially got our parents killed. Adam and Lacey were home when the Black Hats raided, and now they're gone because of her.

My ignorant sister should have killed that traitor. From the way she spoke that day, that was her plan. I don't know what happened after she left with Kase, but she must have spoken with him alone when her second-in-command should've been with her. Piper is impulsive, and while she's good at what she does—for the most part—she hasn't learned to shut off her emotions like I have, and she's usually in way over her head. Kase probably fed her some bullshit that made her feel guilty for wanting to kill him, so she let him go.

"I'm sorry," Liam says. "I thought you knew."

"I've been locked up for six weeks. How the hell was I supposed to—?" I take a deep breath and bite down on my tongue to keep from saying anything else. This isn't Liam's fault… but he did contact her yesterday after our training session. "Is there a reason you called her yesterday morning?"

He averts his eyes and takes a subtle step back. "She's been worried about you—I promised to keep her updated."

"So you told her about what happened with Seb? After what she did to me—to *Ivy*?"

He nods. "I'm sorry, but she's technically my superior and—"

"Jesus fucking Christ, Liam. With all that's going on, you're really worried about the chain of command?" I walk to the dresser and stand with my back to him. "You should go. Pick up a shift, see Addison, something."

"I'm not supposed to leave you alone."

"You need to keep up your appearance in public. If you're gone too long, they'll notice, especially since you're dating the Chief's daughter. We don't need them tailing you again."

He hesitates, probably wondering if I'm going to use my alone time to go off on Piper. I know he's worried about me and that being alone with my thoughts is probably the worst thing for me, but I can't look at him right now. Not only does he remind me of Ivy, but he's stayed in contact with a traitor. Leader or not, what Piper did is unforgivable, and Liam has no right to talk to her about anything involving me.

"Just a few hours," I say, feeling him watching me. "I'll be fine."

11. Second Chance

Nixon

"I'm not approving it and that's final." The Commander's crackling voice comes through the private channel on the radio.

"Sir," I say, "this may be our only chance to rescue her. I just need a little more information."

After Liam left, I radioed Eli to touch base on any new information, and of course, he refused to share much. The only thing he did tell me was that the date of Ivy's wedding has been moved up. Instead of being a couple of weeks out like he'd heard when I was in the Red Zone, it's happening tomorrow.

Twenty-four hours. After that, we'd have legalities to work around and risk having other Society members and civilians question her sudden disappearance. So we have twenty-four fucking hours to save her, and everyone else seems to be taking their goddamn time when I'm ready to launch a mission. Meanwhile, I'm kept in the dark in regards to who she's with, her location, and what kind of state she's in.

All I need is a name. Then Liam can track down the piece of shit holding her hostage.

"I understand if you're carrying some guilt after what happened," the Commander says, "but any operation pertaining to her is in the hands of Eli's group. That's not your zone, and having any of you out there will cause more problems."

"If his group was going to get her out of there, they would've done it by now!"

If it were my zone, I would've put together a mission as soon as possible. I would've led an ambush and killed the bastard myself.

"Eli informed me you've been contacting him, asking for updates on Ivy. Is there a reason for that?"

He knows about me and Ivy.

I force the paranoia back. If he knew, he would say it. He would've already criticized me for my carelessness and demoted me, and I'm not going to offer any information unless I'm asked directly. If I lost my position, it would be impossible for me to assist in an extraction operation.

"She's my second-in-command's sister," I say. "I owe it to him to get her back."

"I'm aware, but—" The radio goes silent, and it's at least ten seconds before he continues. "You know retrieving a victim of the auction is nearly impossible. I can assure you I'm working closely with Red's group to move forward with this, but there will be no interference from you. Do I make myself clear?"

"Yes, sir," I say, defeated.

There's no point in arguing with him, and pushing the subject will lead to further questions as to why I'm so hung up on rescuing a girl I was never supposed to be involved with. I can only use the excuse of her being Liam's sister so many times, and even then I feel like it sounds suspicious. But I can't stop thinking about her, and I need answers. I need her to be safe. More than anything, I need to be with her. She somehow made everything better, and I desperately need her optimism right now.

"Is there anything else you need to talk to me about?"

"There is one thing." I swallow back the anger that has reared its head again. "Is it true that Piper let Kase go?"

There's another long pause before he finally says, "Yes." No explanation or attempt to defend her actions.

"And she's still part of the resistance?" I demand. "At the very least, she should step down as the Blue Zone's leader!"

"The matter is being investigated, and until I have answers, she's under probation."

I grip the edge of the dresser and bite down on the inside of my lip. The furious hammering of my heart reverberates throughout my body. The matter is being investigated? What the hell does that even mean? Piper let a traitor go, which makes *her* a traitor to the resistance. There's nothing to investigate. If I'd done the same thing, the entire resistance would force me to face the same fate the Society had in store for me.

Probation essentially means that her second-in-command has to shadow her in anything she does pertaining to the resistance, and she has to check in with the Commander more frequently than the rest of us. She won't be able to launch any missions by herself, and if the Commander feels it's necessary, she'll have to repeat a training course under the supervision of another resistance leader. Given the circumstances, Eli or Nadia, the Yellow Zone's leader, would be in charge of that.

"You can't be serious," I say through gritted teeth. "Probation? Really? Because of her, my mission was jeopardized! She's the reason behind the capture of another leader and an innocent girl who isn't even part of the resistance, someone who needed our help! What kind of message does that send?"

"You seem to be forgetting that she's already suffering the consequences of her actions."

Our parents. Still no word on them—whether they're dead or alive, in re-education or being tortured.

She *deserves* to suffer. This all could have been avoided, but no. She had to act on impulse, like she always does. I've always told her that would get her in trouble one day, but I never imagined it would be to this degree. She's hurt more than just herself. Adam and Lacey weren't my blood, but I viewed them as my actual parents. I'm who I am today because of them. And Piper took that from me.

"And that's enough of a punishment? Let her feel guilty for possibly getting our parents killed while still allowing her to be responsible for other people's lives?"

"I understand your frustration."

"You *understand*?" My anger boils over. "My life is ruined now! Do you *understand* that? I can't show my face anywhere, the people I cared about are gone, and I'm expected to stay in hiding indefinitely— all while having a group that *needs* me. She took everything from me!"

The rage dulls to a simmer once I've let everything out. I wait in silence for his response, expecting him to scold me for my disrespect. Muffled footsteps make their way around the house on the other side of my closed door. Liam must be back, and I cringe at the thought of how much he might have heard.

All of my members have witnessed my abrasive side at some point—it's needed sometimes, especially when they first join—but not like this. I'm usually able to keep my cool and I hardly, if ever, bring up my personal issues in conversation. If Liam heard any of that, I can expect a speech or at least another hundred apologies for what happened, even though none of it was his fault.

I take a deep breath and release my grip on the edge of the dresser. Getting angry won't solve anything. It won't turn back time and change what Piper did, and it won't bring back our parents or prevent Ivy from being taken to her buyer.

"I do understand—I've lost people, too, same as everyone else in the resistance," the Commander finally says. The assertiveness doesn't leave his voice, but I pick up on a hint of sympathy that's hidden there. "I promise she will face the consequences of her actions, but you need to trust the process. I'll try to get eyes on Ivy, but in the meantime, stop asking Eli about her. Over and out."

Dropping the mic beside the radio, I take a step back and rub my eyes with the heels of my hands. The footsteps have ceased, and I'm dreading going out there to face Liam. Maybe I shouldn't have pushed him to tell me about Piper. It wouldn't have changed what she did. I would've found out eventually, but it would be one less thing I have to deal with right now.

I look at the bed, tempted to crawl under the covers and submit to the nightmares that are waiting for me. I just want to forget about all of this. Ivy, Adam, Lacey, Piper, the past couple of months as a whole. I would do anything to be able to forget.

After a few more moments of hesitation, I emerge from the bedroom. Liam is at the kitchen table with a fast-food bag and a small stack of stapled papers. Sitting with him are Isaiah and Seb. All their eyes shift to me as I step into the room, Seb breaking eye contact as soon as my eyes meet his.

"How much did you hear?" I ask, taking a seat between Liam and Isaiah and across from Seb.

Reaching into the bag, Liam pulls out a sandwich wrapped in white paper and slides it to me. "Just the last bit." He pops a French fry in his mouth and flips a page of the packet. "I didn't know Adam and Lacey were your parents."

With a sigh, I lean back. I've never told anyone that except for Ivy. The Commander only knew because Adam used to be the Blue Zone's leader. It's not something I want other people to know. Adam and Lacey were great and treated me as their own, and Piper and I have known each other for years and have always been close. But for whatever reason, I wanted to keep it a secret, and they respected that.

"Only in a legal sense," I correct him.

"Oh." He looks up. I imagine he has questions about the technicalities, but he doesn't ask. He just pulls a carton of fries from the bag, slides them to me too, and says, "So that makes Piper…?"

I nod, unwrapping my sandwich. "My sister."

"Damn. I'm sorry."

"Me too," I say around a bite of food.

"I didn't mean it like—"

"No, it's fine. This doesn't leave the four of us, though. Got it?" The three of them nod in agreement. "What are you two doing here?"

"We've finished with the bodyguard," Isaiah says. "Out of the two families he'd previously mentioned, the Everett family was the one he knew most about, though not very much. Wyatt Everett, mid-twenties, was closest to Nolan Astor." At the mention of Wyatt's name, Liam's unwavering gaze locks on the logistics expert. "His father is a Level Three Society member and works closely with President Hoffman. Wyatt is set to be married, but his bride remained unnamed."

"Was she purchased from the last auction?" I ask.

"We're not sure," Isaiah says. "The bodyguard could neither confirm nor deny, and was only able to offer what he'd overheard. But there is something interesting about Wyatt."

With a subtle tremor in his hand, Liam passes me two pages from the bottom of the stack in front of him. After wiping the oils and salt crystals coating my fingers on my jeans, I grab the documents and glance over them. Four names—all women—are printed in bold, black letters with the approximate dates of their purchase beside them. Below those are their dates of birth.

"He's had four potential wives over the past five years," Isaiah continues. "But none of them made it to the altar. During Mr. Fuller's time working with Nolan Astor, he witnessed Wyatt Everett enter the home several times, usually accompanied by a woman—his fiancées at the time. Each time, Wyatt left the property alone, and Mr. Fuller noted cleanup crews entering the home in the following days."

"So this guy's killing his future wives?" I ask grimly. It's not surprising in the least, but that doesn't make it any less nauseating.

"That, or reselling them to other Elites, who do as they wish. This upcoming wedding is different from the rest—it's almost been kept a secret. No details have been given to anyone outside of Society members and those with an invitation."

"Almost like the Everetts aren't expecting it to happen," Seb cuts in. "If he disposes of his bride at the last minute—"

Liam jumps to his feet, his chair scraping against the linoleum, and runs a hand through his hair. Turning his back to the three of us, he mutters something under his breath.

"Liam," I say, "what is it?"

He shakes his head. "They have Ivy."

"And we'll get her back." Pushing my food aside, I angle myself toward him. "But we don't know for sure who she's with."

"I contacted my mom when I was gone, like you told me to." He turns to us again, gripping the back of the chair and locking his eyes on the stack of papers. "She received an invitation to the wedding. Ivy's marrying Wyatt."

Everything else fades.

If that piece of shit has done anything to her, I'll kill him myself, and I'll enjoy every second of it.

"Why didn't you tell me this?" I demand.

"I just found out. I was going to after we finished up here, but… I didn't know how bad this guy was."

"And you're sure it's him? Your mom gave you the name?"

He nods and looks up at me. "There's a rehearsal dinner tonight, and she asked me to go with her." I open my mouth to speak, but he cuts me off. "I know you're going to say it's dangerous, but I'm going. I already have a plan in place. Addison's dad gave us permission to go, and we can bypass TCG with the paperwork from him."

"What time is the rehearsal dinner?"

"Seven."

Seb glances at his watch. "That's six and a half hours from now."

"Isaiah, head out," I say as I stand up. "I'll let the group know to lie low until told otherwise by me or Eli. Seb, take Liam to get Addison and whatever we're going to need."

"What are you talking about?" Liam asks.

"Seb's in good standing with the government; he's going to act as your and Addison's bodyguard, and you're going to smuggle me into the Red Zone."

"But the Commander wants you to—"

"Fuck what the Commander wants. This *is* dangerous, which is why I'm not letting you do it alone."

This is perfect. I'll undoubtedly get my ass handed to me later, but it's worth it.

We're getting Ivy.

12. The Decree

Ivy

I lean against the railing of the balcony that overlooks the manicured backyard. The setting sun paints the cloudless sky a fiery orange, acting as a beacon only I understand. A gust of wind slices through me and I clutch my black cardigan tighter. I welcome the crisp air, inhaling deeply, allowing it to pierce my lungs.

The engagement ring glares menacingly at me in the corner of my eye, a reminder of what's supposed to happen tomorrow. But it won't happen—not as long as everything goes according to plan.

I don't know exactly what will come after tonight, but whatever it is, it has to be better than this. Part of me feels like I'm not ready, like I could've done more planning or research, but I'm quick to silence the doubt. Doubt is destructive. If I listen to it for a single second, this entire plan will collapse.

Guests have already arrived. I can hear their circulating chatter from up here but can't go downstairs until Wyatt comes to retrieve me. I imagine he's down there now, mingling with guests and downing a couple of drinks. He's always worse when he drinks, but this time, the more he has, the better.

His dagger-like words from last night have stuck with me all day, and they echo even louder now. *The night I killed that rebel bitch.*

Neither of us spoke of it today, and I'm not sure he actually remembers. He says a lot of things when he's drunk that he barely remembers when he's sober, but I'm not going to risk the consequences of bringing up the resistance. Whether he remembers telling me or not, it doesn't change what he did to her. The new revelation continues worming its way through my brain, reminding me of that night in the alley. I watched him kill her and I did nothing to stop it. Just when I thought I was healing from that night, it's come back to haunt me again.

I make my way back into the warmth of the house, shutting the French doors behind me. Someone passes by the partially open bedroom door and I wait to see if anyone else emerges. Laughter explodes from downstairs, filling the atmosphere with a shallow sense of elation.

I make my rounds one final time to ensure everything is ready for later. The drawstring backpack is tucked safely underneath the bed, and by feeling its contents from the outside, I know everything is there. In the bathroom, I open the cabinets beneath the sink and move aside the stored items for a quick glimpse of the untouched first-aid kit.

The sight of it fills me with both anxiety and security. This is actually happening. In a few short hours, I'll be free. I run a finger over one of the latches, wishing I could go ahead and do it already.

"Ivy," Wyatt calls.

I quickly conceal the box, close the cabinet, and spring to my feet. "In here!" Tossing my curled hair over my shoulders, I pretend to check my flawless makeup in the mirror.

Wyatt appears in the doorway moments later. Dressed in his tuxedo, everything from his hair to his shoes is in perfect order. "Are you ready?"

"I think so," I say as I approach him, giving him a quick kiss on his freshly shaven face.

He studies me, his mouth twisting into a frown before tugging on the sleeve of my cardigan. I reluctantly shrug it off and he tosses it onto the counter, leaving me with only the revealing dress he chose for me.

"Better," he says with a smile. He offers me his arm and I loop mine through it, keeping a hand on his bicep as we make our way to the party.

Clinking glasses and various bits of conversation fill my ears as we descend the staircase at the front of the mansion. Guests pack the grand dining room and living room. Servants bustle throughout the kitchen, replenishing platters of food and topping off champagne flutes that sit on black, circular trays. We pass through the second dining and living room, and everyone who sees us offers a smile, nod, or quick congratulations. My high heels click against the black marble floors as Wyatt drags me along. He moves hastily, as if looking for someone or something, and despite holding on to him, it's difficult to keep up.

We make it to the entertainment room at the back of the ground floor. What's usually a vast space feels tight with all the bodies packing it. The stench of liquor lingers between the cocktails that everyone seems to have in hand and the servants equipped with their trays of champagne, weaving in and out of the crowd. Couples lounge on the leather couches in the center of the room. Tables beside the wall-mounted fireplace are crammed with women drinking, talking, and laughing. Above the enclosed flames is the large slab of marble that's usually used to project anything from movies to Mr. Everett's graphs and charts during his meetings. Tonight it boasts *Congratulations, Mr. and Mrs. Everett* in bold, cursive letters with the Enlightened Society's emblem—an owl encircled in thirteen white stars—in the background.

Wyatt finally stops at the bar, where his father is seated on one of the gray upholstered stools, conversing with the bartender and a man beside him I don't recognize. Carson Everett swivels around, silently excusing himself from the conversation. Like his son, he's dressed in a tux, and his graying hair is held in place with an excessive amount of gel. Surveying us, he beams with the same dazzling grin he showcased the night I was brought here.

"You look wonderful, Olivia!" he says. Though he knows I go by Ivy, he always uses my full name, and I never care to correct him.

"Thank you," I say with a smile, resisting the urge to hide the neckline that plunges way too far.

"Excited for your speech?" Mr. Everett asks, gulping down the rest of the brown liquor in his glass. The bartender immediately pours him another drink, then a second for Wyatt.

"A little nervous," I admit.

"You'll be fine," he says, waving off my concern.

"It'll be short," Wyatt says, circling his arm around my waist. "A couple minutes, just for people to know who you are."

I don't want these people to know who I am. The news of my altercation with the resistance was all over the Northern Unity. People from every zone saw my face plastered on their TV screens and heard my name muttered in their daily lives. Gossip travels fast around the Red Zone—but it dies just as quickly. Aside from the Everetts' friends who visit often, no one has mentioned what happened to me. The Red Zone soon buzzed with juicier tales after I got settled here, such as the impending execution of the Green Zone's lead terrorist, and as difficult as it is to hear, I'd prefer it to stay that way. Continuing to fly under the radar will make tonight easier.

Wyatt plucks a champagne flute from the tray of a passing servant and offers it to me.

"I… I've never drunk before," I say, eyeing the bubbly liquid.

"There's a first time for everything," he says with a wink, and shoves the glass into my hand. "Come on, I want to introduce you to a few people before you're put in the spotlight."

We spend the next half-hour or so making small talk with nearly everyone who vies for our attention. Wyatt does most of the talking, and I only offer my scripted responses to the questions Mrs. Everett somehow predicted I'd be asked.

"I'm happy to be marrying into this family and supporting my husband in all of his endeavors."

"Living in the Red Zone is a dream come true; I couldn't imagine being anywhere else."

"Despite my stubbornness, I knew Wyatt was meant for me. He's been so patient and loving…"

I'm left to mingle alone when Wyatt excuses himself a handful of times to grab another drink at the bar, and nearly every time, he returns with another glass for me. I have to decline his most recent offer as I'm only halfway through my third one, and he drops the fresh drink on a passing servant's tray with an eye-roll. I didn't feel any effects after my first glass; only after finishing three-quarters of my second did a subtle warmth begin to work its way through me, now enveloping my insides and making my skin prickle.

In the normally quiet sitting area on the other side of the entertainment room, Wyatt keeps an arm secured around my waist as he talks with one of his friends. I take another sip of my drink, finding an odd comfort in the way it hushes my thoughts and makes everything around me more tolerable. Loud noises are softened. Words that pass between Wyatt and his friend are like liquid, flowing with ease and adding to the sudden tranquility that washes over me.

The arm around me tightens, and for a minute, I don't remember it's Wyatt's. My sluggish brain leads me to believe it belongs to someone else—a ghost from my past—and I lean into the embrace, taking temporary comfort in the gesture. Only when the staggering smell of cologne mixed with liquor meets my nostrils do I realize who he is, and with his friend watching, I can't recoil without raising suspicion.

"She's doing better than I expected," the man says, his steely marble eyes trailing my body. When his gaze locks with mine, he speaks directly to me. "We were concerned about you the other night, Ivy."

I blink, trying to place where I've seen him before. I know his face, but my brain refuses to fully register it.

"We had a talk afterward," Wyatt says. "I think she understands now. Next time, she won't disappoint us."

The man lifts the rim of his glass to his lips, where that sinister smirk has returned. Nolan.

I scan our immediate surroundings in search of his wife but don't see her anywhere. From where we are, I can't find Mr. Everett either, though I suspect he's still sitting at the bar. The faces surrounding us are unfamiliar—more Elites drinking and chatting.

As if reading my mind, Nolan says, "Bridgett isn't here. She's not feeling well," and I wonder if it's because of the pregnancy or if he did something to her, which only makes me angrier.

I'm angry at Wyatt for what he did to Elizabeth and for choosing me to be his wife. I'm angry at him and Nolan for what they did to that woman the other night. The anger even extends to Bridgett. She was forced into this life just like I was, yet she's ignorantly accepting it, pretending it's all okay when her husband performs his vile rituals in their house.

Not wanting to think about it anymore and welcoming the distraction the alcohol brings, I finish off my glass. Wyatt immediately notices, grabs my empty glass, and disappears to find another servant.

Once he's gone, Nolan takes a step closer, towering over me. "You have no idea how lucky you are to be here," he says. His words are hollow, distorted, and his face becomes fuzzy. "I'm honestly surprised you didn't turn out like the others."

"What happened to them?" I blurt out before I can stop myself. I immediately regret it when Nolan grins.

He shrugs, but the look in his eyes tells me he knows exactly what happened. "That's a question for your fiancé, but let's just say it's a good thing you got your act together when you did." Taking another drink, he adds in a more chilling tone, "And let's hope you don't disappoint him in *other* areas."

A woman in a strapless, form-fitting dress approaches us, grazing her hand along Nolan's arm. The second he looks away from me, I wordlessly excuse myself, stomach churning.

I push through the crowd, frantically scanning the sea of bodies for Wyatt so I'm not accused of wandering off without him, but he's completely disappeared. Even in my high heels, I'm too short to see over the moving wall of people. The floor seems to shift underneath me as I continue to push past Elites who are oblivious to me. Has it always been this difficult to walk in these shoes?

I can't tell which direction I'm going. My legs are unsteady, and I accidentally bump a few people who shoot me glares. A fuzzy sensation wraps around my body. Time seems to be skipping forward in short, detached clips. Warmth floods my veins now, making my cheeks hot and my head spin, but when I touch a hand to my face, my palm feels clammy.

Before I know it, I'm at the doors that lead out to the patio. Wyatt is still nowhere to be found, but standing near one of the sets of French doors, I spot his mother. Her brunette hair is pulled back, making her face appear tight as she smiles at the woman she's talking to. She's not someone I enjoy being around, but she's familiar, and I won't get in trouble with Wyatt if I'm with her.

Mrs. Everett's eyes flick from her acquaintance to me as I slowly approach. Another hollow smile, and she says, "You look beautiful, Olivia."

The woman in front of her turns around to face me, and I freeze.

The light is back in those hazel eyes that are identical to mine. They sweep over me, and I wonder if she can sense how much I've changed over the past few months. She's changed, too, though. Those gentle eyes that used to sparkle when she'd see me are now lit up by greed. Her dark brown curls fall over her bare shoulders, reaching the neckline of her form-fitting gown. Light glints off the cluster of diamonds dangling from her neck, and when I glance down, I notice she's removed her wedding ring. Every single memory from the day I was taken is resurrected, bombarding me.

And then she smiles at me. She actually *smiles*.

A blazing blade of anger slashes through me. The room spins. My pulse quickens. There are so many things I want to say. So many questions. I want to scream. I want to cry. I want to hit her. My throat tightens. Her name is lodged there, cold and bitter.

"Mom?" I force out.

My mother reaches for me. Her fingers graze the back of my hand, and I jerk it away as though her touch has burned me.

"It's so good to see you, sweetie," she says with another smile that reaches her black-bordered eyes this time.

My hatred for her burns mercilessly. She betrayed me. Money was worth more to her than her own daughter.

"Why are you here?" I hiss. Behind her, Mrs. Everett's face hardens, but I don't care.

Pursing her glossed lips, my mother steps forward, threading her delicate fingers through mine. "I know this has all been very difficult, but this is what's best for you. Wyatt has so much to offer you—more than you could ever want."

Are those tears in her eyes? *She* sold *me*! She has no right to be crying. Those tears should be coming from me. But they aren't. I wasted so much time crying over what my mother did to me in the beginning. All that's left for her is resentment.

"Best for me?" I spit. "Or for you?"

She ignores the remark. "You look good," she says, eyeing me. For a second, I think her smile falters. She knows that's bullshit. "You must be so excited to be joining the Society. You've looked up to them since you were a little girl."

Pressure builds in my head. Shaking her off me, I stumble past her and Mrs. Everett, out of the entertainment room and toward the back staircase. I'm not thinking of my next move—I'm just moving. *I have to go*, I repeat to myself, *I have to get out*. That's all that matters.

The crowd thins out, but the air is still heavy. My surroundings continue to sway. The staircase that leads up to the main level is just within my reach; I extend my arm, missing several times before my hand secures the banister. For a moment, with one foot on the first step, the stairs double—two identical sets side-by-side. I pause, blinking hard, but when I open my eyes again they return to normal.

"Ivy?" a man's voice calls, almost drowned out by the hundreds of other voices.

I freeze at the base of the stairs, too afraid to turn around, too afraid to face Wyatt and explain where I'm going. He calls again. Closer.

A hand touches my shoulder, and I reluctantly turn my head.

"Hey," my brother says with a faint smile.

All I can do is stare at him, and for a moment I think I've completely lost it. But then I reach out and touch him. As soon as my fingers graze his jaw, feeling the coarseness of his facial hair, I step away from the stairs and fling my arms around him.

"Liam?" I gasp.

He squeezes me tighter, making tears spring to my eyes. "Yeah, I'm here."

I pull back, studying him. For the occasion, he's tamed his dark, wavy hair and put on a suit. "But why? How?"

"I came with Mom." He says the last word carefully, like he's unsure if that title even suits her anymore. "I wanted to see you."

I've missed him more than anything, and actually seeing him is the best thing to come of the weeks I've been trapped here. But that elation quickly dissolves as my foggy mind dredges up a handful of paranoid thoughts.

Is this a trap—another way for Wyatt to test me? Does he expect me to ask Liam for help? Does he know Liam is part of the resistance?

"I've missed you," Liam says. "You have no idea how happy I am to see that you're…"

"Alive?" I finish for him. His mouth twists into a frown, and before he can backtrack, I add, "Really, Liam, why are you here?"

Taking me by the arm, he leads me to a secluded corner underneath the stairs. His gaze settles on the purple marks on my upper arm and wrist. Unlike everyone else here, he actually appears concerned.

"Are you okay, Ivy?" he asks.

I have no idea how to answer that. "Yeah, fine." I fold my arms over my chest, looking out toward the entrance of the entertainment room. Everything is gradually becoming more difficult to focus on. Passing bodies are blurs. The beat of my heart is magnified. The warmth that enveloped me earlier is now a fierce burn. My hands are cold and sweaty against my arms. The voices of all the guests sound washed out, like my head is submerged under water.

Liam lowers his voice. "Does he hurt you?"

"What?" I turn back to him. He's moved closer, as if trying to shield me from everyone else.

"Wyatt." He nods toward the bruises on my bicep and repeats the question, slower this time. "Does he hurt you?"

My face grows hot. I part my lips to speak but stop myself, the answer crumbling in my mouth.

I want to tell him the truth. More than anything. I want to beg him for help, spill out everything that Wyatt's done, but the paranoia that this is a set-up hasn't left. In fact, it's stronger, and the longer I stare at him, the worse it gets. He shouldn't be here. It's too dangerous, and I wouldn't put it past Wyatt to do something to him.

"No," I lie, forcing a smile. My vision doubles again. It's getting harder to breathe. "No, I've just been… reckless."

"Reckless?"

The fog in my head threatens to take over. I'm running out of time. "Yeah, um—look, you should go." My tongue is like lead in my mouth, heavy and struggling to form words.

"What do you mean?"

"You shouldn't have come here. Go back to the Green Zone."

His eyes momentarily leave mine, shifting down and to the left, and he reaches his hand toward his ear but runs it through his hair at the last second. "What about your wedding?"

A guard passes by, eyeing us as he makes his rounds, his glare lingering on Liam a second longer than me.

The wedding isn't going to happen, is what I want to say. The Red Zone is going to be a warzone after tonight, and I don't want him to be in the middle of it. As much as I want to be able to leave with him right now, I can't. Not when he's here alone and undoubtedly being monitored. Resistance member or not, he doesn't need to get himself killed attempting to help me.

I unsteadily pull him into a hug, having to put most of my weight on him to remain upright. "Don't come," I whisper. "I'll see you soon." Stepping back, I take in the confusion on his face and concern in his eyes. All I can do is hope he understands—that the ability to decipher each other's cryptic messages is still there. "I love you, Liam. Please go home."

Then I turn and climb the stairs.

He calls out for me, but I don't look back. My breaths become shallower with each inhalation, and the lump forming in my throat doesn't help. A weight has settled in my chest. The world around me spins, accelerating every other step.

Stumbling up the second flight of stairs, I reach the top floor. With a hand on the wall for support, I make my way down the empty corridor to my and Wyatt's bedroom. My entire body has gone numb, save for the tingling sensation I can't shake. Lifting my feet from the floor becomes increasingly more difficult; my heels scrape against it with each attempt. I force myself to breathe deeply, but it's as though my lungs have shriveled up. Noises from downstairs are virtually nonexistent. All I can hear is my magnified heartbeat.

I push my way into the bedroom. Rushing blood pounds in my ears, and the warmth inside me twists its way upward like fingers itching to wrap themselves around my brain, to silence every last fragmented thought. My eyelids are unbelievably heavy, and an unintentional glance at the bed makes me want to collapse onto it.

I need to get out.

It's the only thought that emerges from the haze. It's the only thing that makes sense.

I force my wobbly legs to carry me to the bathroom and picture the brilliant shine of the scissors' blade—can practically feel the cool metal against my skin. I swing open the cabinets and yank the first-aid kit from underneath the sink, toppling over bottles in the process. Lowering myself to the floor, I fumble with the latches on the box. Thanks to the trembling of my hands, I struggle a few times before the satisfying click and opening of the kit.

I stare at the scissors. My body won't cooperate. My brain is begging me to act quickly, but my actions are delayed. In slow motion, I reach for the handle, but grab a wad of bandages instead. Again, my vision doubles. Two kits on the floor in front of me. Two pairs of scissors. Two hands desperately grasping for the blades and missing.

My head is swimming.

My body is heavy.

The air is too thick to breathe.

I need sleep. Can't keep my eyes open. I blink hard, hoping to see more clearly. *Can't think.* Prickling needles crawl over my skin. My fingers secure the closed blade of the scissors. I reach for the counter, try to pull myself to my feet.

I need to get out.

Gravity works against me, trying to pull me back down. My legs shake. Finally on my feet, I lean on the counter, my face hovering over the sink. *Can't breathe.* I'm gasping for air. Panic consumes me. I suck in a shallow breath, then another, but it's not enough. I bring the blade to my arm, try to feel for the tracker under my skin, but can't focus.

"I see it's already working."

Turning my head sends a wave of nausea over me. Wyatt stands in the doorway, glowering at me with a fresh glass of champagne in hand.

"What—what are you talking about?" I ask between gasps.

He smiles, but a storm is brewing in his green eyes. "I've been spiking your drinks." He marches over to me, slamming the flute on the counter beside me. Alcohol sloshes over the rim, splashing the counter and my arm.

Grabbing my wrist, he jerks me upright. "You really thought you were going to leave?" he sneers.

My heart thunders in my ears. Unable to speak, I shake my head. This doesn't make sense. He drugged me? When? How? Did his parents know? Did my mother know?

His nostrils flare and his jaw tightens. In one swift motion, he wrenches the scissors from my hand, throws them to the floor, and plucks the flute from the counter, shoving it in my hand.

"Drink," he demands.

When I don't, he forces the glass up with one hand at the base and the other secured around my wrist. The rim is shoved against my lips. I attempt to turn away, but he readjusts, grabbing me by my hair and keeping my head in place.

The alcohol splashes over my face, filling my nose and mouth and spilling down my neck and chest. An involuntary inhalation sends me into a fit of coughing. My nose and throat burn and my eyes water.

Wyatt flings the flute aside. Glass shatters. I'm sputtering, gasping for air.

He drags me into the bedroom, jerking harder when I trip behind him. He shoves me forward, and I hardly catch myself at the end of the bed. Moving past me, he kicks the shoeboxes out from underneath the bed and yanks out the drawstring bag, pulling it open and dumping its contents. Dozens of papers litter the floor as he shakes it out. Heat floods my face again, and my heart hammers against my chest as if trying to rip its way out. Not once does his glare leave me.

"You thought I wouldn't find out?" he yells. "Where were you expecting to go, huh?" He stalks toward me, pulling me away from the bed and shoving me back by my shoulders. "Answer me!"

"I didn't—I wasn't going to do anything. I promise!" Tears burn my eyes. I back away from him, glancing at the closed door.

He shoves me again. "You lying bitch." He slams me into the wall with a resounding thud. "After all I've done for you, you were just going to leave. And for what?" He pulls me away from the wall, only to fling me against it again. Pain radiates from the base of my skull, and black dots float before my eyes.

One of his hands finds its way to my throat, and he leans in close, his face inches from mine. "I've given you *everything*." Droplets of his spit coat my chin, and his hot breath sticks to my skin. "You are *nothing* without me!" He begins to squeeze the sides of my throat, slowly applying more and more pressure with his palm.

My tears spill over. With a shaky hand, I claw at his arm, gasping for air.

"Please," I choke out. "Stop."

Closing the space between us, he presses his lips to mine. With tears streaming down my face, I try to turn my head, but he moves his hand up, turning it back to him and forcing another hungry kiss.

I hit and kick and scratch, which only makes it worse. His other hand moves down my body, finding the hem of my dress and hiking it up.

Breaking the kiss, he studies me and hisses, "You belong to *me*."

I frantically shake my head, which makes everything spin more. Darkness eats at the edges of my vision. My thoughts go quiet, and the next thing I know, I'm being dragged to the bed.

Climbing on top of me, Wyatt pins me down. The face of the woman at Nolan's house flashes in my mind. Then Nixon's. And finally Liam's. The darkness continues to close in. Wyatt's hand glides down my torso. I squeeze my eyes shut, desperately thrashing underneath his weight.

There's the growl of a zipper, and terror engulfs my thoughts. A scream rips through me, cutting at my throat and consuming the rest of my quickly draining energy. My face is met with his palm and pain explodes from my cheek. My ear rings. A hand clamps over my mouth, muffling my cries.

Wyatt lowers his face, his lips tickling my ear, and whispers, "Do that again and I'll kill you."

"I don't love you," I find myself babbling after my mouth is uncovered. The words are muddled in my mouth. My voice sounds disembodied, echoing around me. The darkness closes in, slowly pulling me under, promising to protect me. "I *never* loved you."

I see Wyatt's wild eyes over me, feel his fingers twist in my hair as his other hand brushes my thigh. His touch is fire and I want to cry out. I wriggle beneath his weight, attempt to shove him off. But I'm weak. And tired. And ready for the darkness to consume me.

Just before I surrender to the oblivion, Wyatt laughs. "That's right—you were in love with that bastard terrorist. But he never gave a shit about you."

13. Get Me Out

Ivy

A throbbing between my eyes pulls me out of my slumber.

Turning onto my side, I nuzzle my face against the pillow, willing the pain to go away. With each minute that passes, it intensifies, and soon I notice bursts of pain from different parts of my body—the most noticeable being between my legs.

Fighting past the grogginess, I force my eyes open and try to recall what happened last night. Ribbons of gray morning light stream into the room through the balcony doors. Wyatt sleeps soundly, his back to me.

I push myself up, wincing at the pain that shoots up from my right wrist. Rubbing my eyes, I swing my legs over the side of the bed and pause when I notice the papers strewn across the floor. An image of Wyatt dumping them from the bag flashes through my mind. He found them. But how? When?

I slide off the bed, and the throbbing worsens. My vision gets fuzzy and I press a hand against the nightstand to steady myself. When I look down, I see my shoes on the floor and realize I'm still in my dress from last night.

It's the morning of our wedding.

My plan failed.

Looking over my shoulder, I make sure Wyatt is still asleep before shuffling to the bathroom. The room spins but nowhere near as badly as I remember it from last night. Nausea overpowers me, and I grab the edge of the counter, taking slow breaths as I wait for it to pass. It doesn't. It only dulls, becoming slightly more tolerable.

Recollections of last night begin to roll in, but there are gaps in my memory. I check my reflection in the mirror, taking note of the circular, reddish-purple marks on my neck where Wyatt strangled me. My wrist is a nasty blackish-blue color, with a matching set of markings on my inner thighs when I lift my dress.

My stomach roils at the thought of what happened, and the fact that I can't be sure makes it so much worse.

Heat burns behind my eyes as fresh tears make their presence known. I hear Wyatt stir in the bedroom, the sound of sheets brushing against skin, and panic anchors itself in my gut.

I can't marry him.

Dropping to my knees, I dig through the emptied contents of the first-aid kit. Bandages, ointments, gauze... Where are the damn scissors? Crawling forward, I scan the bathroom floor, blinking away tears and keeping my breathing steady. I spot them behind the base of the toilet and dive for them. The metal screeches against the dark epoxy floor as I pull them toward me.

More movement. I have to be quick.

Sitting up, I press my back against the wall adjacent to the walk-in shower. I separate the blades and press a thumb to my inner forearm, locating the lump underneath my skin. Resisting the urge to shut my eyes, I press one of the blades just above the tracker, at the tip of the scar that's already there.

Anxiety surges through me. Liam's face pops into my head, along with the hope that he heeded my warning. Then Wyatt's. And his hands on me. Another wave of nausea, and I swallow back the acid that creeps up my throat. My frantic heartbeat makes the pounding in my head more excruciating.

I inhale deeply and attempt to steady my trembling hand.

Tightening my fingers around the metal, I close my eyes, push the tip of the blade into my flesh, count to three—

One quick, deep slice. Pain shoots up my arm. Biting down on my tongue, I fight back a scream, and the metallic saltiness of blood fills my mouth. My head reels as the searing pain rips through me. My arm is slick, and the sight of the flowing crimson sucks the air from my lungs.

"You stupid little bitch!" His hands are on me before I have a chance to look up.

Wyatt drags me away from the wall, attempting to wrestle the scissors from my grip. Through the pain, tears, and heavy hands that grab at me, I try to fight him off. I latch onto his arm, sinking my nails into it until I feel bits of flesh collecting underneath them. He shakes me off, cursing and yelling, telling me how ungrateful I am—how I should be happy to have him. How I'm nothing without him.

Shoving him away from me, I crawl across the blood-painted floor before being yanked backward by my ankle. He flips me onto my back. Pain erupts from the back of my head, and he crawls on top of me. I thrash underneath him. My elbow collides with his jaw, and his knee digs into my stomach.

"Get off!" I cry, attempting to jerk the scissors from his grasp.

Twisting his fingers in my hair, he pulls my head from the floor and steadies my face in front of his. A disgusting smile finds its way to his lips. "Obviously your punishments haven't taught you anything. Maybe paying your brother a visit will make you think twice about your actions."

A fire erupts inside me—the same one from the day I agreed to cooperate with Wyatt and his parents. Flames engulf me, charring whatever morality I have left.

"Stay away from him," I growl, clutching the scissors tighter.

His smile widens. "I'll do the same to him as I did to that bitch in the alley." He unravels his fingers from my hair, and my head smacks the floor. "But this time, I'll make sure you see everything."

Terror and anger course through me, fueling the fire. I squeeze my eyes shut.

A scream scrapes my throat and my body works on its own, swinging my arm up and over. The scissor's blades make contact with something soft, pushing deep until I feel a pop beneath the pressure. An agonizing wail erupts from Wyatt. His fingers grasp at my wrist, attempting to pry my hand away before I make one final, aimless swipe.

Thick, warm liquid coats my hand and splatters on my face. Nails claw at my wrist until I drop my hand, the scissors clattering to the floor beside me. Liquid continues to spray onto my face and chest. Wyatt's slippery hand slides down my cheek and neck. His breaths are ragged, gurgling with each gasp for air between coughs that send more droplets onto my skin. His weight shifts on top of me.

My heart hammers against my tight chest. I'm finally able to push Wyatt off, and his body thuds against the floor. His gurgling breaths become shallow with more and more space between each one, occasionally interrupted by another wet cough.

Still, I can't move. My body is paralyzed, as though another entity has taken control and won't let me up. The pulsating pain in my arm returns.

The tracker.

I have to get the tracker out.

I force my eyes open and turn my head to the side. Flinging a hand to my mouth to stifle a scream, I scramble to my feet. The room whirls around me as I stand upright, gazing down at Wyatt's shuddering body. A hand clutches his throat, blood oozing between his fingers and flooding his gaping mouth. My stomach clenches and my mind accelerates, shouting internal commands that barely make any sense. I need to help him. Stop the bleeding, call for help, anything. But another part takes over, forcing me back to the floor, where I crawl to the first-aid kit.

Biting down on the inside of my cheeks, I dig my thumb and index finger into the wound on my arm. My vision tunnels, and I can't hold back the scream that racks my entire body. Feeling the hard, quarter-sized object, I blindly extract it from my arm and fling it to the floor.

My hands shaking, I grab a stack of gauze, cursing as I press it to the wound, and haphazardly wrap and secure it. Hopefully I can get help later. Right now, I need to get out.

Grabbing the edge of the counter, I hoist myself to my feet and force myself not to look back as I stumble out of the bathroom. Wyatt's breathing has stopped, but I tell myself he's not really dead. He can't be. Someone will find him. They'll get him to a doctor and he'll be okay. I close the door behind me, hoping it will prevent me from going back in there, from attempting to help him.

Locating the drawstring backpack near the foot of the bed, I scoop up every document I can find and shove them inside, not caring if they get crumpled, and swing it over my shoulders. Then, as if tugged by an invisible force, I flee the bedroom, still in my dress. Still bathed in blood.

The house is unnervingly quiet. No servants or maids. Mr. and Mrs. Everett must not be up yet either. Still, I put as little weight as possible into each footfall as I descend the stairs, frantically checking my surroundings. My arm burns and I blink back the fresh tears. The air grows heavier by the second, and by the time I make it to the main level, I'm hyperventilating. The fire that ignited inside me has dissipated, leaving the heavy ashes of guilt to settle in my gut.

I make my way to the other end of the mansion until I reach Mr. Everett's study, where I know there aren't any cameras. A rush of adrenaline washes over me as I slip inside and see the exterior door across the room. I sprint to it and am met with a wall of frigid morning air as soon as I open it. I step outside, embracing the cold that stings my skin and invades my lungs. Soft morning light reaches across the front yard, painting the property in a chillingly serene golden hue.

Carefully shutting the door behind me, I take one last look at the mansion before forcing myself to run.

Still unsteady, I press on, focusing on the satisfying burn that snakes its way up my legs as I bolt across the yard. Each time my bare feet connect with the frost-laced grass, my breaths come a little easier.

I scramble over the low fence that separates the Everetts' property from the neighbors', crying out when one of the spikes at the top catches my calf. I have to keep going. Distance is all that matters. I need to put as much distance as possible between myself and this hell.

Blood trickles down my leg as I sprint toward the front edge of the yard next door. Tears pour out again, and in between gasps I find myself laughing. An odd sense of joy floods my veins. I push myself further, laughing and crying as one thought plays on a loop.

I made it.

Reaching the neighbors' gate, I pull myself up, wincing as pain shoots up my injured arm. Clumsily climbing up and over, I make it halfway down the other side before letting go. My feet hit the sidewalk, momentarily throwing me off balance and making my newly wounded leg throb. Turning to my left, I break into another sprint that's short-lived. My lungs feel as though they're about to burst; pressure builds in my head. My injuries are agonizing.

My run turns more into a hobble, but for the moment, I'm okay with it as long as I'm moving away from this place. I don't have an idea as to where I'll go next, but as long as I'm out of the Society's grasp, it doesn't matter.

A car's engine comes to life somewhere behind me, and I unintentionally freeze. It's too early for anyone else to be up.

How did I not notice a vehicle out here?

Ignoring my aching leg, I push myself forward. I don't look back. I've made it out; I can't be taken back there. If Wyatt's somehow been found already, they'll have me killed—executed, just like Nixon.

A door slams shut. Then another. My heart lodges itself in my throat, and I attempt to push myself harder.

"Olivia, stop!" a man's voice yells.

Heavy boots beat against the asphalt behind me. They echo in my head, rattle my bones, but I can't move any faster. The air is like shards of glass in my lungs now, slicing deeper with each gulp.

Another figure intercepts my path, dressed in all black. My mind is screaming at me to do something. The man stands motionless about ten feet ahead, watching me. My pursuer grabs me from behind, lifting me up and pulling me into him as he pins my arms to my sides. Letting out a piercing scream, I kick and attempt to hurl myself out of his arms. A hand clamps over my mouth, and I'm carried toward the car that's stopped on the side of the road.

The second man sprints ahead, opening the back door and raising a walkie-talkie to his mouth. "We've got her, sir."

14. Cage on the Ground

Ivy

"Jesus, she hit me in the fucking nose!" the man in the passenger seat says as his partner slides in behind the wheel. Digging through the glovebox, he retrieves a wad of napkins and presses them to his nose.

I want to scream. I want to throw open the door and launch myself out of the vehicle. But my throat is constricted and I'm paralyzed in the backseat. I attempt to pull in a few deep breaths and figure out where I went wrong, but neither is possible right now. Sobs take over again. My mind is clouded with the remnants of the drugs I was given last night and what I did to Wyatt.

"I told you it was a shit idea," the driver says, already starting up the street toward the entrance of the gated community. He glances over his shoulder at me, and I get a glimpse of his tan face before he redirects his attention to the road. "You okay, Olivia?" He races through the residential area at least twenty miles over the speed limit, taking the twists and turns without slowing down.

The passenger looks back—napkins to his nostrils and fingers pinching the bridge of his nose—and assesses the gauze on my arm and blood all over me. "She's hurt. What the hell happened?"

"Let me go," I say, my voice hoarse and throat sore.

"We're here to help," the driver says, finally slowing the vehicle as we approach the iron gates at the entrance of the neighborhood. They lurch open, and he slams on the gas as soon as there's enough space for the compact car to fit through. "We're with the resistance."

I focus my eyes on him, unsure I heard him correctly. A seed of hope burrows in my chest. But why would the resistance be here? Why now? They've had seven weeks to save me. Is this part of the reason Liam was here last night?

"Who's your leader?" I ask.

The passenger looks at the driver, who nods, then back to me. "Eli."

My hope grows, budding into the beginning stages of relief as well as confusion. This could be a trap. Eli *is* the Red Zone's resistance leader, but he's also a double agent who works within the system in favor of the resistance. If the Society is skeptical about him, though, these men could be posing as his members in order for me to confirm his identity.

"Show me your tattoo," I say.

The passenger awkwardly adjusts himself in the seat and props his foot up on the center console. Lifting the hem of his pants, he pushes his sock down to reveal the three bold, horizontal lines inked into his skin beneath his inner left ankle—the same place Nixon had his tattoo.

Breathing a sigh of relief, I sink back into the seat, and the man slides his foot down. I'm safe for now.

"How did you know I'd be escaping?" I ask.

"We didn't," the driver says. "Eli only sent us to scout out the area and try to get eyes on you… We didn't expect it to turn out like this."

"And you just decided to jump out of your car and chase me?"

"Told you," the driver says to his partner. "Shit idea."

"Oh, shut up," the passenger says, removing the bloody napkins from his nose and balling them up in his hand. "It worked out, didn't it? We figured something was wrong when you ran to the neighbors' yard and jumped their fence… and the blood. What happened?"

"It's not our job to ask," the driver immediately says, and I'm thankful I don't have to explain.

"Where are you taking me?" I ask. At this point, I don't really care. All I want is to be somewhere the Society won't find me so I can get in touch with Liam.

The passenger sucks in a breath and looks to his partner. "Well… due to the unpredicted turn of events—"

"We don't know where you're going," the driver interrupts, jerking the car to the left and running a red light.

"Slow down! Do you really want to get pulled over with her in the car?"

"Eli was just as shocked as we were when I informed him that we had you," the driver says, ignoring his friend's warning.

That must've been who he radioed as I was being shoved into the backseat. He stood outside a few moments longer than his partner with the walkie-talkie.

"All he told me was to take you to another team he'd put together, but after you're in their hands, I don't know. You'll be safe though."

Like the first time I was rescued by a resistance member—Nixon—everything is up in the air. Neither scenario was expected, and once more, I'm having to blindly trust strangers. But this time, I'm willing to go along with it.

"I imagine they'll be looking for you soon, if they're not already," the passenger says. "Brave of you to make an escape the day of your wedding."

What I did wasn't brave. It was gruesome, and I wish I could scrub it from my memory. Mr. and Mrs. Everett should be getting up within the next hour or so. They'll find their son lying in his own blood, and when they realize I'm nowhere to be found, the hunt will begin.

The Northern Unity won't be safe. There won't be anywhere to hide. If the resistance attempts to get me out of the country again, there may be hope. But I can't go anywhere without my brother. He's all I have left.

"We'll have to do something about that tracker of yours," the driver says.

His partner looks back at me again, gaze falling to the red gauze on my arm. "I think that's already been taken care of." His wide eyes pan up to mine before he turns to the driver. "Her leg's hurt, too. She needs a medic."

No questions are asked, and I don't offer any details. As long as I don't have to talk about anything that's happened, I can forget about it. That's not the kind of person I want to be—a killer. That's not who I am. I've been unraveled, stripped of everything over the past couple of months, but I will do absolutely anything to cling to the single thread that's left of who I am.

"We're almost there," the driver says, veering the vehicle to the left again, and I grip the back of one of the seats to keep myself upright. Police activity is nearly nonexistent here compared to the Green Zone, but it's still a miracle no one has noticed this man driving like a maniac.

Slowing down, he pulls into a dimly lit, vacant parking garage and drives up to the second level. Another blacked-out vehicle is already waiting for us, and its front passenger door opens as we approach. A woman circles the front of the car, her eyes scanning the garage as she makes her way over.

"Ready?" my driver asks, exiting the vehicle before I can give a response.

Opening my door, he offers me his gloved hand, and I hang on to him as I slide out. A shiver ripples through me when my feet hit the cold concrete. The woman glances at my injured leg and arm then looks to the man, as though questioning whether the wounds are from him. Mindful of the injury, she takes me by my arm, and the two of them assist me to the second vehicle.

"She's going to need stitches," the man tells her.

"What happened?" the woman asks.

"Her tracker's been removed. We weren't able to see how bad it is, but if not done properly…"

She nods, releasing my arm to open the back door of the vehicle she exited, and offers me a smile as the man helps me in. "Don't worry, love, you're in good hands." She looks to her comrade. "You two hang around here for a while. Drive around until someone spots you, and I'll let you know when she's safe."

"Another speeding ticket for the sake of a mission. Got it."

She nudges his arm as he turns away. "You're good at it."

Climbing into the back seat with me, she closes the door, and the driver—another man—loops around to make the descent to the ground level. Leaning my head back, I close my eyes and try to focus on the movement of the vehicle and my breathing, which has finally returned to normal. The throbbing in my arm is a bit more bearable now, but still excruciating whenever I move it or something brushes over it. The splitting headache that began between my eyes has spread, radiating upward. My anxiety hasn't let up; it still swirls in the pit of my stomach, merging with the guilt I can't get rid of.

"How are you doing, Olivia?" the woman asks. Her fingers graze my shoulder, and my eyes shoot open. She pulls a bag from underneath the seat in front of her and sets it in her lap. The driver looks at me in the rearview mirror but stays quiet.

My eyelids are unbearably heavy, and although I know I passed out at some point last night, I feel like I haven't slept at all. "Tired."

"Seems like you've had a hell of a morning," she says, slipping on a pair of latex gloves and retrieving fresh gauze and a pair of curved scissors from her bag. Her face is soft, and her dark eyes are full of compassion. "Is it okay if I take a look at your arm?"

I nod, and she gently takes my wrist in one of her gloved hands.

"I'm going to have to redress it for you. We'll get you stitched up once we've stopped."

Turning my arm, she wriggles her finger beneath the bloodied bandage, allowing a space for the scissors to fit. The cool metal grazes my skin as she cuts the wrap away with ease. Reaching into her kit one more time, she pulls out an orange plastic bag and stuffs the gauze wrap inside.

"You look familiar," I mumble. "Have we met?"

The smile that finds its way to her face makes her appear gentler. "Briefly. You asked for my help."

A sense of relief floods my body. The punishment I endured from Wyatt was worth it. "You're the server from the steakhouse."

She nods, peeling the soaked gauze pad from my skin, and I suck in a sharp breath through gritted teeth. Unintentionally peeking at the bloody mess of my arm, I let out a small shriek and turn my head when I see separated flesh. A fresh gauze pad is pressed to my arm along with another wave of searing pain, and the woman wraps and secures it. The plastic bag crinkles, and the zipper of the medical bag groans when she stores the bloody bandages away.

"My name's Ember," she says, pushing up her sleeve to reveal the three bold lines on her inner right wrist. "I informed Eli of your situation after our encounter. We would have got to you sooner if we could." Her eyes glide over the newly dressed wound on my arm to the cut on my calf, then back up to study my collection of bruises—and the mix of my and Wyatt's blood staining my skin and dress.

"Thank you," I whisper.

Leaning my head back, I close my eyes again. The relief of being with the resistance takes the edge off my anxiety, but I can't silence the warning bells ringing in my head. I'll at least make it through today—possibly the night, if raids don't ensue—but I can't be kept here forever. The Northern Unity was never an ideal place for me to stay after I was taken.

Now it's deadly.

When Ember wakes me, the car has stopped. Disoriented, I sit up, blinking away the sleep in my eyes and attempting to break up the fog in my head that's somehow denser than it was before. We've arrived at a two-story Tudor home at the edge of a neighborhood consisting of nearly identical houses. The driver leans against his door outside, taking a long drag from his cigarette. Ember slides out and scans the area before offering me her hand and assisting me to the ground. I lean into her as we walk up the paved driveway toward the back of the property. The driver stays behind, casually leaning against the SUV.

The sun sits higher in the sky, its warmth trying to melt away the final frigid weeks of winter. Budding trees line one side of the property, and a wooden fence shields the other from the neighbors. Ember opens the gate that leads to the backyard of the immaculate house and latches it behind us before we continue up the stone walkway. Head cloudy and legs wobbly, I put more of my weight on her as we climb the five brick steps of the small back porch. She raps her knuckles against the door three times, and we wait.

Moments later, the door clicks and swings open, revealing a familiar face—though he looks more distraught than the last time I saw him. Eli's dark eyes travel over my face and chest, then to the freshly dressed wound. When his eyes meet mine, I recognize the same look of sympathy I saw the day I awoke in the Red Zone after being captured by the Black Hats.

"It's nice to see you, Ivy," he says, stepping aside to let us in.

"You too, Eli," I say as Ember and I enter the warmth of the house.

"Where do you want me to take her?" Ember asks him. She guides me through the small mudroom and into a narrow hallway with black onyx flooring.

"Kitchen," Eli responds. "I'll grab my kit." He disappears into one of the open rooms behind us, and we continue down the hall until we reach the last room on the left.

When Ember and I step into the large kitchen, the two men at the table look up at us, their eyes droopy and hair sticking up as if they've just crawled out of bed. The man who looks to be a little older—maybe around Eli's age—looks from the woman to me, and his eyes widen. He and his partner stand up when Eli joins us with a black medical bag in hand. The older man doesn't look away from me. Like Eli, his eyes search every mark on my body, and I pull away from Ember's gentle hold on me and cross my arms, shifting my weight.

Eli sets his bag on the white table that connects to the granite island, and his two members sidestep in opposite directions to give him space.

"Assume your positions outside," he tells the men. "We'll take care of her."

The two men leave without any protest, and Eli unzips his bag.

"Have a seat, Ivy. Let's take care of your arm." He removes various items from his kit, laying them across the table. One thing in particular grabs my attention, making my breath catch in my throat.

A syringe.

"What's that for?" I ask, cocking my head toward the glinting needle. Memories of the facility I was kept at creep into my foggy mind. As one of my nurses, Eli was in charge of keeping me sedated during the days leading up to the auction.

"Local anesthesia," Ember says, pulling out the chair nearest to me and circling around her leader to take a seat on the opposite side. "It's just to relieve your pain and keep you comfortable while he sews you up."

Rounding the conjoined table and island, Eli heads to the sink in the corner beside the covered windows, and while his back is to me, I sit down in the chair that's been pulled out, setting the drawstring backpack in my lap. Running a finger over the nylon material, I eye each item that's been set out on the table, but my gaze keeps returning to the syringe that winks at me under the spotlights. The water shuts off. Eli makes his way back to me, and I rest my arm on the table with my palm up.

He moves a second chair closer to me, its legs scraping against the onyx floor. He slips on a pair of blue latex gloves, grabs a pair of scissors and cuts the gauze wrap from my arm. Before he removes the bloody pad that's pressed to my wound, I avert my eyes, not wanting to make the mistake of looking again. The cool, wet swab that rubs against my skin burns the area surrounding the cut, and the smell of rubbing alcohol stings my nose. I wince as I feel the needle prick my skin.

"What did you do with the tracker after removing it?" Ember asks me, her gaze shifting up from my arm.

"I threw it," I say. "It's in the Everetts' house."

"Were you followed?"

I shake my head.

"You've been drinking," Eli says, reaching for a sharps bag to dispose of the used needle and alcohol swab. He must be able to smell the champagne from last night. The warmth of it has left my body, leaving me cold and empty.

"He made me," I mumble.

I look around the kitchen, trying to focus on anything other than my arm, which is rapidly losing feeling. There's a small desk area built into the counter behind Ember, with a shelf above it that holds different cookbooks and canisters. A half-empty coffee pot near the sink pumps a steady trail of steam. One of the cherry-wood cabinets above the dishwasher is cracked open, revealing stacked plates and bowls.

"Who made you?" Eli asks.

"My *fiancé*." The word is bitter rolling off my tongue, leaving a rancid aftertaste in my mouth.

I desperately try to dig up any sort of recollection from last night after I was pinned down. Maybe it's best I don't remember what happened after that. Knowing Wyatt, he took what he had been pushing me for. And I couldn't fight back. I couldn't say no. A pit of disgust and shame opens up within me, tugging me down into its dark, lonely abyss. If only I'd been faster. If only I hadn't accepted those drinks from Wyatt. If only I'd been more careful in hiding the backpack.

"This blood"—Eli's gloved fingers graze my exposed collarbone, and I flinch—"is it yours?"

Heat floods my face, and I bite down on my trembling lip. "No."

He continues working on my arm without questioning my answer. My arm is almost completely numb. All I can feel is the pressure of the needle puncturing my skin, weaving in and out.

"Is my brother here?" I ask.

Eli pauses, and he and Ember exchange a look. "Your brother?" he asks, continuing with his work.

"Liam, the Green Zone's—"

"I know who he is, but why would he be here?"

"I thought…" He was at the party last night. Despite the spiked drinks, I know I saw him—touched him, even. That was real.

"Thought what, love?" Ember asks.

"He was…" I close my eyes, replaying the moments before I went upstairs. Liam's face forms clearly in my mind, with his dark wavy hair, brown eyes, and the suit I still can't believe he was wearing. That was definitely my brother. "I saw him last night. He was at the rehearsal dinner."

"Was he with anyone else?" Eli asks. "Any resistance members?"

"No, he said he came with our mother."

Even if he had been with other members, I wouldn't have known. I only met a few before I was kidnapped by the Society, and most were from the Blue Zone.

After the snip of the scissors and one final tug, Eli sits back in his chair. He pulls the gloves off and runs a hand down the side of his face. "Ember, can you find Ivy some fresh clothes, please? And have the scouts head out. I want everyone somewhere safe."

"Yes, sir," she says, pushing her chair back and leaving me alone with Eli.

The two of us sit in silence. Eli studies me, still reclining in his chair, with the side of his face propped against his fist. Rather than focusing on my blood-stained hands, bruises, or cuts, he's staring directly at me, his eyes locked on my face as if trying to see into my thoughts.

I shift uncomfortably, dropping my eyes to my lap and fidgeting with one of the drawstrings. "So what's going to happen?"

He lets the quiet linger a little longer before saying, "I'll reach out to the Green Zone, see what's going on with Liam, and I'll inform the Commander of your whereabouts."

"Where will I go?"

"For now, you'll stay here under my supervision until we get things sorted out." Dropping his hand, he stands and begins putting away his supplies. "What's in that bag?"

"Documents… information on the Enlightened Society. I stole them."

"So you've been planning this." The spotlights catch the blade of the scissors when he plucks them from the table, and I have to look away.

"Yes." But nothing went according to plan, and I'm going to have to live with the repercussions for the rest of my life. A tear slips down my cheek and I quickly wipe it away, but not before Eli notices.

"You're safe now, Ivy," he says. Zipping his medical bag, he lifts it from the table. "We'll talk more after you get some rest."

15. Courtesy Call

Nixon

The body of former Police Chief Benjamin Clearson was found in the home of Nixon Reed on January 3rd⋯

The remains were confirmed to be those of the missing Chief on January 5th. Investigators recovered stolen documents within the home that contained information on Chief Clearson⋯

Due to the overwhelming amount of evidence found by in - vestigators, Nixon Reed's right to a fair trial has been overridden and he has been charged with treason and one count of murder in the first degree⋯

"What the fuck?" I look to Seb, who's lying on the bed in our hotel room, staring up at the ceiling. "This is bullshit! They're really pinning me for his disappearance?"

"Seems that way," Seb says, obviously only half-listening.

"Seb, this is serious."

With a groan, he turns onto his stomach and buries his face in the pillow. He's exhausted.

We both are. After staking out the Everetts' last night while Liam was inside, we drove an hour out to check out the wedding venue before heading back to the hotel where Addison was waiting. Long after Seb and I got to our room, I stayed up to smooth over the details of how we'll intercept Wyatt and Ivy's route to the venue. Liam and Addison were in their own room across the hall, and Seb stayed up with me for a couple of hours before crashing.

Even when I finally forced myself to lie down for the night, I couldn't shut my mind off. My memories of being imprisoned mixed with this new sense of purpose kept me awake longer than I needed to be. In the staggering silence of our upscale room, I kept replaying everything I'd heard at the Everetts' from Liam's wire, mainly during his brief conversation with Ivy.

Tossing the police report onto the desk beside the window, I collapse into the chair. The analog clock on the nightstand shows it's half past eleven. Three and a half hours until the ceremony begins.

"Why do you think Ivy told Liam not to go to the wedding?" I ask.

"What?" Seb says, his voice muffled.

"She practically begged Liam to go home."

After that, she never returned to the party. Liam wanted to stick around longer to talk to Wyatt, but with the heavy security and his informal invitation, it was too much of a risk. The last thing we needed was for him to be questioned.

That, and I don't think I would've been able to control myself if I heard that Elite piece of shit speak.

When I had Liam ask his sister if Wyatt hurt her, she hesitated, and when she finally answered, I *knew* she was lying. After we left,

Liam confirmed that Ivy was covered in bruises. It took everything in me not to demand that Seb turn around right then.

"I don't know," Seb says. He sits up and pushes his unruly black curls from his face before rubbing his eyes. "Maybe she's pissed at him for having contact with their mom."

"No… No, she didn't sound angry. More like desperate."

"She also sounded fucked up." Pushing the comforter off of him, he slides off the king-size bed and grabs a bottle of water from the mini-fridge. "I've met the girl once, and it wasn't exactly on good terms."

"I know. I'm just trying to be smart about this, in case the Society is planning something else. It sounded like a warning."

"And Eli would let you know if that were the case."

"Eli doesn't know we're here." Flipping through the police report, I skim over the details of the bullshit charges against me, and stop on a page with a photo paperclipped to it. I study the side-profile of myself. It's an older photo—maybe from two or three years ago; my hair barely touches the tops of my shoulders. I can't tell where it was taken, but I'm focused on something else, smiling.

"Ooh, looks like they've had their eye on you for a while," Seb says, looking at the picture over my shoulder.

"Probably because they knew Liam and I were friends," I say. "The Society kept tabs on his family and everyone they came in contact with after his dad disappeared."

I should've been more careful talking to Liam after his dad went AWOL. I knew better. He wasn't even part of the resistance then, but he needed a friend to lean on, and I wanted to be there for him.

"Think they showed Ivy this?" Seb asks.

"Wouldn't surprise me. They'll do whatever it takes to get into someone's head."

If Ivy has seen any of this, she's bound to believe it without anyone telling her otherwise. She may even think Liam knew. It was hard enough earning her trust the first time, and if they led her to believe this lie, that trust she had in me is probably gone. They knew she was no longer their blind follower, and this could've been their way of breaking her down, completely turning her against the resistance.

I flip to the next page, which mentions the form of execution that had been chosen for me. A vote between twenty-six members of the Society resulted in their decision to burn me alive. Those who attended in person had to pay a fee, and everyone who stayed home was required to watch it broadcast on the news.

There's a knock on the door, and Seb takes it upon himself to see who it is. As he makes his way across the room, I unzip my backpack beneath the desk and stick my hand in, feeling for my pistol. Seb looks through the peephole just as my fingers brush the handle.

"Just Liam," Seb says. He unlatches the door, pulling it open.

Liam and Addison file in, Addison hanging back with Seb while Liam makes his way directly to me. His eyes momentarily settle on the police report on the desk before locking on me.

"We have a problem," he says.

"What kind of problem?" I ask, standing.

"Addison's dad called. He says the Red Zone will be entering a lockdown, and the Police Chief here is giving us two hours to get out before raids start."

"What? Why?"

"He didn't say," Addison cuts in. "All he told us is things are about to get bad."

"What about the wedding?" Seb asks.

Everyone looks at me for guidance.

"Your call," Liam tells me. "I'm with you either way."

If we're stuck here during the lockdown, we'll risk the Commander finding out our location and shutting down the mission, losing our chance of getting Ivy back. Not to mention the fact that I'll more than likely be caught, bringing my team down with me. But we can't leave Ivy here. She needs our help.

The Green Zone's border is just over an hour from here. If we're quick, we can get back to the Everetts', grab Ivy, and get out before the raids start. It'll be a close call, but we can pull it off. Worst case scenario, we ride out the raids at a safehouse here and hope we're not found.

"We're not leaving without her," I say. "Let's pack up our stuff and head out." Reaching under the desk, I pull my backpack out and shove the police report inside.

"We'll meet you two around back," Liam says, and he and Addison turn toward the door.

He only makes it halfway there when his phone rings from his pocket. Pausing, he pulls out the burner and checks the small window on the front before turning around and holding it out to me. "It's Eli."

Probably to warn us of the lockdown as well. If the Red Zone is taking these measures, it will likely spread to the other zones, too.

Taking the phone, I flip it open and press it to my ear. "Hey, Eli."

"Where are you, Nixon?" he asks without hesitation.

"I'm with Liam and Seb."

"That's not what I asked. How far from Richmond?"

Richmond, where he lives. He wouldn't ask that unless he was certain we were in the Red Zone. How the hell does he know we're here?

Liam's at the door with Addison, whispering something in her ear. She nods, gives him a kiss on the cheek, and holds up her keys for me to see, signaling she's going to get the car. At my nod of approval, she leaves.

Holding the phone to my face with my shoulder, I pull my gun from my backpack before zipping it up. "I don't know what you're—"

"Don't lie to me," Eli says. "I know you're in the Red Zone, but we'll talk about your blatant disobedience later. Wherever you are, leave. I need you here as soon as possible."

Seb returns from the bathroom and begins packing his own bag while I do a walkthrough of the room, making sure we're not leaving anything behind. "We already know about the lockdown, but we're not going anywhere until we get what we came for."

"What lockdown?"

I pause at the end of the bed. "Addison's dad told her the Red Zone is entering one. You didn't know?"

"Damn it," Eli mutters. "How long do we have?"

"About two hours."

He lets out a frustrated sigh, and I can tell the mic is covered when he says something in a muffled voice. When he speaks to me again his words are more urgent, but the underlying tone of irritation remains. "You know my address; leave now. Ivy's in our custody, and you and I have a lot to discuss before we move forward."

I turn my back to Seb and Liam, who are patiently waiting. *"What* did you just say?"

"She's here with me."

The first wave of optimism I've felt in a while crashes over me, and everything else I've been dealing with dissolves. I want to ask for the details of how they got her out and why we weren't informed of their operation, but stop myself. That doesn't matter right now.

Ivy's safe, and the only thing I care about is seeing her.

Grabbing my jacket from the bed, I shrug it on and pull the hood up. "Is she okay?" I demand as I sling my backpack over one shoulder and conceal my gun in my waistband. Seb does the same, and Liam focuses on me, hope flashing in his eyes.

"She will be once she's with people she knows," Eli says. "Just hurry."

"We're on our way," I say and shut the phone, shoving it into Liam's hand as I move toward the door.

"What did he say?" Liam asks, following me.

"They have your sister."

16. Glasshouse

Ivy

There are voices.

I can't tell how many. They're too muffled for me to make out who they belong to. Part of me is tempted to go downstairs and see who else is here, to listen in on whatever they're discussing, but I don't want to get up. Every part of me aches. I've been lying here staring up at the whirling ceiling fan for what feels like forever.

I don't know how long I've slept, and I feel both better and worse than when I first lay down. Better because the overwhelming fatigue has loosened its grip on me; worse because the weight of everything that's happened has taken its place.

Eli hasn't discussed anything else with me, including whether he was able to get in touch with my brother or anyone else from the Green Zone. After showering, Ember performed a full physical on me, which was probably the most humiliating thing I've ever endured. But she didn't ask any questions—not about the bruises on my neck, arms, or between my legs. Instead, she gave me some fresh clothes, asked if I needed anything, and assured me she and Eli would be close by while I slept.

My shower washed away Wyatt's blood but did nothing to cleanse me of the vileness that seeps from every cell in my body. The fresh clothes Ember brought me—the same all-black outfit the scouts were wearing earlier—felt soiled as soon as they made contact with me, as though they absorbed all of the disgust that clings to me. Wyatt's acidic touch is forever seared into my skin—every hit, every unwelcome advance. Neither my mind nor body will forget, no matter how much I beg them to.

Turning on my side, I pull the covers up to my chin and stare at the wooden nightstand beside the bed. My gaze locks on the small white pill beside the glass of water. I noticed it when I first woke up but still haven't taken it. Eli or Ember must have left it while I was asleep, and while I know they aren't malicious, I'm too afraid to take it, too afraid to accept anything that's given to me without knowing exactly what it is.

Right now, I want answers. I want to know where my brother is and why he was at last night's party if he wasn't called by Eli. I need to know where I'm supposed to go from here. The Red Zone isn't an option for obvious reasons.

Pulling my sleeve up, I run a fingertip over the threads in my arm, wincing as pain prickles up around the jagged, sewn flesh. Although the tracker's no longer there and Wyatt no longer has control over me, I still feel chained to him and his family. They've stolen who I am and left me hollow and broken. The breaking has only just begun, though.

With each moment that passes, it all becomes heavier. Since being awake, all I've wanted to do is cry, but the tears won't come. I feel everything and nothing all at once.

A knock on the door makes me jump, and I clutch the comforter tighter. I hold my breath and squeeze my eyes shut as the handle turns and the door opens. One of the floorboards creaks, but I refuse to open my eyes, expecting more poking and prodding from Ember.

The footsteps come closer, slowly, as though trying not to disturb me. They stop behind me on the other side of the bed. Whoever it is, they don't say anything immediately. They just stand there. Their eyes burn into my back.

A hand brushes my shoulder, and I tense under the touch.

"Hey, V."

My heart swells at the familiar voice, and I turn over to Liam. A sad smile finds its way to his lips. He takes a seat at the edge of the bed, and I sit up, pushing the covers off. Shuffling closer, I throw my arms around him, burying my face into his shoulder.

"Oh my God," I say, breathing in his scent. He smells like home, like candles and black coffee and a little bit of cologne. "Oh my God, you're here!"

"I came as soon as I could." He squeezes me tight. "I'm so happy you're safe."

Finally, the tears come, but they're tears of joy. For a moment, everything else melts away, and for the first time in two months, I'm happy. With Liam here, I know I'm safe.

He pulls back, his dark brown eyes scanning my face, lingering on my neck, then traveling down to my forearm and bruised wrist. He doesn't ask questions, doesn't pry any details from me like he normally would. When his eyes meet mine again, he says, "I'm sorry." The smile falls. "I'm so sorry."

"Stop. It's not your fault."

His gaze drops to the stitches again. "Are you okay? That's probably a dumb question. I mean, can I do anything? Do you need anything?"

"I'm just happy you're here." I sit beside him with my legs dangling over the edge of the bed and lean my head against his shoulder. "What about you? Are you okay?"

"I'm fine. Just been worried about you. If we'd known where you were… If the Commander had let us, we would've gotten you out."

There is a part of me that's angry—or maybe hurt—no one came for me. It formed when I finally realized I was stuck at the Everetts'. But that feeling isn't as strong right now; it's buried under the guilt and trauma that churn together to create an unbearable numbness.

We sit like this for a few minutes—my head against his shoulder and his arm loosely around me. I have so many questions for him and I know he probably does for me, too, but I don't want to ruin this. I don't want any talk about my time in the Red Zone or whatever has happened with the resistance. All that matters is that he's here.

"About last night," he says, breaking the silence. "I would've stayed longer if I could, even taken you with me, but—"

"It was too dangerous." I was very much aware of the extra security on the property. But what if he had stayed? Nothing would have changed the fact that I was drugged, but would Wyatt have still taken advantage of me? Would Liam and I have been able to make it somewhere safe, considering Eli apparently wasn't involved?

"I won't let anything like that happen to you again," Liam says. "I promise."

There's another knock on the partially opened door, and Eli pops his head in. "Sorry to interrupt," he says. "Liam, could you help Sebastien and Addison in the attic?"

"Addison's here?" I ask.

"She is," Liam says, standing. "We wouldn't have been able to make it here without her."

"Wait, I want to see her." I stand, too, and pain shoots up the leg that was cut when I jumped the fence.

"Soon," Eli says, "but we need to talk with you first."

We? As in him and Ember?

Throwing one arm over my shoulders, Liam gives me a final light squeeze. "We'll be upstairs. We're not going anywhere."

"You can't stay?" I ask.

He looks to Eli then back to me. "The faster we get everything ready for tonight, the sooner we can leave."

So they do have a plan. As tempted as I am to ask what it is, I don't. I trust them, and if they can get me away from the Society, I don't care where we go.

Liam exits the room, and Eli shuts the door behind them. Murmurs circulate outside, but I can't hear what they're saying. There's a third voice, I think—a man's. I pace the bedroom, ignoring the slowly dulling pain in my leg. Although I'm still tired, I don't want to lie back down. I've been lying around all day, and now I want to be productive, to help any way I can in getting us out of here.

The door opens again, and I freeze at the foot of the bed. Eli enters with the drawstring bag in hand. He studies me briefly, eyes moving to every exposed injury on my body before looking away.

A second figure emerges, carrying a notebook and pen, and shuts the door, and my breath catches in my throat. His dreadlocks are twisted at the crown of his head, exposing the jagged scar that starts near his right earlobe and ends at his jaw. His icy eyes search me just as Liam's did, surveying my injuries, and I jerk my sleeve back down.

My heart races, being rebuilt and broken over and over in a matter of seconds. This can't be real. This *isn't* real. It has to be some sort of hallucination caused by stress and trauma, or the drugs Wyatt slipped in my drinks last night. *He's supposed to be dead.*

I blink hard, but he's still there. His eyes finally meet mine, but they're not comforting like when we were together in the Blue Zone. They're frozen again, detached and cold. His face is hard. The mask he finally removed back then has returned, and it's as though we've been teleported to our first day together after I was abducted by the Black Hats.

Before I can stop myself, I close the space between us and wrap my arms around his waist, burying my face in his chest. He tenses, sucking in a breath.

"You're alive," I say. It comes out quiet and strangled—an odd mixture of a question and a statement.

The room is suddenly spinning as my brain tries to comprehend what's going on, and I hold on to him for support. I'm desperately searching for the safety in his touch, the comfort in his once-intoxicating smell, but it's not there.

He was captured with me. I heard him being sentenced to death at the auction. Wyatt and his parents went to the Green Zone to watch him die. How is he here?

Nixon gently pats my back before wriggling from my grip and taking a step back. His face remains blank, and he looks at Eli, standing off to the side.

"You didn't know?" Eli asks.

I shake my head, keeping my eyes trained on Nixon. He's lost weight—not an alarming amount, but it's noticeable. His nose appears to be slightly crooked, and a healing scab cuts through his bottom lip.

"They told me you were dead," I say.

"It was all over the news," Eli says. "The Green Zone's group organized an operation to free him on his execution day."

I look at Eli, who's leaning against the small black desk on the wall to my right. "I didn't… I wasn't allowed to watch the news. But they kept telling me—" I stop myself. He doesn't need to know that Wyatt constantly made it a point to remind me about Nixon's fate.

"We have a lot to talk about," Eli says. "Nixon and I are going to ask you some questions, okay?"

"What kind of questions?"

"Same stuff we'd ask anyone who'd been in your situation." He pulls the chair out from under the desk and rolls it toward Nixon. "Why don't you take a seat?"

I look between the two of them—Nixon in the desk chair by the door, Eli still half-sitting on the desk—suddenly unsettled by their presence. I remind myself I'm safe. They're not here to hurt me. They're only here to help, and my brother and best friend are close by.

I finally sit on the edge of the bed.

"Let's start at the beginning," Eli says. "I know you spoke with an interrogator after the auction. What sort of questions did he ask?"

I shrug. "Just about the day I was taken from the Black Hats—if I was hurt or threatened and if I had any contact with other resistance members. I told him I went willingly and never met anyone else."

"Anything else?"

The file about my dead father pops into my mind. "No."

"Did he say anything to you—something that would possibly make you doubt the resistance or what we do?" When I hesitate, Eli adds, "You can tell me. Even if you didn't truly believe him, I need to know what was said to you."

Aside from bringing up my father's alleged murder, the interrogator told me Nixon had manipulated me during my time with him. I don't want to deal with that embarrassment on top of everything else.

"He didn't say anything like that," I lie.

"Okay. What happened after your interrogation?"

Tapping a finger against my leg, I glance around the room, unsure of how much I should tell them. If I go into every detail, I know I'll completely lose it because that night, all I wanted was to be with Nixon. I cried in the dark, reaching across the bed where he should've been. I remember it so vividly. Every broken emotion that slashed through my heart, every tear that was absorbed by my pillow, that insatiable need to feel him there, to be with him.

Now that he's here, I don't know what I want or what I feel. I'm happy he's alive and safe, but that's the extent of it. Everything else I felt toward him has been buried under the numbness, but it's all there somewhere, murky and distant. It has to be. I dreamed of seeing him again in so many different scenarios. Some were beautiful, others were brutal, but I loved them all just because he was there, even if it wasn't real.

"I was taken to my private buyer," I say cautiously, "where I met Carson Everett. He told me he'd purchased me for his son, and he took me to his guesthouse where I was kept for two weeks, locked in from the outside." I hear the click of Nixon's pen. "They wouldn't let me out until I earned their trust."

"At what point did you meet Wyatt?" Eli asks. My stomach clenches at the name.

"The day after I arrived," I say, looking back at him. "That's when I learned I was supposed to marry him. I tried to refuse, said something stupid, and…" Bringing my thumb to my mouth, I begin nibbling on my nail, something I haven't done since agreeing to go along with Wyatt's game.

"And what?" Eli asks.

"He hit me." As I say it, the day replays in my head, fast-forwarding through the past couple of months in a matter of seconds. From the corner of my eye, I see Nixon write that down, and I wonder if this is as difficult for him to listen to as it is for me to talk about.

"Was that the only time he hit you?"

"No." I press the heels of my hands to my eyes just before the tears can spill over.

"You're safe, Ivy. He can't hurt you here."

That only makes the tears flow more. The dead can't physically hurt you, but they live in the depths of your mangled mind, waiting to slaughter your sanity.

"You said you had to earn their trust to get out of their guesthouse," Nixon says. His voice sends a chill up my spine. It sounds the same as when we were first together—glacial and authoritative. "How did you manage to do that?"

"I just told them I was ready to cooperate and did whatever they said," I say, dropping my hands to look at him. He has one leg propped on the other with the notebook open in his lap.

"Like what?"

"I don't know—anything. How to dress, how to talk, how to act. I did whatever I had to in order to avoid Wyatt's punishments."

"Did they ever ask about the resistance?"

"No."

"Did you ever bring it up?"

"No."

"Even if it was by accident?"

"What are you suggesting?" I search his face for some sort of comfort, some emotion, but there's nothing. It's a solid, impenetrable barrier.

"It's just a question," Eli says. "No one's insinuating anything."

"I never brought it up," I say.

"Were you ever able to leave the property?" Eli asks.

"Only with Wyatt or his parents."

"Did you have contact with any other members of the Society?"

"A few, yeah."

"Why?"

Shrugging, I allow my eyes to wander the room again, stopping on the bag of stolen documents. "Marrying Wyatt meant I'd become part of the Society. They wanted me to familiarize myself with everyone."

I met so many people while with the Everetts I can't remember who was in the Society and who wasn't. They all seemed the same—cardboard cutouts posing as people.

"Let's skip ahead," Eli says. "Walk us through last night; start at the beginning of the rehearsal dinner. I want to know what happened up until my scouts saw you."

My stomach shrivels and my body goes cold. I look between the two men, who patiently wait. Eli's leaning back with his palms against the top of the desk. Nixon is studying me with the pen hovering above his page of notes. His gaze burns through me, and I want to hide under the covers. I don't want him watching me, don't want him dissecting every little thing I say like he did with Kase. More than anything, though, I don't want to admit to what I've done. Especially not to him.

"I wasn't downstairs at the very beginning," I finally say. "I had to wait for Wyatt to come get me, so I stayed in our room as people arrived and made sure everything was ready." I motion to the bag behind Eli.

"So you planned all of this?" Nixon clarifies.

"Sort of." I take a deep breath, tapping my leg again with two fingers, one after the other. "When Wyatt came for me, he brought me downstairs, where we talked with his father and guests, and he made me drink… a lot."

"Did he give you anything else besides alcohol?" Eli asks. "Last night or any other time you were there?"

"Are you asking me if I've been using drugs?"

Eli shrugs one shoulder. "I could tell you were under the influence of something other than alcohol. If he made you do anything and you complied to avoid his abuse, you can tell us."

"I never used anything," I say. "I was drunk, that's all. I'd never drunk before, and I hadn't eaten anything."

A small piece of me wants to tell him about what Wyatt did to my drinks last night, but that would open the door to a whole new conversation that I'm not ready to discuss. Neither of them say anything or ask any other questions, so I continue with a condensed version of last night.

"I didn't feel well after drinking so much, so I went upstairs to lie down. I ended up falling asleep in my dress and woke up before Wyatt. I cut the tracker out in the bathroom, grabbed the bag I had hidden, and escaped. The scouts saw me when I climbed the neighbors' fence. I didn't realize who they were until they shoved me in the car and told me they worked for you."

"Okay," Eli says, pushing himself off the desk. "When you were brought here—"

"Hold on," Nixon interrupts. "At what point did you see Liam?"

"Umm…" I close my eyes for a moment, trying to visualize exactly when my brother approached me. "He found me right when I was heading upstairs. Wait, how did you know—"

"A scout and I were staking out the place and had Liam wired. You told him to go home."

Eli raises his eyebrows. "Is that true, Ivy?"

I pull my knees up to my chest. "Yes."

"Were you not happy to see your brother?" Nixon asks, taking on an accusatory tone.

"I was, but—"

"You know he's part of the resistance. Did it not cross your mind that he could've helped you? That maybe he was there to get you out?"

"I didn't want him to get hurt!" My eyes brim with tears, but I'm quick to wipe them away with the back of my hand. "I didn't know you were with him. But it's not like you were going to help me anyway." The last line comes out with a razor-sharp edge, but Nixon doesn't seem the least bit fazed by it. In fact, he smirks. What the hell is his problem?

"You disappeared after that," he says. "You went upstairs and didn't return, so I pulled Liam out—couldn't risk him being found out. So what happened up there?"

"I told you, I went to sleep," I say.

"This morning, you were covered in blood," Eli says. "Where did that come from?"

My heartbeat picks up. Wrapping my arms around my legs, I try to think of something to say. I can't talk about that right now. I can't relive it.

"My arm," I mumble. "I was trying to be quick when cutting out my tracker, and it ended up getting messy."

Eli nods slowly, glancing at Nixon then back to me. "When I asked if it was your blood, you said it wasn't."

Shit. "I must not have been paying attention. I had a lot on my mind and I don't think I'd sobered up yet."

"What's Wyatt like?" Nixon asks.

My gaze shifts to him and his growing list of notes. "What kind of question is that?"

He's leaning back, tapping his pen against the notebook. "I just want to get an idea of what kind of person he is."

"I don't know—an asshole."

"Can you be more specific?"

I roll my eyes and let out a long breath. Is this his way of asking if I felt anything for Wyatt? Of all people, he should be the last to think that.

"He's narcissistic," I say. "Psychotic, manipulative, controlling."

My hatred toward Wyatt is still fierce, so why do I hate myself for what I did to him? If he'd just stayed asleep, I wouldn't have had to kill him. Murdering him hasn't rid me of the control he has over me. I can still feel it whittling away at what's left of me, and I may never be free of it. Not until I lose myself completely—if I haven't already.

"When you lay down last night," Eli says, "did Wyatt go to bed with you?"

"No," I say. "The party was still going on."

"You said he was controlling, and someone was always watching you. I can't imagine he'd let you out of his sight, especially since you were surrounded by so many Elites and Society members."

I tighten my arms around my legs, feeling my heart hammer against them. "I guess… Maybe he didn't want me getting out of hand in front of everyone but wanted to keep up his image."

Eli moves across the room and stands beside Nixon. He glances over the notes and, without looking up, says, "Is there any part of you that cares about Wyatt?"

I scoff. "You think I *loved* him?"

"Not love, necessarily," Eli says. "But from the times I spoke with you before the auction—and from speaking with your brother, Addison, and Nixon—you seem like a pretty compassionate person. You don't like seeing other people get hurt. Does that extend to him, too?"

"No!"

"It's not uncommon for victims to begin caring for their captors. Stockholm Syndrome is—"

"I do *not* have Stockholm Syndrome!" I yell, balling my hands into fists. "I hated him—I was afraid of him."

Nixon jots that down.

Do they think I sold them out? Is that what this sudden interrogation is for?

There was never a part of me that loved Wyatt or even remotely cared for him. He was a disgusting person. The thought of having feelings for him, being intimate with him, jerks my mind back to last night before I passed out. His hands on me, his breath against my skin, his lips devouring mine while I tried to fight back.

Tears sting my eyes. All I want is to scream at Eli and Nixon to get out, curl up under the blankets again, and cry. I want to claw at every inch of my flesh until the pain replaces that of Wyatt's touch.

Eli looks up at me, his expression unreadable. "Are those bruises from him?"

"Yes," I force out.

"Did you two get into a fight? Maybe as you were trying to leave?"

I turn my face away from them, closing my eyes. *Not now. I can't do this now.* It's humiliating. I couldn't fight him off, couldn't stop him from doing what he wanted to me. But Nixon and Eli won't stop until they get answers, and I imagine it'll be worse for me if I refuse to say anything.

"No," I say. "I told you, he was asleep."

"So you're saying you cut open your arm and pulled out your tracker without him ever waking up? That sounds pretty excruciating. Surely he would have heard you and tried to stop you, especially on the day of your wedding."

I shrug, wiping my face with my fingers. "Guess he was a deep sleeper."

"Was?"

My eyes snap open, and panic begins to squirm in the pit of my stomach. "He was this morning. He didn't hear me."

"You said that you hated him and were afraid of him," Nixon says, studying his notes, "as if that's not the case anymore."

"What do you mean?"

He looks up at me. "I mean, you said it in the past tense, like maybe you hated him and were afraid of him at first but that changed."

I'm fully focused on Nixon and his cool, casual demeanor. I recognize it from when I listened in on him questioning Kase. He's not here to provide any support or help me; he's here because everyone knows he's good at picking up on inconsistencies. They're trying to trap me.

"You're interrogating me like you did Kase," I say to Nixon. Anger bleeds into my words, but I don't care. "You think I'm like him, that I sold you out?"

"I don't think we're getting the whole story," Nixon says matter-of-factly, "and until we do, I don't know what to make of this."

"Are you serious?!" *I* was the one who defended Nixon whenever Wyatt talked him down, and I suffered plenty of beatings because of that. Now he's acting like I'm the enemy. "Whose fault do you think it is that I was taken there? Because it sure as hell wasn't mine."

"That's enough," Eli says, stepping forward. He doesn't yell, but an assertiveness replaces his gentle tone. "I want the truth and I want it now. Until I get it, I will not clear you to leave the Northern Unity, and you may want to cooperate sooner than later. There's word that the Red Zone will be placed under lockdown because of what happened this morning, which will make it a lot more difficult to get you out."

A flare of hope attempts to arise at hearing that I'm supposed to be leaving the country, but it's quickly snuffed by the ever-growing tension in the room.

I press my forehead against my knees. I didn't want to kill Wyatt; I don't even want to accept that I did it. Something inside me suggests maybe he's still alive, that his parents found him after I left and were able to get him help.

I still can't believe that this is happening and that Nixon is really here. The Everetts took pride in telling me he was going to die. I should've known better than to believe them. I should've expected the resistance to save him, even if no one came for me.

I try to remind myself again that I'm safe here. No one will find me. Liam is upstairs if I need him, and he's not going anywhere. As soon as I'm out of here, I never have to worry about the Enlightened Society again. But with every optimistic thought I squeeze in between the flashbacks, my mind conjures up a million more things that could potentially go wrong.

"I'm telling the truth," I mumble. I don't bother wiping my tears away this time. They trickle over my nose and lips.

"I don't have time for this," Eli says. "If I don't know your involvement with these people, I can't rightfully send you to the Commander's camp."

"My *involvement*?" I lift my head. "I was sold to them!"

"I'm aware, but I need to know what happened after that. I need to know how you were able to get out with top-secret documents, somehow without being seen." Eli marches over to the desk, swiping the drawstring bag from the top. "When you're ready to cooperate, let us know."

He starts toward the door, and Nixon stands, returning the chair to the desk before following him.

"Wait," I blurt out.

Eli stops with his hand on the handle, and Nixon freezes in the space between the desk and the exit. Their eyes are on me, and my chest tightens.

I have to give them something to make them trust me. They already have the documents I stole, but apparently that's not enough. I focus on Nixon, standing only a few feet away from me, and once again search his face for some sort of strength. It's empty.

"The blood wasn't mine," I whisper. My hands are noticeably trembling, and I clasp them in front of my legs.

"Whose was it?" Eli asks.

I squeeze my hands tighter together and feel metal rub against my fingers. Looking down, I realize the engagement ring is still there; it's suddenly heavy, weighing down my hand. The sight of it repulses me. Yanking it off my finger, I fling it to the floor. It clinks against the wood and bounces, coming to a sliding stop at Nixon's feet.

"Let me talk to her alone," he says.

My heart thunders in my chest. More tears pour out. I want to protest. I don't want to be left alone with someone who's basically a stranger again. But at the same time, I want it to just be me and him, as if being alone will rekindle what I used to feel with him.

"Fine," Eli says, although he doesn't sound too sure. "I'll be close by if you need anything. Ivy, I suggest you take that pill."

"What is it?" I ask in a shaky voice.

With his back to me, he opens the door half an inch. "Just take it."

"I'm not taking anything until I know what it is."

He lets out an audible sigh and hesitates, but finally says, "Emergency contraception."

Nixon

I stare at the door for a few moments after Eli exits, forcing myself to take several deep breaths. Rage clouds my vision. My heart pounds violently in my ears. Every rapid-fire thought is fully focused on hunting down that bastard and plunging a knife into his chest. The need to watch him suffer, to watch the pathetic life drain from his eyes, consumes me.

The only thing that snaps me out of the hate-filled trance is the soft, strangled cry that escapes Ivy. Seeing the way she trembles, her face buried in her hands, waters down my anger—for now.

Plucking the engagement ring from the floor, I drop my notebook and pen on the desk and roll the chair across the room. Stopping a few feet from the bed, I sit down, searching for something to say to her. I wasn't meant to hear Eli's words, and I can't imagine what's going through her head right now. She must be humiliated, traumatized for sure, and clearly there's a part of her that blames me for everything that happened. I understand why. I blame myself, too.

"Ivy, look at me," I say.

She sniffles and slowly lifts her head, but avoids my gaze. Her face is red and blotchy. Tears continue to stream down her cheeks. Folding her legs in front of her, she drops her hands in her lap, and her eyes fall to the engagement ring between my fingers.

"I need you to tell me *something*," I say. "Otherwise, Eli won't let us go anywhere, and we don't want to be stuck here much longer."

"I thought you were dead," she mumbles.

"I know, but I'm here. I have your brother to thank for that."

"How come he could save you but not me?" It comes out as a whisper, almost like she doesn't really intend for me to hear her.

"He wanted to—we all did—but we didn't have a location or even the name of your buyers. It wasn't until Liam contacted your mother that my group found out. Apparently Eli's group put a plan in place after you approached Ember, but…" But she escaped before anything was put into action. I still don't know what their exact plan was—not that it matters anymore.

"Do you want to talk about that?" I ask, nodding toward the tiny pill on the nightstand behind her.

Without looking back, she shakes her head, and her puffy eyes travel around the room. She sinks her long, painted nails into her palms.

I study the circular marks on her neck and the bruises on her wrist. When her sleeve was pulled up earlier, the same marks snaked up her forearm, and I have a feeling there are plenty more on other parts of her body. The anger threatens to take over again, and I try to push it down. Looking at her right now only gives it strength.

"Tell me where the blood came from," I say.

Her nails go deeper into her skin. I roll the chair closer and lean forward, resting my elbows on my legs.

Her chin quivers. The silence drags on. With each passing second, I have to refrain from reaching out for her. Even something as small as brushing my hand against hers would be too much. I'm here to get answers, not drag out whatever it was we had before our capture. Normally, I can turn off my emotions at any given moment, but right now it's impossible.

"You're not in trouble," I say gently. "Whatever's going on, I can help."

A shuddering breath escapes her. She opens her mouth to speak, but a sob interrupts and she brings a hand to her mouth to stifle it. Finally, she chokes out, "Wyatt... I killed him."

Stunned, I don't say anything for a minute. I'm frozen, repeating the line in my head several times before it actually sinks in.

"Jesus, Ivy," I mutter, leaning back.

I'm glad the bastard's dead, but I wish I'd been the one to take his life. Not only for what he's done, but so Ivy wouldn't have to bear that trauma on top of whatever else she's gone through. The fact that he pushed her to that point—to where she saw that as her only way out—enrages me more. Ivy's one of the kindest, most caring people I've ever met; how could anyone treat her that way?

And the Red Zone's resistance—where the hell were they when all of this was happening? I know it's difficult to track down victims of the auction after they've been sold, but Ivy approached Ember four days ago. Why did it take until today for them to just get a couple of scouts out there, and why was I not informed of any of their plans until *after* Ivy was in their custody?

Covering her face with her hands, Ivy folds forward, more sobs escaping her. I glance at the door, knowing Eli's comment about being nearby was actually a warning for me. He's likely standing right outside, listening, and at any moment, he could barge in here and end the questioning if he feels like anything's getting too personal. Right now, though, I don't care—not about his warnings or about his threats of informing the Commander.

Standing, I slowly move to the bed and take a seat beside Ivy, placing a hand on her upper back. For a moment she gravitates toward me but immediately pulls back, shaking my hand off. A burst of frustration floods my body.

The comfort I used to be able to give her is gone. All because of *him*.

"I'm sorry," she says between hiccupping breaths. "I'm so sorry."

I've told her before that I never wanted her to kill anyone, so she probably thinks I'm mad at her, but that couldn't be further from the truth. I hurt for her. Maybe there's even a part of me that's proud of her—not for killing Wyatt, exactly, but for the courage she's found. I just hate that she had to find it like this.

"Tell me what happened."

"I woke up and went to the bathroom. I cut open my arm and he woke up and saw me." She pauses, shifting beside me. Her fingers find a loose thread at the end of her sleeve. "He tried to drag me out but I fought back. We were fighting over the scissors. Then he pinned me down... He threatened to hurt Liam, told me he was going to make me watch. And—" Her voice hitches on the last word. She sits up, hugging herself. Self-soothing.

"You're not in trouble," I remind her.

"I don't know what happened," she says in a shaky voice, squeezing her eyes shut. "I didn't even think about it; my body just acted on its own."

"What did you do?"

"The scissors... I... I slit his throat." She presses a hand to her mouth again as another shuddering breath takes over.

I search for something to say to take her pain away but know there's nothing that will. I've had this same talk with several of my members, but they were all trained to some degree—they knew that the potential of having to take someone's life always loomed. Ivy only had desperation to act on.

"There was so much blood," she whispers. "And even after everything he did, I still wanted to help him." Shaking her head, she smears the tears streaking her cheeks with her hands. "God, what is *wrong* with me?"

"You're a good person."

She lets out a sarcastic half-laugh and redirects her gaze to the ceiling fan. "I'm not."

"You *are*." I angle myself to face her directly. "It was self-defense. I know that doesn't make it any easier to process, but think about it—do you think he would've shown you any mercy? If he was already hurting you, what would've stopped him from taking it further?"

"He wouldn't have killed me."

Before I can ask why she'd possibly think that, the door opens, revealing Eli—shoulders tense and hand gripping the handle. He glances between the two of us, likely noting how close we are, and I have a feeling I'm going to get a lecture on it later.

"Attic. Now," he says. "We have company."

A muffled knock from another part of the house captures his attention. Ivy and I jump to our feet, and he swiftly exits the room. As his footsteps fade down the hall toward the stairs, another, more forceful knock sounds.

"What's he talking about?" Ivy asks as I return the chair to its place and swipe my notebook from the desk.

Voices not belonging to Ember or Eli come from downstairs. I hold a finger to my lips, and Ivy nods at my silent command. With a hand on her shoulder, I steer her toward the door and out of the room. I survey our surroundings as we hurry toward our destination, keeping each step light.

The ladder of the open attic is at the end of the hall, just off to the side of the banister that looks over the staircase. Eli's nowhere in sight, but I can hear him talking with the 'visitors'—soldiers most likely. We knew raids were coming, but knowing what I do now, I expect this to be far worse than we originally predicted.

A door closes downstairs. Eli's pleasant voice slowly trails off, and I quicken my strides, forcing Ivy to do the same. When we reach the ladder, I nudge her forward. She quickly climbs up and I'm right behind her. On the second-to-last step her foot catches the lip, and a gasp escapes her as she stumbles backward. Reaching up with one arm, I steady her, giving her a gentle push upward.

Liam appears at the top, extending a hand to his sister, and I crawl in after her. As soon as I'm inside the attic, he passes me a gun before ushering Ivy toward the back of the narrow space. I squat at the edge of the entrance, setting the notebook down and motioning to Seb, who already has a gun in hand. Lying on his stomach across from me, he reaches down as far as he can, grabbing the ladder and folding it. Together, we slowly pull it up, working against the hinges that want to slam the door shut. We carefully close the hatch just as the voices get closer again.

Seb and I remain crouched on opposite sides of the entrance, weapons ready. I jerk my chin toward the dangling chain of the single light. Addison reaches for it, and there's a quiet click before we're shrouded in darkness.

I keep my breathing steady, but my heart slams against my chest. Despite the temperature outside, the attic is stiflingly hot and its air thick with the tension between all of us. This isn't the first raid I've had to endure, but it is the first since having a bounty on my head. This isn't about me, though. They're looking for Ivy. If they're already searching for her all the way out here, that means they've scoured the inner cities of the Red Zone. We're two hours away from her buyers, so they must have acted as soon as they figured out she was missing— and found their dead son.

A floorboard creaks beneath us. With Seb beside me, I'm confident we can at least slow them down. Liam, while he's never actually had to pull the trigger on anyone, is a good shot and can help out if needed.

Voices float up to us. Leaning forward, I strain to hear what's going on. One pair of footsteps passes under the attic door, but Eli stays close, probably standing directly underneath it.

"So you said we're under lockdown?" he asks. "All because of a missing person?"

"Yes, sir," another man says from a little farther away.

"Come on," Eli says, taking on a friendly tone. "General Reese has never ordered a lockdown for something so juvenile. It would have to be much more severe to go to these lengths."

There's a long pause. Sweat beads at my hairline, and the air becomes heavier with every second of silence. I can't tell how many there are, but if it's like the raids in the Green Zone, there should be three soldiers—two tearing apart the house and one keeping an eye on Eli and Ember, if she's still here. With three of us in the resistance up here and Eli down there, we could take them.

"If the person in question isn't located tonight," the man says, "we can expect this in every zone."

"How bad is this, Jeremy?" Eli asks.

"All we've been told is that there was an incident within one of the thirteen families."

"And they think it's because of this girl?" Eli asks.

"At this time, they're not sure."

The footsteps that passed by minutes ago—or maybe they belong to someone else—return.

"Looks good," a second, gruffer voice says. "Mind if we have a quick look up there?"

Shit. Holding my breath, I tighten my grip on the gun, ready to act if anyone who isn't Eli makes their way up here. I'm fully confident we can overpower them, but since this isn't an isolated raid, there are more than likely more soldiers outside, searching the rest of this neighborhood. The second they hear gunshots, they'll swarm this house. There's no way we can take out a horde of armed soldiers.

"Not at all," Eli says.

Someone tugs on the cord attached to the underside of the door, and it slowly begins to open. Through the small crack, light shines up into the dark space, and I carefully pull away from the entrance. The gap grows another inch, hinges whining. I look at Seb, who locks eyes with me, ready for my command.

Another inch. Then two. It's unnervingly still. Slow, calculated breaths are the only thing keeping my nerves at bay. It doesn't matter how many times I do this; it never gets any easier.

Seb steadies his gun, aiming at the entrance. I glance back at the other three, who are crouched along one of the shelves that line the back of the attic. Liam has his eyes trained on the door with a gun of his own, and the other two are behind him.

When the door has opened enough for the ladder to be unfolded, I draw in a final deep breath, gently resting my finger on the trigger. No matter what happens, none of my people die today.

"Hey!" a third voice yells.

Everything freezes—the door, the movement downstairs, my heart.

"Company's about to clear out for shift change and R-and-R. Are you two ready?"

"Yeah, all clear!" someone else calls back. "Thank you for your cooperation, sir."

"Of course," Eli says.

The cord is released and the door slams shut. As soon as we're sealed inside, the air quickly becomes hot again. No more voices. No more rooms being searched. Even after the footsteps disappear, none of us move. I remove my finger from the trigger but keep my gun ready.

It could be a trap—luring Eli downstairs, taking his attention off the fugitives he's harboring in his attic while a soldier investigates alone. As far as we know, no one in the Society has ever suspected Eli of being in the resistance. He's worked closely with their kind for years and he knows plenty of military personnel. But with everything so different now, I don't want to take any risks.

We all remain frozen in silence. Minutes pass without any word on what's happening. My heart has slowed to a steadier pace but I remain on high alert, listening, waiting. Those soldiers will be back to conduct a more thorough search, and it's going to be a damn nightmare getting out of here. In the Society's eyes, Ivy is their property, and like before, they will do anything to get her back.

Finally, the door is pulled open and the ladder unfolded.

"All clear," Eli calls as he makes his way up to us.

Standing, I find my way to the chain dangling from the ceiling in the center of the room and turn the light on. Seb is already on his feet, and Liam, Ivy, and Addison slowly rise to theirs. Despite the cramped space—with its shelves stocked with supplies from weapons to nonperishables and the two backpacks and rucksacks on the floor—the atmosphere suddenly feels lighter, more breathable. From the top step, Eli's eyes briefly find their way to each one of us then survey the opened, half-packed bags.

"Nixon, come with me, please," he says, turning to head back down. "The rest of you finish packing; take as much as you can."

Scooping up the notebook, I pass my weapon to Seb and follow Eli down. We walk toward the room Ivy was in, but Eli stops halfway down the hall, spinning around to face me. He doesn't speak immediately. Instead, he glances up at the attic behind me, extending his hand. Understanding what he wants, I pass him the notebook, and he flips it open, looking over what I wrote.

"She killed him," he says in a low voice.

"Yes." I knew he was listening.

"You were sitting pretty close to her." He flips a page.

"I was comforting her."

The notebook snaps shut, and Eli holds it in front of him. "That's not your place."

"It's the same thing I do with all of my members when—"

"But she's not one of your members. She's your mission, nothing more."

"She's been through hell. She needs someone right now."

"So leave that to her brother. I need you to be a leader, especially as you guide her, Liam, and Seb outside of the walls. You can't afford to be distracted. Understood?"

"Yeah."

"I'm serious, Nixon. You're going to be meeting the Commander. If he knew—"

"I've got it." Letting out a long breath, I drag my hand down my face and switch topics. "Who's watching over my group while Liam and I are away?"

"Nadia's already sent her second-in-command. That, along with Piper's probation… We're spread thin right now, so this escape needs to go as perfectly as possible." He lets that last line linger. "I'll finish making copies of those documents and send Ember up to check your wounds. Go finish packing."

18. Tell Me What You're Running From

Ivy

"It's going to be okay," Addison says, holding me close like it will somehow prevent me from slipping away again.

I stare ahead at the shelf that lines the wall of the narrow attic, focusing on the towering boxes of bullets. Nixon and Liam are packing up Addison's car with all our supplies, and Sebastien and Eli are downstairs.

In the small amount of time my best friend and I have had alone, not much has been said. Like Liam, she apologized profusely, even though none of it was her fault, and asked if I was okay—a question I don't really know how to answer. I'm here in one piece, yet I feel as though I'm a heap of shattered bits with edges jagged like glass. I'm alive but feel like a ghost.

"They're going to keep you safe," Addison says, rubbing my back. "And we're going to see each other again, okay? Soon."

I wonder if she honestly believes that. It sounds more like something she feels obligated to say in this moment, something to ease the pain of leaving her behind.

"Okay," I mumble, but I don't believe it. Addison's optimism is something I've always loved about her, but right now, it's annoying. Infuriating, even. I know she wants to make me feel better, but I don't want to be lied to. I don't want to go through each day hoping it's the day she and I will be reunited. We both know it won't happen. Not with her being the Police Chief's daughter.

Things already felt different between us when I first saw her, and everything became even more strained when I learned she wouldn't be escaping with us. Once again, the Society has succeeded in taking away someone I care about.

"We should get going," I say, pulling out of her embrace.

She nods, offering a small smile, and I lead the way out of the attic. Addison reaches out and gives my hand a squeeze as we enter the kitchen.

Eli and Sebastien stand over the map that's sprawled out on the table, going over last-minute preparations. It's insane to make this journey before dark. But after the raid less than an hour ago, Eli insisted we had to leave as soon as possible. I couldn't hear anything that was said when we hid in the attic—just faint murmurs between my frantic breaths—but I knew they were looking for me. The Red Zone doesn't normally have raids. In fact, I've never heard of one taking place here. What was worse was when Nixon came back up, informing us of a lockdown that would likely spread to the rest of the country. He didn't say why, but I already knew the answer to that, too.

The Society knows what I did. They know I murdered Wyatt. Whether everyone else aside from Nixon knows that, I'm not sure, but I don't plan on sharing it with any of them. I'll keep that vile part of myself locked away and hope Nixon respects me enough to keep it between us.

The two men look over at Addison and me.

"Ready?" Sebastien asks, folding up the map. His nearly black eyes brighten as he offers a toothy grin. He doesn't seem nervous at all—more like he views this as a road trip rather than a potentially deadly mission.

"Yup," Addison responds for both of us. Another hand squeeze. Her voice isn't lively like it normally is. It's hollow, bleak.

"Alright." Sebastien tucks the map into his back pocket while shaking Eli's hand and thanking him. Turning to us, he says, "Nixon and Liam should almost be finished." He starts out of the kitchen, and Addison and I follow hand-in-hand.

Right as we're about to cross over into the hallway that leads to the back door, Eli says, "Ivy, can I talk to you for a moment?"

I freeze, heart racing. *Not another interrogation. I can't do that again.* But I've quickly learned not to question him, so I free my hand from Addison's and take a few tentative steps toward him.

"I'll send her out in a minute," Eli tells the other two.

They hesitate a second longer then continue out of the kitchen. Eli wordlessly turns his back to me and circles the conjoined table and island, grabbing a glass from one of the cupboards. He fills it with water from the dispenser on the stainless-steel fridge and swipes something from the counter out of my line of vision before returning to me. A comfortable distance away, he stops and holds out his hand. The tiny white pill rests in his palm. I completely forgot about it after Nixon and I started talking about Wyatt.

"You don't have to take it if you don't want to," Eli says. His face is softer than when he was interrogating me, and his eyes are full of sympathy. "I just want you to know you have the option."

Of course I want to take it. The last thing I need is to be carrying a part of Wyatt inside me. Although I know it wouldn't be offered to me had Ember not felt it was justified after the examination, it feels like taking it would confirm what I already suspect Wyatt did to me, and I don't want to believe it's true. I don't want to imagine how I was violated while unconscious or for anyone else to find out. It's humiliating enough that Nixon knows, and I wish I'd just kept my mouth shut instead of questioning Eli.

I snatch the pill from Eli's hand, pop it in my mouth and wash it—along with the bitter truth that accompanies it—down with the water.

"Mild cramping, nausea, and fatigue are common side effects," Eli says, taking the glass from me. "And I highly suggest seeing a doctor once you get to the Commander's camp for STI testing."

My face burns, and I shift my weight from one foot to the other. I remind myself that despite Eli being in the resistance, he does actually work in the medical field. This is normal for him.

"Okay," I say.

"Is there anything else you want to tell me? Or maybe Ember, if that makes you more comfortable?"

"No."

"Then you're free to go. Good luck out there."

Before he can change his mind, I turn and head out of the kitchen, stopping in the doorway to say, "Thank you for everything."

Outside, the sun hangs low, sending flares of pink and orange across the clear sky. The neighborhood is quiet; no wailing sirens or shouting of lingering soldiers following the raid like in the Green Zone. I slip through the gate and stop beside the front of Addison's car. She's already assumed her position in the driver's seat, but Sebastien, Liam, and Nixon are huddled behind the vehicle, talking amongst themselves. Sebastien and Liam's backs are to me with Nixon in front of them, all three wearing the same black outfit as I am.

Nixon glances up at me then whispers something to the other two, and they disperse. He and Liam round the car, and Sebastien walks toward me, holding out a black hooded jacket.

"You'll be in the back with us," he says as I pull it on.

"Us?" I ask.

He opens the door behind Addison and motions for me to get in. "Me and Nixon."

My stomach knots at the thought of being trapped between the two of them—specifically, being so close to Nixon. Addison's had the same car since we were in high school, and I know from our times of piling into it with our friends that it's a tight fit. It's going to be even worse being stuck back there with two grown men.

Liam's already taken the passenger seat beside Addison, and Nixon opens the back door on the opposite side of the vehicle. I reluctantly slide into the middle seat just as he enters. Our knees bump, and I reflexively cross my legs.

"Sorry," I mutter.

"You're fine," he says without looking at me.

We haven't spoken after what I admitted to him. Despite the moment of him attempting to comfort me, the cold look he had when he entered the room is still stamped into my mind.

As soon as Sebastien gets in, Addison backs out of the driveway and starts down the road.

With my legs still crossed, I round my shoulders, trying to take up as little space as possible. Despite my attempt, my arms still rub against Sebastien's and Nixon's, and my thighs are pressed against theirs. Claustrophobia quickly settles in and I try to find something to focus on as a distraction. I settle for staring at my hands in my lap, picking at the skin around my nails. No matter how much I try to keep my eyes down, though, I can't help peeking up at the two of them every now and then.

Sebastien has his full attention on the world outside his window, the gun he pulled from its holster in his lap. The more I look at him, the more I think I've seen him before. He's oddly familiar, with his curly black hair tied into a knot at the top of his head, tan skin, and round eyes, but I can't recall where I recognize him from. His name sounds familiar too, a whisper from the past. Did Liam talk to me about him before? Or Nixon? We've barely exchanged any words with one another, and there was no formal introduction. I only picked up his name when Eli addressed him. When I asked Addison if she knew him, she said she'd only met him once other than today. He's a scout on Liam's four-man squad in the Green Zone, but that was all she knew.

Nixon shifts in the seat to my right. I'm suddenly hyper-aware of how close we are, more than I am of Sebastien, and no matter how much I contort myself, I can't put enough distance between us. Just a couple of months ago, I craved his touch. Now I want to be as far away as possible.

It's not just him; I don't want anyone touching me. What felt like hundreds of hugs from Liam and Addison were enough physical contact for a while. I enjoyed it at first—it felt familiar, like a piece of home—but it quickly became suffocating, and it took everything in me not to shake myself from their embrace.

"I'm going to miss you guys," Addison says after a little while, breaking the silence. Some of the bubbliness has returned to her voice, but nowhere near as much as usual.

Liam reaches across the center console and laces his fingers through hers, making circles on the back of her hand with his thumb. "We're going to miss you, too."

A pang of jealousy shoots through me, and I'm immediately reminded of how I found out they'd been secretly dating. Even Nixon knew. During my absence, they seem to have gotten even closer. Liam never left her side at Eli's until it was time to move everything to her car.

I know it's dumb to be upset that they continued on with their lives while I was being held hostage by the Everetts. Although it felt like it, the world didn't come to a grinding halt because I was gone. Everything kept trudging forward—lives, relationships, careers—as if the world remained in perfect order. Like human beings aren't trafficked and innocent people aren't killed, like families aren't torn apart or turned against one another over money.

"Have you come up with a story in case your dad asks what happened to Liam?" Nixon asks, turning his attention to the windshield.

"Yeah," Addison says. "He met up with his mom and is staying with her a while to make amends."

"And if they check in with his mother?"

"He came back home to us, where he refuses to leave the apartment, depressed over his missing sister."

"Good. And you'll go back to the Green Zone, continue gathering intel from your father, and wait for one of us to contact you."

"No communicating with any other resistance members—got it."

"You're part of the resistance?" I ask.

Addison glances at me in the rearview mirror with a trace of a smile. "Not *technically*. But with Dad's position… you know."

She's like their spy, and Liam's okay with it, which irritates me more as I'm reminded of how much he told her while shutting me out. I thought I was over that after yelling at him for it in the Blue Zone, but now the anger and jealousy return.

An old thought creeps to the front of my mind—one I felt guilty for originally. Liam could have prevented this. Had he told me about his work in the resistance from the beginning, he could've helped me before I was kidnapped by the Black Hats. I don't know how—I'm not even entirely sure it would've been possible—but that doesn't make it sting any less.

"Turn up here," Nixon tells Addison. "Park behind one of these buildings."

"We need to split up," Liam says, already removing his seatbelt. "Two and two."

"Good idea," Nixon says. "One scout per pair. I've got your back while you take care of the door. Seb, think you can escort Ivy?"

"You got it," Seb says. His hand wedges between me and him and his seatbelt clicks. Wrapping his fingers around the door handle, he sits up straighter.

This is happening. This is *actually* happening. The anxiety of escaping I'd temporarily forgotten returns. It floods my veins. Every muscle feels so rigid I fear I may not be able to move. My limbs tingle with the unwelcome sensation, and my thoughts race.

What if we're recaptured? What if I don't make it? What if the plan doesn't work? We've tried getting out before and failed. Addison's father knows she and Liam are here. What if he sends someone to retrieve them after being notified of what's happened in this zone?

The vehicle comes to a complete stop. Addison throws her arms around Liam as he leans in for a kiss, whispering indecipherable words into his ear before he pulls back and gets out. Seb immediately follows his lead, and I hear the trunk pop open.

Addison reaches for me next, and I lean forward, allowing her to awkwardly embrace me for what could very possibly be the last time.

"We're going to see each other again," she tells me. Her voice cracks. "I love you."

"I love you, too," I say, right as Nixon calls for me.

Addison wipes tears away when I pull back, smearing her mascara underneath her eyes.

I tear my eyes away from her, forcing myself to scoot across the seat and out the open door to my left. A weight settles in my chest. My heart struggles to beat through the immense pressure, and with each step toward the three men around the trunk, my legs feel heavier.

Liam passes me the second, smaller backpack, similar to his. Seb and Nixon shoulder the rucksacks, and I notice Nixon wince once it's secure on his back.

"Sure you can carry that?" Liam asks him as he pulls his laptop from his bag.

Nixon shoots his second-in-command a glare while holstering his pistol. "I'm fine." He grabs a gun from the trunk and steps back. "Ivy, hood up."

Slipping my backpack on, I do as I'm told, tucking all my hair underneath my jacket's hood as he has. Seb finishes fastening the buckles of his rucksack across his chest, retrieves his own submachine gun, and shuts the trunk. Without saying anything else, Nixon and Liam start off to the left, disappearing into the treeline.

"Let's go," Seb says, already walking in the opposite direction. "Stay close."

With one final look at Addison's car, I reluctantly follow him. Every step forward makes my heart race faster and the pressure more unbearable. Seb moves swiftly, scanning the wooded space as we go. Although I don't know him, I'm happy I'm paired with him rather than Nixon.

I keep up with his quick pace, trying to focus on anything but the fear swirling in my stomach. Branches above us slice the sky into orangish-pink chunks. The thawing ground squishes beneath my boots, and I'm paranoid the sound will give our location away to any potential soldiers or police in the area. I try to listen for any other noises—footsteps, vehicles, voices—but the Red Zone is chillingly still. Even after curfew, it's normally vibrant and alive with the night-time crowds and gatherings.

Moving helps with the anxiety. All of my bottled-up energy is slowly released. As long as we continue moving, I can keep my mind off everything else; the only thing I need to focus on is getting out of here. Everything else can be dealt with later when we're safe at the Commander's camp—although no one has laid out any details of this mission for me. All I know is what Nixon told me: we're escaping the Northern Unity. We're heading through the service tunnels that run underneath the walls; the Commander's camp lies somewhere on the other side.

A gunshot splits the air, and I jump, whipping my head in all directions. Not realizing Seb has stopped, I bump into him, and he reaches out to steady me. Half a beat passes before a second shot echoes in the open. Knifelike fingers of panic clench around my heart. A few moments pass with Seb's hand on my shoulder and his face angled away from me. No voices or returning fire. Everything is quiet again.

"Probably just Nixon taking out the cameras," he whispers, dropping his hand. "Let's keep moving."

As we push forward, I stay closer to him. There's a break in the trees twenty yards ahead, opening up to an empty road, and on the other side of that is another barrier of trees—a mix of coniferous and deciduous that are preparing to bloom. Through the natural border, I can make out the dull gray wall. Its presence is both comforting and daunting. On the other side is freedom and safety, but also other potential threats. The danger doesn't stop when we cross over, and I have a feeling the Society won't stop their search for me any time soon.

"Get down," Seb says, dropping to his stomach a few feet from the edge of the woods. He aims his gun at the open space before us, and I lower myself beside him. Pain shoots up my arm, starting at my stitches and radiating to my wrist, and I bite back a groan.

Between the trees across the street, I spot a chain-link fence encompassing a steel door built into the wall. Nixon stands inside, facing us, scanning the surroundings. Behind him, Liam has his back to the road as he stands beside the door. When he angles his body slightly to the right, I can make out the corner of his laptop's screen extended in front of him.

"What's he doing?" I whisper.

"Hacking the door's keypad. As soon as we're inside, we need to be quick but quiet. Nixon will lead; I'll have your back."

"You're sure there isn't anyone inside?"

"No clue." He studies the road as though expecting someone to infiltrate the area at any moment. "But if there is, we'll take care of it."

"What about on the other side of the walls? Are there soldiers there?"

"Not usually, no. *Technically*, it's outside the Society's jurisdiction."

From where I'm lying beside him, his hood shields his face. As he looks around, he keeps his head low, periodically pausing to study Nixon and Liam. Liam swings his backpack off one shoulder and shoves his laptop inside. He says something to Nixon, who then motions in our direction.

"That's our cue," Seb says, climbing to his feet. Offering a hand, he helps me up. "I'll be right behind you."

We cautiously make our way to the edge where the dirt turns to asphalt. Seb checks each end of the road, and with a small nudge from him, I run. My bag thumps against my back, the bottles of water inside beating against my spine. The cut on my leg throbs, sending bolts of lightning up my calf.

Relief floods my body when we enter the enclosed space. Seb shuts the gate behind us and keeps his eyes on the road. No one speaks. In fact, it seems like no one even breathes as Nixon heaves the door open with a grunt, revealing the eternal darkness that awaits us. He clicks on a flashlight that's attached to the strap of his rucksack and points the beam into the tunnel. A metal platform is illuminated, its rusted staircase plunging into the underground sanctuary.

Squealing tires and slamming doors shatter that sense of relief.

"Freeze!" a man barks. "Drop your weapons!"

I instinctively turn my head toward the unknown voice. At the same time, my wrist is grabbed and I'm jerked forward. I catch sight of four soldiers approaching just as I'm pulled into the darkness.

"Drop your weapons!" a soldier repeats.

Panic blankets my thoughts. I force myself to keep my eyes forward, the temptation to look back gnawing at me. Liam fumbles with his flashlight on the strap of his backpack as he drags me deeper, finally clicking it on halfway down the stairs. Several gunshots pop outside, one after another, and I jump. Someone yells out in pain. Liam pulls harder to keep me moving.

"Let's go!" Nixon yells from behind us.

Fully inside in the tunnel, Liam releases me and we run, our frantic footsteps echoing off the stone walls and ceiling.

A few more rapid-fire shots sound before the door screeches shut, and boots clobber against the metal stairs. The air gets colder, like breathing in ice. I mimic each step Liam takes in front of me, focusing on the beams of the flashlights. Our shadows dance across the walls, warped by the maze of pipes and beams. Liam glances back and slows to a jog, allowing the other two to catch up.

"Seb, take the lead," Nixon commands.

Seb pushes past us, and we pick up our pace again.

Fear and anxiety spread, twisting their way around my insides like weeds. I focus on my breathing, my brother in front of me, and Seb in front of him. Nixon follows close behind us as we round a corner into another lightless portion of the tunnels. We stay close to the wall, only inches from touching the large pipes.

Bolts of pain continue to shoot up my leg each time I put weight on it, and my arm throbs. I keep going, forcing my legs to move faster, telling myself we can rest soon. A prickly feeling crawls up my neck. Again, I resist the urge to look back.

We round another corner. Looking away from the light in front of me, I squint in an attempt to see through the darkness, but it's impossible to make out anything other than the walls that feel like they're slowly closing in. I think I see movement from the corner of my eye along the top of one of the far walls when the flashlight hits it.

When I look around, there's nothing there. Only shadows and light slicing through the black.

Something echoes through the tunnel system—the grating sound of metal against metal—and a gasp escapes me.

"Keep moving," Nixon commands.

Fear tightens its hold on me. I try to stay close, try to match their sprint, but the throbbing gets worse.

Blinding white light penetrates the tunnel, followed by ear-splitting alarms.

"*Go!*" Nixon yells, barely audible.

I sprint forward, adrenaline pumping through me. Lights continue to strobe, disorienting me to the point that I can hardly see in front of me. The flashlights no longer offer any help in navigating the labyrinth. I think I hear voices but I can't tell where they're coming from. Terror engulfs my senses, pushing everything else aside.

I stumble, reaching out with one hand to steady myself against the cold pipes lining the wall. The alarms reverberate in my aching skull. The two shadowy figures up ahead make another turn. Bursts of light make my head swim.

An arm wraps around my midsection, propelling me forward. I lean into Nixon, allowing him to guide me as we race through the distorted maze. We round the same corner.

"Liam!" Nixon yells as we run toward them, his voice vibrating throughout my body. I stumble again, blinking through the blinding light, and Nixon's arm tightens around me. The space between us and my brother doesn't seem to be shrinking. "Liam!"

Liam stops, reaching out for Seb to do the same, and spins around as we approach them. We come to a halt, and Nixon pushes me to the ground.

"Door's just up ahead, but I don't have time to open it," Liam yells over the alarms.

"Already on it. Seb, charges."

Seb reaches into a compartment of Nixon's bag and hands him a rectangular box with protruding wires. Liam squats beside me, shielding my body from the other end of the tunnel, and pulls the pistol from his tactical belt. Nixon runs ahead, and Seb positions himself on my other side with his back to me, pointing the submachine gun the way we came.

"Ivy!" Liam yells. Even sitting this close together, it's hard to hear him over the sirens. "Once the door's off, we're going to make a run for the exit. Do not stop. Do not look back."

He pulls off his backpack, unzips the main pocket and takes out four respirator masks. Handing two to me, he secures the yellow straps around his head, and I pass one to Seb before putting on my own.

Another figure emerges from the end of the tunnel we came from, and my heart seizes. Seb inches forward. A steady light focuses on us, concealing the silhouette behind it.

Seb fires, the staccato sound twisting my stomach. Shouts cut through the chaos and the stable light dances out of view, disappearing behind one of the walls. A short pause, then Seb fires again.

My ears ring and I scoot away, pressing myself as close to my brother as possible. Nixon barrels back toward us, coming to a skidding stop. Liam hands him the extra mask as he crouches beside us. Before he has the straps secured, a deafening blast tears through the air, ricocheting off the concrete and stone and overpowering the sirens.

It shakes the earth. The vibration pulses through me. It rattles my bones and throws me off balance. Smoke engulfs the space behind Nixon, and even with my mask on, the odor assaults my nose.

Tugging on my arm, Liam hauls me to my feet and drags me forward with Nixon leading the way. Muffled gunshots continue, moving with us. Remembering what Liam said, I don't look back.

I'm led into the wall of smoke, and although Liam has a tight grip on my wrist, it's difficult to keep up. The air is unbelievably sweltering. Despite the mask filtering the air, I struggle with each ragged breath. My eyes burn. I can't see anything. The strobing lights struggle to cut through the smoke. Panic grips me with no sign of letting up.

I can't hear anything anymore, not even my erratic pulse. The world has gone silent, broken by the blast. The farther we make it, the more sweat and soot stick to my skin. Time stands still yet accelerates as we sprint through the dense, dark cloud.

We stop where the billow of smoke moves upward, escaping through what used to be the door sealing us in here. The staircase and platform identical to the ones at the entrance are now a gnarled mess of metal. Heat radiates from the explosion site, wrapping around me. Suffocating me.

"Seb!" Liam shouts. His voice is faint, as if we're underwater.

"I'm here!" Seb calls back. He runs toward us, swinging his gun behind him, and leaps up. Nixon and Liam each boost him up by the bottoms of his shoes, and he's sucked into the black cloud. A moment passes and he calls down, "Clear!"

"Ivy, you're up," Nixon yells. He stands with his back against the wall and leans forward, linking his fingers together and holding his cupped hands in front of his body. Liam pushes me toward him, promising he'll be right behind me.

Holding onto Nixon's shoulder, I secure my foot in his hands and unsteadily pull myself up. Not waiting for me to get my bearings, he lifts, and I grasp at the wall in search of something to grab on to. My fingers grip the edge of the exit, and a scream escapes my lips as my flesh is seared on the scorching metal lip that remains of the door. Stretching my arms as far as they'll go, I struggle to hoist myself up. Nixon pushes up on my boot; I press my other foot against the wall for extra support. A hand wraps around my forearm, narrowly missing the stitches, and jerks me upward. I'm dragged out of the tunnel and over the burning metal.

"Got her!" Seb yells, pulling me away from the exit.

I crawl to my feet, coughing and gasping for fresh air. The mask has made breathing more tolerable, but I can still feel the smoke burning my nostrils and filling my lungs with each inhale. Liam's pulled up next and immediately finds me.

"Are you okay?" he asks.

He's right in front of me but sounds so far away. My ears continue to ring. The sirens sound distorted. Seb shouts something, but I can't tell what.

"Shit, your hands." Liam grabs my palms, inspecting my burned fingertips in the beam of his flashlight. "I have some burn cream in my—"

"I'm fine," I say, pulling my hands back. My voice sounds muffled, and I'm not even sure he can hear me. "We can take care of them later."

Nixon emerges from the tunnel with little help from Seb. He does a quick survey of us, making sure we're all accounted for, and we run.

19. Another Reason

Ivy

The burn cream Liam gave me after we were far enough from the wall temporarily soothed my fingers, but now that pulsating heat is returning. I keep my hands open at my sides, trying not to touch anything that will make the pain worse. My respirator mask thumps against my chest with each step, and although we're likely miles away from the wall by now, I can still smell the smoke. It clings to my hair and has been absorbed into my clothes.

We ran without stopping until we were sure we weren't being chased and have been walking for what feels like forever. Night fell a while ago, and once again, our only source of light is the flashlights on the men's backpack straps. Aside from a few whispers here and there about where we're going, where we'll be stopping, and Liam asking if I'm okay, there hasn't been any talking.

We've stuck to the roads, which are riddled with cracks and holes. The yellow lines are almost completely faded, and weeds have made a home in the crevices. Tangled overgrowth claims the land, reaching across the broken asphalt as though searching for something to devour. No buildings are in sight, and the trees out here carry their own eerie essence with their gnarled branches and trunks split as if they've been struck by lightning.

Out here it's open. But rather than feeling free, I feel exposed, unprotected. Those walls were a prison, but that prison offered security. They kept me safe from whatever lurks out here. They were all I knew.

I'm lucky to have gotten out. Others aren't as fortunate. There are still people in the homes of their buyers. More victims will be sold in four months at the next Elite Auction while the Society distracts its citizens by broadcasting the open slots for residency in the Red Zone. Black Hats will still kidnap, torture, and kill those they view as a threat—resistance member or not—and citizens will be shipped off to re-education, either having a chip planted in their brain or forced to work at a labor camp.

The cycle will continue, all while the Northern Unity appears to be a perfect place. No hunger, homelessness, or unemployment. Everyone knows the Enlightened Society will take care of them. What they don't know is that all those things come at the price of their blood and innocence.

"Hey," Seb says, "let's stop for a minute."

Nixon turns around, and I squint against the beam of his flashlight. "Yeah, we'll take ten. Ivy, let's take a look at your leg." He leads me to one of the trees on the side of the road, kicking away rocks and twigs to make a more comfortable surface to sit down on. "Liam, med kit."

I lower myself to the ground and lean against the trunk. Every part of me already aches—more than earlier today—and exhaustion is quickly creeping in. Sitting alleviates the pain in my leg and somewhat takes away from the soreness of my muscles.

Liam pulls the kit from Seb's rucksack and passes it to Nixon, who kneels beside me. Popping the box open, Nixon pulls out a pair of latex gloves and slips them on. Sebastien keeps his back to us, scanning our surroundings, and Liam stands on the other side of me, watching as his leader prepares the gauze with a tube of ointment.

I wince when my pant leg is rolled up, instinctively pulling my leg back.

"You're okay," Nixon says, straightening it out again.

The dressing that was applied after my shower has begun to peel away from the laceration. Blood has crusted on the inside of my pant leg, and under the flashlight, my skin appears pink. Nixon carefully pulls the rest of the gauze away, but I avert my eyes before I can see anything, focusing on Seb instead. Even though I'm not looking, the action reminds me of the first time I stayed in a safehouse with Nixon—when he dressed a shallow wound on my wrist after we fought over a flashlight. That memory triggers more, but I quickly shut them down.

This is different. Everything's different. I want to recoil, to beg him to stop touching me. I don't care if the wound gets infected; I don't want anyone's fingers on my skin.

"How bad is it?" Liam asks.

"Not bad," Nixon says. "Just irritated from sweat and friction." His gloved finger rubs the ointment over the wound, and I tense when he presses fresh gauze to it. "We'll travel a little farther before resting for the night. Think you're up for that?"

"Yeah," I say, though I'm not entirely sure. The high from escaping the Northern Unity has worn off, leaving my body heavy and mind reverting back to the scene at the Everetts'.

The kit goes back in Seb's rucksack, and he joins the rest of us beside the tree. "How much farther?" he asks.

"Another mile, maybe," Nixon says, standing. "That'll put us eleven from the outpost."

"What outpost?" I ask. No one mentioned that to me, or really anything about this mission other than getting out of the Northern Unity and reaching the Commander's camp.

The thought of more walking makes my body feel even heavier. I want to beg Nixon to let us sleep here for the night. We haven't encountered any soldiers, and I doubt we will this late and this far from the border. I'm not exactly sure how far we've traveled, but it has to be enough to be out of the Society's jurisdiction.

Glancing at the men standing around me, I can tell they're exhausted, too. Seb's shoulders are slumped forward. Liam continuously shifts his weight, and Nixon sounds weary.

"Resistance outpost," Liam tells me, offering his hand to help me stand. "They'll help us the rest of the way."

"We'll head out again at sun-up," Nixon continues, "and we'll take turns keeping watch tonight. Seb, you'll take first; I'll take second. Liam, you're last. Three hours each."

"You need as much sleep as possible," Seb says. "One of us can take second."

"No."

"But—"

"I said *no*. Let's go."

Seb gives a subtle eye roll as Nixon passes him, and we follow him back onto the road—Liam walking beside me and Seb behind us. Our pace is more sluggish than it was before, with our boots scuffing the asphalt every few steps. We pass more trees, more overgrowth, and turn onto another vacant road. Since the wall disappeared from our view, it's seemed like we've been walking in circles. Everything looks the same.

"So does anyone know what this camp is like?" I ask. "Like, how many people are there? Or who the Commander even is?"

"I've already told you very few have actually met him," Nixon says. Earlier, he was moving quickly, staying about five feet ahead of us at all times. Now, he's just over an arm's length away. "As for how many are there, I don't know."

"I heard he used to be a Black Hat," Seb adds.

"Bullshit," Liam says. "We've never had someone in the resistance who was a Black Hat."

"That was the rumor in the Green Zone when I first joined," Seb says.

"That was eight years ago." Nixon glances over his shoulder. "If the Commander was a rogue Black Hat, the Society would've hunted him down already."

"Unless he's a double," I blurt out.

I said something similar the first time Nixon explained who the Commander is—or at least what little he knows about him. Eli is one of the few who has actually met the man, and he didn't offer any sort of insight. Then again, I didn't bother asking, but some sort of information on this stranger we're supposed to be trusting would've been nice.

"Don't trust the resistance anymore, Ivy?" Nixon asks. There's a moderately lighthearted note to his words, but they still make me regret saying anything. He doesn't trust that I'm still on their side, despite me killing an Elite and him seeing how distraught I was about it.

"I do," I say, "but there's a lot I don't know."

"Well, in this case, we're right there with you."

For someone who doesn't trust easily, it's surprising Nixon is so willing to follow orders from someone he's only ever talked to over a radio. He has to know more about the Commander than he's let on. When he joined the resistance in the Blue Zone, his adoptive father was his leader; it made sense that he'd trust him. But when he became a leader himself and was transferred to the Green Zone, the Commander became his immediate superior, and he admitted to originally hating the resistance—he blamed them for the loss of his biological parents. How was a man he'd never met able to earn his undying loyalty?

Nixon motions for us to stay put as he breaks away from our group at an intersection. Pausing at the warped stop sign to the left, he repositions his light, illuminating a lone gas station. Its sign has faded and the parking lot has crumbled like the road. From where I'm standing, the building behind the single row of gas pumps looks to be in decent shape. Weeds and vines cover the corner of the store facing us and a fallen tree blocks the far side of the lot, but everything appears to be mostly intact.

Lingering a moment longer, he finally signals for us to follow. The four of us creep through the darkness, the slowest we've moved all night. All three men are on high alert, scanning our surroundings with their weapons ready. A chill runs through me as we near the building. The double doors of the entrance no longer exist, only an open space leading into blackness. All of the windows lining the front wall are intact, and the posters and signs taped to them are yellowed and peeling. The poles between the ancient gas pumps have chunks of paint missing, exposing the rust underneath.

"Wait here," Nixon says. We stop by the pumps to shield us from the store. "I'm going to clear the building."

"I can do it," Seb volunteers.

"No, I've got it. Just wait here." Before anyone can argue, he starts toward the store.

"He realizes he's going to burn himself out, right?" Seb mutters.

"You know him," Liam says. "Always trying to prove himself."

"Seems he's gotten worse since the other day."

"What happened the other day?" I ask.

They look at me, then share a glance as if deciding whether or not they should tell me.

"He's just been… different since he got back," Seb says. "Don't get me wrong, he's a great leader, but—" He shakes his head and looks at Liam.

I peer between the gas pump and pole. Nixon's light slices through the darkness, drifting throughout the interior and temporarily disappearing. I'm not the only one who's noticed he's different. I don't know him as well as these guys do, but if even I can pick up on that, something's wrong.

"He's been through a lot," Liam says.

"But what happened the other day?" I ask.

"Don't worry about it." The tone he uses is familiar—one that insists it's none of my business. It's the same one he used the last day I was home, when I was trying to pry information out of our mother about Dad's disappearance.

For now, I listen. I'm too tired to argue, and as long as we get to the Commander's camp unharmed, I don't care what happened with Nixon. It's an awful feeling, but if he's going to be cold and distant, why shouldn't I? If I've learned anything the past couple months, it's that I need to worry about myself first. Other than my brother, everyone and everything else comes second. That's the only way I can ensure my safety. Relying on other people only leads to being disappointed.

Nixon emerges from the store, waving us over. Liam and I go first, with Seb close behind. Every step across the parking lot brings both dread and relief. I'm thankful to finally be stopping, but staying out here in this seemingly barren territory makes my stomach churn.

"We'll rest here," Nixon says when we approach, and he turns around, leading us inside. "There's a ladder that leads up to the roof. We'll keep watch from up there."

Shards of glass crunch under our boots, and I press my sleeve to my nose to block out the rancid stench hanging in the air. Shelves have been picked clean. Garbage litters the browned tile floor—everything from wrappers to bottles and cigarette cartons. Cardboard boxes are toppled over behind the dust-layered counter, their contents missing, and the glass case behind it has been broken into.

We stop at the very back, where a wall of coolers meets a half wall, separating the area that leads back to the loading dock. Resting his gun against one of the coolers, Nixon unbuckles his rucksack and drops it to the floor, and Seb follows suit. Liam pulls a handheld flashlight from his backpack, sets it upright, and the rest of the lights go out.

"Ivy, bag," Nixon says.

Slipping it off, I pass it to him, and he lowers himself to the floor beside Seb. Liam and I sit across from them, leaning back against the cloudy glass doors. Sitting, again, alleviates some of the pain that has spread throughout my entire body. My feet throb in a satisfying way once my weight is off them. Nixon unzips the main pocket of my backpack and pulls out four bags of beef jerky, protein bars, and water, distributing them before opening his own.

When I tear open my bag of jerky, the scent of teriyaki fills my nose, making my stomach grumble and almost masking the smell of rot that surrounds us. The first bite makes my mouth water and my stomach beg for more before I can even swallow.

We eat in silence. The only sound filling the small store is the crinkling of our bags and the occasional water bottle. Across from Liam, Nixon keeps his unwavering gaze on the front of the store. In the dim light, I can make out the bags under his eyes. His hood is thrown back, and with his hair tied up, the scar along his jaw is completely visible. If it weren't for the other two being here, this would be almost exactly like the first night we stayed together, hiding from the Society.

"I can't believe we're actually out here," Liam says.

"I can't believe we're out here with two fugitives," Seb jokes. "Look at us—two high-standing citizens with these *criminals*." He feigns a look of disgust then cracks a smile, causing a dimple to appear on his left cheek. "Especially this one." He points a piece of his half-eaten beef jerky at me, and my heart stops. "The girl who miraculously escaped her captors. I never took you for the rebellious type."

"I'm sorry, do I know you?" Leaning forward, I study him closer. I know I've seen him before. "You just… you look familiar."

Smiling again, he nudges Nixon with his elbow. "Aw, she remembers me."

Finally turning his attention to the group, Nixon smirks and finishes chewing before joking, "With a face like that, how could she not? You probably haunted her dreams for weeks."

Seb's face lights up with amusement and he lets out a laugh that whittles away at the lingering tension. "Bold words coming from someone I've barely even seen with a girl."

"I'm around a girl now, aren't I?" Nixon says, loosely waving a hand in our direction, and heat rises to my cheeks.

"Liam doesn't count."

"Man, fuck you." Liam laughs, crumpling his empty water bottle and flinging it at Seb. He dodges it, and the plastic cap clanks against the wall between him and Nixon.

"To answer your question, though," Seb says, redirecting his attention to me, "I was your guard at TCG."

"Oh," I say. "Right. I should've remembered that."

Nixon briefly mentioned him after I was rescued from the Black Hats. But Seb isn't anything like I remember from then. When I was being held at TCG, he was dull and emotionless, perfectly blending in with the other guards. Now he's full of energy, despite the tiring evening we've had.

Seb shrugs, peeling the paper back on his protein bar. "Wasn't exactly the best introduction, and you've been through hell since then. By the way, rumor has it you cut out your own tracker—is that true?"

"Seb," Liam warns.

"What?" he says through a mouthful of food. "I just want to know if your sister's more of a badass than you."

"Yeah, it's true," I say, popping the final piece of jerky in my mouth. Setting aside the bag, I gulp down more of my water before opening my own protein bar.

"Damn." Seb raises his eyebrows. "I'm impressed. Definitely more of a badass than Liam. Maybe even up there with Nixon."

What looks like a tiny smile plays at the corner of Nixon's mouth, but he doesn't acknowledge the statement or look for my reaction.

"I doubt that," I say.

"I don't. I mean, you escaped the *Elites*. We had to rescue this fucker." He nudges Nixon again then scoots away from the wall, leaning forward. "How did you manage that anyway?"

"Um…" I drop my gaze to my lap, picking at the wrapper of the protein bar. "Guess I got lucky."

"Okay, but *how*? I mean, with today being your wedding day—"

"Seb," Nixon interrupts, "that's not your place. Drop it."

"He doesn't have a filter," Liam tells me. "Just tell him to shut up when he gets on your nerves."

"Well," Seb says, sliding back to his spot beside Nixon, "I vote for training her and making her our new second-in-command. Scout, maybe?"

"No," Nixon says, twisting the cap off his water.

"Or logistics. We've always said we needed more women, and ever since…"

He doesn't finish, but we all know who he's referring to. Elizabeth, the Green Zone's only female resistance member. But none of them know what *actually* happened to her. They know she was killed, and they assume it was at the hands of the Black Hats.

"She can't join," Nixon says. "Not my group, at least."

"Why not?" Liam asks defensively.

For the first time since arriving here, Nixon finally looks at me, his expression blank. "I don't want her to—that simple."

My chest tightens. The air becomes thick with his words, threatening to suffocate me. His eyes remain trained on me. Whether to mock me or search for a reaction, I can't tell.

"Okay," Seb says, dragging out the last syllable. "That was harsh."

"Yeah," Liam says. "You don't have to be a dick about it."

Standing, Nixon unzips the largest compartment of one of the rucksacks and pulls out two compressed sleeping bags. "Not like she'll be going back there anyway."

My heart skips at the reminder that I'll never be going home, but my mind is quick to revert back to his previous words. It's not really what he said but *how* he said it, like the idea of me being part of his group, being near him, is appalling. The hurt quickly morphs into anger that's desperate to be unleashed.

Nixon slides the sleeping bags toward Liam and me, then pulls another from the second rucksack.

"I know what happened to her," I blurt out. "To Elizabeth."

"We know," Liam says. "You told us."

"No, I mean, I know who did it."

I know this isn't the time to talk about her—we have enough going on as it is—but I know something they don't about their friend, their comrade…

"The Black Hats," Seb says. "Right?"

"That's what we thought," Nixon says. His eyes narrow. "So who was it?"

No longer hungry, I fold up the last half of my protein bar and grip it in my hands, focusing on the ridges of the wrapper against my skin as I match his glare. "Wyatt."

"That prick you were supposed to be marrying?" Seb asks.

I nod. "He told me himself… two nights ago."

"You said you never talked about the resistance," Nixon says.

"I didn't."

"Then why would he bring up one of my members?" He takes a step forward, fists clenched and nostrils flaring. The shadows cast across his face make him appear more intimidating—lethal, even.

I instinctively recoil, but my back hits the wall. I'm trapped.

"Seb, head up for your guard shift," Liam says, pushing himself to his feet and stepping in front of Nixon.

Seb grabs his gun and one of the flashlights, momentarily hesitating before he rounds the half wall. His footsteps fade and the screeching of hinges echoes through the building.

"Why the hell would he tell you that?" Nixon yells, trying to maneuver around my brother.

Unable to tear my eyes from him, I squeeze the protein bar tighter until dull bursts of pain return to my fingers. There's a small part of me that wishes I could backtrack, but the stronger, angrier part won't let me. It insists that, for whatever reason, he deserves to hurt, and I don't question it.

"Nixon, calm down," Liam says, placing his arm against Nixon's chest.

Nixon pushes him away and crouches in front of me, his icy eyes filled with rage. "What did you tell him about her?"

"Dude, stop," Liam says.

"Nothing," I say, focusing on the sting of my fingers and the way it distracts me from the intensity of his glare.

"I swear," Nixon growls, leaning in until there's barely a foot of space between us, "if you told those fuckers *anything*—"

"That's enough!" Liam grabs Nixon by the shoulder and pulls him back. "We're all exhausted. We can talk about this tomorrow."

Nixon shakes him off and rises to his feet, turning toward the third sleeping bag against the half wall, but Liam blocks his path.

"And don't you *dare* talk to my sister like that again."

20. Vertigo

Nixon

<u>Black Hats: Covert Defense Against Domestic Terrorism</u>
I. Training
Ten subjects are annually selected from each zone of the Northern Unity at eight years of age. Following the selec tions, the subjects enter a decade-long training course where they learn to sharpen their survival skills, gather in telligence, and perfect the art of assassination.
By the final year, at the age of eighteen, one subject per zone will remain by the process of eliminating his/her classmates over the course of ten years. . .

> Guardians of the subjects who refuse to cooperate are put
> through re-education. In the rare occasion that re-education
> fails, the guardian is exterminated. . .

Letting out a long breath, I lean against the idle air unit behind me. I already knew about the corruption that is the Black Hats, but this? This is revolting—kidnapping children to train them as killers so they can do the Society's dirty work. How the hell did Ivy get these documents?

I try to recall any kids mysteriously disappearing when I was growing up, but no instances come to mind. As the title of the document suggests, though, they're covert. Everything the Society and Black Hats do is carefully planned without the public ever knowing. While everyone is living in their illusion of safety and harmony, children are being recruited to murder. Even the Commander doesn't know about this—or if he does, he hasn't shared it with us.

I return the document to the rest of the collection spread out on the concrete in front of me. Including Addison's file about Ivy and Liam's missing father, there are sixteen for me to look over, and I haven't been able to bring myself to read a single one all the way through. Maybe it's exhaustion or the anger that the information triggers—or a combination of the two—but I can't focus for longer than five or ten minutes at a time.

The more I read, the more I want to be back in the Northern Unity, working with my group to prevent things like this from happening. I know I kept pushing for an extraction mission to be launched for Ivy, but now I realize how pointless that was. Yes, Liam deserves to have his sister back, but launching the mission was ultimately for my own selfish reasons. Ivy's not the same person as before, and although she admitted to killing Wyatt, I have a strong feeling she's still only giving me part of the story. Until I know everything, I can't trust her, and for whatever reason, she doesn't seem to trust me either.

Grabbing my gun, I push myself to my feet and step around the documents to pace the roof for the hundredth time. As I make my way to the opposite end, I glance at my watch. Two hours down, one to go—although I know I won't be sleeping much after Liam takes over.

With every sluggish step, I survey my surroundings. My flashlight cuts through the trees and illuminates the empty street to my left. Seb didn't report any activity after his shift, and everything's been quiet since I took over. Maybe there aren't any threats out here, but I don't want to take any chances. With my luck, the second I let my guard down we'll be ambushed.

When I reach the other end of the roof, I stop at the ledge, do a final sweep of the area, then turn around and start back toward where I was. Halfway across, near the raised edge that obscures my view of the parking lot, I notice a beam of light cutting through the darkness below. My stomach drops. The beam jerks from side to side as it makes its way to the west end of the building, then steadies.

Crouching, I hold my gun in front of me and carefully move in the same direction. Past the raised edge, I prop the gun up on the ledge and peer over with my flashlight, ready to fire at any intruders.

Huddled against the wall below with a flashlight between her knees, Ivy stares out into the wasteland.

With a frustrated breath, I sit back on my heels and massage my temples. I'm tempted to just let her be; I don't care to talk to her or even see her right now, and she's not exactly doing anything wrong. But the first day we were together—when she attempted to run away from me—flashes in my mind, and I can only imagine the hell Liam would give me if that were to happen again. Or worse, if someone with bad intentions happened to pass by and see her.

I quickly gather the documents and shove them in the drawstring backpack before crossing the roof and climbing down the ladder. In the store, I check on the other two as I pass by. Liam's on his stomach, snoring beside Ivy's empty sleeping bag. Seb is across from him near the half wall and turns his head when my light passes over him.

Trying to avoid stepping on the trash, I make my way to the entrance of the store while putting together what I'm going to say to Ivy. What she said about Elizabeth is still at the front of my mind. Maybe I was too harsh, blowing up on her without getting the full story first, but Ivy knows how protective I am of everyone in my group. I opened up to her about Elizabeth before, and she used it against me.

Outside the doorway, I turn left and slow my pace. My light falls on Ivy sitting against the wall, but she doesn't move. She just stares out into the night with her arms crossed in front of her.

"You need to go back inside," I say, stopping beside her.

She doesn't say anything; doesn't even look at me.

"Ivy, now."

"I don't want to," she mutters. Still stubborn, which only irritates me more.

"Stop being childish and get back inside."

She looks up at me. Her wavy blonde hair spills out from her hood and conceals some of the bruises on her neck. For a fleeting moment, she looks the same as when we were together in the Blue Zone—warm and gentle—but her hazel eyes immediately harden, and any familiarity dissipates.

"Make me," she says in a low, mocking voice.

"What's your problem?" I demand. "I got you out of the Northern Unity and you're treating me like shit."

Chuckling hollowly, she looks away and says, "Leave me alone."

"Not until you get your ass back inside."

Removing the flashlight from between her knees, she folds her legs in front of her and crosses her arms over her chest.

"So, what, we're back to how we were when we first met?" I ask. "I leave my entire group behind again in order to help some ungrateful kid?"

"I didn't ask for your help," she says. "I got myself out of the Everetts'; I could've escaped the Northern Unity by myself, too."

Deep down, she has to know that's not true. She escaped the Everetts, but if Eli's scouts hadn't been outside, she wouldn't have made it out of the neighborhood, let alone the country. I don't know where this feigned arrogance is coming from, but it's only pissing me off more. Only hours ago, she was sobbing while Eli and I questioned her. She was nearly inconsolable when admitting what she did to Wyatt. She's strong but broken, and pretending to be anything else isn't going to help her. And while I understand if she blames me for what happened, she has no right to be angry for the things that were out of my control.

I did what I could. I was only out of captivity for a few days. I made an effort, going against the Commander's orders, but she doesn't see it like that. Instead, she seems to think I'm working against her. Like *I'm* the enemy.

"I'm not too thrilled with how everything played out either," I tell her, surveying the still world around us, "but we can't change any of it now. It is what it is."

"You could at least pretend you don't hate me," she says, dropping her hands in her lap.

"What?" I snap my head back toward her. "I never said I hated you." She's annoying the hell out of me right now, and I'm still pissed about what she said earlier, but there's not a single part of me that hates her.

"Not directly," she says. "But you made it pretty damn obvious when Seb brought up me joining your group."

Another pang of anger shoots through me. "Is that why you brought up Elizabeth? Because you misinterpreted what I said?"

As much as I hate it, I can't help but compare her to Kase right now. In a final attempt to hurt me after I questioned him, he brought up Elizabeth's death, blaming me for it. And it worked. Ivy, the person who comforted me after that, has done the exact same thing.

"You never cared about joining the resistance before," I say, unable to refrain from raising my voice. With a few more strides, I prop my gun against the wall and crouch beside her. "Why the hell do you care about it now? You killed someone, and now you think you're resistance material?"

Like before, she digs her nails into her palms. "Why don't you want me to join then?"

Because I care about her. Because despite her iciness and potential dishonesty, I want to protect her. I don't want her to hurt anymore, and while I can't take away the trauma she's already experienced, I can prevent anything like that from happening again. She didn't deserve what happened to her, and she doesn't deserve to endure what comes with being in the field.

But I don't tell her that. I can't. The anger toward this entire situation and Eli's words echoing in my head won't let me.

So instead, I say, "Because you can't do it," and immediately hate myself for it.

The words linger, and the longer the tense silence stretches on, the more I wish I could take it back. Once again, I'm tempted to reach out to her, to hold her in an attempt to take away even a fraction of her pain. But then I'm reminded of how she pulled back at my touch at Eli's, how she tried her best to avoid any physical contact in Addison's car. The holes in her stories. What she said about Elizabeth.

Dropping my hands between my legs, I pop my knuckles, avoiding my two broken fingers. Ivy shifts on the ground, quickly wiping a sleeve across her cheek and sniffling. I tear my eyes away from her, focusing on a web of fissures in the parking lot's asphalt.

"I was telling the truth about her," Ivy says quietly.

"If you didn't talk about my group, why would he tell you that?"

From my peripheral vision, I see her picking at her nails and the chipped polish. She hesitates, then says, "Remember that night I called Liam when he was at your house? The day you took us to our aunt's?"

The night before we hijacked the plane that was shot down by the military. Liam was with me, finalizing the code that rerouted the aircraft.

I nod.

"I told Liam I thought Elizabeth's killer had seen me," she continues. "I… ended up being right." She pulls her knees up to her chest. "Two nights ago, Wyatt and I were lying in bed, and he said something about remembering the first night he saw me. I didn't know what he was talking about at first. He told me he saw me before I hid, saw how scared I was, and wanted to take me with him then, and that was when he knew he wanted me. I knew what he meant then, but I played it off like I didn't."

"Tell me exactly what he said about her," I say.

"I'm sorry. I didn't want to bring it up like—"

"Just tell me!" I don't bother hiding my anger. I'm exhausted and sick of her dancing around my questions.

"'The night I killed that rebel bitch.'" It comes out as a whisper, but I hear it clearly.

On my feet, I turn my back to her and force myself to draw in several deep breaths, gripping my flashlight until my hand cramps. I focus on the cold air filling my lungs, but the heat coursing through my body overpowers it.

That fucking coward.

He stalked and murdered one of my members, then sought out Ivy as his next victim. An irrational side of me is still pissed she took the opportunity to kill him from me. I wish I'd gone into the house with Liam last night and hunted down that piece of shit.

"Why did he target her?" I ask through my teeth.

"I don't know," Ivy says. "He said he wasn't a Black Hat, but he liked to go out and 'help' them, like it was a hobby."

"Did he mention any other members?"

"No."

"Tell me the truth. Anyone. Liam, Seb, Kase, Piper—"

"You." Her voice cracks. "He talked about you a lot."

I turn around, and she averts her eyes. "More than telling you I was dead?"

She hesitates, but nods.

"What did he say?"

Knowing anything about me could mean he knew about other members of my group. He could've kept tabs on all of us just like he did Elizabeth, and if he shared that information with anyone else in his circle, it's only a matter of time until someone starts targeting my members within the walls.

"I don't want to talk about this," Ivy says.

"I don't care."

She looks up at me, her eyes wet with fresh tears. "Nixon, please. I really don't want to."

"You don't have a choice!" I yell. "I have a group back home that could be in danger. If I'm not able to warn them because you're withholding information, their blood is on *your* hands."

"What's going on?" a deep voice asks from behind me.

I turn to see Liam walking toward us, eyes moving between me and Ivy. I wait for Ivy to speak, giving her a chance to tell him her side of whatever this is, but she doesn't say anything. Liam stops beside me and studies his sister.

"I came down to check on her after seeing her from the roof," I finally say. "I can't get her to go back inside."

"You okay, V?" Liam asks her.

She nods, wiping a stray tear that managed to escape. "Needed some fresh air."

"Is there anything you want to talk about?"

She looks at me as if contemplating whether she should tell him what I said, although I'm certain he heard the last part. He'll give me shit for it, but in the end, I'm his superior, and he knows just as well as I do what it could mean for our group if the Society knows anything about us.

"No," Ivy mumbles, looking away from me.

"Okay," Liam says. "Head inside; you need sleep." She glares at him, but with less intensity than she did at me. "Now."

She rolls her eyes but climbs to her feet and pushes past me with her head down. Grabbing my gun, I turn to follow her inside and go back up the roof, but Liam grabs me by the shoulder.

"What the hell was that?" he asks in a hushed voice.

"Nothing." I shake him off.

"What's your problem tonight?" he demands. "You've been a dick to her ever since we got out here."

"She's withholding information."

"She's been through a lot. Give her some time to process everything before pushing for answers."

I can't help but laugh. "Like you guys did with me, right?"

"That's different. You're our leader, and we needed to make sure…" He stops himself, taking a step back and glancing at the entrance over his shoulder.

"Needed to make sure what?" I ask.

That I'm still worthy of being their leader? That I didn't sell them out? I went through hell *because* I refused to tell the Society anything about them, but that's clearly not enough proof.

"Nothing," Liam says. "Just back off."

"I'll 'back off' once she starts being honest with me."

He lets out a long breath in response, obviously knowing he won't win this argument. If I can't report to the Commander that she told us everything she knows, he'll question her himself. It'll be a lot easier on her if she comes clean now.

I push past Liam. When I reach the entrance of the store, he says, "Get some rest. I'll cover the rest of your shift."

21. Wasteland

Nixon

"Nixon!" an urgent voice whispers, followed by a scratching sound and a zipper. A hand shakes my shoulder, sending radiating pain down my shoulder blade. "Nixon, wake up!"

I force my eyes open, blinking several times before looking around. The morning's low light spills into the building, just enough for me to make out my immediate surroundings. Seb is asleep across from us. Liam should still be on the roof. Ivy's sitting up, leaning over the space between our sleeping bags with her hand on my shoulder and gaze locked on one of the empty shelves we're behind.

"What's wrong?" I whisper, pushing myself up and rubbing my eyes.

"There's a girl in here."

"What?" The cloud of fatigue instantly dissolves, and I reach for the pistol in my tactical belt between us.

"No!" She grabs my wrist. "She's a kid."

"We don't know if she's alone." Shaking her off, I remove the gun. "She took one of the bags?" I ask, noting that one of the backpacks is missing from the center of our sleeping area. Another growl of a zipper and the sound of papers rustling.

She has the bag with the documents.

"Yeah," Ivy says.

Standing, I tuck the gun in my waistband behind my back. Ivy stands, too, but doesn't move from beside her sleeping bag. I inch forward, making sure my footsteps are light and scanning the store for anyone else. Everything appears exactly the same as last night, only now the destruction of the place is more visible, from the scattered garbage to what looks like old blood staining the tile in the first aisle.

I stop at the second aisle, slowly rounding the shelf. Hunched over the bag with her back to me, a girl pulls out a wad of papers and tosses them aside. They flutter to the floor, landing on top of a few articles of clothing that have already been removed. Seconds later, the drawstring bag is tossed aside as well, and she continues her search through the backpack.

"Hey," I say gently. "What are you doing out here?"

The girl spins around, stumbling backward, and her brown eyes widen, darting back and forth. She's young—no older than six or seven.

"It's okay," I say, spreading my hands and crouching on the floor. "I'm not going to hurt you."

A stained shirt, two sizes too big, hangs off one shoulder, exposing the prominent bones of her upper chest. Her knotted brown hair hangs over her hollow face, concealing most of the bruise beside her right eye. She tightens her bony fingers around the strap of the backpack, as though she's ready to run off with it.

"Where are your parents?" I ask.

No answer.

"Can you tell me what you're looking for? Maybe I can help you."

Her fearful eyes fall to the mess of papers and clothes beside her then drift back in my direction, settling at my feet. I look over at Ivy, who's still standing in the same spot, watching me with her hands clasped in front of her.

"I'm supposed to find food," the girl finally says in a timid voice.

"Okay," I say, turning to her. "Well, there isn't any in there, but if you want, I can have my friend over here bring me the right bag. Does that sound good?"

The fear doesn't leave her eyes, but she nods, so I motion Ivy over. Handing me her backpack, Ivy sits beside me, and the girl's eyes dart to her before focusing on me again. I unzip the backpack and do a quick inventory of what we have. Four more bags of beef jerky, two cans of cashews, eight protein bars, and eight bottles of water. Each rucksack has two canteens. Those can replace a few of the bottles, and we'll be okay until we at least get to the outpost.

"Are you Army guys?" the girl asks.

"Nope, not Army guys," I say, setting one bag of jerky and one can of cashews beside me.

"My daddy doesn't like them. They take people away."

I glance up at her. "Take them where?"

She watches intently as I pull out two water bottles and protein bars. "Inside." Her eyes pan up to mine. "Are you from the inside?"

I look at Ivy, unsure how to answer.

"No," Ivy says, getting the girl's attention, "we're just passing through. How many people from the inside have you seen?"

The girl shrugs a shoulder, her collarbone threatening to pierce through her skin.

"Did they do that to you?" Ivy asks, nodding at the bruise on the girl's face.

The girl reflexively lifts her hand to the injury near her eye and holds her fingers there.

"It's okay," Ivy says, sensing the child's uncertainty. She scoots forward and pulls up one sleeve, exposing the bruises circling her wrist. I have to look away. "The bad people hurt me, too."

Studying Ivy's wrist, the girl nods. "Did they take people from you, too?"

"They did," Ivy says, "in more ways than one."

I shoot her a glance that she doesn't reciprocate, wondering if she's referring to me or someone else entirely, like Adam and Lacey.

"Can you go get your brother and wake Seb?" I ask Ivy. "I can take care of it from here." Picking up everything I've pulled from the bag, I stand and look at the girl, who's now fully concentrating on the food. "Follow me."

The girl releases the strap of the backpack and stands. Wrapping her slender arms around herself, she hesitates before following. I find a discarded plastic handbasket in one of the aisles along the way and dump the food and water into it. When we reach the exit, I hand the basket to her. She stares up at me with her big brown eyes.

Since joining the resistance, I've developed this mindset that the Northern Unity is the absolute worst place to be with all of its corruption, secrets, and bloodthirsty tyrants. But out here, it's obviously no better. Those outside the walls are destined for a life of struggle to the point that children are forced to scavenge for food. Meanwhile, the Society still sends their soldiers out here to kidnap the vulnerable—probably to send them to the auction.

I don't know anything about the Commander's camp, but if he's as passionate about helping people as he claims, why isn't he helping those who are barely surviving out here? What makes the citizens of the Northern Unity more deserving of his help than those living in this wasteland?

"Thank you, mister," the girl says.

I offer her a smile. "You're welcome. Just don't tell anyone where you got that from."

She nods and runs out of the store, rounding the building to the right. I step outside, waiting at the corner for a few moments as she trots toward the back. Pulling out my gun, I scan the parking lot and what I can see of the surrounding treeline. No one else is in sight; no movement or anything out of place.

Liam drops from the ladder as I make my way to the back of the store. Seb sits up, stretching his arms over his head, and Ivy's already rolling up her sleeping bag.

"What happened?" Seb yawns.

"There was a kid in here," I say, returning the pistol to my tactical belt and fastening it around my waist.

"I didn't see anyone," Liam says.

"She came from the back—probably waited for you to turn around."

"Shit," Liam mutters. "I'm sorry."

"Not your fault. Seb, get up; you're coming with me." Kneeling, I open one of the side pockets of his rucksack.

"Where are we going?" Seb asks, standing and swiping his own belt from the floor.

"I want to follow her—scout out the area."

"Are you serious?" Liam asks. "This isn't one of your missions back home. We need to move out."

Pulling two short-range walkie-talkies from the sack, I shove one toward him, clipping the second on my belt. "What—scared you can't protect your sister yourself?"

Rolling his eyes, he puts on the smart-ass smirk that always annoys me. "Because you did such a great job with that, didn't you?"

"Liam!" Ivy says from behind me.

"Radio me only if you need to," I say. "Stay inside. I want everything packed up by the time we get back." Without waiting for his response, I stride out of the store, Seb following.

We round the building just as the girl did and head straight toward the treeline. I breathe deeply, welcoming the chilly air that fills my lungs despite the dull pain that radiates up the left side of my ribcage. Seb subtly glances at me every so often as he keeps up with my quick pace. Whether he's making sure I'm okay or waiting for any cues, I'm not sure.

The girl isn't in sight when we step off the asphalt, but her footprints are fresh in the soft dirt—clusters of brown grass have been flattened. The ground is littered with twigs and decayed leaves, absent of any other tracks.

"So, why are we following this kid?" Seb asks in a low voice.

"I want to see where she came from. Check out what we're dealing with out here."

The bruise near her eye and her frailness are stuck in my mind. For whatever reason, I need to make sure she's okay, that she has someone to return to who can care for her. If she is in danger, I don't know what I expect to do—bringing her with us will only slow us down—but I can't in good conscience leave her out here alone and unprotected.

"How old?" Seb asks.

"Six or seven, maybe." The impressions in the ground take a sudden left, go straight for a few yards, then make a right.

"And what did she want exactly?"

"Food. Ivy saw her first and woke me."

Seb studies the footprints and the ground surrounding them. "Doesn't look like anyone else has come this way. Think she's alone?"

"She mentioned her dad and said something about soldiers 'taking people away.'"

"Eli did mention re-education camps around here."

I shake my head. "The Society wouldn't re-educate people from outside the walls." Or would they?

From my prior knowledge and what I've read of Ivy's documents, I know re-education takes a few different forms. AI chips are first choice, with labor camps following close behind. But these people out here—however many there are—don't pose a threat. As far as I know, there have never been any cases of people trying to infiltrate the border or overthrow the Society aside from the resistance. Re-educating non-citizens would be a waste of time and money.

"I was thinking more along the lines of the auction," I say.

"Makes sense. You can only abduct so many citizens before people get suspicious, I guess."

Unless you keep them distracted with cozy lives and re-educate anyone who dares to question those disappearances.

The trees break off into a small clearing, where a two-story house sits in the center of ruins. Around a fourth of the home has been crushed by a fallen tree, and the portion that's still standing isn't in much better shape, with its dry-rotted wooden front porch and the chunks of shingles scattered throughout the overgrown yard.

I spot the girl climbing the steps of the porch and duck behind one of the trees, peering around it. A man approaches her from inside, holding on to the door frame for support. She holds out the basket as she nears him, and he snatches it from her, frantically digging through its contents. His mouth moves, but I can't make out what he's saying. Snapping his head up, he scans the neglected yard, yanking the girl up the last couple of steps.

Only when he raises his voice do I hear, "You know you're *never* supposed to leave without me!"

"But you're hurt!" the girl cries. "And we needed food!"

"That's not your responsibility! You could have been—" He breaks off, releasing the girl's arm and forcing his fingers through his shaggy hair.

Without thinking, I stand and step out of the trees.

"*Nixon!*" Seb hisses.

A twig snaps under my boot, and the man spins in my direction, pushing the girl behind him. I raise my hands, moving with slow, calculated steps.

"We're just here to help," I call, glancing over my shoulder at Seb, who reluctantly follows.

"That's him!" the girl says with the semblance of a smile, peering around the man. "That's the man who gave me the food."

"We don't need your help," her father spits back. He clenches his fist around the handle of the basket and inspects me and Seb. Like the girl, he's thin, with baggy, tattered clothes. "And, what—you gave my daughter food then followed her back here?" He shields her body with his again.

I stop about a yard from the steps, keeping my hands up. "We wanted to make sure she got back safe."

"That's very kind of you," he sneers, "but you can go now. I'm not letting you take my little girl, too." He nudges his daughter toward the open door, but her eyes don't leave me.

"We're not here to take anyone. You look hurt; is there anything we can do for you?"

Setting the basket down, he limps toward the edge of the porch and leans heavily on one of the beams. Despite whatever injuries he has, he stands tall, squaring his shoulders, and he glances at Seb before zeroing his eyes in on me—specifically, my holstered gun.

"You're not from out here."

"No, we're from the Northern Unity, but we're not soldiers. We work for the resistance."

"I don't care who you are; I don't want to be tangled up with anyone from the inside. Your people have already done enough damage."

"Your daughter mentioned soldiers in the area. Did they take someone from you?"

Shaking his head, he turns around, leaving the basket on the porch.

"I've had people taken from me, too," I call after him. "My parents, and my adoptive parents after that."

He pauses in the doorway.

"What they do is wrong, and you have every right not to trust me, but if you let me, maybe I can help."

"What can you possibly do to help?" he says over his shoulder. His daughter has a hand on the door frame, peeking out between it and her father.

"I'm a leader of the resistance. When my friends and I get to where we're going, I can look into whatever happened for you."

I look back at Seb, who crosses his arms and shakes his head. He and I both know I can't promise anything, especially if it concerns the disappearance of someone undocumented. But I can't let this go. I've devoted my life to helping people. It doesn't matter whether they're citizens of the Northern Unity or not, they don't deserve to have their lives ruined by the Society.

The Commander might be pissed at me for talking with non-members about what we do. My squad might think this is impulsive and idiotic—hell, even *I* know it is—but after everything that's happened, I can't see anyone else hurt.

The man hesitates, keeping his back to us. Finally, he turns, and says defeatedly, "We had a run-in with some soldiers a while back. They came out of nowhere and took my wife and son."

"How long ago?"

"Eight months."

That lines up with the timeframe of the auction six months before Ivy's.

"And how did your daughter get hurt?"

"We were at a settlement a few days ago; another group of soldiers stormed the place, and a lot of us got hurt in the process."

"But they didn't take anyone?"

"We didn't stick around long enough to find out." He shakes his head and drags his sleeve across his eyes.

"I'm sorry. Really, I am. If you want to come with us, we can check out your injuries and take you both somewhere safe."

From my peripheral vision, I see Seb shoot me a warning glare. We need to head out, and having an injured man and a kid will only slow us down. Not to mention that the Commander wouldn't be very happy about us showing up with two strangers.

"No," the man says. "We don't like staying in one place, and I want to get close to the wall in case they bring them back."

But his wife and son won't be coming back, at least not without the help of the resistance. They're stuck inside those walls. Once the Society has you, you belong to them forever. There are the rare—*extremely* rare—occasions where someone does escape, such as Ivy, but not without immense emotional scars.

"At least give me their names," I say. "I'll see what I can find out once we reach our destination, and I'll come back here in a few days."

"April and Jace Dawson," the man says. "April is thirty-two. Jace is six. Hold on, I have a picture." He fishes in his pocket and produces a folded photograph.

Stepping forward, I take it from him and unfold it. Under the thin layer of caked dirt, I can make out the family—the man, his wife, and his son and daughter, the girl clearly a couple years younger than she is now.

"Okay," I say, shoving the photo in my pocket. "I'll be back with whatever I find out in three days—four at the most. Will you still be here?"

He looks down at his daughter and gives her shoulder a squeeze. "Four days. Any longer and we'll have to leave."

"I understand. If you do, tie something to the door handle and leave a note. I'll look for you."

He nods, moving forward to grab the basket of food. "Thank you. And be careful; not everyone is friendly out here."

"I'll see you in a few days." Turning away from them, I retreat into the trees.

"What the hell was that?" Seb demands once the house is out of sight behind us. We keep a brisk pace back to the gas station. The sun's already inching its way up into the sky, its pale rays slicing through the trees. "You can't carry out a mission without the Commander's approval, and I seriously doubt he'll agree to this."

"Let me worry about that," I say. "And you seem to be forgetting that our mission in the Red Zone was launched without his permission. Against his orders, actually."

Seb jumps in front of me, bringing me to a halt. "You can't save everyone, dude."

He said something similar when I found out that Maverick and Drew died during my rescue.

"I can try." I attempt to maneuver around him, but he jerks me back into place. Rolling my eyes, I shake him off but don't move. "What?"

His irritable expression melts into sympathy. "If this has to do with Ivy, you have to let it go."

Panic pulses through me, but I keep my face neutral. "What's that supposed to mean?"

"I mean…" He rubs the bridge of his nose and exhales. "I get it if you're trying to redeem yourself after what happened with that mission, but this isn't the way to do it. I know it's not my place to tell you what to do, but we have her now. She's safe, and whatever happened to her isn't your fault. You got us out of the Northern Unity. Focus on *that*."

"I'm just trying to do what's right," I insist, pressing on.

He doesn't push the subject any further as we walk, and even though I want to defend myself and my actions more, I don't talk about it either. That will only confirm his suspicion.

Maybe there *is* a microscopic part of me that feels I need to redeem myself for my failed mission, but the simple desire to help those people outweighs it exponentially. That's what the resistance does.

"So, are we going to talk about what happened the other day?" Seb asks after a while.

"I zoned out for a second. That's it."

He chuckles, kicking a rock. It skids across the dirt ahead of us, thumping against a tree trunk. "That bullshit excuse might work on Liam, but not me."

He's right. Although Liam and I are best friends, he tends not to push sensitive subjects. Once he joined my group nearly a year ago, a small barrier formed between us like I knew it would. I'm not just his friend anymore; I'm his superior, and he's in this stage of trying to prove himself to me like all new recruits do in their first twelve months.

But Seb is different. He was already part of the Green Zone's group when I moved there, and while he respected me from the beginning, he's never been afraid of voicing his opinions.

"I'm sorry," I say. "It was fucked up and completely out of character for me."

"I'm not holding it against you, but it was pretty unnerving. Whatever's going on, you can talk to us."

"Yeah, I know, but I'm fine."

He lets out a dramatic sigh. "So damn stubborn as always. Look, I'm gonna be blunt with you."

"Nothing new there," I mutter.

"Which is why I'm one of your favorites."

I laugh. "Never said that."

"But seriously, I need to know that when we're actually in a situation like that, you're not going to snap again. The last thing we need is our leader being out of it when our lives are on the line."

The back of the gas station, complete with mildew and overgrowth, comes into view.

"You have nothing to worry about," I say. "It was a one-time thing."

"Alright. Just know I'll call your ass out if something like that happens again." He says it jokingly, but I know he's serious. "Also, little bit of advice for you—don't expect Ivy to open up if you can't do the same."

"Yeah, thanks."

My situation is completely different from hers, though. We were both held against our will in the Red Zone, but I've already answered for my time there. Ivy, on the other hand, has only actually admitted to killing Wyatt, and while that's crucial information, it doesn't account for the rest of the time she was there. The documents are useful, too, but it's not enough. I still don't know what Wyatt said about me or what he knew about my group. I don't know exactly who else she was in contact with from the Enlightened Society or what she told any of them. Even if they manipulated her to give up information without her realizing it, I need to know.

"What do you mean you don't know?" I hear Ivy yell as Seb and I walk along the side of the building. "He's *your* leader!"

"That doesn't sound good," Seb says, and we pick up our pace.

Liam gives his sister a response I can't hear that makes her yell, "What else are you hiding from me?"

Seb and I jog around the corner and into the store, glass crunching under our boots. The other two are at the back, near the mostly-packed bags. Ivy's gripping a stack of documents, crumpling the edges. Liam takes a couple of cautious steps toward her as we approach.

"Guys," Seb calls out.

"V, calm down," Liam says. He reaches out to her, fingers barely brushing her arm when she jerks away.

"What's going on?" I ask, stopping beside the last shelf before the wall of coolers.

Ivy spins around, narrowing her eyes and closing the gap between us. "What the fuck is this?" She shoves a stack of papers into my chest. "Where did you get these?"

Grabbing the papers, I take a step back and skim over the top one. My stomach clenches. They're the documents about their father's alleged death.

"I told you," Liam says, pulling his sister back, but her glare doesn't leave me. "Addison stole them from her dad and gave them to us."

"*Is* he dead?" Ivy asks. Her entire body is visibly trembling.

"I don't know," I tell her, and I really don't. I tried looking into his disappearance for Liam but came up with nothing. It's as if he vanished. Honestly, after the first year without any intel, I felt that he probably was dead, but I've never had the heart to tell Liam or Ivy that. "Whatever happened to him, I had nothing to do with it."

"But he was the type of person the resistance targets, right? He was the Green Zone's Police Chief, and you told me yourself he was involved in the auction."

Is she really entertaining the idea that I killed her dad? Did the Society brainwash her that much in her short time with them?

Folding the papers, I pass them to Liam, and he returns them to his backpack. "I also told you the Commander has to approve everything I do, so you can ask him about it yourself when we meet him. I never targeted your dad, and I only ever paid attention to him *after* he was gone."

"They claimed they have evidence!" She shakes Liam's hand off again. Her chin quivers.

This isn't the first time she's heard about her father.

"He didn't do it," Seb jumps in. "I was with him that night, and rumors were already circulating the next day."

Ivy shakes her head, raking her fingers through her hair. "There were pictures of his body!"

The chilly air instantly gets colder. I look at Seb and Liam, who are both staring at me in confusion. Seb hasn't seen the documents, but

Liam has. There were no pictures, and in her emotional state, I seriously doubt Ivy took the time to read over every single word in that file. The only two photos that were given to us were of Chief Clearson in uniform and me a couple of years ago.

"What are you talking about?" I ask.

Her face falls, knowing she's been caught in yet another lie.

"You knew about this already, didn't you?"

She doesn't say anything, looking to Liam for backup.

"Answer me!"

"Yes," she mumbles.

"When?"

"The interrogator told me—"

"Unbelievable."

"Did you actually see the pictures?" Liam asks.

"No," Ivy admits. "I couldn't bring myself to, but he made it sound like they were real."

"When are the lies going to stop, Ivy?" I hiss. "My patience is already thin, and every word that comes out of your mouth only pisses me off more."

"I'm not lying," she snaps. "I just—"

"Stop!" I take a couple of steps toward her, waiting for her to meet my eyes before saying, "You want to be a part of my group so bad? Start by telling the truth for once. Because as it is right now, I don't even care to be around you." Pushing past her, I grab one of the submachine guns from the floor beside the four bags. "Let's head out."

22. Hate Me

Ivy

I thought daylight would make this place less frightening, but it only amplifies its eerie essence. Tangled trees, a few gutted buildings, fallen lampposts, and twisted overgrowth reach out in every direction. Dark clouds have begun to roll in, threatening to consume the morning sun.

Seb walks beside me, toting the rucksack and submachine gun as he did last night. Nixon and Liam walk together a few yards ahead but keep distance between each other as they talk. What was said last night and this morning before we left hasn't been brought up again, but the tension is still very much present between all of us. Nixon's words, dripping with venom, replay in my head.

"If I'm not able to warn them because you're withholding informa-tion, their blood is on your hands."

"Start by telling the truth for once. Because as it is right now, I don't even care to be around you."

I'm not lying. I'm afraid. Afraid of being outside the walls. Of the Commander's camp. Of the person Nixon's become. Of myself.

It's only been twenty-four hours since I murdered Wyatt. How can they expect me to just get over that? Not to mention that they don't know everything I went through, everything I had to do in order to survive. As much as I want to let it all out, I can't. Any time I've started to explain, the words sliced at my throat, each syllable razor-sharp, wanting to rip me apart, and Nixon's coldness hasn't made it any easier.

The reality that we've actually made it out of the Northern Unity—that we're freely roaming an uncivilized territory—still hasn't settled in. What's even harder to believe is that I'm no longer under Wyatt's control. I was supposed to be married by now, forced to stay at whatever five-star, resort-style hotel his parents had chosen for our honeymoon. Instead, his parents are probably arranging his funeral.

Guilt is eating at me. Whenever I'm not focusing on something else, the image of him lying in his own blood creeps to the front of my mind. The urgency of escaping yesterday was enough to distract me from it, but now, with everything relatively calm, it all comes back. Stronger, hungrier. Not only the last time I saw Wyatt, but the girl I saw at Nolan's house—the blood gushing from her nose and trickling down her legs, her collection of bruises, and her unforgettable, haunt-ing wail after I left the room. I wasn't the one who took her life, but I had a knife to her throat. And I didn't do anything to stop Wyatt and Nolan.

"So, Ivy," Seb says, grounding me in the present again, "what's so special about you?"

"What do you mean?" I ask.

"I mean, why does the Commander want you out here so bad?" Smiling, he raises an eyebrow. "Something you're not telling us?"

I let out a nervous laugh. "No, why?"

He shrugs. "Missions like this aren't very common for us, especially with those as high-profile as you."

"Well, it's not just me, right?" I nod toward Nixon. "He had to get out, too, after escaping his execution."

Seb sucks air in through clenched teeth, making a soft hissing sound. "About that…"

"What?"

Slowing his pace to put a little more distance between us and the other two, Seb lowers his voice and says, "Nixon didn't exactly *want* to leave. He never planned on it."

"But he's wanted just as much as I am," I say, matching his volume.

"Yeah, but he has a group to look after. He's a natural leader, and despite the fact that there's a bounty on his head, he wanted to stay."

The guilt spreads, gnawing at my gut. Is that why he's so cold—because I took him away from his group?

Nixon has always made it obvious how much he cares for his team. Although Adam told me his adoptive son isn't exactly confident in his own ability to lead, he's done a good job. He takes on all of the most difficult tasks so none of his members have to. Not only is Nixon a leader, he's a protector, too.

"So if he and Liam are out here," I say, "who's running the Green Zone?"

"The Yellow Zone's second-in-command."

"But he'll be going back, right? Your group needs him."

"Not my business. I'm just here making sure you get there in one piece. But back to my question…" He smiles again, and the dimple on his cheek returns.

"I have no idea what the Commander wants with me." I shove my hands into the pockets of my jacket.

Not once did I ever wonder why the Commander wanted me at his camp. I can understand taking me in as a refugee after Nixon saved me from the Black Hats. But now, as someone who's lived with one of the thirteen families of the Enlightened Society, I realize that I should be viewed as a threat. *I* know I didn't give up anything about the resistance, but a man who oversees the entire organization has no reason to assume that. He should automatically be wary of me, like Nixon and Eli.

The same fear I felt the day I was first told I'd be leaving the country returns. This time, it crashes over me. One brutal wave after another, it pulls me under. There's no turning back. We're in the middle of nowhere. No protection. No clue as to what awaits us.

Clenching my hands tighter in my pockets, I focus on the dull pain in my leg, the ache of my muscles, and the burn in my feet, which I'm sure are blistered by now. Keeping my attention on the pain is the only thing that fully grounds me, but it doesn't take away the idiotic urge to spin around and sprint back to the safety of that prison.

I trust they'll take care of you. Nixon's words from when we were in the Blue Zone echo in my head. *If I didn't think it was safe, I wouldn't send you out there.*

Does he actually believe that now? Or is he back to his mindset of not caring whether I'm safe, like when we were originally forced together? If he truly would have rather stayed in the Green Zone, his goal is keeping his group safe, and he's made it abundantly clear I'm not part of that.

"Speaking of Nixon, though," Seb says, "he was telling the truth about your dad. He and Elizabeth were at my house the night he disappeared."

A pang of something I can't name stabs at my heart.

"Just the three of you?" I ask. "Doing what?"

He laughs—a lighthearted, carefree sound that, like last night, elevates the mood. "Just hanging out—had some drinks, talked. I know you've only seen us in action, but we *are* normal people, too."

I know from my aunt that it's possible to get hold of alcohol, but I never expected resistance members to do it. I guess I should have; it's not like following the law is high on their list of priorities.

I stare ahead at Liam and Nixon as we make another right, sticking to the edge of the road. Nixon glances back at us, his eyes passing over me.

Aside from the subject of her murder, he never talked to me about Elizabeth, and even then it was vague. Liam didn't really say much about her either except that she was a friend, which I now understand was code for 'comrade.' But Nixon did come into our family's flower shop to buy a wreath for the memorial he'd planned for her—and when Kase blamed him for getting her killed, it practically destroyed him.

"Were Nixon and Elizabeth together?" I ask, trying to sound casual.

"Like, in a relationship?" Seb shrugs. "I'm not sure. I mean, they were close, I guess, but I think it was more of a protection thing."

"Protection from what?"

"Nothing in particular, really. She was the only girl in our whole group, so some of the guys gave her shit, especially on her squad, so he had to step in on several occasions. If they *did* have anything, though, they kept it a secret. It's against the rules."

Not a direct yes or no—not that it should matter. It's not really any of my business, but that doesn't snuff the smoldering jealousy that's found its way to my chest.

Another thing my interrogator told me pops into my head: *Terrorists* hint at the potential of a romantic relationship in order to manipulate their victims. I don't want to believe I was manipulated. I can't have been; everything Nixon told me about the Society is true. The auction, the Black Hats, all of it. And what I felt for him then was real too—the most authentic thing I'd experienced since I was taken from my home. Did he feel the same way, though?

We continue down the narrow road in silence, with me and Seb hanging back. Whatever Liam and Nixon are discussing, I don't want to hear it, especially if it pertains to what happened at the gas station. I force my attention back to my sore body. The soles of my feet are raw despite the thick socks that were given to me, and the sewn-up cut on my arm is especially irritated today.

After at least another two miles, a confined dirt path extends from the left side of the road, and we follow it. Slender trees surround us in all directions, their branches bare. Chipped bark and dead foliage litter the path and are packed deeper into the soft earth as we walk.

Water gurgles somewhere nearby, almost making this place feel serene. Closing my eyes, I breathe deep and allow the sounds and smells of nature to envelop me. For a moment, it reminds me of when I was in the Blue Zone away from the city, but cleaner—lighter.

"How're you holding up, Ivy?" Liam asks, looking over his shoulder at me. Seeing how much farther behind we are, he stops, and Nixon does the same seconds later.

I muster a smile as we get closer. "Great."

"Keep up," Nixon says flatly.

He's about to turn around to start walking again when Seb says, "Can we stop for a minute?"

Nixon faces his scout. "Why?"

"Gotta piss," Seb says, already handing Liam his submachine gun and stepping off the trail into the dense trees.

"How much farther?" Liam asks. He pulls the map from his back pocket and struggles to unfold it with one hand.

"About five miles," Nixon says, readjusting his gun and pressing a hand to his side. He draws in a deep breath and winces, but Liam doesn't notice. "Commander's camp is a two-hour drive from there."

"And they'll be supplying a vehicle?" Liam folds the map and shoves it back in his pocket.

"According to Eli."

Brushing past Liam as they continue their discussion about the outpost, I move ahead at a leisurely pace, taking in my surroundings. I reach out, running my fingers over one of the ashy tree trunks and taking comfort in the rough, mottled bark against my skin. The entire time I was at the Everetts', I longed to be out in the open, to be free from the prison of that mansion. During our journey, I've never felt that freedom. Until now.

No crumbling roads or buildings. No reminders of a world that used to exist long before our own. Just nature in its purest, simplest form. I take a few more steps forward; the babbling water gets closer, and the serenity is enhanced. It pulls at me, drawing me farther away from the men behind me.

"Ivy," Liam calls. "Where are you going?"

Trance broken, I reluctantly walk back toward him. "Nowhere."

The snap of a twig makes me freeze a few paces from him, and Liam and Nixon whip their heads around, raising their guns.

I follow their gaze, searching for the source of the sound. Trees obscure my view. Everything is quiet, save for the water. At first I think it's just Seb making his way back to us, but there's no sign of him. My next thought is of soldiers. They've tracked us down and are here to drag us back to the Northern Unity.

A hollow thud, like something knocking against a tree trunk, comes from behind me and I jump. Nixon's head snaps in my direction while Liam's eyes remain forward, but I can't bring myself to look back.

Removing a hand from his gun, Nixon extends his arm toward me and motions for me to come closer. I force my legs to move, cringing at the slightest squish of mud beneath my boots. I hold my breath as I walk, as if it will help me remain unnoticed. The silence, something that was peaceful moments ago, is now ghostly.

When I reach Nixon, he grabs my arm and pulls me behind him. The sudden touch surprises me, reminding me of when we hid from the tracking dogs in the Blue Zone. There's a low rumble in the distance, like an engine. I glance at the road beyond the entrance of the trail but don't see anything.

Pulling the walkie-talkie from his belt, Nixon presses the button on the side and says, "Seb, come in."

Static crackles. No response comes.

"Seb, do you read me?"

A gunshot splits the air, and I cringe towards Nixon without thinking. Shouting follows, the words swallowed by a gust of wind that whistles through the knocking branches. Fear floods my veins.

Nixon spins around and sprints toward the noise. Liam nudges me in the same direction and falls in step behind me. We follow the path of flattened brown grass and soggy, broken leaves. Impressions in the bare sections of ground make me think we're on the right track to reaching Seb until I notice several others. My heart skips a beat.

"Seb, come in," Nixon tries again on his walkie-talkie.

I stay close behind him, matching his every move while trying not to trip over exposed roots and scattered rocks. The shouting gets closer—an angry bellow. Another gunshot echoes. The wail of a man sends a chill down my spine.

"Seb, do you read me?"

My heart pounds in my ears. Between each beat, I think I hear more footsteps. More voices farther away. I glance back at my brother, who's on my heels, his features stern. One thought repeats itself in my head: *Seb's dead, and we're next.*

The ground dips down up ahead, with more gnarled roots as an obstacle. Nixon slows down, scrambles down the slope, and turns to me, offering his hand. Without thinking, I take it, feeling a sting in my burned fingers, and start my shaky descent. The front of my boot catches underneath one of the roots halfway down. I jerk it free, and pain shoots through my ankle. I let out a yelp but keep moving.

I jump down to the mostly level ground and out of the trees. I listen for more yelling or gunshots, but there's nothing. Only our footsteps and my blood roaring in my ears.

Stopping, Nixon shoots his arm out to the side, and I come to a stumbling halt behind him. My ankle throbs again. He takes a couple of cautious steps forward, and I peer around him.

Seb is on the ground, pinning a man down with a knee in his back and pistol to his head. The man's face is turned away from us. The hand that's pinned underneath him seems to be clutching his thigh. Seb looks up at us, face stiff. Blood trickles from his nose.

"What happened?" Nixon asks, walking toward them. "Why the hell did you come out this far?"

Liam and I follow, but I keep my distance.

"Motherfucker was following me," Seb says. "I led him out here and he rushed me." He motions to a knife in the foliage a few feet away.

"Were those gunshots from you?" Liam asks.

"Yup." Shifting his weight off the man, Seb stands and flips him onto his back, pressing a foot to his chest. The man cries out in agony, gripping his thigh. Crimson seeps from between his dirty fingers. Seb aims his pistol at the man's forehead. "I'm going to ask you one more time—why did you follow me?"

The man holds his hand up, palm out, to shield his face. Mud cakes his hairline. His brown shirt that was probably white once is torn at the shoulder, exposing part of a tattoo—a collection of blue swirls around a dagger. "Please! I have a family."

"We all do," Seb says, kicking the man's hand away from his face and planting the other foot on his wrist. The man wriggles underneath him, crying out. "That doesn't make you special."

The man's chest spasms, and his eyes widen as he swipes at Seb's ankle, which only makes Seb apply more pressure.

"Stop!" I cry, shoving my way past Liam and Nixon. "You're hurting him!"

Liam pulls me back by my arm, planting me between him and Nixon. The man turns his face to me, a lifetime of struggle in his weathered face. He gives me the same pleading look as the woman from Nolan's house, which makes my stomach clench.

All he's trying to do is survive. Same as us. We can give him what he needs for his family, just like we did with the girl at the gas station. We can help.

"Supplies," the man sputters, keeping his eyes trained on me. "We need supplies. Food, medical equipment, weapons…"

"We can't help you there," Nixon says.

I glare at him. What does he mean, we can't help? We're not far from the outpost, and we have more than enough supplies for a five-mile walk. What happened to the resistance helping people? This man may not be trapped inside the walls, but the Society's greed and corruption have still affected him.

Seb steps off the man but doesn't lower his weapon. Wiping the blood from his nose with his hand, he looks up at us. "What do you want to do with him?"

The man's eyes never leave me. I try to make myself look away, to pay attention to Liam or Nixon or Seb, but my gaze keeps finding its way back to him. Maybe they can live with themselves letting this innocent person suffer, but I can't. If it were me, I'd want someone to have some compassion.

"Your call," Nixon says, turning to walk the way we came. "Whatever you do, make it quick."

No.

Liam follows Nixon, and Seb faces the man on the ground, steadying his gun.

"Ivy, let's go," Liam calls.

He has a family. People who need him.

"Please don't do this," the man begs, attempting to push himself from the ground before Seb presses his boot back to his chest.

Ankle pulsing, I sprint toward them, throwing all of my weight into Seb and grabbing his wrist. He stumbles backward and grasps at the empty air for something to steady him.

"Ivy!" Liam yells over pounding footsteps.

We crash to the ground, Seb's rucksack breaking his fall and my body colliding with his as I attempt to wrench the gun from his hand. He tries to shove me away, but I cling to his arm and straddle his torso. Arm across my upper chest, he holds me off until I'm grabbed by my backpack and jerked off him.

Nixon pulls me away and releases my backpack. "What the fuck is wrong with you?"

Ignoring him, I march over to the man who was left on the ground. He's sitting up, scrambling backward with the blood from his bullet wound dotting the dead leaves. Slipping off my backpack, I kneel beside him and unzip the main compartment. With trembling hands, I pull out the first few items I can grab—a bag of jerky and two protein bars. I set them beside him and, without waiting for him to say anything, stand and sling my bag over my shoulders.

"You can't do that," Nixon says, blocking my path as I start in the direction of the trail. "We have just enough for the four of us."

"So I won't fucking eat," I say, pushing past him.

He grabs my wrist, yanking me back toward him, which only makes me angrier. I twist out of his grip, slam my hands against his chest, and yell, "Don't touch me!"

"Keep your voice down," he orders, pulling me forward by the strap of my bag. His icy eyes bore into mine. "What was that?"

"He was going to kill him."

"To protect *us*."

"That doesn't make it any better!" Tears fill my eyes. My gaze drifts past him to the spot where I left the food; it's gone, along with the man, only the spatter of blood left behind. Seb's on his feet beside Liam, his submachine gun returned to him. "It doesn't make you any different from the Society."

Nixon's grip on me loosens. Averting his eyes, he sighs. "This isn't really about that man, is it?" he asks in a low voice.

I jerk free from him. "It is," I spit back, annoyed at how he always dissects everything I say, like he's looking for some hidden meaning. "And about how you claim you want to help people but do the exact opposite."

Jaw tight and fist clenched at his side, his glare zeroes back in on me. "You don't know anything about me."

"Clearly."

"That's enough," Liam says, grabbing my arm and dragging me toward the trail. "Whatever's going on with you two, you can deal with it *after* we reach the outpost."

Seb and Nixon push their way to the front, taking the lead up the incline. We climb the uneven ground, and I'm careful this time not to trip over any exposed roots. The more we walk, the more my ankle throbs. I resort to limping, only putting weight on the toes of my injured foot to ease the unrelenting pain. Taking notice, Liam throws my arm over his shoulder.

"Since when are you one to give orders?" I ask him when we make it to the top.

"Since when do you pull crazy shit like that?" he retorts.

What's crazy is the willingness to kill someone without reason. Even worse is that he, like Nixon, is completely fine with it, as if their actions don't affect other people. As if that man didn't have people counting on him to bring back basic necessities. In no way am I a hero in this scenario, but I'm confident I did the right thing. An innocent person gets to live, and his family can eat.

"Look," Liam whispers, "I understand you've been through a lot and Nixon's being a bit of a hard-ass on you, but when you're given orders, you follow them. That's the only way we're all going to survive out here. I can only stick up for you so much."

I let out a bitter laugh. "I don't need you to stick up for me."

"God, you're still so stubborn." He flashes me a mocking smile, and the familiarity of it brings my boiling anger to a simmer. "Just chill with the outbursts for at least the next few miles, alright?"

Even out here, in the middle of nowhere with little to no certainty about what's to come, he's still the same person I left behind—sarcastic and irritating in a way that I love. It's nice to know I have at least one person who hasn't flipped on me.

"I've missed you," I say, squeezing his shoulders.

"I've missed you, too."

A break in the trees comes into view, with the trail on the other side. Leaning on Liam eases the pain in my ankle but doesn't take it away completely. Exhaustion creeps up on me, and I wish I'd been able to sleep last night.

Five more miles, I tell myself. Then we'll be at an outpost with other members and can hopefully get some actual rest before heading out again for the Commander's camp.

Dangerously dark clouds swallow the sun now, and the wind has picked up, jolting tree branches and kicking up leaves from the ground. In the small gaps between gusts, I can make out the sound of gurgling water again, just as mesmerizing as it was earlier.

Seb and Nixon step onto the trail first. They freeze when a voice yells, "That's them!"

Liam tightens his arm around my torso and reaches for his holstered pistol. Emerging from the trees, we follow the gaze of the other two, and my heart lodges itself in my throat.

We're near the start of a dirt trail. Two pick-up trucks are parked at the entrance, trapping us in. I count six people waiting beside them and another two in one of the beds—five men and three women in total—all holding weapons of some sort. Rifles, arrows, and knives are pointed at us with one collective objective pulsing through the air: Kill.

Positioning me behind Seb and Nixon, Liam stands beside them, all three aiming their own weapons at the group.

A man steps forward, breaking away from his gang with a rifle pointed directly at Nixon. "I wouldn't do that if I were you," he says in a gravelly voice. His narrowed eyes travel over us.

Unlike the little girl from this morning, he's muscular, with semi-new-looking clothes. In fact, everyone he's with appears to be fairly healthy and clothed appropriately, from thick jackets to shoes that are fully intact.

"We don't want any trouble," Nixon says. "We're just passing through."

The lead man chuckles. "See, I'd believe you—if you hadn't shot one of my men."

I frantically search the people behind him again, spotting the man Seb pinned down in the bed of one of the trucks. A woman is tending to his wound, and he squirms under her touch. He's alive but injured. They're not going to let us walk away from that.

"He was stalking one of my guys," Nixon growls. "It was self-defense."

The leader smirks. "You know, I was going to kill all of you for what you did." His eyes click to me. "Until my scavenger told me the girl's the one who saved his ass and convinced me otherwise."

My shoulders relax and a sense of pride rushes through me. *It was the right choice.* But the weapons aren't lowered, and the threatening smirk remains plastered on his face.

With the wave of his hand, a woman and another man come forward, taking positions on either side of their leader. "Instead," he says, "I've decided to bring you back to our settlement."

"We're not interested," Seb says.

"It wasn't an offer. We still need supplies, and you four are going to help us with that."

"We already gave your scavenger what we had left," Liam lies.

His smile widens, exposing a missing top tooth. "I was thinking more along the lines of a trade." Two more men break away from the group, circling us. Nixon remains focused on the three people in front of him while Seb and Liam watch the other two. "Some soldiers will be here in the next couple days, and if we supply them with what they want, they give us what we need." His eyes sweep over us again. "And with four of you, we should get plenty in return."

My stomach drops.

I'm not going back to the Northern Unity. I can't. These people may not know who we are, but as soon as those soldiers arrive, they'll recognize me and Nixon—maybe even Liam. They'll kill us.

A bald man with a scraggly red beard stops beside me, and Liam keeps his pistol trained on him. A knife is clenched in his gloved hand, brownish residue caked on the side of the blade. Once again, the woman from Nolan's house pops into my mind, and I'm paralyzed, helpless—just like that night.

Nixon turns around, but before his eyes are even on me, the bearded man jerks me back by my waist. A gasp escapes me as the blade is pressed to my throat. Liam's finger brushes the trigger of his gun.

"Shoot me," my captor says, "and I'll cut her throat."

"I suggest you drop your weapons," the leader says. "No one has to get hurt here."

The man and woman on either side of him stand straighter, as if preparing to attack at his command. One of the other scavengers has taken his place beside Seb, the two of them staring each other down, unflinching. That leaves four more by the trucks. No matter how confident Nixon, Seb, and Liam are in their abilities, they won't win against these people.

That pride I felt moments ago has dissipated. A man got to live in order for the four of us to die—or at the very least, be sent to the auction or re-education. Maybe if I'd let Seb kill the scavenger, we'd have been able to move forward before his group found us.

Nixon's eyes dart between me, the man behind me, and Seb. I catch him gnawing at the inside of his cheek, strategizing his next move.

"Do it," I say. "We can't win; we're outnumbered."

Shaking his head, he directs his glare back to me. If we didn't have to appear as a united front at this moment, I know he'd tell me how stupid a suggestion that is—probably even how selfish. And maybe it is. But we *are* outnumbered, and he's obviously injured, even if he tries to hide it.

Either way, these guys are going to get what they want. The only difference is that if we give in now, none of us have to get hurt.

As if reading my thoughts, Nixon turns to the three people behind him, sets his gun on the ground, and removes his tactical belt, dropping it to his feet. Seb immediately does the same, raising his hands in surrender, but Liam hesitates.

"Liam," Nixon says, facing his second-in-command, "put the gun down."

Seconds stretch out. The blade pushes against my skin, making it difficult to swallow past the cool metal. Panic blossoms, and tears burn my eyes. I try to slow my breathing, try to remain as still as possible while locking eyes with my brother, silently begging him to drop the gun.

Nixon wraps a hand around the barrel of the pistol and forces it down, pulling it from his grasp, and Liam finally removes his own belt. The blade comes away from my throat, and I draw in a deep breath.

"Let's load 'em up," the leader barks, retreating to the vehicles.

My backpack is yanked off my shoulders, and the three remaining scavengers take the others' bags. The man behind me forces my arms behind my back. Something clinches around my wrists, pinning them together and digging into my skin. Seb, Nixon, and Liam get makeshift handcuffs too—two zip ties looped together.

With a scavenger behind each of us, we're shoved toward the trucks, lifted into one of the open beds, and forced to sit along one side. Crammed between Seb and Liam, my hands are pinned underneath me. The zip ties pinch my wrists and rub against the bruises from Wyatt.

Two scavengers climb into the back of our truck with us, rifles in hand. The engines roar to life, and at the sound, regret anchors itself in me.

Just before the vehicle lurches forward, the scavengers produce a pile of folded black fabric. The man across from me pulls a makeshift bag over my head, and all I see is darkness.

23. Falls Apart

Nixon

The bag is ripped off my head once I'm shoved into a room. I stumble forward after Liam, landing on my knees with a grunt. Seb and Ivy are pushed in after us, and the door slams shut. The click of a lock sounds, followed by the snap of two latches.

Pushing myself to my feet, I do a sweep of the small, empty room. A single barred window is on the far cedar-paneled wall, allowing the gray light inside. On the wall adjacent to the entrance is a bathroom, the door hanging from a single hinge. A warped ceiling fan dangles above us—bulb busted and chains missing—and footprints of all sizes decorate the dust-coated wooden floor.

Crossing the room, I peer out the window at the small cluster of other cabins. In the middle of the semicircle sits an extinguished fire pit with four large logs surrounding it. Children laugh as they chase each other, and men and women chat. I search for the faces of our captors, but don't recognize anyone. The only thing that stands out is the wardrobe of these people—fully intact and gently used. Nothing like the little girl and her father.

We're trapped in here, with guards likely on the other side of the door. No weapons. No one to contact for help. All because Ivy made an idiotic decision to let that scavenger go.

"Are you happy now, Ivy?" I demand, spinning around. She's standing against the wall beside the bathroom, putting most of her weight on her left foot. "Was letting that guy live worth us being captured again?"

Turning her face, she squeezes her eyes shut and purses her lips.

"You can't act on impulse!" With two strides, I'm in front of her. "That's how *this* happens. When I tell you to do something, you listen!"

"He didn't deserve to die," Ivy mumbles. A single tear slips down her cheek.

"And we didn't deserve to be taken as prisoners. But here we are." Shaking my head, I glance around the room again—this time, searching for something I can use to get me out of these damn zip ties. I flex my arms and attempt to pull my wrists apart with as much strength as I can muster, but all that comes of it is the plastic digging deeper into my skin. "Is this what you wanted? For all of us to be dragged back to the Northern Unity? Was this your plan the entire time?"

I'm barely thinking about what I'm saying, but as the words come out, they almost make sense. She's refused to answer my questions honestly, withheld information, attacked my scout, and urged us to give up our weapons. In what way did she think any of that would play out in her favor unless she was already planning for this to happen?

"No," Ivy says, facing me with wide, watery eyes. "How could you think that?"

"With one stupid decision after another, I don't know what else I'm supposed to think," I snap. "Ever since we got to Eli's, you've been working against me. Why is it so hard to accept that we're not your enemies here?"

More tears flow, and she looks to her brother for support.

"Dude, chill," Seb says from beside the door. "This isn't helping right now."

Liam doesn't jump to her defense, though. He remains by her side but takes on the authoritative demeanor I've seen him use with our group—back straight, face blank, and chin slightly lifted.

"You really messed up, V," he tells her firmly.

"I didn't mean to," she says. "I didn't want this to happen."

"Nixon," Seb says. He's focused on Ivy—specifically, her hands, bound behind her. "She only has one zip tie."

"What?" Sidestepping, I follow his gaze. Sure enough, a single black zip tie is secured around her wrists while Seb, Liam, and I have two.

"What does that mean?" Ivy asks, craning her neck to look behind her.

"Guess they don't think you're strong enough to break out of a single one," Liam says.

"That's because I'm not," she says.

"You're going to try," I say, turning back to the window, "but not yet. I want to figure out what kind of schedule they have going here."

"You really think we stand a chance of escaping?" Ivy asks. "We were outnumbered on the trail and don't know how many are here."

"You're not really in any position to be arguing," Liam says, taking me by surprise, though I don't look back.

"You don't even have your guns," Ivy says.

"One step at a time," I say. "And this time, you're going to listen to me."

Rain falls from the black clouds. The group of people has thinned out, some of them huddled under the covered porches of the cabins while others have disappeared inside. I look around for the trucks we were brought here in, but my view is limited and obscured by the bars.

"So what's your plan?" Ivy asks.

Turning, I sit against the wall beside the window so I still have a somewhat clear view of the outside. "For now, we wait."

We sit there for what must be hours—Seb a few feet from the door, head leaning back against the cedar wall and eyes half shut; Ivy beside the bathroom with her head resting on her brother's shoulder. The only sound is the rain hammering against the roof and an occasional rumble of thunder. We remain silent, listening for our captors.

Hunger gnaws at my stomach. My throat feels like sandpaper. A dense fog of fatigue hangs over me.

Leaning forward, I clench and unclench my bound fists. A prickly sensation creeps up my arms as the feeling in them slowly returns. The pain in my ribs from earlier has subsided, but I know once I'm in action again, it'll return. I just hope it holds off until we're out of here and close to the outpost… however far that is from this place.

Closing my eyes, I try to map out the path we took here in my head—how many turns and in which direction, how long we were in the back of that truck—and remember how many voices I heard. There were eight people on the trail and maybe a dozen outside before the rain moved in. At least twenty. And they're armed.

Meanwhile, we're trapped in here, and the person responsible is six feet away from me, sitting quietly. I steal a glance at her, which only makes my anger return, and I have to force myself to focus on something else. But at the same time, the anger is the only thing that really grounds me. If I don't hold on to it, the anxiety of being captured and what awaits us takes over, something I've never felt before my six weeks in the Red Zone.

Fresh memories of the beatings, the burning breaths of water, and the faceless men dragging me back to my cell invade my mind. My throat constricts and the wounds on my back suddenly burn, as if it's happening all over again. Pulling my legs up, I press my forehead into my knees and cling to the anger and frustration toward Ivy. Even if I partly understand her reasoning for what she did, it keeps me from retreating into the shadows of my mind.

For the hundredth time, I pull my wrists apart, and the ridges of the zip ties bite into my skin. I let out a frustrated breath but try again. Nothing.

"Someone's coming," Seb says quietly.

Sitting up, I focus on the door. Heavy footsteps stop on the other side, and the snap of the first latch sounds. Then the second. There's a moment of shuffling, shoes scuffing against the floor, but the click of the lock finally comes and the door squeals as it's pushed open.

The leader from the trail steps into the room, taking in the four of us spread across the small space. When his gaze lands on me, his mouth contorts into a malicious smile.

"Ya know," he says, running a hand over his slicked-back hair, "I was looking forward to having the four of you here the next couple days, letting you help out around the settlement until the soldiers came for you."

I clench my fists, making the zip ties dig into my skin. We have to get out of here. If the soldiers are already on their way, we're fucked.

The man flicks on the flashlight he's holding, sets it upright and crouches in front of me. One of his men remains in the doorway with a tactical belt around his waist, holding one of our submachine guns.

The leader chuckles. "Don't worry, I'm not going to kill you— then I wouldn't have anything to trade."

"Whatever you'd get for us, I can get you more," I say. The Commander wouldn't help anyone who works with the Society, but if bluffing can buy us some time, I'll use it to our advantage.

"Normally," he says, "I'd make a deal, but we both know I'll receive more than enough for you four. Isn't that right, Nixon?"

I grind my teeth and force myself to keep my breathing steady.

They saw the documents. Not just the ones Ivy stole from the Everetts, but the report about Chief Clearson's alleged death with my picture.

I glance at the rest of my team. Seb and Liam remain stoic, but Ivy's looking at me, hazel eyes dull and apologetic, her chest rising and falling with each rapid breath.

"So," the man in front of me continues, "I contacted one of the commanding officers at the closest—what do you call them, re-education centers?" He waves a hand in the air. "Anyway, they were pleased to hear we have a few of their fugitives. Especially the girl." He looks at Ivy, and his menacing smile grows. "Can't say I blame them."

Ivy holds his gaze, and Liam slides closer to her until their legs touch.

"Well," the leader says, pressing his palms to his knees as he stands, "I thought you at least deserved to know of the new arrangements. They should be here in a couple hours. Hope you're looking forward to going home."

Seb looks away from the armed scavenger, and his gaze clicks to Ivy before locking on me, eyebrows raised in silent questioning.

A couple of hours rather than a couple of days, and I don't even have the foundation of a plan in place. These people are hoarding our weapons and supplies, and we have no clue where exactly we are. We'll have to improvise. Making it out of here is going to be difficult but not impossible, as long as the other three are willing to cooperate.

I give Seb a subtle nod.

"So, are you going to feed us?" he asks, stopping the man just in front of the scavenger, and I hold back a groan. That's really the best he could do?

The leader considers the question for a moment, eyeing Seb with amusement. Then he waves his scavenger forward and says, "Find them some food," before exiting the room and locking us inside once again.

24. Any Second

Nixon

"Try again," Liam tells Ivy, impatience creeping into his voice.

Ivy struggles against the zip tie. "I *am* trying."

"Do we even have a plan?" Seb asks, now standing beside the window.

"Shut up!" I command, leaning my head back against the wall. "I need to think."

We don't know how many more scavengers will be returning with food. Regardless, they'll definitely be armed—guns, knives, or some other makeshift weapon. If Ivy can get out of her restraint, that will give us a little leverage, but not much. She has no training, so it's not like she can fight off these men without help. And she's hurt, but I don't know the extent of her wounds—only that she hasn't been able to put her weight on one foot since we went off the trail.

I think back to the day of the Elite Auction, when she and I took out several guards during our escape attempt. She acted instinctively when I asked for her help. Training or not, her actions helped us get as far as we did. If she can do that again and use her adrenaline to her advantage, that may be enough.

"Ivy," I say in a low voice, forcing myself to my feet, "do you remember the guard you helped me take down at the facility in the Red Zone?"

She stops her struggle and looks up at me. "What?"

"Do you or not?"

"Yeah, but what does that have to do—"

"I need you to do that again."

She shakes her head. "I can't."

"You can and you will, unless you want to go back there. Can you stand?"

She sits on her knees then plants one foot on the floor, pushing herself up. When her right foot is underneath her, she winces and shifts her weight.

"Turn around," I say. "Let me see your hands." When she begins to argue, I interrupt by ordering, "Just do it."

With an eye roll, she faces the wall, showing me her hands behind her back. Bright pink lines stripe her wrists.

"Okay," I say, "what you want to do is press your wrists and shoulder blades together, clench your fists, and pull your arms apart as hard as you can with your elbows out. That should break it at its locking mechanism."

Wiggling her hands, she evens the zip tie across her wrists and takes a deep breath. Her back tightens as she pushes her wrists together and she clenches her fists. Another deep breath and she pulls her wrists apart, the plastic digging deeper into her bruises.

"You need to do it quickly," Seb says. "One swift motion. Don't overthink it."

"Again," I say, moving to her side. "Keep your feet shoulder-length apart, and this time, try pulling up as you do it."

She gets into position again, spreading her feet apart, and repeats the movement, groaning when the restraint remains intact.

A strike of lightning briefly illuminates the room, and a clap of thunder follows seconds later. Faint footsteps come from outside the room, barely audible over the rain hammering against the roof, and Ivy whips her head toward the door.

"There has to be another way," she says, relaxing her arms.

"There's not," Liam says, standing. "You might want to hurry."

"Seb," I say, "I want you near the door. Liam, you're across from it."

They take their stances. The footsteps draw closer, each one amplified, echoing in my head. This will work. This has to work.

"Ivy," I say, "this is literally life or death. You know they're going to kill us if we go back there. Do it again, with all the strength you have."

Chewing on her lip, she faces forward and pushes her wrists together again. She squeezes her eyes shut. White-knuckled, every muscle in her body tenses. She forces her wrists apart while bending her arms. The zip tie pushes back, but she keeps going, squeezing her eyes tighter and furrowing her brow.

A snap breaks the silence, and the broken plastic ring is flung across the room.

Ivy holds her hands in front of her, and lets out a breath, smiling. "I did it."

"Good job," I say. "Now, I want you against the wall behind the door. When it opens, you're going to do the same thing you did in the Red Zone— —throw the guard off balance, and we'll help from there."

"And what if there's more than one?" she asks.

"We'll figure it out."

She hesitates for a moment, but is shocked into motion by the snap of one of the latches. When the second latch is undone, she's flattened against the wall, and I take my place across from her, between Seb and Liam.

"You can do this," I mouth to her as the lock clicks.

The doorknob turns. My heart hammers against my aching ribs, and I say a silent prayer, begging for this to work. The door creaks open; the bearded guard has returned, holding a chipped plate of scraps in one hand and a flashlight in the other.

He's alone.

Stepping inside, he nudges the door almost fully shut with his foot.

"Now," I say, and the guard looks up at me.

Ivy throws herself at the man, hands out in front of her. He stumbles when she collides with him, and the plate clatters to the floor. Flashlight still in hand, he swings it out, narrowly missing Liam, who takes advantage of the opportunity by slamming him into the wall with his shoulder. With Ivy's help, they wrestle the man to the ground, and the four of us surround him. Seb presses a knee into his neck, Ivy holds his arms down, and Liam keeps a foot on his back.

The guard struggles against them, pushing back against Ivy, but with each movement, Seb applies more pressure on his neck. He opens his mouth, either to gasp for air or yell, but no sound comes out.

I place a foot on his head and lean down. "One sound, and I crush your skull. Got it?"

With the side of his face mashed against the floor, he attempts a nod. His body relaxes, and Seb lets up a bit.

"Ivy, grab the knife from his belt," I say.

When she releases him, I pin one of his arms down with my knee, and she feels for the sheathed knife toward the front of the tactical belt. My gaze darts from her to the slightly open door and back. I strain to listen for any other enemies, but so far, everything is quiet.

Grabbing the hilt, Ivy wiggles the knife from its encasement, the guard doing nothing to assist her.

"Cut Seb loose first," I instruct.

Seb angles his hands toward her and pulls his wrists apart, giving her as much space to work as possible. Grabbing one of his wrists, she holds him in place and positions the blade over the center of the makeshift cuffs. She hesitates. Her hand trembles. She stares at the hovering blade, as if intimidated by it.

Just as I'm about to say something, she snaps out of her trance and saws away at the zip tie. The sound of plastic grating against metal falls in rhythm with the pounding rain. Our guard shifts his weight with a groan, and I apply more pressure to his head.

"Wes!" an impatient voice calls from outside the room. Not directly beside the door, but still too close for comfort.

Ivy continues her shaky slicing at Seb's zip ties, even more frantic now. Finally, he's free, one of the ties falling to the floor and the other dangling from his wrist. Spinning around, he grabs the knife from Ivy, instructing her to hold the guard down as he rushes to me. With a couple of precise slices, my arms are free, and he moves to Liam. Reaching into the guard's belt, I retrieve the holstered pistol.

Another flash of lightning consumes the room. A gust of wind makes the rotting structure groan.

"Wes!" the voice yells over a clap of thunder. It's closer. The guard reflexively tries to turn toward the door.

"Don't even think about it," I say, wrenching the flashlight from his hand and passing it to Ivy. "Where's our stuff?"

The man scoffs. "I ain't tellin' you shit."

"Let him go," I tell Ivy.

I motion Seb over, and we haul the man to his feet. Once standing, I move behind him and circle my arm around his neck, securing the chokehold by pushing his shoulder forward and grabbing my opposite arm.

The disembodied voice calls out again; footsteps are audible now.

"You can tell me," I say, tightening my grip as he struggles, "or you can die."

Ivy averts her eyes and stands behind her brother.

"Okay, okay," he sputters, desperately pulling the crook of my arm from his windpipe. "Main cabin, across the campsite. Wraparound porch—you can't miss it."

"Where in the cabin?"

"Back room, main floor. They keep it guarded. That's all I know."

Releasing my arm, I tuck the pistol in my waistband. With the bit of wiggle room, the guard throws himself forward, but I pull him back, cupping his chin in one hand and pressing the other against the back of his head. Using the heel of my hand, I thrust his chin over his shoulder in one motion, and an audible crack cuts through the room.

His body goes limp and thuds against the floor, and Seb is quick to reclaim his tactical belt, sheathing the combat knife.

The heavy footsteps are right outside. Liam backs away from the door, standing tall and shielding Ivy's body with his. Stepping over the guard's body, I flatten myself against the wall beside the door frame, Seb a few feet in front of me.

The footsteps stop. Whoever's on the other side hesitates, and I prepare myself for an attack as soon as they step inside.

The door inches open. The ripping of the tactical belt's Velcro tears through the room. Seb winds up his arm, holding one of his throwing knives by the blade beside his ear. Tightening my fingers around the handle of the gun, I take a deep breath and hold it steady.

The door's kicked wide, and the knife flies from Seb's grip, lodging itself in the intruder's chest in less than a second. Dropping one of our stolen submachine guns, the man gasps, gaping at his wound as he reaches for the protruding hilt. Seb sprints toward him, yanking the knife out and immediately slicing his throat.

Blood spurts from the side of the man's neck and he presses a hand to it, slumping against the door frame with a gurgling inhalation.

"You couldn't have been cleaner about it?" I ask, grabbing the submachine gun and glancing at Ivy. Her eyes are locked on the bleeding man, her mouth covered with trembling hands, and for the first time since being reunited with her, I know exactly what's running through her mind. Liam pulls her into a hug, but her eyes don't leave the body.

"You're welcome," Seb says, wiping the bloody knife on his pants. "Are we really going to waste our time getting our stuff back?"

"At least the documents; the Commander needs them. Give me that knife." I hold the gun out to him, and we trade weapons. "Liam, please tell me you still have that map."

Liam releases his sister and fishes the folded paper from his back pocket. "Yeah."

I didn't exactly expect these people to be thorough in what they did, but not searching us was a stupid mistake. Lucky on our end.

"Here." I shove the pistol into his hand as he and Ivy approach me. "You're with me. Use that only if needed. Seb, take the map and

Ivy. You two stick to the treeline behind these cabins and wait for us at the edge of the camp."

"What? No!" Ivy says.

"Just go," Liam says, giving her a final hug before nudging her forward. "We'll be right behind you."

Seb pokes his head out of the room. "All clear."

"Her ankle," I say as Ivy joins him in the doorway.

"Yeah, got it," Seb says. He throws one of her arms over his shoulder and wraps his own around her waist, pushing the stock of the gun into his armpit. With one final check for guards, he leads her out of the room, and Liam and I follow close behind.

We step out into a large, empty room. Like our makeshift cell, it's absent of lights and mostly abandoned. A single folding chair sits in the far corner beside the entrance to a tiny kitchen that's clearly out of commission. Several buckets crowd the floor, catching the steady streams of water pouring from the ceiling.

Liam sticks beside me as we make our way across the room and circle the rusted spiral staircase. Keeping Ivy upright, Seb leads the way with his gun ready. The rain drowns out the sound of our footsteps... and those of anyone else who's potentially in here.

We pass through the next and final room—another empty space with fissures in the floor and the overpowering smell of mildew. Spotting the exit, I jog ahead, twist the doorknob. Locked.

"Shit," I mutter.

"Can we pick it?" Liam asks.

I shake my head. "If it's like the door to the room we were in, it's probably latched, too, and we don't have time to find out."

"Windows are nailed shut," Seb says, parting the curtains with the muzzle of his gun. "Here, take her for a sec."

Liam grabs Ivy by her arm and backs away from the window.

"Make sure no one's nearby," I say, squinting in the darkening room.

Seb rotates his gun. "Looks good. Just gotta be quick." Pulling the weapon back, he smashes the stock into the lower pane, and a resounding crack penetrates the room. He repeats the action again and again, each time with more force until, finally, the satisfying sound of shattering glass comes and only a few jagged pieces remain.

Brushing the shards on the windowsill away, he ducks and steps through. Ivy's next, making it out with his assistance. Liam quickly follows, and I'm right behind him, adrenaline bursting in my chest as soon as the shards of glass on the porch crunch underneath my boots.

I scan the area as we make it down the stairs. The main cabin is directly across from us on the other side of the firepit, approximately fifty feet away. To the left, there's a gravel path at the entrance of the camp that's swallowed by the dense trees, and to the right, four parked pick-up trucks.

"That way," I shout over the rain. "Stay hidden and wait for us."

Seb immediately sprints to the left with Ivy, and they disappear between two cabins. Liam and I run in the opposite direction, diving between another pair of buildings.

We stick to the exterior walls, ducking beneath windows and moving as quickly and quietly as possible. Every couple of steps, I glance back the way we came, expecting to find someone coming to investigate the noise we made. Our boots sink into the mud with each footfall. My clothes are already soaked and heavy, and the cold rain stings my face.

Over the storm, I struggle to listen for any voices as we loop around the back of the camp. I can't make out anything other than the rain and rumbles of thunder that are increasingly closer together.

Lightning flashes again. I look up at the thick clouds masking the dusk sky, trying to figure out how much time has passed since we were told the soldiers were coming. It can't have been more than an hour, but without knowing exactly, that puts more of a restraint on how much we have left.

Breaking away from the cabins, we pick up our pace. Bolts of pain stab at my ribs. I press a hand to my side, forcing myself to breathe past it, to keep moving. My body feels heavier by the second. No matter how fast I run, it seems like I'm not fast enough.

Thirty feet ahead, after the curve of the semi-circle, I can make out the wraparound porch through the hazy rain. So far, everything looks clear, but that doesn't stop the paranoia from pulsing through me. The thought of armed soldiers surrounding us invades my mind. I shake my head, willing it away, trying to focus on the task at hand. But it comes back almost instantly, along with everything that happened in the Red Zone. The fear of returning—of reliving that hell—assaults me, paralyzes me.

My legs lock. I stumble forward, kicking up mud.

Not now, I think. *I can't do this now.*

I catch myself with my hands, the knife digging into the ground. I push myself up on my knees. Slow, deep breaths—I take slow, deep breaths and focus on the knife clenched in my hand, the sensation of cold mud seeping between my fingers, the droplets of rain trickling down my face.

"Nixon!"

I look up. Liam races toward me, jerking me up from under my arm, and grips my shoulder to balance me.

"You okay?" he asks.

"Yeah, just tripped." I avoid looking directly at him. He doesn't believe that, and I don't need to see the confirmation of his doubt. "Keep moving."

I shake him off me and run toward the main cabin before he can object, before he can insist we just turn around and find the others. The first few strides are shaky, but I manage to steady myself.

About ten feet from the cabin, we slow to a jog. The storm is unrelenting now. Tree branches bend violently against the howling wind. With heightened senses, I survey the area. Normally I'd want to take the time to scout out the place and weigh our options, but we don't have that luxury.

"Stay right behind me," I tell Liam, lowering into a crouch.

We close the gap, fighting against the wind and diagonal rain, and climb the slick steps to the porch where the covered back door awaits us. Staying low, I make my way to the right side of the building as stealthily as possible.

Liam and I attempt to peek through the two windows closest to the door, but the blinds are shut. All I can see on the other side is a faint orange light and idle silhouettes. Liam makes his way down to the far end, pushing up on the closed windows as he goes. All locked. Unlike during the training session with him and Seb, I can't divert the attention of the people inside without breaking the glass, and doing that would alert anyone in the cabins nearby.

There's movement from the room. A distorted shadow passes the window, stops halfway, then changes direction. I hold a hand up to Liam, and he freezes. I can't tell which way this guy is facing; we hardly have a plan and can't risk being seen out here. If we can corner the guards, we have a better chance of getting what we came here for.

A muffled voice comes from farther in the room, and the man by the window howls with laughter before moving away.

At least two of them. With Liam's gun, we could easily take them out if we catch them off guard. But again, we risk alerting others, and I don't want Liam to have to use his gun on anyone unless he has to. I'd rather do this myself and just have him as backup. Either way, we don't have much of a plan, which puts us at a disadvantage.

I wave Liam over and we round the corner, stopping at the door. Standing, I nudge him against the wall so he'll be behind the door when it opens. Voices circulate inside, fading in and out.

"Stay here," I say in a low voice.

He looks at me like I'm crazy, his gaze briefly flicking to my right side. "I'm going with you." He steps forward, but I push him back.

"I need you to watch my back. I'll call for you if I need you."

I move to the other side of the door and press my back to the wall. Gripping the muddy knife, I bang the side of my fist against the glass panel. The voices stop. There's no movement. Liam grips his gun with both hands, pointing it down in front of him with his eyes trained on the door. I bang on the door again—harder.

A silhouette approaches with cautious steps, each one slower than the last. I inch closer, the doorframe rubbing against my shoulder. The handle jiggles. A beat of silence passes, and the door's pushed open. I lunge forward, grabbing the man—no, *woman*. That makes three scavengers.

Pulling her into me, I hold the knife to her throat, and we enter the cabin where two men wait. One shoots up from the table he's sitting at, knocking over one of the electric lanterns. The second, who's already standing, swipes a gun from the collection lining one of the walls and aims it directly at me.

"Put it down," I demand, stopping a few feet from the door, "or I'll kill her."

The unarmed woman doesn't struggle against me. She moves in sync with me, and her chest rises and falls in steady intervals underneath my arm.

The gunman smirks. "Kill her—I don't care."

Except he does. Otherwise, he would've shot me already.

I spot our supplies. The stolen documents are haphazardly scattered on a white folding table pushed against the wall to my left. Beside it lie our opened, deflated bags. Pallets of canned foods and bottled water loom over us. Then there's the array of firearms to my right.

The gunman looks over his shoulder at the man in the corner. "Go let Alex know his prisoners escaped."

Alex must be their leader, and shit's about to get bad if he's nearby. Stumbling over the chair he was in, the man flings open the door opposite us and runs out.

The woman begins tugging at my arm, twisting from side to side in my hold. Throwing herself to the left, she forces me to move with her, and I tighten my arm.

"Go ahead," the gunman taunts. "Kill her."

Yanking on my arm with one hand, she swings her elbow back. I barely dodge it, having to temporarily loosen my grip on her, but I keep the knife to her throat. She forces us into a crouch and hurls her elbow back again. It digs into my ribs, and pain explodes from my right side. I reflexively start to reach for it, but stop myself, grabbing the woman and pulling her back into me. In the split second she's free from my grasp, she turns so our backs are to her partner.

"Shoot this motherfucker already!" she yells, continuing her fight.

I try to force her upright while attempting to sidestep her continuous attacks. Another blow to my ribs. My eyes water and I hold back a groan. I hear the click of a gun being cocked.

Grabbing a fistful of the woman's hair, I jerk her head back and make an instinctive swipe across her throat. Her screams are quickly replaced by gasps. Blood coats my hand, and she falls forward.

The crack of a gunshot penetrates the air. Still crouched, I squeeze my eyes shut. But no pain comes—except for in my ribs. A breathy moan comes from behind me, followed by a thud. I open my eyes and look back at the gunman with a hole in his chest.

Liam stands in the doorway, gun raised, aiming at the empty air. His eyes are wide, vacant, mouth slightly open.

"Liam." I jog over to him, shaking him by his shoulder. "Hey, look at me." Pushing the gun down, I move in front of him, and his eyes search my face as if he's unsure of who I am.

"I killed him." It comes out as a low murmur, almost like a question.

"You did what you had to. We can talk about it later, okay? Right now, we need to get our shit and get the hell out." Prying the gun from his hands, I drag him to the white table and grab one of the backpacks from the floor. Together, we shove every document we can find inside.

With only a few papers left, footsteps return, frantically pounding against the wood floor. I shove the backpack at Liam, and he throws the final documents inside.

"Go," I say, handing him the knife and pushing him toward the exit. "Meet up with the others; I'll be right behind you."

The man who was in here before comes into view, barreling toward the room with two more behind him.

"Go!" I yell at Liam, and fire a shot at the first man who steps into the room. He clutches his leg but doesn't go down. Another returns fire, and I dive behind one of the stacks of canned food.

Liam's gone. Peering around at the entrance, I fire three more times, one directly after the other. My ears ring.

The men take cover on the other side of the wall. Abandoning my shelter, I shoot again at the empty doorway and stagger toward the collection of guns. I spot my MP5 among the collection of firearms and, with one final shot, trade the pistol out for it. With a quick check of the full magazine, I throw the sling over my shoulder and dart out of the cabin.

Just as I reach the doorway, a voice I recognize as the leader's—Alex—booms, "Round up the search crew!"

I leap off the wraparound porch and sprint to the left where the edge of the semi-circle promises freedom. It's too dark to see it now, but I know it's there.

The rain is colder, like fragments of ice piercing my skin. Stabbing pain lances through my ribs, choking the air from my lungs. I bite down on my lip, sink my teeth as deep as I can stand to divert my attention from it, but it's useless. Hunched forward with an arm around my abdomen, I run faster.

Shouting ensues, warring with the wind. Puddles splash against my legs, soaking my pants as my feet pound at the ground. My throat's dry. My legs threaten to collapse.

Truck engines roar to life; the fear of capture sparks again, but this time, I use it to push myself forward and redirect my focus to my squad waiting for me up ahead. With each imagined soldier, I move faster until the lashing rain and shuddering trees blur around me. With the phantom feeling of water flooding my lungs, I force myself to suck in a gulp of air.

"Liam!" I yell over the violent storm. "Seb!" I reach the final cabin. The ground morphs from mud to gravel. "Liam! Seb!"

A beam of light cuts through the night to my left with three figures behind it.

"Right here!" Liam yells before the light clicks off again.

I run toward them, passing through the trucks' blinding headlights as they flick on. Seb grabs my arm and pulls me into the treeline, and we move through the maze with Liam and Ivy in the lead.

"According to the map, we're just over a mile from the outpost," Seb says from beside me.

I don't respond. My mouth is fused shut from the tension and anxiety coursing through me. Adrenaline's finally kicked in, dulling my aching side and sharpening my senses.

Gunshots pierce the air behind us. Faceless men yell, but their words are washed out. Seb and I alternate cover-fire while simultaneously dodging skeletal trees and keeping up with Liam and Ivy. Our shadows stretch across the ground and trees from the flashlights of our predators. I can't tell how many are on foot behind us, and I have no idea where the trucks went. I don't even know which direction we're moving in. But I trust Liam knows the way.

My legs burn. The cold bites at my face and hands. Shots continue to ring out, muffled by the rain. I fumble with my gun, unable to feel my fingers around the handle and front grip, and can only tell I've fired from the kick. Ivy looks back and I yell at her to keep moving.

A hand clamps down on my right arm, throwing me off balance and pulling me away from the group. Jerking free, I lift my gun, aiming for the head as I slam it into my attacker.

"This way!" Liam calls.

I catch up with them and we veer right, coming out of the trees and onto a road. The gunmen chasing us don't follow; the last I see is them seeking cover behind trees when I fire a final round before we make another right.

We make a left at the next intersection. The road becomes wider, more exposed. Exhaustion laps at the edges of my mind. I'm suddenly aware of every ache and pain in my body, but I force myself to move, to run faster.

We aren't going back to the Northern Unity.

Bright lights flash behind us. Tires squeal against the slick asphalt.

Seb spins around and sprays a barrage of bullets. One of the trucks swerves. Liam pulls Ivy to the side of the road and we follow close behind. Zigzagging through the trees, Seb and I stick close to the road's shoulder, still taking turns covering our group.

There's a steep decline ahead with fallen trees blocking the opposite side of a stream. Ivy and Liam edge closer to the road now, preparing to sprint toward the bridge that will take us to the other side. The gunshots from our assailants have slowed, but not for long. As soon as we're back in their line of fire, we'll need to move quickly and seek more cover.

"I'm out!" Seb yells.

The bridge is only a few feet away. "Stick with the others," I say. "I'll cover you."

Liam looks back at us. I give him a nod, and he pulls Ivy out into the open and onto the bridge. Seb goes ahead of me. I fire a few more times from the treeline, take a deep breath, then bolt out onto the road.

Bullets spray from over the tops of the trucks. Casings litter the broken asphalt. I aim for the head of one of the gunmen. He goes down, but I can't tell if I actually hit him. Before turning to my squad again, I aim for the headlights next, knocking out both on one vehicle.

I catch up with Seb, closing in on Liam and Ivy. We're nearing the halfway point of the bridge, but the closer we get to the end, the farther away it seems. Lightning streaks the sky, disorienting me as it cuts through the blackness. The deafening crack that follows shakes the earth, reverberating throughout my body.

And once it fizzles out, I hear a wail of agony behind me.

I spin around. Seb's kneeling on the ground, clutching his abdomen. Dread washes over me.

"*Seb!*"

I run to him, yanking him up. He stumbles forward. Blood oozes between his fingers, dripping to the ground.

"I've got you," I pant, swinging my gun over to my other side.

He leans into me, staggering, grunting as we move. Our pace slows dramatically, but I pull him forward, taking on nearly all of his weight. With the gun in my left hand, I turn and shoot a few more rounds without a clear target. Both vehicles come to a screeching halt.

Repositioning my hold on Seb, I drag him forward but immediately slow down when I'm blinded by LED lights at the end of the bridge. Liam and Ivy have stopped their pursuit, now backing away from the truck in front of us—their bodies only shadowy figures against the beams.

How the hell did they get ahead of us?

A door swings open from the passenger side, and a voice screams at us to get down. Not a second later, the gunfire returns— only this time, it's endless. Liam pushes Ivy to the ground, covering her body with his. I pull Seb down with me, and he cries out when we smack the asphalt.

Bullets fly over us, clanking against metal, the ground, and whatever else they make contact with. Seconds stretch on. I lift my head, trying to get a glimpse of the people in front of us, but I can't see past the lights.

Someone shouts over the chaos. Screeching tires fight against the sound of the gunshots. The stench of burning rubber and gunpowder fills the air. Seconds later, the only sounds are the unrelenting rain and footsteps.

I pull my legs underneath me and sit up. Arm's length from me, Liam looks up but doesn't move. I blink, shielding my eyes with my hand. Four figures emerge from behind the lights at the other end of the bridge. I glance at Seb as he winces and rolls onto his back, clutching his wound. A sheen of sweat coats his skin. His shirt is soaked with blood, clinging to his body. With his eyes squeezed shut, he breathes heavily through gritted teeth.

"Someone's been shot!" a woman yells, running toward us.

I grab her arm when she reaches for Seb.

"We're here to help," she says, shaking me off. Motioning two of the men over, she says, "Get him in the truck and apply pressure. Let them know to get a bed ready."

They lift Seb from the ground and haul him to the open vehicle. Liam, Ivy, and I climb to our feet. I immediately start toward the truck where Seb's being loaded into the back of the cab, but the woman and remaining man block me.

"Who are you and why are you out here?" the woman asks, taking on a completely different demeanor. Her glare passes over the three of us but settles on me—specifically the gun hanging from my shoulder.

"Does it matter?" I try to push past them, but the man shoves me back.

"We just saved your asses," he says. "Least you can do is tell us who you are."

I glance at the truck again, then at Liam and Ivy behind me. The soldiers will be here soon, and as of right now, those assholes from the settlement know exactly where we are.

"Nixon," I say.

"Green Zone's leader?" the woman asks. I nod, and she looks at the other two. "Can you confirm your identities?"

Liam unzips his jacket and pulls his shirt down, flashing the tattoo beneath his right collarbone. "Liam, second-in-command. This is my sister, Ivy."

"The other guy is Sebastien," I tell them, "one of my scouts."

"Let's get to the outpost then," the man says, "before your scout bleeds out."

25. Translate

Ivy

Seb's excruciating groans from the cab burrow into my head with every bump we hit. I grit my teeth together each time. Nixon's calming voice follows, his words drowned out by the truck's engine.

Huddled close to Liam in the covered truck bed, I keep my eyes closed and attempt to calm the anxiety that worms its way through me.

"How did you find us?" Liam asks.

"Heard the gunshots," one of the two men back here says. "How'd you get tangled up with those guys anyway?"

"We were followed earlier today. They contacted the nearest re-education camp and told them who we are."

"Your leader mentioned something about that. Don't worry, the soldiers won't bother us."

"How do you know that?" I ask.

They can't promise that. It isn't over. It will never be over.

"We have an agreement of sorts," the man says. "We don't bother them out here; they don't bother us."

The truck comes to a slow stop, and my eyes shoot open. One of the men across from me clicks on a flashlight, and I squint against the sudden brightness.

"We're here," he says, opening the back of the truck.

His partner slides out and he follows, reaching a hand out to me once he's on the ground. I reluctantly take it, and he helps me down. Liam appears beside me, swinging his backpack onto his shoulders.

The rain hasn't stopped and makes me shiver in my already-drenched clothes. I look around at what I can see of our surroundings. A chain-link fence topped with barbed wire surrounds the chunk of land. In the center is what looks like an abandoned warehouse, four stories tall with every window boarded. Four more vehicles are parked at the front of the building—another pickup truck, a beaten-up compact car, an SUV with a hood that doesn't match the rest of it, and a Humvee. My heart skips at the last one.

Liam and I follow the two men around the truck to where Nixon is helping one of the other strangers carry Seb to the entrance. The woman beats on the metal door, and moments later, it's pushed open. The eight of us file inside, and they lift Seb onto a gurney that's waiting beside two men in dark blue scrubs. Nixon explains to them what happened, but I'm hardly listening.

Sweat sticks to Seb's now-pale skin. Eyes half open, he frantically searches the faces looming over him. An oxygen mask is pressed to his face, and one of the nurses pumps the connected bag. I tear my eyes away, unable to look at him without the guilt sending waves of nausea over me.

We're in a massive room with stained epoxy floors that reflect the dimmed utility lights. The smells of motor oil and gasoline linger heavily. Shelves packed with various automotive parts line the back wall, and beside them, at least a dozen gas cans. A platform with chipped yellow paint is to our right, looking over the expansive room, and underneath it is the entrance to a corridor, the double doors propped open.

"Get him to medical," the woman says. "You three follow me."

"I'm going with him," Nixon says, starting after Seb as he's wheeled away through the open doors, but the woman blocks his path.

"They need as much space as possible to work. You'll be able to see him soon." She places a hand on his shoulder and guides him in the opposite direction, and the doors to the right close.

Liam and I follow them through another pair of doors to the left. I don't pay attention as we walk, just keep my eyes ahead on the woman in front of me. I've crashed from my rush of adrenaline. My body feels as though it's made of lead; pushed beyond its limits, it's completely numb, save for my ankle. My thoughts are a disoriented mess. The only clear image in my head is Seb's bloodied torso and his face, twisted in torment.

If I'd just let him kill that scavenger, we'd have never been captured and he wouldn't have been hurt. None of us would have had to exert ourselves the way we did. But I couldn't allow a seemingly innocent man to be murdered. Now, Seb may lose his life instead.

We're led into a janitor's closet, the overpowering odor of bleach and other chemicals replacing the gasoline and oil. In the center of the floor is a trap door, just like in Adam and Lacey's house. The woman hooks her fingers underneath it and pulls the hatch up. Clicking on her flashlight, she points it down the steps that plunge underground.

"Emergency bunker," she explains as we descend, her voice bouncing off the rough concrete walls. "You'll stay here—eat, shower, get some rest. There's some clothes, but I can't make any promises on what will fit."

"How long will we be here?" Liam asks from beside me.

"Until you're all medically cleared. You'll be seen after Sebastien's taken care of. A vehicle will be provided for you, and from here, you'll go directly to the Commander's camp."

At the bottom, we stop at a reinforced steel door. The woman angles her flashlight at the keypad mounted to the wall and punches in a four-digit code. A beep echoes through the chamber, followed by the click of the locking mechanism, and she pushes down on the handle, heaving open the door and wedging a stopper underneath to keep it in place. Sticking her hand inside the room, she feels around and the lights flick on.

Nixon and Liam follow her in without any hesitation, but I don't. I remain just beyond the threshold, my gaze lingering on the glowing keypad. A code is required to get in and out. The woman was blocking it as she typed it in. How do we know we're not going to be held captive here? How do we know these people are really who they say they are? They could be working undercover for the Society or planning to trade us for supplies like the last group we ran into.

I glance back at the stairs, only the first few visible in the light pouring out of the bunker. Are they planning on guarding this place in case we try to escape? Will we be able to come and go as we please, or do we have to wait until someone comes to retrieve us? I've been held against my will three times; I'm not letting it happen again.

"Ivy?" Liam says. The three of them are in a room that seems to serve as both a living area and kitchen. "You okay?"

"What if this is a trap?" I ask without thinking.

Nixon and the woman turn to me as soon as the words come out.

"It's not," Liam says, walking toward the door with an outstretched hand. "These are our people."

I shake my head and unconsciously take a step back. "*Your* people, not mine."

I'm not one of them. That was made perfectly clear.

"We're all on the same side," Liam says, wrapping an arm around my shoulders and trying to lead me toward the bunker, but I refuse to go any farther than the doorway.

"She was sold in the Elite Auction," Nixon explains to the woman, "so she's a bit… cautious."

"Understandable," the woman says with a hint of sympathy. Her eyes travel over my body. "We're here to help." Gathering her short brown hair in her hands, she turns her head, exposing three small black lines behind her left ear. "This is the safest place for you right now."

Releasing her hair, she motions for Nixon to follow her and continues, "As I said, generator is up and running. Help yourselves to showers and food." She opens the door to the left, Nixon follows her inside, and I hear, "Your radio is in here, and the code to the door is written…"

The door clicks shut behind them, and their voices are muffled.

"Feel better now?" Liam asks, slipping his arm from my shoulders. He drops his backpack on the coffee table and collapses onto one of the sofas with a sigh.

Seeing that tattoo should've put my mind at ease like when I saw Ember's in the Red Zone, but it didn't and I don't know why. These people saved us—they're providing us shelter and taking care of Seb. Maybe being with Wyatt has made me permanently doubtful of anyone new. Or maybe I just need to sleep off this persistent paranoia. I wasn't exactly the most trusting person in the world before I was sold in the auction, but I at least wasn't skeptical of every person I met.

I reluctantly make my way into the bunker and take a seat beside Liam. Resting his head against his fist, he stares blankly at the open archway that leads into another section of the compound. With his other hand in his lap, he pops each individual knuckle with his thumb.

"Are you okay?" I ask.

He pauses his anxious ritual. "Yeah, just tired." He drops his hand from his face and turns to me, but his gaze is distant, like he's not fully here. Dark circles hang under his puffy eyes. We were already exhausted this morning after hardly any sleep, and escaping our captors has taken even more of a toll, but I know the difference between him being tired and upset.

"What about you?" he says.

"What about me?"

"Two months stuck with an Elite prick, escaping the Northern Unity, all the shit that happened today… Seems like you can't catch a break. And you look terrible." He forces a mocking smile.

I roll my eyes but find myself smiling, too. "For once, I agree with you. Fortunately, this is temporary, unlike…" I wave a hand toward him and feign a look of disgust. "What does Addison see in you?"

He laughs, and the rigidity in his body melts away. "Aww, is someone jealous?"

"Jealous of what, exactly?"

"That I'm *clearly* the better-looking sibling."

"Sure you are—coming from the one who didn't even have his first girlfriend until his sophomore year. And that lasted, what, two weeks?"

"At least *I* wasn't the one Dad caught at a guy's house after lying about staying with Addison."

I laugh and shake my head at the memory, remembering the night Dad showed up at my then-boyfriend's house while his parents were out. Still in uniform, he forced his way into the house, hauled me to his car, and made me endure the ride home in complete silence. He always had an intimidating edge to him and wouldn't hesitate to raise his voice, but Liam and I always knew he was *really* pissed when he was quiet.

"God, I thought he was going to kill me," I say. "I was grounded for a month."

"It was pretty stupid on your part," Liam says. "I mean, he was best friends with Addison's dad."

All because I left my phone on silent. He'd tried calling me several times to check in, and when I didn't answer, he resorted to calling Addison's father to make sure I was okay.

"You could've covered for me, dick," I say.

"Hell no. I wasn't getting in the middle of that."

I shoot him my middle finger and he swats my hand away. "It's not my fault he was so overprotective."

Leaning forward, I unlace my boots and pull them off, being extra careful with the right one. "You'd think if he cared so much, he would've stuck around." Pain stabs at my throbbing ankle and I wince, kicking the shoes underneath the table. "Nixon told me he worked the auction."

Liam's face falls. His focus travels to my swollen ankle as I scoot back and prop it up on the sofa. Not saying any more, he stands and walks to the kitchen area, opening the top door to the freezer.

"You knew that already, though," I say.

Liam sighs. "Yeah." He returns to his seat and passes me an ice pack that I press to my ankle. "But not much else."

"So, why do you think he left? If he wasn't killed or anything…"

"I don't know. Maybe he was ashamed of what he did."

"But he was all-in. He basically worshiped the Society."

"I don't know," Liam says again, mildly irritated. He runs a hand through his hair and leans his head back. "Doesn't matter, though. Nothing from the Northern Unity matters anymore."

The door across the room opens, and Nixon emerges with the woman.

"And the soldiers?" he asks.

"They don't normally bother us," the woman responds, "but if they happen to stop by, we'll take care of them. You all just focus on resting, and someone will be down to retrieve you once they're finished with Sebastien. Can I get any of you anything else?" Her eyes break from Nixon and sweep over Liam and me on the sofa.

"I think we're good," Liam says. "Thank you."

"Let us know if you need anything," she says, walking toward the exit and kicking the stopper from underneath the door. It slams shut with a resounding clank.

Nixon lingers outside the room they exited a moment longer before joining us, but he doesn't sit down. Instead, he rounds the sofa opposite us, keeping his back turned. His shoulders rise and fall with each breath, and an arm remains wrapped around his torso.

"It'll be a few hours until Seb's out of surgery," he says. "We won't know anything until then."

I shift uncomfortably and glance at the closed door. Seb will be okay—he has to be. I repeat that over and over in my head, although it doesn't ease the sinking feeling in my stomach.

"We'll be looked over after that," Nixon continues. "Once cleared, they'll have a squad escort us to the Commander's camp a couple hours south."

"Seb will be fine," Liam says. "He's strong."

Nixon shakes his head and faces us. "We've already lost two more members; I don't want to lose any more."

Two members? Who else did they lose? I know Elizabeth was one, but that was months ago.

"And we won't," Liam says. "He'll pull through, and we're going to see him as soon as he's out of surgery."

Nixon nods in agreement, but his hardened expression says otherwise. I know how much he cares about every single person in his group. I remember how distraught he was over Elizabeth's death. He feels like he's personally responsible for anything that happens to his members, even if it's completely out of his control. That's one thing I've always admired about him—his protectiveness.

He'll blame himself for this, too, even though it's not his fault. It's mine.

"Nixon, I'm sorry," I say.

His eyes click to me.

"For everything. I didn't mean for us to get caught or for anyone to get hurt. I just—"

"Stop." Circling the sofa, he unzips his jacket and drapes it over the armrest. Despite the injured side he keeps grabbing and the way his shoulders droop forward, he remains standing. He drags a hand down his face, exhales, and says, "What you did was reckless and, frankly, stupid. You acted impulsively and put us in danger… But I understand why you did it."

Of course he does. He made that obvious before we made our way back to the trail. Still, if he understands why I couldn't let that man die, why did he accuse me of trying to get us recaptured? I messed up, I get that, but getting dragged back to the Northern Unity is the last thing I want.

"If you're wanting to move forward with this mission, though," he continues, "you have to follow orders. If any of us tell you to do something, you do it without arguing. Understood?"

"Yeah," I mutter.

Finally, he sits, unzipping the backpack in front of him. "Why don't you go take a shower? Your brother and I need to talk."

In my peripheral vision, Liam turns his head and begins popping his knuckles on his other hand.

"About what?" I ask.

"Nothing that concerns you at the moment," Nixon says.

"He's my brother; I think it does concern me."

He looks up at me, pausing with a few loose documents halfway out of the bag. "Didn't we just agree you wouldn't question orders?"

I scowl. It was more of a suggestion than an order, and when it comes to Liam, I *should* be involved, especially if it's about this mission. I've hardly been told anything as it is, and after today I should be kept in the loop. Maybe if I had actually been told what was going on from the beginning, I wouldn't have acted on impulse. If someone could just put my mind at ease, I wouldn't be stuck in this constant fight-or-flight mode.

"It's fine, Ivy," Liam says, standing. "Come on, I'll show you where everything is."

Without waiting for me, he walks toward the archway and reaches for a switch on the other side of the wall. The narrow walkway lights up. From here, I can make out the bunks built into the walls on either side, and beyond that is another open room.

I shoot Nixon a final glare and force myself to stand, setting the ice pack aside. Liam opens one of the two slim cabinet-style closets nestled between the bunks as I catch up. He rummages through the articles of clothing and pulls out a pair of sweatpants and a gray T-shirt that are close to my size. The closet slams shut, and he leads me through the bunk area and into the open space at the end.

Liam pushes open the opaque glass door to our immediate right, and we enter a small changing area. Eight gray lockers line the back wall. Two splintery benches are bolted into the middle of the sickly green tile floor.

"Showers are to the left," Liam says, handing me the clothes and nodding to an identical opaque door. "Toilets to the right."

"Are you going to tell me what that was?" I ask as he turns for the exit.

Sighing, he faces me. "What are you talking about?"

"Don't play dumb. What the hell does Nixon have to talk to you about that I'm not allowed to hear?"

"I don't know—he hasn't talked to me yet. And with the way you two have been, I figured you wouldn't want to be anywhere near him."

"I don't, but if there's something wrong—"

"There isn't."

He's lying. I always know when he's lying, and it's even clearer now, thinking back to how he used to act when he was hiding his involvement with the resistance. I also know not to push him. I've done that before and it only led to him closing himself off more. He's shown me the same courtesy thus far, so I'll leave it alone for now.

"You'll at least tell me if it has to do with the rest of this mission, right?" I ask.

"Of course. Now go shower, and try to finish before they're ready to look over us."

"Nixon said they won't be done with Seb for a few hours."

"And you always take forever." He pulls the door open and exits the changing room. "Don't use all the hot water."

I roll my eyes, making my way into the shower room. I flick on the lights, swipe a folded towel from the rack and set my clothes on the single shelf that stretches across one of the walls. I turn to the six shower stalls behind me, white curtains open and a bar of soap and bottle of shampoo in each one. I hang my towel on the hook between two stalls and turn the handle until there's a steady spray of water. As it warms up, I peel off my waterlogged clothes.

Unbuttoning my pants, I pause and glance at the door. No lock. My first night in the Red Zone, when Wyatt snuck into the guesthouse, pops into my head, and a sense of unease washes over me. I tell myself this isn't the same, that I'm with people I know and trust… for the most part.

Steam billows from the shower, matting stray hairs to my face and making my skin itch with a yearning for warmth. Wriggling out of my pants, I take one final look at the closed door. Shivering, I step into the stall and yank the curtain shut behind me.

I focus on the heat that envelops me as I wash my hair, periodically opening one eye to make sure the curtain is still closed and no one's lurking outside. When I rinse the shampoo, I strain to listen for any noises other than the gurgling of water that rushes down the drain in the floor. At one point, while scrubbing dirt from under my uneven nails, I think I hear the door open—but when I peer around the corner of the stall, everything is exactly as I left it. Paranoia continues to eat at me, though.

Quickly rinsing the soap from my body, I shut off the shower and grab the towel, securing it around me. Like at Wyatt's, I still don't feel clean. That constant feeling of disgust is stronger now.

Throwing on my clothes, I wring the excess water from my hair and comb through it the best I can with my fingers before discarding the towel on the floor and making my way back to the others.

"I'm here to help," I hear Nixon say as I make my way through the sleeping quarters. "What happened back there doesn't have to define you."

I pause at the threshold. What happened where? The settlement? The Northern Unity? Liam's definitely seemed off since getting here, but Nixon's making it sound like more than just fatigue or general anxiety.

Rubbing his eyes with the heels of his hands, Liam sinks back into the sofa. "It was just a shock." He opens his eyes and begins to say something else but stops when he spots me, arm's-length from the archway. "How long have you been there?"

Nixon follows his gaze and sits up straighter.

"Just got out," I say, walking into the room.

The documents they recovered are spread out on the coffee table. As I return to my seat next to Liam, I make out one of the headlines about the Elite Auction—one of the most recent files I stole without reading.

Liam and Nixon stare at me, probably wondering how much I heard of their conversation and whether or not I'll bring it up. I do want to ask about it, I want to know my brother's okay, but it's not my place right now. Nixon is his best friend, after all; I can at least trust that if it's bad enough, Liam will confide in him.

Standing, Liam retrieves the ice pack from the freezer again and tosses it to me. "I'll grab you some food."

"I'm not exactly hungry," I say, catching the pack.

"You're eating," he says, disappearing into the room off to the side before I can argue.

Scooting back so I'm leaning against the armrest, I extend my leg and drape the ice pack over my ankle. Nixon plucks a few papers from the table and props one foot up on his leg. Leaning back, he pretends to read over the material, shuffling the same three pages every few seconds.

I shift in the awkward silence and glance at the closed room Liam went into, every passing second more excruciating. Looking around the room, I try to focus on anything else until he gets back, but my eyes keep finding their way to either Nixon or the rest of the documents—especially the ones pertaining to the auction. I try to read the upside-down print, but my eyes burn from exhaustion and the letters seem to merge together.

Two bold words grab my attention, though: **Transitional Adaptation.**

"What's that?" I ask.

Nixon looks at me, then at the documents on the table. "Um, the files you stole…?"

"I know, but—" I point to the one that caught my interest. "That one."

He grabs it and holds it up for me to see. "Process of the auction. Why?"

"I never read those ones. I meant to, but… never mind—what's Transitional Adaptation?"

"Wait, you haven't read these?"

I don't mean to raise my voice, but the irritation creeping over me takes control. "Just tell me what it is!"

No one explained that part of the auction to me, and I need to know what it is. I need to know what they do to victims like Bridgett in order to make them so compliant.

"I'm gone for two minutes and you're already arguing again?" Liam asks. He sits at the other end of the sofa and shoves a box of cheese-flavored crackers and a bottle of water toward me. "At least eat this."

"Liam, what's Transitional Adaptation?" I ask as he passes Nixon two identical containers.

"What?" he asks.

"I know it's a two-week course that victims go through before the auction, but what *is* it? What does the Society do?"

"Eat and I'll tell you," he says.

I glare at him while opening the box and ripping open the plastic bag inside. Grabbing a handful of crackers, I pop a few into my mouth.

Satisfied, he takes the box from me and says, "Sensory deprivation tanks. Victims are locked in them for ten days, starved of all stimuli and left only with their thoughts. The remaining four days, they're reintroduced to the world and basically reprogrammed to believe whatever the Society wants them to. Your mind breaks when you're in those tanks for an extended period. All sense of time is lost—minutes feel like an eternity. So when you come out, you're easier to mold."

So that's why Bridgett practically worships the Society and Nolan.

"Not everyone is put through it, though," Liam adds.

"What do you mean?"

He looks to Nixon as if asking for approval before speaking. "Certain private buyers prefer their *participants* to be… unaltered. They want them to be afraid—like they get off on it."

I lower a cracker from my mouth, mind reeling. My eyes burn more, this time with tears that I desperately try to hold back.

That woman who was murdered at Nolan's house was 'unaltered.' She had to be. The screams that still ring in the depths of my mind weren't of someone who had been molded to accept her fate. They were screams of pure terror, and that's exactly what Nolan and Wyatt wanted.

"Is there any coming back from it?" I whisper. "Back to who you were, I mean."

"Don't know," Liam says around his food. "Never met anyone who went through it."

"It's probably possible," Nixon says. "Reintroducing them to familiar people and places could help, but it would still be difficult. Be thankful you didn't have to do it."

Pressing my lips together, I look away. I didn't have to endure it, but that doesn't make my time in the Red Zone any better.

I force myself to eat the final bit of my food, washing it down with water as an acidic burn begins to crawl up my throat. Liam holds the box out to me again, but I turn it down. My stomach churns.

Four months until the next auction. More victims will be put through the torture of having their lives ripped away, their minds broken and rebuilt to the liking of their buyers. All while I'm here, relatively safe. Guilt sets in again, mixed with the trauma of the past couple of months. Wyatt's punishments, his hands on me, his blood coating my skin, the woman at Nolan's house…

I hate myself for being here. I hate myself for not doing more to help that woman or Bridgett or the resistance. I hate myself for being so weak and broken and useless.

There are going to be more. There will *always* be more. As long as the Society is in power, nothing will change. People will continue to be tortured and killed, and there's nothing I can do to stop it.

I stand, the ice pack slipping from my ankle and plopping to the carpet. The floor sways underneath me, and black momentarily eats at the edges of my vision.

"What's wrong?" Liam asks, reaching for my arm.

I shake my head and step away from him. "Nothing—tired. I'm going to lie down."

"But the doctor—"

"Can look over her later," Nixon interrupts. "Get some rest. We'll wake you."

I escape to the sleeping quarters, picking the lower bunk closest to the entrance. Close enough for me to hear what's going on in the other room, but hidden behind the wall, so no one can see me bury my face in the pillow as my tears spill over.

26. Paralyzed

Nixon

"Is she asleep?" I ask Liam in a low voice when he returns from his shower.

"Yeah," he says, resuming his spot across from me and running his fingers through his damp hair. "What exactly happened to her? I know you gathered at least some information when you and Eli questioned her."

I set the document I wasn't really paying attention to on the table. Since Ivy lay down, I've been watching the entrance to the bunker, waiting for someone to fill us in on Seb. His condition is the main thing I've been focused on, temporarily distracting me from Ivy and the hell she's been through.

"Not my place to tell you," I say.

"She's my sister, and I'm your second-in-command. You're supposed to keep me in the loop."

"I also have an obligation to respect her privacy. If she wants to talk about it, she will. I didn't get much out of her anyway."

Regardless of what I think, it's not my place to share what she told me, even if it's with her brother. Knowing him, he'll talk to her about it, thinking he can fix it somehow, and that will only sever the final thread of trust she has in me. Whether she admits it or not, I know it's there.

"Right," he says, untwisting the cap of his water, "like you haven't been grilling her the past couple days." He takes a drink, then admits, "I'm worried about her."

"I get that, but you should worry about yourself before others."

As soon as I say that, he averts his eyes and reaches for a document on the table—one about the Black Hats, which he's already read.

"Liam," I say. When I tried to have this conversation with him earlier, he kept deflecting.

He pulls his hand back but doesn't look at me. Twisting and untwisting the cap of his water, he glances at the bunks where his sister is. "I've seen you and members of my own squad kill people before, but actually doing it myself..."

"It's not the same."

"But you prepared me for it. I knew we have to face death, that I'd have to kill eventually, but that doesn't make it any easier."

"I prepared you for how to do it if it ever came to that, not how to deal with it."

Training to kill and actually killing are two entirely different things. When he trained with me, it was either basic target practice or using chalk rounds on a few other members. No live rounds were ever used on an actual human being. His main focus is as a hacker anyway; the basics he learned in handling firearms and hand-to-hand combat were only for his protection should he be put in any danger.

"I keep trying to tell myself I did what I had to," he says.

"You saved my life," I say, leaning forward. "*Again*. And I know you're going to hold that over my head for the rest of my life."

He cracks a smile, but drops his gaze. "Can't let my best friend die on me."

"It sucks, I know, and there's not really anything I can say to make it better. But if anyone understands how you feel, it's me and Seb. Or even Ivy."

He looks up, eyebrows scrunched together. "Ivy?"

"She's your sister; she loves you unconditionally. Talking to her might help." And it may convince her to share what she did. Unlike Liam, Ivy hasn't had a chance to talk about anything outside of an interrogation. If she has someone she trusts and can open up to, I can rest a little easier.

"Maybe," Liam says. "I don't know… I feel like shit." He lets out an awkward laugh.

"I'd be worried about you if you didn't." I try my best to give him a smile, and although I know it's dulled by my obvious fatigue, he relaxes a bit more. His shoulders lose their rigidity and he stops fidgeting with his bottle.

"I never expected it to actually happen. I can't stop thinking that it somehow makes me a bad person."

"What else could you have done?" I ask.

He stares at me blankly.

"Nothing. There's nothing else you could have done. I could've died, but you would've blamed yourself for that, too. Taking a life is never easy, at least not for people like us."

"People like us," he mumbles. "How are you even sure we're the good guys in the grand scheme of things?"

"Because we don't kidnap and sell people. We do everything we can to prevent it and help others. Things get messy in the process, but it's better than being complacent."

Shaking his head, he runs both hands down his face. "Sometimes it's hard to believe that."

A small beep sounds, and the steel door of the bunker's entrance opens. The woman who brought us down here steps inside, followed by a man who looks around my and Liam's age. At the sight of his dark blue scrubs, I stand up.

"How is he?"

The woman smiles. "He's made it out of surgery and is doing well."

I exhale with relief, breathing easier than I have since I got here.

She gestures to the man beside her. "This is Gabe, one of our medics, who assisted in the surgery. He'll take you up to the medical ward where you can see your friend and be examined."

"I'll wake Ivy," I tell Liam.

"No," he says before I can turn around. "Let her sleep. She needs it."

"I can wait down here with her if you want," the woman offers, "in case she wakes up."

"That'd be great," Liam says. "Thank you."

Gabe holds the door open for me and Liam as the woman moves further inside. The door slams shut behind us.

"Sebastien pulled through just fine," Gabe says as we climb the steps behind him. "The general anesthesia should be wearing off soon. It was a clean through-and-through at the edge of his abdomen, missing any internal organs. He was lucky. We'll keep him upstairs to monitor him throughout the night."

"Will he be able to travel?" Liam asks.

"Yes, but 'when' is entirely up to the doctor. He'll be in considerable pain for a while, so he'll need to take it easy."

We emerge from underground and exit the janitor's closet. In the open room riddled with various mechanical parts, I'm tempted to jog ahead but force myself to match Gabe's pace. Although I trust these people and am comforted by the good news, I have to see Seb for myself to know he's truly okay. I've seen too many of my comrades die to take someone else's word for it.

With each step toward the corridor on the opposite side of the room, my heartbeat increases. Nervousness breaks the fog of exhaustion, but I try not to let it show. Every part of me expects the worst. I can't help but doubt Gabe's words. What if something happens overnight? What if the bullet grazed an organ and they missed it?

The long corridor seems to go on forever. We pass at least a dozen doors until Gabe stops at one that's ajar. Peeking inside, he nudges it open and steps aside for us to enter.

A single tabletop lamp lights a portion of the room, softening everything in its dull orange glow. Seb lies in one of the two hospital beds, hooked up to an IV bag and heart monitor. The color has drained from his face. A green hospital gown is draped over his body, and the dirt and blood have been scrubbed from his arms and face.

"He'll be drowsy for a bit," Gabe says from the doorway. "A side effect of the anesthesia, as well as exhaustion."

"But he's conscious, right?" I say.

"He did briefly wake up post-surgery and was responsive yet disoriented, which is expected."

Approaching the side of the bed, I notice the nasal-prong oxygen mask secured to Seb's face. His chest rises and falls with ease and his eyes move rapidly underneath his lids. He's definitely alive. Still, my fear that something could happen to him overnight won't ease up. Gabe says something about informing the doctor that we're ready for examination before leaving the room, but his words are faint.

I could've prevented this.

I could've grabbed more ammo from that cabin. I could've had Seb take the lead while I covered for all of them. Or I could've killed that scavenger myself.

"I know what you're thinking," Liam says beside me. "You're blaming yourself, just after giving me a speech about how I shouldn't." There's a trace of humor in his tone.

I shake my head. "It's not the same. I'm responsible for what happens to all of you."

"I'm your second-in-command and his squad leader. I share some responsibility here."

Strictly in terms of the chain of command, I know that's true, but I don't want to share that responsibility with him. Not this way. Liam was preoccupied with his injured sister anyway. Covering Seb was solely up to me.

"You heard Gabe," Liam says. "He made it through surgery; he's going to be fine."

It's more than that, though. I know people get hurt in the resistance, and I've accepted that. But that doesn't extinguish the burning need to protect every single one of my members.

Two of my members—Maverick and Drew—were lost while my group saved me. Elizabeth died while trying to escape the Black Hats. Those three, though still difficult, are a bit easier to accept. I wasn't with them; it was pretty much impossible for me to do anything, given the circumstances.

With Seb, there's no excuse. I was *right there* and he still got hurt.

"I think our biggest issue is going to be convincing him to take it easy," Liam quips, pulling me out of my thoughts. "He always likes to be part of the action." When he doesn't get a reaction from me, he places a hand on my shoulder and drops his mocking tone. "You're a good leader, Nixon, no matter what's happened."

There's a light knock on the door. I don't look away from Seb, but from the corner of my eye, I see Liam turn his head and his hand drops from my shoulder.

"It seems you've all had a hell of a day," a familiar voice says— one I haven't heard in months.

My breathing stops. I look up from Seb, staring straight ahead at the shadows cast across the blank wall. It can't be him. There's no way. The Black Hats had the house surrounded when Ivy and I were captured.

I make myself take a breath and turn around slowly, coming face to face with my adoptive father.

"Adam," I croak, surprised I'm even able to speak.

Adam smiles and pulls me into a hug. Although the embrace is loose, the contact with my wounds causes me to tense, and he notices, studying me as he pulls back.

"I'm glad you're safe," he says, then extends a hand out to Liam. "Good to see you again, Liam."

"Yeah, you too," Liam says as they shake, sounding just as surprised as I am.

"Is Lacey with you?" My overtaxed brain frantically tries to put everything together. The possibility of them being dead always loomed in the back of my mind, but I never entertained the idea. I didn't want to acknowledge it, despite never being given an answer as to what happened after Ivy and I were taken. All I knew was that Piper was questioned and denied ever knowing anything about the resistance. How did she not know they were alive this whole time? Or did she know all along and never told me?

"She's at the Commander's camp," Adam says, "and I know she'll be happy to see you." He looks between me and Liam and, as if just realizing what he's implied, adds, "All of you."

"He knows," I tell him, remembering how Liam, Seb, and Isaiah accidentally found out about my relationship to them. "Part of it, at least. How are you here?"

"Come with me," Adam says. "I'll examine you and we can talk. Liam, you'll be next."

Liam nods, and I follow Adam out. The room he leads me to is considerably smaller than Seb's, with an examination table shoved against the wall and a small counter beside it that holds a stack of papers, pens, and a clipboard. Next to that is a handwashing station with a slightly crooked cabinet above it.

"Take your shirt off and hop up on the examination table," Adam says with his back to me. He flips a page on the clipboard.

I pull my shirt over my head and set it on the table before climbing up, the thin white paper crinkling under my weight.

"One of your medics, Carter, relayed your injuries to us," he says, reading over the notes in front of him. "Two broken ribs and fingers, broken nose, severe lacerations on your back, bruising… Any newly acquired injuries?"

"No," I say. "Does Piper know you and Lacey made it out?"

"She does not."

He writes down something I can't make out. Setting the pen aside, he turns on the sink and wets his hands before pumping a generous amount of soap into his palm.

"How *did* you two make it out?"

"We didn't. We were captured just like you were. The only difference is that we were held at TCB, awaiting trial, whereas you and Ivy were taken directly to the Red Zone."

Of course they were going to give them a trial. A highly respected doctor and a genetic engineer can't just disappear without raising questions.

"So, how did you get out of there?" I ask. I don't doubt there are resistance members within TCB—I have a few members placed in transport centers in my own zone—but they wouldn't be capable of breaking detainees out. Their only purpose there is to gather and relay intel.

"Special Operatives," Adam says, scrubbing his hands. "Highly trained, covert members of the resistance who report only to the Commander."

"Why have I never heard of them?"

"That would defeat the purpose of being covert, wouldn't it?" After rinsing off the last of the soap, he shuts off the water and dries his hands with a paper towel. "I didn't know they existed until then either. The only other person who's aware of their presence is Eli, but even he doesn't know their identities. We were able to be rescued because of where we were. Like Eli's group, they can't get too close to things such as the auction."

As far as I know, no news has circulated about two fugitives from the Blue Zone. There wasn't even any talk of a trial. Then again, the Society launched a manhunt for Ivy and Liam prior and boasted to everyone in the Northern Unity that they had detained me, a high-profile *terrorist*, only for everything to collapse over the past few days. Informing the public of even more resistance activity, especially from two people held in high regard, would lead to panic and distrust. That would cause more fractures in the fragile foundation of lies the Enlightened Society is built upon. And now that it's well known I escaped my execution, they'll try even harder to keep it a secret and strengthen their cover story as to why Adam and Lacey are no longer in the Blue Zone.

Tossing the paper towel in the small trash can, Adam turns to me and pulls a stethoscope from the pocket of his lab coat. His eyes travel over me, lingering on the yellowing bruises on my right side. "Knowing you, you didn't rest like you were supposed to. How bad has the pain been?"

"I'm fine," I lie.

"Nixon," he says, taking on a fatherly tone.

"It's been… manageable. Worse when I move too much."

"Scale of one to ten?"

"I don't know—six?"

He puts the earpieces of the stethoscope in, and I sit up straight, which puts a strain on my side. Holding the diaphragm to my chest, he listens to my heart in a couple of areas before moving to my back. He hesitates, finally getting a good look at the extent of the injuries.

I tense under the cool metal. Some I know have already begun to scar; the deeper ones, though, I've felt reopen several times.

"Relax," he says. "Deep breath."

I do as I'm told, wincing at the stab of pain, and exhale slowly through my mouth. He repeats the command two more times, moving the diaphragm around, then steps back, returning the stethoscope to his pocket.

"Your lungs sound good," he says. With one hand on my shoulder, he presses the other to my injured side, feeling around my ribcage. "Keep overexerting yourself, though, and you could cause some damage."

"I didn't have much of a choice on our way here." I suck in a sharp breath when he presses on a tender spot.

I don't bring up the training session. It doesn't change anything now, and Adam knows me well enough to suspect I didn't waste any time getting back into training.

"Not much I can do for the pain," he says, stepping back. "I'll get you some ibuprofen. Be sure to ice it and *rest*. How are the others?"

"Liam's okay physically," I say. "Exhausted like the rest of us."

"And Ivy?"

"She hurt her ankle on the way here and has some injuries from her… buyer, but I don't know how bad."

Returning to the counter, he pulls a black stool out from underneath and sits down, jotting something down on the clipboard. "Have you had a chance to talk to her after you and Eli questioned her?"

I'm about to ask how he knows about that but stop myself. Eli filled the Commander in before we left, so it makes sense for Adam to be kept in the loop, if only because of our relationship.

"Barely," I say, pulling my shirt back on. "We aren't exactly on good terms at the moment."

"How hard have you been on her?"

I shrug, averting my eyes. "No different than my members."

"But she's not one of your members—she's a victim of the auction."

"She's withholding information." Though I still don't exactly know what. I can't shake the feeling that if Wyatt mentioned me, he had to know other members, too.

"I don't doubt that, but do you honestly believe there's a malicious intent behind it?"

When I don't say anything, Adam sighs and rolls the stool a little closer. "Don't force it; she'll talk when she's ready. Making her relive it all on your time, rather than hers, will only drive her further away, to the point where she won't want to talk to you or Liam at all. You and Eli got what you needed out of her."

All we really found out was that she killed Wyatt. The fact that he abused her wasn't a surprise, and the bruises on her arms and neck spoke for themselves.

"I know you want to fix things," Adam continues. "You've always been that way with your comrades and sister, but..." He runs a hand through his graying hair. "This is different. I don't know any of the specifics, but I know Ivy's been through a lot. Right now, she needs someone to comfort her, not interrogate her."

"Shouldn't you be having this conversation with her brother then?"

Adam smirks and twines his fingers between his legs as he leans forward. "We may not be blood relations, but you're still my son. I could tell how you felt about her when you were staying with us."

I attempt to laugh it off, but that does nothing for the paranoia that's resurfaced. Continuing any sort of relationship with Ivy is forbidden.

"You care about her," he continues. "Maybe that's as far as it goes—I don't know—but don't let these assumptions of yours get in the way of that. Keep in mind that you're the first member of the resistance she put her trust in. She needs you now more than ever."

"Again, she has Liam."

Adam shakes his head. "Liam wasn't captured like you two. He can listen, but he can't relate to her like you can. And I know you could use someone, too."

"I'm fine."

I slide off the examination table and walk toward the door, but Adam intercepts my path and places a hand on my shoulder.

"You're going to hurt yourself more by pushing her away," he says. "At least lose the leader attitude with her."

"Can I get back to Seb?" I ask, not bothering to hide my irritation. Knowing Adam is the one who operated on my scout has eased my anxiety a bit, but I still want to be nearby just in case, and Ivy is the last thing I want to talk about right now.

Adam sighs but allows me to pass, following me out of the room.

"I'll see you four at the Commander's camp in a few days," he says as we walk, "but you'll meet him first."

"Why in a few days?"

"I have to finish up my time here. I rotate out with a few other doctors—one week here, three at the camp."

"You just happened to be working the week we show up?"

"I actually volunteered after the news reached us about Ivy escaping and you being in the Red Zone." He shoots me a stern glance. "You went against orders."

I look away from him, focusing directly ahead as we near the open door to Seb's room. "How much trouble am I in?"

"I'm not going to lie to you, he was pretty angry, but..." He pauses and purses his lips—a habit of his when he's figuring out how to word something. "Ultimately, he's just glad you were close enough to move things along quicker."

That's not all of it. He's not telling me something. Part of me wants to ask what exactly the Commander said, but that will turn into a whole new conversation I don't want to have tonight. I'm exhausted, weak, and don't want to deal with the added stress of the lecture I know I'm going to get once I meet him. I already know I went against orders and will have to deal with the consequences. For now, though, I want to forget about it.

Liam's pacing at the foot of Seb's bed when we return, stopping when he sees us. Seb's still unconscious and, thankfully, still breathing. I walk farther into the room, halting a few feet from him.

"You're next," I tell Liam, cocking my head toward the door.

"You can head back to the bunker, Nixon," Adam says as Liam passes by me. "I'll send him down once we're done."

Without looking back, I say, "Would it be okay if I stayed up here with Seb?"

"We'll be in and out every two hours to check on him," Adam says. "He's in good hands."

"I want to be here when he wakes up."

Seb likely won't remember much of what happened, and waking up in an unfamiliar place alone won't help. He's never met Adam before, or any of the other medics as far as I know. The last thing we need is him waking up and thinking we've been recaptured. Ivy and Liam will be fine by themselves in the bunker.

"Okay," Adam says after a pause. "Get some rest."

I hear the click of the door and Adam's muffled voice on the other side. Their footsteps fade. For a few moments, I remain frozen in place, watching the steady rise and fall of Seb's chest. I watch for any other movement, even if it's just the twitch of a finger. Nothing comes.

I crawl into the second bed on the other side of the nightstand and lie on my uninjured side, facing Seb. Exhaustion has already made itself known in my aching body and cluttered mind, but I can't tear my eyes from him. I know I need sleep, that I'll be useless if I'm not rested, but the fear that something will happen the second I let my guard down wrenches in my gut.

Staring at my unconscious scout makes our last training session replay in my head. The image of my knife pressed to his throat flashes before my eyes, and I ball the sheets in my fist at the reminder. If Liam hadn't been there, I don't know what would've happened. There's a small part of me that's confident I would have been able to snap out of it on my own, that I wouldn't have actually hurt him. But the overwhelming majority says otherwise. In that moment, I didn't know where I was; I couldn't even recognize one of my own members.

I squeeze my eyes shut. Uncertainty twists its way into my conscience, rooting itself at the core of my being.

I snapped again when Liam and I were running toward the main cabin. With everything happening all at once, I didn't really process it or recover. My focus was just turned elsewhere for the time being. If that hadn't happened, would I have been in a better headspace to cover for Seb? I blamed Ivy for it at first, but he wasn't her responsibility. Regardless of how we ended up in that situation, *I'm* the one who's responsible for what happened. It was up to me to ensure we weren't captured too. Ivy made a mistake, but this is *my* squad. I'm the one who's supposed to protect them at all costs.

If I can't do that, how the hell can I call myself a leader?

27. Take It Out on Me

Nixon

The usual nightmare paralyzes my body, its effects lingering after waking. With my eyes sealed shut, I repeat the familiar process of slowing my breathing and reminding myself of where I am.

I'm at the outpost. Adam is here. My squad and I are safe.

Most of me knows that to be true, but remnants of the nightmare linger, tugging at my groggy mind. It was almost exactly the same as the last time—being tortured and beaten—but there was more to it. Instead of being dragged back to my cell after forcefully inhaling the icy water, I was handed a knife, long and jagged and heavy. Everything went black after that, as if I'd closed my eyes or the lights had been shut off. Wretched screams echoed around me, clawing at my ears and shredding every last thought. When I could see again, I was staring at my crimson-coated hands and the knife at my feet. Somewhere up ahead, someone called my name. I looked up toward the voice, only to see five bodies strewn across the bloody floor. Elizabeth, Maverick, Drew, Seb, and Ivy.

Acid burns my throat. Even now, I can hear that voice, distorted by my roaring pulse. I clench my fists, relieved to have partial use of my body again.

Someone grabs my shoulder. "Nixon."

I force my eyes open, blinking several times before I can make out the ceiling above me.

"You okay?"

The hand moves from my shoulder. Disoriented and still somewhat stiff, I turn my head in the direction of the voice, preparing myself to relive the final gruesome moments of my dream.

Seb stands over me with one hand pressed against the wall beside him, eyes wide and tan skin two shades lighter than normal. The tube to his IV stretches across the gap between the beds, but all the other wires that were connected to him have been removed.

"Yeah," I say after a moment, finally realizing I'm awake. My voice is hoarse, and my throat stings. "Yeah, I'm good." I push myself up and rub my eyes.

"You looked like you were in pain," Seb says, sitting back on his bed, "and your body got all tense for a minute. Bad dream?"

"No," I lie. "My ribs are giving me hell after yesterday, that's all. How are you feeling?"

"Amazing, thanks to whatever drugs they're giving me." He grins and lies back, pulling the blankets over him. "I'm still fucking starving. Adam promised me food, but damn, it's taking forever."

I glance at the analog clock across the room. Half past eight. I have no idea what time it was when we got here or how long I've been asleep.

"He said you volunteered to stay up here last night," Seb says.

"Figured you'd be more comfortable seeing a familiar face when you woke up."

"Aww." He faces me, his cheek pressed against the pillow, and conceals a wince with another smile. "Your face wouldn't be my first choice, but I'll take it."

I attempt to laugh at his remark but can hardly bring myself to even smirk. I'm grounded here in the present. The nightmare is still fresh in my mind, though.

"You shouldn't be moving around yet," I tell Seb. "You need to rest."

He rolls his eyes. "I feel fine."

"You were *shot*."

"Pretty badass, huh? Although not as much as Ivy. That girl's my new idol."

"None of this is funny!" I snap, swinging my legs off the bed. "For once can you please be serious?"

His smile dissolves. "Damn, dude, chill."

"You could've died."

"But I didn't." He props himself up on his elbow. "What's up with you?"

All I can do is stare at him, clenching my fists at my sides. I grind my teeth, unsure of what to say.

I was scared of losing him—still am. Same goes for Liam and Ivy. For weeks, I thought I'd lost my parents, only to find out they're alive and well but my sister is a traitor. I'm afraid for my group back home. I'm afraid of the memories that haunt me day and night, that they'll push me to snap again in a way that hurts everyone around me.

"Nothing," I mutter. Dragging a hand down my face, I let out a long breath. I'm not getting into any of that with him right now. "I'm going to head down to the bunker and finish reading over those documents. Don't move. I'll send Liam up to see you in a bit."

"If you see Adam," Seb calls after me as I open the door, "tell him I'm about to starve to death."

"Will do."

I navigate the long, empty hallway at a sluggish pace. Reading more about the disgusting secrets of the Society isn't something I care about doing right now, but staying up here with Seb will only lead to him asking me more questions that I'm not ready to answer. I don't care to share, and he needs to focus on himself at the moment. If the other two are still asleep, I'll at least get a little time to myself.

I eye each door I pass, wondering what's on the other side and what exactly the groups stationed out here do. Eli didn't share any of that with me, just said where we were supposed to go and assured me we'd be safe. It doesn't really matter either way—I don't plan on being here long—but I can't help but speculate.

They rotate medical teams every week, so there has to be more going on here than helping people from inside the walls. Resistance members don't travel outside the Northern Unity often—it's risky, and that risk is likely greater now that we've escaped. If there are re-education camps nearby, I understand having scouts, logistics, and even hackers out here. Maybe the medics are on standby in case something happens to one of them during a mission. But there are other people out here, too—neither resistance nor citizens. They know that. Do they offer any assistance to the people struggling to survive on their own?

Back in the bunker, the main lights are off, but an electric lantern casts a soft blue light across the room from the coffee table. All the papers Liam and I left out have been cleaned up.

I find the backpack propped against the table and sling it over one shoulder. On my way toward the door across the room, I grab an ice pack from the freezer.

Flicking on the light of the makeshift office, I drop the bag beside a white folding table that holds a radio, notepad, and cup of pens, and sink into the padded metal chair. Despite not actually wanting to read, I pull a wad of papers from the backpack and smooth them out across the table. Pressing the ice pack to my side, I lean my head against my fist and look over the first document in front of me.

<u>Elite Auction: 01/05/2067</u>
•**Noah Burnley—#970** Male; 18yo; Yellow Zone
•**Julia Blaylock—#971** Female; 16yo; Blue Zone

- **Tess Simmons—#972** Female; 21yo; Blue Zone
- **Aiden Hart—#973** Male; 20yo; Green Zone
- **Olivia Clearson—#974** Female; 19yo; Green Zone (**SOLD**)
- **Tristan Harper—#975** Male; 15yo; Yellow Zone (**SOLD**)
- **Shelby Clark—#976** Female; 23yo; Green Zone (**SOLD**)
- **Alicia Marsh—#977** Female; 14yo; Yellow Zone (**SOLD**)

Ivy wasn't the only one sold to a private buyer, but she was the only one out of that group who was forced to attend the auction. They wanted her there for no reason other than to hear what was going to happen to me—an attempt to break her, to make her lose hope. I've suspected that ever since then, and now it's confirmed: There were three others who were sold to private buyers.

Another thought crosses my mind, something I haven't considered until now, and my stomach drops. How the hell did the Society know there was anything between Ivy and me? It wasn't until we arrived at Adam and Lacey's that we actually began to tolerate one another, and that was mainly because we were both shaken up after walking in on that ambushed safehouse. As far as the Society knew, Ivy was my hostage. No one knew about our last few nights in the Blue Zone, and our only public display of affection was when we were backstage right before the auction. They'd already planned on having her attend before that.

I squint at the names printed on the paper as if that's going to give me the answer I'm looking for, thinking back to every person we encountered between the Green and Blue Zones who could've potentially tipped them off. Adam, who was technically retired from the resistance at the time, still had contact with the Commander and the Blue Zone's Group. He was aiding and abetting a fugitive and a terrorist—an act of treason—which makes him just as bad in the eyes of the Society. Same goes for Lacey. But they were supposedly freed from TCB and evaded their trial.

Grabbing one of the pens from the cup in front of me, I flip the top page of the notepad and make a note for myself to get more information on the so-called Special Operatives. My stomach twists into a knot as I write. I don't necessarily think they were in on this, but I want to be cautious.

Kase was the one who confirmed Ivy's location to the Black Hats, but he never saw the two of us communicate. He couldn't have known. The only time he saw me with her was when he was being escorted out by Piper's team.

Piper.

The only time Piper met Ivy, I admitted that Ivy knew about my legal relation to her, Adam, and Lacey. Now I realize how dumb that was. As soon as I said that, Piper commented on how Ivy must be 'special', since I'd never shared that with anyone else. Was that enough for her to draw a conclusion? After I was rescued, she said Eli had told her about our kiss at the auction. I took her word for it—it was believable—but what if that was a cover? She let Kase go after knowing he'd flipped; what would stop her from informing the Society about me and Ivy?

I stare at the radio, blood boiling. My sister's a damn traitor, yet she's allowed to remain in the resistance as a leader. Sure, she's under probation, but how does that fix anything? She still holds authority over an entire group. Their lives are in her hands, and at any moment, she could betray them, too.

Flinging the pen down, I shove all the papers aside and lean back. How does it make any sense that *I* was interrogated as if I'd sold out the resistance after being tortured for six fucking weeks, while Piper faces hardly any repercussions? The Commander claimed the matter is being investigated. Bullshit. I can guarantee that if it was me, I'd be removed from the resistance without hesitation.

I grab the mic of the radio and reach across the table, finger hovering over the power switch. I could contact the Commander, demand answers right now for everything that's happened—but I immediately discard the idea. We'll be seeing him in person soon anyway. I'm tempted to call Piper… not that she'd tell the truth about anything, but at least I could unleash my anger on her. She deserves it, and the longer I sit here with it, the more potent it becomes.

I hear the door open and snap my head in that direction, still gripping the mic.

Ivy freezes in the doorway, clutching the door handle. "Sorry," she says, "I heard the door and…"

Her eyes are red and swollen, and her bottom lip is raw like she's been gnawing on it all night.

"It was me," I say. "I stayed with Seb last night."

"Oh." She releases the handle and crosses her arms over her chest, eyes shifting to the two doors behind me—the storage closet and generator room. "How is he?"

"Alive." I turn back to the radio and set the mic down. "He's going to be fine, just has to take it easy for a little while."

"I'm sorry," she whispers. "I feel awful."

"Yeah, well, you almost got him killed."

"You think I don't know that?"

Sinking back in the chair, I drop the ice pack on the table and massage my temples. I don't want to deal with this right now. Her apologies are meaningless if she can't be transparent about anything, and the issue of how the Society found out about everything is still at the front of my mind as well as my resentment toward Piper.

How many members of the Society know? All of them, or only those directly linked to the last auction? I glance at the document with the names of the most recent victims. My eyes land on the 'SOLD' next to Ivy's name.

"What did Wyatt say about me?" I ask abruptly.

"What?" Ivy asks. "Where's that coming from?"

"You said before that he talked about me. What did he know?"

"I… I don't know."

Chuckling, I shake my head and stand. "I'm so fucking tired of your lies."

"I'm not lying!"

"How can I be sure of that? Everything you've said has been inconsistent, and there's a lot I still don't know." I take a step toward her, half expecting her to retreat, but she doesn't. She matches my glare.

"You haven't exactly given me a chance to talk."

"Bullshit. You've had plenty of chances. Including now."

"No—I've been *interrogated*, like I did something wrong. Like it was *my* fault I was sold."

"No one said that."

"It didn't have to be said; it's clear from how you've treated me ever since we were at Eli's."

"Because I immediately picked up on your—" I stop myself, closing my eyes and taking a deep breath. Adam's right, the leader attitude doesn't work with her, but it's difficult to shut that part of myself down.

"Well, *I* immediately picked up on how you'd changed," Ivy says. "How you could barely look at me, how you spoke to me like I'd turned on you and the rest of the resistance. Everything that came out of your mouth was an accusation."

"I was doing my job." I glance past her and listen for any movement outside of the office. "Look, if you want to talk, that's fine, but at least close the door so you don't wake Liam."

She stares at me for a moment like she's debating it. I'd like to think I wouldn't care either way, but if we can at least resolve some of this tension, maybe things will be easier going forward. Rolling her eyes, she steps into the room and closes the door with her foot. She turns her head, running a hand through her wavy hair.

I open my mouth to repeat my same question about Wyatt, but she strides forward, stopping a couple of feet from me.

"What the hell is wrong with you?" she demands. "You've been a complete dick ever since we saw each other, not to mention that you threatened me when we were at the gas station!"

"You threw Elizabeth's death in my face over a misunderstanding."

"That's an excuse?!" Her voice rises with each word. "And let's not forget that you said it would be *my* fault if anyone in your group got hurt, all because I don't fucking know why he killed one of your members."

"What the hell did you expect me to think?"

"I expected you to trust me!"

"Well I don't. Not right now at least."

I hate it, but it's the truth.

She falters. The steely glare softens for a moment, showing me just how much I've wounded her.

"Fuck you!" She slams her hands into my chest, and I stumble backward, grabbing her wrists and jerking her forward so her face is inches from mine.

"Don't you *dare* push me," I snarl.

"He raped me," she spits.

It feels like a punch to the gut, knocking the air from my lungs.

Tears well in her eyes, but she shoots me a mocking smile. "Is that what you wanted to hear? He drugged me and raped me the night of the rehearsal dinner because he found the documents I'd hidden." She yanks herself free from my loosened grip and rubs her wrists. "What else do you want to know? That he beat me every day? Or that he constantly reminded me of how you were going to die?"

Turning her back to me, she takes a few steps toward the door and rakes her fingers through her hair.

I already knew that's what happened to her, but actually hearing her say it brings on a whole new wave of rage, mixed with an unbearable haze of guilt. It clouds my conscience, making everything else dissolve. I want to yell and hit something and hold her all at once. I want to go back to the Northern Unity and burn the entire country to the ground for what they did to her and what they're still doing to countless more victims.

"Ivy," I begin in the gentlest tone I can manage, but the rage is a fire lacing my veins and lashing up my spine.

"Stop," she says, shaking her head. She spins around, curling her fingers into her palms. Fresh tears streak her face, but she holds her head high and looks directly at me as she speaks. "You want to know what he said about you? He called me your *whore*. He and the interrogator both said you manipulated me, that you never cared. And he said he watched you die. That you died not giving a shit about me."

So Wyatt knew about us, too. It could be because rumors of the kiss at the auction spread, but that doesn't explain why Ivy was made to watch it all unfold.

"Ivy," I try again, firmer this time. I take a step toward her.

"No," she interrupts, narrowing her eyes. "You don't know what it was like." She scrubs her face with her hands, only for more tears to flow. "I thought of you constantly. I worried about you. I hoped Eli would get you out. Every single day I hated myself for going along with what Wyatt wanted, but I did it to survive and to gather information for the resistance." Sniffling, she shakes her head, and her eyes travel around the room. "I thought of how if you were there, you'd tell me how stupid it was, that it was dangerous. And it was. But I wanted to do something other than just sit there and wait for the help that wasn't coming.

"I don't know what happened to Elizabeth or anything about the rest of your group. He never brought any of them up besides that one time. And after all that, after crying for you every night, you think I'm this… this traitor." Her voice cracks on the final word, and she turns away again just as a sob racks her body.

For a moment, I'm frozen in place. Everything slowly sinks in. The rage comes and goes in waves, each one weaker than the last. Its fire is replaced with a cold void. I'm furious at what the bastard did to her, but in this moment, I'm consumed by her hurt. Each of her sobs and hiccupping breaths, muffled by her hand, makes my chest tighten.

I hesitantly walk up to her, searching for something I can say to ease her pain, something to restore the light she was full of before any of this happened. But no words can erase this. With a hand on her shoulder, I turn her around to face me, and despite everything Eli warned against, I circle my arms around her and pull her close.

She tenses at first, squirming as if she might recoil, but soon leans into my embrace. Burying her face into my chest, she wraps her arms around me, balling the back of my shirt in her hands. She trembles with each sob that pulses throughout her body and I tighten my arms, wishing I could take it all away.

"I'm sorry," I whisper. "I'm sorry you had to go through all that and I couldn't protect you. I'm sorry I've been so hard on you." I rub her back, hopelessly willing away all of her grief.

Sniffling, she turns her head and presses her cheek against my chest. With each beat of my heart, her breaths come a little easier, and her trembling gradually subsides. Her tears seep through my shirt, making it stick to my skin.

"I'm sorry I haven't been completely honest," she says after a moment. "I was scared, and you didn't seem the same. Like, when I first saw you…" She subtly shakes her head as if dismissing the topic, but I know exactly what she's referring to.

She hugged me as soon as I walked in the room, like my presence was relieving and comforting, and I didn't reciprocate. No matter how much I wanted to, I couldn't with Eli there. What we're doing right now is way beyond the boundaries he reiterated. Still, this moment, regardless of how heartbreaking it is, is the closest I've felt to normal in a while.

"I didn't want it to be like that," I tell her, "but it's against the rules and Eli was there."

She looks up at me. "What do you mean?"

"He knows about… us—what happened while we were together, to an extent. Rumors started after those guards pulled us apart at the auction, and he warned me not to let anything else happen."

She nods slowly and steps back. "Which explains how Wyatt got that idea."

If I'd known that would get her into more trouble with him, I wouldn't have let it happen. It was impulsive; I wasn't thinking of the guards surrounding us or how it would get out. All I cared about at that moment was her and how I thought I'd never see her again. I wanted those final minutes together to mean something.

"Yeah," I say, "but I'm pretty sure the Society, or at least the Black Hats, knew before that."

"How?"

"I don't know for sure, but"—I walk to the table, swipe the document with names of the victims from the last auction, and hand it to her— "there were three other people sold to a private buyer, yet you were the only one who attended the actual auction. Why do you think that is?"

"To hear your sentence," she says, skimming over the names. "I figured that when the interrogator told me I had a private buyer." As she says it, her eyes widen. "But they wouldn't do that unless they had some idea that… Who could've told them?"

"My guess is Piper."

She looks up, eyebrows pulling together. "Piper? As in your sister?"

I shove my hands in my pockets. "It's a long story, but she let Kase go, which is how we got caught. She's still in the resistance but under investigation. Anyway, I think because she made a comment about how I'd shared some personal stuff with you, she had an idea there was something going on, and she leaked that to the Black Hats. Plus, she had some things to say about what happened between us at the auction, claiming she heard it from Eli."

"Are you okay?"

"I'm managing."

The way her eyes briefly narrow, I know she doesn't fully believe that, but she doesn't push it. "So, I'm guessing other resistance members know about… us?"

"No, just Piper and Eli."

"But the Commander has to, right? I mean, even if they didn't tell him, he'd have to know if the Society does."

"Shit." With my palms pressed against the end of the table, I lean against it. That hadn't crossed my mind, but now she's brought it up, it makes sense. Although Eli made it sound like the Commander wasn't aware… "Guess we'll find out when we meet him."

Reaching behind me, Ivy returns the document to the table with the others. Her arm brushes against mine and she freezes, a small gasp escaping her.

"What's wrong?" I ask.

"Where did you get that?" The paper flutters to the table and slides onto the chair when she opens her hand. I turn around and scan the haphazard pile of documents, unsure of what she's talking about. Leaning across the table, she retrieves a photograph that's peeking out—the one that was given to me by the man Seb and I met.

"When Seb and I followed that girl," I say. "Her dad gave it to us. His wife and son were taken by soldiers and I promised to help find them."

How long has it been since then? A day? Two? So much has happened, it's all blurring together. I promised to be back there in four days, and I'm running out of time. We still have to meet the Commander, and allowing me to look into the two disappearances and travel back toward the walls is going to take some convincing.

New tears pool in Ivy's eyes. She points to the woman on the far right with a trembling finger. "I know her."

28. The Unknown

Ivy

Each shallow breath sends a sharp pain through my chest. I blink away the fresh tears blurring my vision. Every part of my brain is begging for this not to be true. It can't be.

But there's no mistaking the smiling face that stares back at me—a phantom that's returned to haunt me. Only, when I saw her, that innocent smile was concealed by bloody duct tape and those eyes were full of terror and desperation.

I shove the picture into Nixon's hands and back away from him. I force my fingers through my hair, twisting them in my roots until my scalp stings.

He won't find that woman. She's dead.

"Ivy, what's wrong?" Nixon asks, setting the picture down. "How do you know her?"

I remember her begging for her life, crying for her two children—the children in the picture before their family was ripped apart. The little girl's face creeps into my mind, her hollow eyes and fragile frame. A girl who will never see her mother again, who's too young to understand what happened to her. A girl with a missing brother, who may or may not have faced the same fate.

My heart climbs into my throat. "The Red Zone," I squeeze out, untangling my fingers from my hair. "She was auctioned."

Nixon's eyes widen. "You met her?"

I nod.

"Who is she with?"

I shake my head and squeeze my eyes shut. That night replays in my head. The vivid memories are shards of glass that slice away at my sanity, leaving nothing but a bloody corpse.

"They did awful things." I'm shivering. My body is ice cold. It feels like there's not enough air.

"Can you tell me what happened?" Nixon asks. He sounds so far away, but the tenderness has returned to his voice. I wish he'd keep talking, let me get lost in his words, distract me from the rest of the world.

"Wyatt was mad at me for talking to Ember. He took me to his friend's house… Nolan… and showed me—her. As a punishment." I open my eyes. The tears are endless. The room sways. Panic floods my veins. There's not enough air. "They told me I should—be grateful, that I—could've ended up like her."

Nixon slowly walks toward me, and I take another step back. I want to reach out for him, to melt into his embrace, and run away at the same time.

"She was tied up," I rasp, the image invading my mind. My throat constricts. "Bloody and bruised. Almost naked."

Her agonizing wails ring in my ears. Nixon's mouth moves, but I can't hear him over them. It feels as though another entity has invaded my mind, holding me hostage in a body I'm desperate to escape.

"There was a knife." My words get caught in my throat and my voice hitches. "Wyatt put it in my hand and told me I was going to do the same thing to her as they did to you. Nolan held her head back and Wyatt forced me to hold the knife to her throat. He told me to prove that I was a 'good girl.'"

The walls are closing in. Disgust slithers up my body and burrows itself into me, clenching around my deflating lungs and thundering heart. More gasps for air. More tears. I swallow back the scream of absolute anguish that claws at my throat as I stumble backward, my back colliding with the wall behind me.

My ears ring. Sweat prickles underneath my arms. My legs are wobbly. I open my mouth for a gulp of air, but my lungs won't function. Everything spins. I claw at my throat, hoping to feel something from my jagged nails digging into my flesh, but no pain comes. I'm numb yet hyper-aware all at once.

I can't breathe. My chest burns. Why can't I breathe? My legs give out, and I sink to the floor as the walls cave in around me.

"Hey, hey, you're okay." Nixon drops to his knees in front of me with one hand on my shoulder and the other cupping my cheek. "Look at me. Focus on me."

I want to pull him closer and allow him to take it all away, as if he has the power to absorb every violent emotion crashing over me. I also want to run, because having him look at me after what I just admitted and not knowing what he's thinking makes my stomach clench. With a hand clamped around my throat, I frantically stare around the room, avoiding the picture on the table.

"Ivy, focus on me," Nixon repeats. He swipes a thumb underneath my eye, smearing my tears. "You're safe. I'm here. Your brother's here. Seb's okay. We're all here to keep you safe."

I gasp for air again. My eyes find his, wide and sympathetic. The rigid mask he's worn this entire journey is gone. He doesn't quite look the same as before we were separated, but it's close.

"I didn't do it," I choke out. The overwhelming need to explain myself takes over. I struggle to form words, to inhale. I can't let him think I killed that woman. "He pushed me out of the room. But I heard her screams. There was blood on him when he—"

"Okay," Nixon says. "It's okay. I believe you." He pulls my hand from my throat and presses it to his chest. "Here, can you breathe with me?"

He inhales deep through his nose; his chest expands underneath my hand and deflates when he exhales through his mouth. He repeats, and I try to mimic him. Focusing on the rise and fall of his chest, I manage a tiny breath. The small rush of oxygen to my lungs brings temporary relief, but the panic of it not being enough grows.

"Keep going," Nixon says, giving my hand a light squeeze.

I pull in another shaky inhalation.

There's a quick knock on the door before it opens, and Nixon takes his eyes off me for a fraction of a second.

"What's going on?" I hear Liam ask, his voice thick with alarm. "What happened?"

My gaze wavers from Nixon, but he pulls me back in by saying, "Ivy, focus on me." Remaining calm, he glances at Liam. "Panic attack; she's okay. Go get Adam."

Liam's footsteps fade, and I hear the beep of the keypad and the steel door slam. Each breath gradually comes a little more easily. Relief washes over me when my throat unclenches. The pressure in my head begins to dissipate.

"Adam?" I ask.

Nixon offers me a small smile. "Yeah, he's here. Lacey's at the camp. Keep going, you're doing great."

The news helps me breathe a bit easier too. My lungs swell with their first full surge of air, and the anxiety continues to dissolve. More grounded in the moment, I'm suddenly aware of just how close Nixon and I are, my hand on his chest and the steady beat of his heart under my palm.

After a final conscious exhalation, I wiggle my hand free from his and wipe my tear-stained face.

"How did they get away?" I ask. My voice is still shaky. I rest my head against the wall behind me, relieved the claustrophobia has let up.

Nixon sits back, putting a little space between us. "Special Ops, apparently. They got them out while they were awaiting trial at TCB."

"Did you know?"

He shakes his head. "Not until last night."

So all this time, he hasn't even known whether his parents were even alive. When he was stuck in the Red Zone, he was left to question their whereabouts while also facing a looming death sentence, and I don't even know what exactly he went through while he was there. Having been in the Society's custody, I imagine it was hell—and Seb and Liam mentioned he's been different since being back. But he pushed it all aside to carry out this mission, to make sure I made it somewhere safe.

"How're you holding up?" I ask.

It's the same thing I asked him the day Kase was interrogated. It feels like a lifetime ago, and it's hard to believe this is the same person. It's hard to believe *I'm* the same person, that I existed at a time before now—a time before being a heap of jagged, shattered pieces I'm not sure will ever fit back together.

"I'm good," Nixon says with another small smile, one that seems like he's trying to convince himself more than me. "Glad everyone's here in one piece."

"I meant after everything you've been through… I don't know exactly what happened, but—"

"Another time, okay? Right now, let's just focus on you."

"I'm okay." The room no longer spins. My breaths are mostly even, and while that night at Nolan's still circulates in my head, it doesn't hold the power over me that it did minutes ago. "Do you still think I turned on you?"

His eyes soften and trail down to the exposed stitches in my arm. "No. I shouldn't have thought that in the first place."

As much as I hate it, he had a reason to. Not just because I wasn't cooperative, but because one of his closest friends from the Blue Zone *and* his sister have betrayed him. His skepticism makes sense.

I let out a long breath. "Are we okay?"

His eyes meet mine and he hesitates, probably deciphering what I mean by that. *I'm* not even completely sure what I mean by it. I just know I don't want to fight anymore.

"Yeah," he finally says, "we're good. And if you ever need to talk about anything, I'm here. I'll help where I can."

The groan of the bunker door causes both of us to turn toward the office's entrance. Liam and Adam stride in, stopping just past the doorway. Being told Adam is here is one thing; actually seeing him is another. He looks the exact same as when we were in the Blue Zone—salt-and-pepper hair, clean-shaven face, and the dark blue scrubs. He smiles as he approaches us, strengthening the impression that nothing has changed.

"Good to see you again, Ivy," he says, offering me his hand. He helps me to my feet, and Nixon stands at the same time.

"You too, Adam."

"Do you mind if I take a quick look at you?"

I glance at Liam then Nixon, not wanting to be apart from either of them. I remind myself that Adam is safe, someone I can trust—but what if those memories come back? What if I can't stop them? He's a doctor and here to help, but he's not someone I've ever run to for comfort. He's never seen me at my darkest points like Liam and Nixon have.

"We'll be right outside," Liam says, noticing my hesitation. "We're not going anywhere."

I give a reluctant nod. Adam has to clear me to leave the outpost. If I put it off, we'll only be kept here longer. The panic attack has passed; I'm okay now.

Nixon follows Liam out of the room, and the second the door shuts, the air becomes thicker. I take a deep breath and squeeze my eyes shut for a moment to ground myself.

"Do you know what caused the panic attack?" Adam asks, gesturing toward the metal chair in front of the table.

My legs are heavy as I make my way across the room, but they're at least steadier now. When I take a seat, the photo of the woman and her family catches my eye. The tightness in my chest returns, and I cover the picture with one of the documents.

"Nixon and I were talking about some things from the Red Zone," I say, side-eyeing the paper that's covering the photo. Now I'm tempted to pull it out for a second look. *Maybe I was wrong. Maybe it wasn't her.* "It got a bit overwhelming, but I'm fine."

Adam nods, pulling a stethoscope from the pocket of his shirt. As he listens to my heart and breathing, I focus on the door and push aside any intrusive thoughts that threaten to take over.

Wyatt is dead, and as much as I hate that I killed someone, I'm relieved I won't have to face him or his abuse ever again. I escaped the Northern Unity and the Enlightened Society. I'm a murderer and a fugitive who will never be able to return home, but I have my brother with me, and maybe one day I'll somehow see Addison again, too.

The past few months have destroyed me. I'm hollow, a fractured shell. The secrets and anger and hatred I've clung to the past few days were the only things that made me feel something. Now that I've let it all out and admitted to everything, it sets in that I've completely lost myself. I don't know who I am or who I'll become.

All that's certain is I'll be going to the Commander's camp, where I'll wait to be told what comes next. But everyone keeps insisting I'll be safe, and for the first time in a while, I believe it.

29. Ruins

Ivy

I pull a final shirt from the tiny closet and shove it into the backpack I've been given. Although food and clothes will be provided for us at the camp, the members here suggested we take some supplies just in case.

"Ready, V?" Liam stands in the archway, backpack dangling from one shoulder.

Shutting the closet, I zip up my bag and shrug it on. "Yeah."

I follow him to the bunker's exit, where he unlocks the door and holds it open for me. As soon as it closes behind us, we're swallowed by the darkness. I feel along the walls with each cautious step, focusing on the light streaming in from the open hatch at the top.

"Are you going to tell me what happened earlier?" Liam asks from behind me.

"I will when you tell me what was bothering you last night," I half-joke.

My panic attack wasn't brought up again after Adam examined me. It was as if it didn't happen, which I'm fine with. In the few hours of downtime, I iced my newly wrapped ankle, as Adam advised. Liam, Nixon, and I ate and speculated on what the Commander's camp might be like and what's in store for us. When Nixon stepped away to speak with the Commander, Liam and I talked just like we used to back home, reminiscing on times before I was kidnapped, as well as him filling me in on what I missed while I was gone, which apparently wasn't much. The Green Zone's resistance carried out a few small-scale backlogged missions while Nixon was away, but couldn't do much else without him. Aside from plotting Nixon's rescue, Liam spent most of his time at work or with Addison.

Underneath all the lighthearted conversation, though, there was the underlying tension of him wanting to know what happened. Not just with my panic attack, but my entire time in the Red Zone. One day I'll tell him everything, but I'm not sure when. As much as I love and trust my brother, I know he'd somehow think it was his fault. He'd blame himself even though it was out of his control, and I don't want to see it eat at him. More than that, I don't want to admit that the person he's been reunited with isn't really his sister, but rather someone masquerading as her with nothing but darkness lurking inside.

Liam chuckles. "Okay, fair." Then he takes on a slightly more serious tone, saying, "I just want to be sure you're okay. If Nixon made you upset—"

"He didn't," I interrupt. "It wasn't him. Things got a bit overwhelming, that's all."

We emerge from underground, and the chemical smell of the janitor's closet stings my nose. Shutting the hatch, we walk side-by-side down the empty corridor. Every step sends a ripple of anxiety through me. Only a two-hour drive until we're at the Commander's camp. This is the moment I've been anticipating for months, but it doesn't make it any easier to process.

Voices circulate in the main room of the warehouse at the end of the corridor. I immediately recognize Adam's, followed by Seb's laughter, the sound sending a rush of relief over me. I know Nixon said he was okay, but hearing him snuffs out my remaining doubts.

The three of them are waiting at the single back door nestled between two shelving units. Back pressed against the door, Seb notices us first, flashing a grin and nudging Nixon beside him. The two of them are equipped with their own backpacks, and each holds a submachine gun. Unease worms its way through my gut at the sight of the weapons, but I tell myself they're just a precaution. We may not be far from our destination, but anything could happen between here and there.

"There's my new favorite person!" Seb says, looking directly at me as we approach.

"Didn't she attack you?" Liam says.

"She did, which only makes me like her more. Pretty ballsy to tackle someone holding a gun."

"Sorry about that," I say. Heat creeps into my face. "How are you feeling after…?"

"Being shot?" Seb grins again, and the dimple in his cheek reappears. "It wasn't my first time, but I'm good."

"'Good' is an overstatement," Adam says. "You can expect a lot of pain during the next few weeks. Don't get ahead of yourself."

"Yeah, yeah, I got it." Seb pushes himself from the door with a wince, and his empty hand moves to his abdomen. "Let's get the hell out of here."

Adam opens the door, and we file outside after him. The midday sun offers a subtle warmth, promising that this brutal winter will soon come to an end. Behind the warehouse, a chain-link fence encompasses the plot of graveled land with several rows of battered vehicles. There are at least a couple dozen of them, some with crumpled hoods and missing tires, others severely eroded by rust; heaps of metal and plastic litter the ground between them. As we walk, I spot a few cars that appear to be in decent shape—mismatched fenders and front ends, but intact.

At the very back, the gate is open and the compact car and Humvee I recognize from last night await us. Four men, whom I suspect are our escorts, finish loading up the two vehicles, and Adam breaks away to talk with them.

"Ivy, you're with me," Nixon says, slipping his bag off and dropping it in the open trunk of the car.

My stomach drops. Since leaving the Northern Unity, I haven't been alone with him—aside from this morning.

"Why is she with you?" Liam asks, stopping beside me.

"We still have some things to talk about." Nixon extends his hand for my backpack. I hesitantly pass it to him and he stores it with his, shutting the trunk and facing the rest of us. "And I don't want to hear Seb whine."

"Is this because of my comment about your face earlier?" Seb asks.

Nixon smirks. "No, but now that you've brought it up again, I definitely don't want to be stuck with you."

"So put Ivy with him," Liam says.

"You really want to do that to her?" Nixon says jokingly.

I glance at Liam. His face is rigid, and he grips the strap of his backpack. "It can't wait?"

"It's fine, Liam," I say. "We're all going to the same place."

"They're ready," Adam says, making his way back to us. "The Commander's aware that you're on the way."

I throw my arms over Liam's shoulders, and he returns the embrace with one arm. As we hug, I block out the others' voices and close my eyes, praying that this won't be the final one we share.

"I love you," I say into Liam's shirt, "and I'll see you in a couple hours."

"I love you, too," he says with a squeeze. "Don't let him get to you."

I pull back and open my mouth to ask what he means, but I'm interrupted by Seb shouting, "Liam, let's *go!*" from the back of the Humvee.

Liam rolls his eyes. "See you soon, V." He shuffles toward the vehicle and walks around to the other side. The door opens and he swings his backpack off, throwing me one final glance before climbing in.

A hand rests on my shoulder, and I turn to see Adam.

"I'm glad you're safe, Ivy," he says with a smile.

"Thank you," I say. "For everything."

"No thanks needed. Good luck, and I'll see you in a few days."

With a final goodbye, I walk toward Nixon, who's waiting beside the open back door of the car, talking with one of our escorts—a man with a short red ponytail and trimmed beard.

"Ready?" Nixon asks.

I nod. "I think so."

"We'll take good care of you, Ivy," the escort says, flashing a quick smile as he opens the driver's side. "James and I have made this trip hundreds of times."

Nixon steps aside and I slide into the back, stopping at the middle seat. To my right are a large red medical bag, a rucksack, and several ammo boxes stamped with different numbers. The other man—James—is in the passenger seat with a rifle propped between his legs.

Closing the door, Nixon readjusts his gun on its sling beside me. The Humvee rolls forward first, and our driver follows once it clears the gate. Gravel crunches beneath the tires, kicking up dust as we leave the outpost.

I cross my legs and fold my arms in my lap, trying to take up as little space as possible like I did in Addison's car. Nixon remains pressed against the door, watching the world blur past us.

"So, you guys rebuild vehicles here?" he says.

The driver glances up at his rearview mirror. "Mostly as a cover in case anyone comes poking around. We only use a few of the ones we rebuild."

"What about the rest?"

"Use the parts we can," James says without looking away from the windshield, "and trade the rest for resources. Antiques go for a lot."

"Trade with who?" Nixon asks.

"Canada and Mexico, mostly."

The Commander has ties with other countries? How much power does this man have exactly? Being an enemy of the Enlightened Society in the middle of a wasteland, I expected him and his isolated group to be completely off the grid.

Nixon doesn't react to the information, though. He just watches the window with a hand on his gun.

"So the Commander's camp..." I say, and the driver's eyes flick up to me. "You've been there—what's it like?"

He offers a smile that reaches his eyes and glances at his partner. "You'll have to see for yourself, but I can tell you now that it's nothing like what you're expecting."

"Have you ever had trouble from the Society there?" Nixon asks.

James shakes his head, shifting in his seat. "Pretty quiet out there. The first forty miles outside the wall is the area you really need to worry about."

Where the re-education camps are, as well as people like the scavengers. Although I imagine there are still stragglers past that forty-mile threshold, which makes me wonder if the Commander or resistance in general helps them. Citizens of the Northern Unity seem to be their main priority, but who's helping the vulnerable out here? Who's preventing them from making deals with the Society or being kidnapped for the auction?

"Are you from the Northern Unity?" I ask, bracing myself against the front passenger seat as the road gets bumpier.

"I'm not," James says, stretching his arms above his head, "but Micah here is." As he turns to the driver, I notice a glossy scar that stretches from his receding hairline to his bushy eyebrow. "How long have you been out here now—three years?"

Micah nods. "Something like that, thanks to my dad."

"What made him want to leave?" Nixon asks. "Aside from the obvious."

"Commander needed some help outside the walls and trusted him enough to do the job." Micah waves a hand in the air, dismissing the topic. "Long story, but you made a good replacement."

Nixon sits up straighter. "Your dad was the Green Zone's leader?"

"Yup—though he was nowhere near as ambitious as you, from what I've heard."

"What exactly have you heard?"

"Don't listen to him," James says. "He doesn't know shit aside from what's gone down the past couple months."

"That's all I need to know," Micah says. "This guy's made more waves than my old man ever did. And you"—he glances over his shoulder at me with raised eyebrows—"have been all anyone has talked about the past few days. Even the Commander was shocked when Eli told him."

My heart stops, and I sink back in my seat. He knows. The Commander knows everything without me having had a chance to fully explain myself.

"Sensitive subject," Nixon says.

"Which we're not supposed to talk about anyway," James puts in, reaching over the center console and turning one of the dials below the air vents.

The whir of the heat on full blast drowns out the sound of every bump we hit on the neglected road. I focus on the Humvee directly in front of us through the dirt-streaked windshield, but in my peripheral vision, I see Nixon look at me with a solemn expression.

I search for something else I can say to change the subject, but I'm not in the mood for small talk and honestly don't care about anything other than getting to the camp. The car already feels too cramped. Every second I sit here, I quickly become more restless, and I wish they had just allowed our original squad our own vehicle with the four escorts in the second. Or at the very least, I wish I could've been paired with Liam. With him, there wouldn't be any suffocating tension. But Nixon chose me for a reason.

Taking a deep breath, I inch closer to him and whisper, "What did you need to talk to me about?"

"That woman you saw," he whispers back. "Was there any mention of her son?"

"No." I focus on his calm expression to keep the flashbacks at bay. "I mean, she did say she had two kids when… when everything was happening. But that's it."

"And the guy you mentioned—Nolan. What was his last name?"

"Astor."

Pressing his lips together, he nods and sits back. "Did you meet his wife?"

"Bridgett? Yeah, once." I angle myself toward him. "How do you know about her?"

"Seb and Isaiah interrogated Nolan's bodyguard, who attended my execution with him. They reported Nolan had purchased a woman from another family a week prior, and Bridgett was briefly mentioned."

That fits with what Bridgett told me—that the woman was one of the ones who was passed around to multiple people. She even went as far as saying Nolan and Wyatt did her a favor by ending her suffering.

Nausea creeps over me, and I rest my cheek against the back of my seat. I remember Wyatt telling me that woman wasn't a citizen anyway—no one would miss her. I knew it was messed up then, but now I know she has a son trapped in the Northern Unity and a daughter out here, it's so much worse. Abducting their own citizens isn't enough for them. They have to rip apart families outside the walls, too, in order to satiate their disgusting desires.

"She was a victim, too," I whisper. "Bridgett."

"I'm guessing that's why you asked about Transitional Adaptation last night?"

I nod, concentrating on the cool leather against my cheek.

"What was she like?"

"Totally brainwashed. Like, worse than I was when you first met me."

Nixon smirks. "That's hard to believe."

The small joke makes me giggle, and the lingering tension begins to recede. We sit in silence for a few minutes with the hum of the engine and steady gust of heat. Micah and James have begun talking amongst themselves, but I don't pay attention to their conversation.

I glance up front to make sure the Humvee is still ahead of us and wonder if Liam is still upset that I'm not paired with him. My fear of losing him again makes me wish I had been, but for now, I'm content with being with Nixon, as long as another argument doesn't ensue.

What happened this morning has already exhausted me, and right now I feel just as vulnerable as I did then. I didn't expect to explode like that, but I'm glad I was able to let it all out. Does Nixon see me differently because of it, though? Because of how I reacted and everything I said?

It wasn't my fault. I did what I had to do in order to survive. But there's still a part of me clinging to the person I was before, the person I was when we first met, and I don't want that to change.

"Wyatt attended your execution, too," I say. "I'm almost surprised he didn't force me to go."

"Probably thought it would make him lose control of you," Nixon says. "Although it's clear he never really had that to begin with."

He leans his head back, facing me, and searches my eyes for a moment. The intensity of his gaze has softened, and for just a second, I think I see a glimpse of the tenderness I became familiar with in the Blue Zone.

"You're really brave, you know that?" he finally says, in a low voice so the others don't hear.

I roll my eyes. "I don't feel it."

I spent six weeks cowering and giving in to every one of Wyatt's commands. It wasn't a complete waste of time, since I was able to gather information, but why didn't I try to escape sooner? Or try harder to find a member of the Red Zone's resistance?

"You are," Nixon says. "You went through all that by yourself and escaped without any help."

"Eli's scouts were outside," I remind him.

"But you didn't know that. You were determined to get out no matter what. And even when you saw Liam there, you didn't ask him for help. You tried to protect him by telling him to leave, and faced it on your own."

I shrug one shoulder. "Guess you rubbed off on me a bit."

He smiles, but it's tinged with remorse. "I'm proud of you. You'd make a great resistance member."

Heat creeps into my face. I avert my eyes, focusing instead on the hand on his gun. "What I said this morning, when I was rambling about the Red Zone and mentioned you… thinking about you… I—"

His hand slides from the weapon and drops to the seat between us. After a moment of hesitation, he moves it closer, his fingers brushing against mine, and an electric current shoots through me. Part of me wants to recoil, to keep this barrier that's formed between us. But the overwhelming majority of me yearns for this to happen, begging me to try to find comfort in his touch again.

It's against the rules. We could both get into trouble. But right now, I need it. Despite my uncertainty of everything else, this is the one thing I'm sure of.

I tuck my fingers into his palm, and he closes his hand around them.

"I thought about you, too," he whispers, gently running his thumb over my skin. "All the time."

30. Waking Dream

Ivy

"Ten minutes," I hear Micah say.

I shift in my seat, eyes closed, not having realized I'd dozed off. For a moment I don't know where I am, and it's not until each of my senses slowly turns on that I remember what's happening. The hum of the engine and the overwhelming smell of old leather remind me I'm in the back of the car with the escorts up front. I open my eyes, blinking away my blurry vision, and the driver's seat comes into focus.

We're almost at the Commander's camp. Anxiety twists in my stomach, knowing I'll soon have to face him and rehash everything I've already explained. I don't know which I'm more afraid of—explaining it all to the head of the entire resistance, or what his reaction will be. As far as he's concerned, I'm a liability, a threat to his organization.

Nixon moves beside me, and when he does, I realize my head is resting on his shoulder. I groggily sit up and push my hair from my face. Embarrassment settles in, intensifying when I look down at our hands still folded over one another.

He turns to me, expression unreadable, and I curse myself. This wasn't supposed to happen, and I wonder if he's thinking the same thing. I remember resting my head against him for a moment when I was answering questions about Nolan—where I first met him, how many times I saw him, what I knew about his family—but I don't remember falling asleep.

"Did I wake you?" Nixon asks, pulling his hand free.

"Um, no," I say, directing my attention to the windshield. "Sorry, I didn't mean to fall asleep." The road is smoother out here than it was near the outpost. Fewer potholes speckle the asphalt, and freshly painted lines separate the two lanes. "Did I miss anything?"

"Small detour, but that's it."

Micah veers to the right, taking a ramp onto the interstate. A sea of trees sprouts on either side, concealing the ground below. Mountains jut up on the horizon, and the late afternoon sun slices through the dense fog that hangs over them. The openness and endless nature are tranquil, and for a moment, it reminds me of when I first arrived in the Blue Zone with Nixon.

"We were talking about Nolan, right?" I say, looking at Nixon.

Eyes closed, he shakes his head, his hair rubbing against the leather seat. "We don't have to keep talking about it if you don't want to. I think I have all I need."

Sitting back, I pull one leg onto the seat and rest my head on my knee. As much as I hate reliving it all, it does feel nice to have someone I can open up to—someone who's been through something similar and can understand where I'm coming from.

"What else did that bodyguard say about him?" I ask.

"Not much," Nixon says. "He did mention Wyatt and Nolan were close, which you already know."

'Close' is an understatement. Liam and Nixon are close, but they don't indulge in assaulting and murdering women like Wyatt and Nolan did. Nolan's just as dangerous as Wyatt was, if not more. By now, he must have heard about Wyatt's murder, and I imagine he'll stop at nothing to find who did it. With my tracker left at the scene of the crime, it won't be difficult to pin me for it.

As long as I stay at the camp, the Society shouldn't find me. I never want to find out what punishment awaits me if I ever face Nolan again. I'm sure he wouldn't allow me a painless death. But I don't want to live in hiding forever either.

The car gradually slows, coming to a complete stop. An indistinct voice comes from outside, and I look up toward the front of the car. We're stopped at the bottom of a ramp off the interstate. Several men with guns are positioned near the exit along a towering barbed-wire fence, one speaking to the driver of the Humvee from the booth of a security checkpoint that looks eerily similar to the ones in the Northern Unity. After a moment, the barrier rises and we're allowed through. I lean forward, sliding my leg off the seat.

"Holy shit," I say. "Nixon, look."

Micah makes a right off the ramp, and we follow the Humvee onto a four-lane road surrounded by fully intact buildings.

"It's a fucking city," Nixon says, peering around the driver's seat.

James looks back at us with a proud smile. "Welcome to the Commander's camp."

A handful of other vehicles zip past us. Passersby of all different ages amble down the sidewalks and shuffle in and out of buildings. Strings of lights are wound around the bare branches of the trees that dot the sidewalks.

I search the area for any sign of soldiers or militarized law enforcement, but there aren't any aside from the guards at the entrance. Nor are there any flags that bear the Northern Unity's symbol fluttering in the wind. The atmosphere even feels lighter. Genuine smiles brighten the faces of people we pass, and their heads are held higher than those of the citizens back home.

Elation bursts in my chest, and every muscle in my body relaxes. Everything I've been fretting over for the past few days dissolves, washed away by the odd serenity that envelops this new place.

We made it. We're free.

"How?" Nixon asks. "How do you guys have a fully functioning city?"

"Lots of work and dedication on the Commander's part," Micah says. "It took a while to restore what was left here from the Old World."

We drive through the downtown area, where buildings are packed tightly together and vegetation is more scarce. Neon lights and signs boast that everything from restaurants to shopping centers are open for business, and the brightly painted exteriors bring more life to the space. Despite the restorations to the old city, though, the antiquity of it is still apparent from the elaborate ornamentation from the Old World and the fissures in the bricks and concrete.

"The Commander will be able to answer all of your questions when you meet him tomorrow," James says.

I relax a bit more. At least I have time to mull over what I'm going to say and prepare for whatever questions might be asked.

Micah follows the Humvee onto a one-way street where the towering buildings' shadows stretch across the asphalt. To my right, picnic tables dot the sidewalk. Families, couples, and people dressed in business attire lounge in the plaza, talking, laughing, and eating as if there isn't a cult of Elites a few hours from here that would auction them off without a second thought. As if there aren't others outside the Northern Unity's walls who are struggling to survive.

Seeing people act so normal, so carefree, is both comforting and infuriating. I'm relieved that we've made it here, that we have a safe place to stay without the constant worry of being captured or beaten or tortured. But simmering anger wars with that relief. The Commander has a fully functioning city, the resources to care for those in need. So why are there so many still suffering? Why are there people in the wasteland who resort to making deals with the Enlightened Society as a desperate means to survive?

We pull into a parking garage, and Micah parks the car in a spot marked as 'reserved' beside the Humvee.

"I'll take them in," James says, propping his gun against the dashboard and opening his door.

Micah presses a button beside the steering wheel, and I hear the trunk pop open. Seb slides out of the Humvee beside us and Liam walks around the back, taking Seb's backpack and gun for him. Although I knew they were directly in front of us the whole time, seeing them brings another wave of relief.

"Ready?" Nixon asks me.

I nod, and we both thank Micah as we slide out. James's voice echoes throughout the concrete space as he chats with one of the other escorts through the Humvee's rolled-down window. The voices of people outside drift into the parking garage, and I find myself staring out at them again, still wondering how all of this is possible.

"Dude, can you believe this?" Seb asks as he and Liam approach us.

Nixon pulls our bags from the trunk and passes me mine while shouldering his. "Definitely not what I expected," he says, shutting the trunk. "Did your escorts tell you anything about this place?"

"Not really," Liam says. "Just that the Commander will explain everything. You?"

"No," Nixon says. He looks around, gripping his gun, as if expecting soldiers or Black Hats to appear any second. "But I have a weird feeling about it."

"What, you don't trust them?" Seb asks.

It *is* weird, and I definitely have questions, as I'm sure the other three do, but they haven't given us a reason not to trust them. They've had plenty of time to turn us in if they wanted to—and with Adam's presence at the outpost, Nixon should be the least skeptical.

"Not necessarily that," Nixon says. "Just a feeling."

"The Northern Unity's over a hundred miles from here," Liam says. "I don't think we have anything to worry about."

"You four," James calls, "this way."

Seb and Nixon follow him toward a set of double glass doors across the garage, and Liam and I fall into step behind them. The glass doors slide open as we near them, along with a second set on the other side.

We enter a hotel lobby, and its warmth envelops me. Our shoes squeak on polished tile slabs, and the sharp smell of lemongrass pulls me in. Several lounge chairs and end tables have been set up toward the front of the lobby, near another entrance that looks out onto the one-way street.

The man and woman behind the white, marble check-in desk greet us with warm smiles, and I'm suddenly uneasy. Although they appear harmless, with their navy-blue button-up shirts and glimmering gold name tags, I've seen too many faces like that with an ulterior motive hidden behind them. I look to Seb and Liam beside me for their reactions, but their expressions are blank.

"Good to see you again, James," the woman behind the desk says. Her eyes drift to Nixon beside him, then the three of us.

"You, too, Mia," James says, propping an arm on the desk in front of her computer. "I need rooms for these four. They're resistance members from the Northern Unity, seeking asylum and scheduled to meet the Commander tomorrow."

Mia's eyes widen, but her smile doesn't falter. "Of course. Presidential suite?"

"Perfect."

While she types away on her keyboard, her coworker produces two keycards from the drawer between them. Handing them to James, he looks at Nixon and says, "Room service menus are in the suite. Feel free to order whatever you'd like. Our rooftop restaurant is open until eleven o'clock, as well as our bar and lounge. If you need anything at all, let us know."

"Thank you," Nixon says.

"I'll show you your room," James says, pushing himself off the desk. "Have fun, you two," he adds to the desk clerks.

We follow James to the three elevators to the left. The middle one slides open as soon as he pushes the button, and we pile inside. I scrunch myself into the corner with Liam beside me, and once the elevator closes, the space feels tighter. I focus on my breathing as we're lifted, praying we don't stop for anyone else to enter as the green number above the door creeps up with each floor we pass. Thankfully, we don't.

On the seventh floor, James leads us down a long hall that's decorated with potted plants and abstract paintings and stops to unlock the dark wooden door at the very end.

"Welcome home," he says, pushing the door open.

I follow Seb and Nixon in with Liam behind me. A short hallway stretches before us with a door to my right and an identical one at the end. We take a left, which opens out into a living room and dining area. A picture window with smaller windows on either side looks out onto a large balcony, decorated with more plants and four sets of tables and chairs.

"We're staying *here*?" Liam asks, dropping the backpacks and guns on the wooden dining table. Seb collapses onto the small, charcoal-gray sectional couch that looks like it's more for decoration than comfort.

"Yup," James says, and points a thumb toward the hall behind him. "Two separate king beds and bathrooms. Help yourselves to whatever you want. I'll be here quarter till one tomorrow to pick you all up for your meeting. My contact information is written down in both rooms if you need anything from me specifically."

"And until then?" Nixon asks.

James shrugs one shoulder and hands him the keycards. "Relax here, visit the spa, explore the city. Whatever you want. The Commander is covering the cost of the hotel, food, and entertainment, so if anyone asks, tell them you're with him."

"Why?" I ask. "Why is he paying for everything?"

Letting us seek refuge here is one thing, footing the bill for everything we do is completely different, and my skepticism grows. Maybe he does this for everyone who escapes the Northern Unity—however many that's been—but it's all still odd, like Nixon said.

James smirks. "Your mission is a high-profile one. He wants to make sure you're safe and comfortable."

That's not an answer, though—at least not to me. But it's been made clear that we won't get any real answers until we meet him tomorrow. I glance at the clock hanging on the wall above the dining table. Around twenty past three. Less than twenty-four hours until our meeting.

"Well, if you don't need anything else, I'll head out and see you all tomorrow," James says.

"Wait," Nixon says, facing him. "Is Adam's wife here? Lacey Reed?"

"She is. Why?"

"I want to see her. I'm their son."

"No shit," James says with a smile and a hint of disbelief. "That explains why Adam spoke so highly of you. Their place isn't far from here; Micah and I can take you if you want."

Nixon looks back at the rest of us as if asking for approval.

"Go," Seb says. "I'll be in charge of these two."

Nixon rolls his eyes. "Liam."

"I'll make sure he doesn't do anything stupid," Liam says, sitting on the edge of the couch. "We'll meet up with you here later."

"I'll let Micah know," James says, walking toward the exit. "Meet us in the garage when you're ready."

A moment later, the door to our suite clicks shut, and Nixon sets his stuff down next to the rest on the dining table. I shrug off my own backpack and drop it onto one of the two leather club chairs in the corner of the living room.

"Ivy," Nixon says, "do you want to come?"

Liam looks at him, his fingers digging tensely into the corner of the couch cushion.

"What?" I ask.

I wouldn't mind seeing Lacey again, but I don't want to interrupt his time with her either. With everything he's been through, including finding out that Piper is the reason we were captured, he deserves some alone time with his mom, someone he can fully open up to.

"You don't have to," Nixon says, walking to the counter at the back of the dining area and placing the second keycard by the coffee maker, "but I know she's going to ask about you."

Part of me doubts that, but she did open her home to me when I was hiding from the Society, and made the transition from law-abiding citizen to fugitive easier. I should at least thank her for all that she did.

"Uh, sure," I say, looking at Liam.

He forces a tight smile and says, "Have fun. I'll see you later."

Does he know something? Is it because of how he found me and Nixon in the bunker?

"Looks like you're my dinner date, Liam," Seb says, nudging Liam with his elbow.

"No drinking, Seb," Nixon says. "I don't need you hungover tomorrow."

"Yes, sir," Seb says sarcastically, and I hold back a smile. "But I expect a full night of partying after we meet your boss."

Liam stands and wraps an arm around my shoulders. "Be careful. We don't know what this place is like yet."

"Yeah, you too," I say. "And have fun with your *date*."

Liam drops his arm, and I follow Nixon toward the exit before I can change my mind.

31. Be Somebody

Nixon

Ivy and I start up the gravel driveway toward the blue two-story house, and Micah and James's car pulls away behind us. The rocks crunch under our boots, filling the awkward silence that has wedged itself between us.

I control our pace, taking slow, casual steps while I figure out what I'm going to say to Lacey. I'm torn on whether I should act as if what happened isn't a big deal or if I should apologize. Ultimately, her and Adam's capture wasn't my fault, but I was the one who came up with the idea of seeking refuge at their place after the safehouse was ambushed. There were other safehouses we could've stayed at, but I didn't want to take the risk of those getting found out, too. I thought I was keeping the Blue Zone's group safe by staying away, but it backfired.

"Nervous?" Ivy asks. Her hands are shoved in her jacket pockets, and her nose has already turned a light pink from the cold.

"What makes you think that?" I ask.

"You're chewing on your lip. You do that when something's bothering you."

I press my lips together, not having realized I was doing it or that she's ever noticed. "Studying people's mannerisms now?"

She lets out a light chuckle. "No, definitely not on your level. Just something I picked up on from… before."

The way she says the last word makes me want to ask her to elaborate. I know what she means, but I want to hear how she describes it, whether she'll specifically mention how we used to be. Just to test the waters. Neither of us has touched on the subject again, but by the way she held my hand and leaned into me on our way from the outpost, I know there has to be at least a remnant of whatever it was that we had.

Now that everything's begun to settle, I realize that every part of me hopes there *is* something left between us. As much as I've tried to push those thoughts away, I felt them in the bunker when I was holding her again. Despite the circumstances, that trust was there, and it's only strengthened since leaving the outpost. When she held my hand in the car and fell asleep curled up against me, there was no place I would have rather been in that moment.

"A little nervous," I admit.

"About seeing Lacey?"

I shrug. "That, and meeting the Commander tomorrow."

We step onto the covered plywood porch, and I knock on the oak door.

"This feels a bit like déjà vu," Ivy says.

She's right—this feels exactly the same as when we first showed up at Adam and Lacey's together. Only this time, we're actually safe, as hard as that is to believe.

The door swings open, and Lacey freezes in the doorway, covering her mouth. Her wide brown eyes fill with tears and she pulls me into a hug, squeezing tighter than her small frame should allow her.

"Oh my God!" she says. "You have no idea how happy I am to see you."

I wrap my arms around her, trying not to wince at the dull pain that returns to my ribs. "I'm happy to see you, too."

She pulls back and holds my face in her hands. A couple of stray tears trail down her cheeks, but she smiles through them. "I was so worried about you. I cried with joy when Adam told me he was going to meet you at the outpost. Like I am now." She laughs and wipes her face with one hand, turning to Ivy and pulling her into a gentler embrace. "I'm so glad you're safe, sweetie. This must have been so difficult for you."

"It's great to see you again, Lacey," Ivy says with the first genuine smile I've seen from her these past few days.

Lacey holds her close a moment longer before breaking away, wiping more tears that have spilled over. "Come inside," she says, ushering us in.

We step into a bright, cozy living room that branches off to an open eat-in kitchen. Lacey's high heels click against the wood floor. She slips them off, pushing them against the side of the white sofa before continuing to the kitchen. Ivy and I take a seat at the bar, which makes this feel even more like when we first arrived in the Blue Zone. Ivy throws me a sideways glance, and I know she's thinking the same thing.

"Are you two hungry?" Lacey asks, pulling her dainty silver watch off her wrist and setting it on the granite counter. She opens the fridge and leans against the door, searching its contents. "I just got home from work, so I haven't cooked anything yet." Without waiting for an answer, she begins pulling items out and lays them on the counter—ravioli, marinara sauce, and shredded mozzarella, all packed in unlabeled glass containers.

"Don't worry about it, Lacey," I say.

"After everything you two have been through, I want to cook for you." She grabs two pots from one of the lower cabinets and fills one with water from the sink in front of us. "Although it won't be anything too extravagant; I don't do much grocery shopping when Adam's not here."

She moves the pot to the stove and clicks on the eye. "We were so relieved when we heard you'd be leaving the Northern Unity," she says, tying her long black hair into a ponytail before dumping the marinara into the second pot. "We were especially surprised to hear about you, Ivy."

"So I've been told," Ivy says with an awkward smile. "Our escort said even the Commander was shocked."

"I'm sure he was," Lacey says. "I take it you haven't met him yet?" She looks at me when she asks the question, but her eyes briefly click to Ivy as she leans back against the counter.

"Tomorrow," I say. "What can you tell us about him?"

"He's not as scary as you're probably expecting," Lacey says. "I don't frequent his office, but from the couple times I've met him, I know he's a kind man who's dedicated to his work."

Of course she's not around him often—she never officially joined the resistance. I should've squeezed some answers out of Adam back at the outpost, but I was too focused on whether Seb was going to make it through the night.

"So, I'm guessing you don't know much about this place either," Ivy says. "Like how there's a fully functioning city off the Society's radar."

"Not the technicalities, no," Lacey says, "but I'm sure you'll get the answers you're looking for tomorrow."

"It *is* off the Society's radar, right?" I ask, leaning forward and folding my arms on the counter. "You have to admit, this all seems too good to be true."

Lacey smiles and stands in front of me, resting a hand on my arm. "I promise you you're safe here. You have nothing to worry about."

That's not a yes or a no. She knows something. She has to. Maybe not as much as the resistance members here, but at least a shred of information. There's no way she'd commit to staying here other-wise—she questions things too much.

"Are we expected to stay here permanently?" I ask.

"I don't know, sweetie," she says. "I'm assuming Ivy will, but I don't know about you and your members who came with you." Turning, she pulls off the rubber lid of the glass container and dumps the ravioli into the boiling water. "Of course, there's a selfish part of me that does want you to stay."

Ivy looks at me, eyebrows raised. "You plan to go back?"

I shrug, sinking back in the barstool. Until now, I haven't really thought about it. Since I'm a fugitive, it's probably not likely that I can return to the Green Zone, but I'm still a leader. I have a group that needs me—and like Eli said, the resistance is spread thin with Nadia's second-in-command assuming responsibility for them and Piper's probation. All I really cared about when launching this mission was making sure Ivy was safe, and although I want to stay with her, I can't abandon my team.

"What about Liam?" Ivy asks.

"I don't know," I say.

He has an alibi, thanks to Addison. Assuming Eli could get him back inside, it would be easier for him to return without too many questions being raised. But he's Ivy's brother; she doesn't deserve to have him taken away again.

"It's all up to the Commander," Lacey says, "and whatever he thinks is best."

"I'm not losing you two again," Ivy whispers to me.

I wish I could make the same promise to her as I did when we originally planned to come here, but I've quickly learned that making promises you can't keep only hurts yourself—and others—more.

I'm tempted to reach for her, to hold her hand and offer some sort of comfort like I did earlier, but I don't. I can't. Not in front of Lacey.

"We'll just have to see what happens," I tell her. "Maybe I can talk to him." It's the best I can offer right now without knowing much about the Commander or what exactly is going on here.

"Might be easier said than done," Lacey says, glancing at us as she stirs the ravioli with a wooden spoon in one hand, pulling three plates from the cupboard with the other. "The Commander is pretty understanding, but the stunt you pulled to get here is still an issue."

"You heard about that?" I ask.

"Just from Adam. I don't know all of the details."

It didn't seem like Adam knew all the details either, which is good. I just hope Eli didn't share too many with the Commander. Even though it appears that most, if not all, members of the Society know about me and Ivy, I'm still holding on to the hope that he doesn't.

"What stunt?" Ivy asks.

"He went against the Commander's orders," Lacey says in a lighthearted tone. "Rather than staying in the Green Zone like he was supposed to, he put together a team to get to the Red Zone to save you."

"What?" Ivy says with a laugh. "*You* went against orders? While preaching to me about how I should follow yours?"

"I had my reasons." I can't hold back a smirk. "You, on the other hand, were being stubborn."

"I had my reasons," she repeats in a mocking voice. I'm almost surprised at how relaxed and comfortable she is right now. Lacey has that effect on people, though, and I'm happy to see Ivy beginning to revert back to her old self.

"Seems to me you're the stubborn one here," Lacey says to me as she sets a plate in front of each of us.

"I get it from you," I say, and she laughs. The sound of it breaks up some of the tension and makes all of this feel a bit more normal. "You think I'll get kicked out for it?"

Lacey presses her lips together and looks between the two of us, her eyes lingering a second longer on Ivy. "Disciplined? Yes. Kicked out? No. I think your dedication says a lot more about you than your disobedience."

The sentiment takes the edge off my growing anxiety. I hope she's right, but I'm naturally preparing for the worst. If not because of the forbidden mission then for the rumors from the auction. It never hit me that he might know about the kiss until Ivy suggested it. Now it's one of the main things running through my head, and what makes it worse is that those feelings have been rekindled. Looking at her now—seeing her smile, hearing her laugh—I can't deny them.

"And I wouldn't expect any less from you," Lacey says. "Sometimes following your heart is better than following orders."

"Yeah," Ivy says, bumping my knee with hers. "Sounds like your mom knows what she's talking about."

Lacey winks. "I normally do."

"Okay," I say, raising my hands in surrender. "I don't need you both ganging up on me."

"Why not?" Ivy asks, sliding off the stool. "It's fun."

I roll my eyes but return her smile, feeling calmer.

"Can I use your bathroom?" she asks.

"Of course," Lacey says, nodding toward the small hall behind her that leads to a back door. "First door on your left."

Stirring the sauce and adjusting the heat, Lacey glances at me from the corner of her eye with a playful smirk.

"What's that look for?" I ask. I know it all too well—normally something she does when she already knows something I haven't told her.

"Nothing," she says, shaking her head. A beat of silence passes, then, "Are you two…?"

The panic I felt when Adam insinuated the same thing returns, although I'm less surprised to hear it coming from her. She automatically assumed Ivy and I were together the first time she saw us, and she knew we'd been sneaking outside when we were staying with them. No point in trying to play dumb.

"No," I say in a low voice. "I don't know. I… want to be."

"But?"

I sigh, propping my head against my fist. "We've been fighting, and it's mostly been my fault."

"I see." She removes the ravioli from the stove and drains it in the sink, steam temporarily masking her face. "Did you apologize?"

"Yeah, but that doesn't change any of it."

She sets the pot aside. With her hands pressed on the counter, her dark, tender eyes lock on mine. "It takes a strong man to say he's sorry, and an even stronger one to show it. Don't focus on what you did wrong; focus on how you can show you were sincere in your apology. You care about her, and she clearly cares about you, too."

"What makes you say that?"

She smiles. "Maybe Adam didn't notice how you acted with each other, but I did. Especially after you questioned Kase, and Liam and Addison showed up. If that were no longer the case, do you really think she would've come here with you?"

"She likes you."

Lacey raises her eyebrows, clearly not buying the excuse.

I sigh, sitting back. "You know just as well as I do that we can't be together. It's against the rules, and I might have to leave."

"It sounds more like you're trying to find a reason why you shouldn't care about her anymore."

I'm not trying to find a reason—I already know it. But I still do care about her, maybe even more than I did before, as if what we've endured has simultaneously pushed us apart and brought us together. Whatever bond or feelings or affection I had, it's stronger. Despite having argued with her for days, I feel closer to her.

"She's my mission and Liam's sister," I say. "Even you know it's against the rules."

"I see." Lacey grabs a few forks from one of the drawers and distributes them. She's quiet for a moment, and I wonder if she's somehow heard the rumors about us, too. "But you do care about her."

"Yes. More than I should."

"Then it's up to you to decide if she's worth the risk of getting into trouble. Only you can make that decision."

After we finish eating, we sit at the table for a couple more hours, talking to Lacey about anything we can think of that isn't related to the resistance. It mostly consists of Lacey asking Ivy about her life when it was normal—what her parents were like, how she and Liam grew up, and comparing their relationship to mine and Piper's when we were younger.

When Ivy's dad is briefly brought up, she shifts in her chair beside me and runs her fingers through her hair. She hasn't spoken of him since our argument over whether I killed him, and I'm still not sure if she believes me or the Society. But she answers the question—a simple one about what it was like being the Police Chief's daughter—and jokes that her dad was a hard-ass, yet someone she could always turn to. She even mentions the hot chocolate he always made as a remedy for any hardships and tells Lacey about the night she made it for the two of us, which makes Lacey flash me a knowing smirk.

"Adam told me Piper doesn't know you're here," I say when my sister's brought up again, unable to help myself. "Or even alive."

Lacey purses her lips. "She doesn't."

I understand why. If she's under investigation and indeed a threat to the resistance, she could tip off the Black Hats. But I was kept out of the loop too.

"You kept it from me, though," I say, unable to hide the hurt in my voice. "Was it because you thought I'd flipped too?"

"Sweetie, no." Lacey reaches across the table, clasping my hands in hers. Her eyebrows arch together, and pain flashes in her eyes. "That's not it at all. We wanted to. I even refused to leave the country at first—Adam can attest to that. But... we couldn't. The Commander didn't want Piper to find out where we were going. Just in case."

"You thought I'd tell her?"

"We weren't sure if you knew what she'd done yet." She squeezes my hands, as if silently pleading for me to believe her. "If it had been possible, I wouldn't have left until I had you with me. But they were expediting the trial, and there was already talk of shutting down borders. The Special Ops had to act quickly."

"Do you know why she did it?" Ivy asks. "Why she let Kase go?"

Lacey takes a deep breath and sits back. "It seems he and Piper had an ongoing relationship."

Unbelievable. She lectured me the day I was freed about my relationship with Ivy when she was doing something worse. Kase was one of her subordinates. A relationship like that is strictly forbidden. No exceptions. She should've learned that years ago from her experience with Jazmine.

"So she protected a traitor because she was sleeping with him," I say, frustration coating my words. "And she's still a leader."

"Not for long," Lacey says. "This is her second offence; the Commander won't overlook that."

"This is bullshit," I mutter.

"I know you're upset with her, but—"

"*Upset?* Ivy and I went through hell because of her!"

Without faltering, Lacey continues in a gentle tone, "*But* she didn't do it with the intention of harming you two, or the resistance. I'm not defending her by any means, but I know that much. And she will face the consequences for what she's done. The Commander isn't happy about it either." Her gaze drifts between the two of us before she focuses on me again. "Don't worry about that now, though. Focus on taking care of yourself."

I turn my head, looking out at the setting sun through the window in the living room. My selfish sister nearly had our parents killed and is the reason Ivy and I went through what we did. Anger pulses through me, strengthening the more I think about it, but I grind my teeth, preventing myself from saying anything else. This isn't Lacey's fault; she doesn't deserve me taking it out on her.

"We should get back to the hotel," I tell Ivy. Looking at her, the anger diminishes but doesn't fully disappear.

Lacey walks us out onto the front porch. "I don't mind driving you," she says.

"You go," Ivy tells me. "I want to walk."

"I'm not letting you go alone," I say.

"It's safe here," Lacey assures me, "but I don't blame you." Wrapping her arms around me—more gently this time—she kisses my cheek. "I love you so much."

"I love you, too," I tell her.

She pulls Ivy into a hug, whispering something in her ear, and brushes a strand of blonde hair from her face when she releases her. "It was good seeing you again, sweetie. Adam will be home in a couple days. We'd love to have you both over when he gets back."

Home. The word feels strange. I don't think of the Northern Unity as my home anymore, but this place doesn't quite feel like it either. Refuge, sure, but 'home' is a stretch, especially if there's a chance of me going back to the confinement of those walls. As of right now, this is temporary.

"Yeah," Ivy says, "we'd like that."

"Be careful, you two," Lacey says, rubbing my back before I step off the porch.

"We will," I say, and Ivy and I start down the gravel driveway.

32. Weight of the World

Ivy

I step out of the dark room, carefully shutting the door behind me, and Liam's snoring is muffled by the barrier. As desperate as I've been to get some uninterrupted rest, I can't turn my brain off. Everything continues to play out before my eyes, from the little girl we saw the first day outside the walls to the gang of scavengers. And in between those, my time in the Red Zone creeps to the front of my mind, Wyatt's face haunting me.

With my arms wrapped tightly around me, I shuffle down the short hall, glancing at Seb and Nixon's closed door as I pass it. For a fleeting moment I'm tempted to knock, to see if Nixon is as restless as

I am tonight. I want to be close to him again, but he needs his rest. He must be the most exhausted out of all of us, and earlier he stressed the importance of being reenergized for when we meet the Commander tomorrow—something I still can't believe is happening.

The city lights pour in through the picture windows, illuminating the living and dining rooms. As I pass through, I grab Nixon's jacket from where it's strewn over the back of the couch, shrug it on and roll the sleeves up over my wrists. His earthy scent immediately envelops me, bringing back the memory of when I first wore it—when we crossed over to the Blue Zone and he had me put it on when we went into the convenience store.

Unlocking the sliding glass door, I step out onto the terrace, tensing as the door squeals against its track. The cold concrete against my bare feet sends a shiver through me, but I ignore it. Pulling Nixon's jacket tighter, I cross the terrace and stop where the two railings meet at the corner, leaning over the cool metal.

The view is even more breathtaking than it was when we initially arrived. A handful of stars dot the sky that's washed out by the lights. The downtown area is alive with people walking the streets, their distant laughter and chatter finding its way to my ears. Patrons file in and out of bars and nightclubs. Music pulses through the air, sending a wave of euphoria over me. And just past the border of the city—of the Commander's camp—are the mountains, with the moon peeking out over them. From here I can make out the dense fog hanging over the range, appearing as plumes of smoke.

Out here we're free—truly free. No curfews or raids. No soldiers or Black Hats prowling the streets. There's no threat of re-education or execution. We can start over. At least, that's what everyone keeps saying.

The sentiment is comforting to an extent, but that doesn't mean I can forget everything I've been through and what others are going through.

And although we've been promised safety here, how long will that really last? Liam, Seb, and Nixon are all still part of the resistance. Just because we're here doesn't mean their work has stopped. Sooner or later, they'll be expected to carry out more missions, which may or may not be back inside those walls, and I don't think I can handle that. If anything were to happen to them, I don't know what I would do. Even if they're not sent back out there, how can the Commander be so confident the Society won't make their way here?

A hand brushes my back and I jump, panic igniting in my stomach.

"Sorry," Nixon says in a sleepy voice as he leans against the railing beside me, "didn't mean to scare you."

"Did I wake you?" I ask.

"Sort of. I heard the door."

"Sorry."

He shrugs and looks out toward the mountains. "I'm a light sleeper now anyway. What are you doing up?"

"Can't sleep. I thought coming out here would help… kinda like when we were in the Blue Zone."

"Performing our little ritual without me?" A smile tugs at his lips. "*And* stealing my jacket?"

Heat floods my face, and I'm thankful it's too dark for him to see. We stand in silence, leaning against the rails and watching the streets below us. Our arms are inches from one another, and I'm tempted to move closer like when we were in the car earlier. After our final explosive argument, though, I don't know exactly where we stand. Everything was laid out in the open, we made up, and I finally found the comfort I've been desperately missing. It's different from how it was before, but undoubtedly there. That alone showed me there has to be at least a sliver left of what we had, buried somewhere underneath all of the pain and torment we concealed with our spiteful words.

The words Lacey whispered to me as we were leaving her house replay in my head. *He needs you. Don't let him push himself too far away.*

"I've missed our ritual," I say, keeping my eyes forward.

"Me too," Nixon says after a beat of silence. He chews on his lip again. It's the first time I've seen him do it since we got to Lacey's. Until now, he's been noticeably calmer—shoulders less rigid and voice lighter.

"Thanks for what you did today, by the way. In the bunker, I mean. It helped a lot."

"You don't have to thank me." He turns his head. "I know I've made it difficult these past few days, but you can still talk to me whenever you want. I promise I won't jump to any conclusions." There's a trace of humor in his last sentence.

"You had every right to." What happened to me wasn't his fault, yet I was taking it all out on him without even considering what he's been through. "You can talk to me, too. About anything."

He nods slowly, folding his hands over the black metal bar. A few more moments of strained silence pass that I'm desperate to fill, but I can't think of anything to say. We're in this weird limbo, and I don't want to push anything, especially considering his nerves about meeting his boss tomorrow and what he learned about his sister.

I shift my weight to my other foot, taking the pressure off my sprained ankle, which Liam made me ice again when I got back. Other than asking how Lacey is, he didn't say anything about me going with Nixon. From the way he reacted when Nixon invited me, though, I know he didn't like the idea, and I wonder if the two of us being out here right now would bother him.

I glance back at the door. I'll have to go back in soon. If he wakes up for any reason, he'll notice I'm gone and come looking for me. The protective part of him has always been there, but it's more apparent now.

"I almost slit Seb's throat," Nixon mumbles.

"What?" I snap my attention to him. I can't have heard him correctly.

"Yeah." His gaze is locked on the mountains on the horizon. "I called for a training session with him, Liam, and a few other scouts the third day I was back, just so I could get myself used to everything again. It was fine at first, nothing I hadn't done before. Seb was on the opposing squad and grabbed me from behind when I infiltrated the house we were using, like he was supposed to... And I snapped." He shakes his head, and the corner of his mouth lifts in a sad smile. "I forgot where I was, what we were doing, and I pinned him down and pulled my knife. I didn't even recognize him when I was on top of him. If Liam hadn't been there to pull me out of it..."

That must've been what Seb and Liam meant when they said he's been different. He's struggling just as much as I am. He's just better at hiding it.

"But you didn't do it," I say, turning toward him. "You were able to stop yourself. Seb's fine."

"With Liam's help," Nixon emphasizes. "You should've seen their faces after I came out of it. I've never seen them so afraid."

"They understood, though, right? After what you went through?"

He doesn't respond.

"You haven't talked to them about it, have you?"

He closes his eyes and taps a finger against one of his knuckles. "No."

I exhale, looking at the door again. This may be my only opportunity to learn about what he's gone through, to understand him. If I shut it down, he might not want to talk about it again, and he clearly needs someone right now.

"Do you want to sit?" I motion toward one of the white tables with matching cushioned chairs.

He hesitates, but follows me. Pulling out the chair that faces the front of the terrace, he slumps back against the cushion. I take the seat next to him, dragging it closer so the armrests touch, the metal legs scraping against the concrete. Folding my legs underneath me, I prop an elbow on the table and study him. His eyes are distant. Not like when he was interrogating me, but closer to when he first told me the real story about his parents. Other than that, his expression is unreadable like it usually is—a mask hiding the pain underneath.

"Do you want to talk about what happened in the Red Zone?" I ask.

"I was interrogated," he says in a low voice after a short pause, "and beaten and tortured when I didn't comply. Deprived of sleep and food, whipped, dunked underwater, isolated. Eli visited me when he could, but that was it. I knew I was going to die." He shifts in the chair, not looking at me. "When Seb grabbed me—I don't know... That's all I could think about, being dragged out of my cell for another round of that."

Resting my cheek in my palm, I remain quiet. A flood of grief and anger fills my chest, mingling with one another until they're nearly impossible to tell apart. I want to reach out and touch him. The idea of him being locked in a cell by himself with no idea of what was coming next or what was happening to his group is excruciating. Six weeks of endless torture, only to be hauled back to the Green Zone so he could face death at the hands of the real criminals.

"I never wanted to hurt him," Nixon says, and his voice cracks. "Every time I close my eyes, all I can see is the guards in the Red Zone, or me hurting the people I'd do anything to protect." He balls his fists in his lap. "Seb and Liam have noticed I've been off. They've tried to get me to talk, but I… I just can't."

"You think you're less of a leader now." I don't mean to say it out loud, and as soon as I do I silently curse myself for it, dropping my hand from my face. "I'm sorry, I didn't mean—"

"No, you're right. What kind of leader turns a weapon on his own comrade?"

"One who's struggling because he endured all of that to *protect* that exact same comrade and others." I lean forward, grabbing one of his hands, and hold it with both of mine in the space between us. "Nixon, you're a good leader. You're hurting, and that's normal."

He finally looks at me. The shadows cast over his face distort his features. "Two of my members died the day of my execution. Because they were trying to save me. After that, what I did to Seb, seeing you hurt, Seb getting shot… I don't know if I'm made for this. Not if I can't protect the people who trust me with their lives."

"That's not your fault. None of this is." I believe that with every part of my being. Regardless of what I might've said when I was angry, I know he's done everything he can to keep everyone safe. "I'm sorry about your members—I know how much that hurts you—but they risked their lives for yours because they believe you're worth dying for. And they trust you. Seb and Liam wouldn't have come here with you if they didn't. And despite how angry I've been the past few days, *I* trust you. Completely."

"I was supposed to protect you," he says. "My mission was to keep you safe."

"It was out of your control. But you came for me. As soon as you found out where I was, you put together a team and came to the Red Zone against the Commander's orders."

I still don't know the whole story behind that, and make a mental note to find out from either him or Liam later. But to think I was so pissed off at Nixon and his group for not making an effort to rescue me! He was doing everything he could, even if it meant disobeying his superior.

Nixon smirks and wipes a hand across his face. "Yeah, not looking forward to that conversation."

"Like Lacey said, it says a lot about you. How can he be mad about that?"

Except that what Nixon did could also be seen as another indication that something happened between us before our capture. If the Commander heard the rumors but didn't think much of it then, he must suspect it now. Nixon probably won't face the same penalty as Piper since I'm not actually part of his group, but it won't look good.

"Piper questioned me after I was saved," Nixon says. "Before I found out what she did."

"Questioned you about what?"

"Whether or not I told the Society anything." He leans forward against the table, but doesn't move his hand from mine. "Obviously I didn't, and I knew it was procedure for me to be questioned but—I don't know. After that, I can't help but think that she and everyone else believe I sold them out. They were all… cautious when I got back. Happy to see me, but it was different. Kinda like I was with you, I guess."

"But you didn't sell anyone out."

"No, of course not."

But he feels guilty regardless. That, on top of what happened with Seb, makes him feel like he's not strong enough. He's the strongest person I've met, though. I thought that when we were together before, but I believe it even more now. I don't know anyone else who could go through what he has and still put on a brave face while continuing to protect others. Just like before, he puts everyone else's needs above his own.

I adjust myself in my chair so I'm as close to him as possible, my knee pressing into the metal armrests. "Do you remember what you said to me at Adam and Lacey's after you interrogated Kase?"

He shakes his head.

"You told me about how Kase was one of the strongest, and how you didn't think you'd be able to survive if the same thing happened to you. But you did." I squeeze his hand. "You endured so much more and survived, without giving the Society a single piece of information. You are *so* much stronger than you give yourself credit for."

He smiles. "I remember you saying something like that."

"And I was right."

Despite everything that's happened, there was never a single part of me that doubted Nixon in that regard. Even if he did hate me, even if he hadn't put together this mission for me, I always knew how much he cared about his group. No one in the Society could ever break that. He was willing to die alone if it meant keeping them safe. Nothing says more about him as a leader than that.

"Even though we weren't together," I say, "I believed in you the whole time. And I know your group believes in you, too."

Nixon stares at me, his gentle smile lingering. His eyes soften, giving me a glimpse of the man I remember, and my heart flutters.

"It's hard to be upset when I'm around you," he says. "Thank you."

"Don't thank me," I say. "Just… communicate with me. And I'll do the same."

He wiggles his hand from my grasp and slides his fingers between mine. It sends a rush of warmth through me, numbing me from the cold. "Deal."

"I think you need to tell Liam and Seb what's been going on, though. They deserve to know."

"You're right." He looks down at our entwined hands and purses his lips as if wanting to say something but trying to figure out how. Finally, he whispers, "I've missed you."

"I've missed you, too." Hesitantly, I reach up and cup his face, tracing the scar along his jaw with my thumb and taking comfort in his skin against mine. "So much."

Although it's been days since we were reunited, this is the first time it's actually felt real. Everything is still as we share our vulnerabilities and our secrets stitch us back together in a strange, new way—a way that will make us stronger.

I don't know what my future holds after our meeting tomorrow. Like before, there are plenty of things I'm unsure of. All I know is that, however things pan out between us, I never want to let Nixon go. As long as I have him and Liam with me, maybe everything will be okay.

33. Family First

Ivy

The car rolls up to a white, secluded three-story house. Smoke billows from the chimney, obscuring the bright blue sky and hanging over the mansion like a cloak. James stops just short of the carport up ahead, parking beside a pair of stone walls that open up to the manicured front yard. Liam and Seb peer out the window past me, but Nixon keeps his eyes forward in the front passenger seat.

After last night on the terrace, my nerves about the meeting have slightly subsided. But now that we're here, outside the Commander's headquarters, their presence makes itself known as a boulder that settles in the pit of my stomach. The pop of Liam's knuckles beside me signifies that he's just as anxious as I am. Even Seb appears uneasy, with the way he drums his fingers against his knee.

"Let's go," James says, shutting off the car.

He leads us to the front of the mansion, walking along a flagstone path that leads to a matching set of stairs with blooming willow trees on either side. Corinthian columns adorn the stone veranda, where several sets of cast aluminum furniture are sprawled out.

James pushes open one of the double mahogany doors and we file in, entering a foyer that opens up into a cozy living room. A maroon couch with fluffed throw pillows faces the crackling open-hearth fireplace.

Taking a right, we climb the oak-paneled grand staircase, passing the row of double-hung windows along the platform before making it to the second floor. With each step, the tension pulsating between all of us intensifies. I can feel it in the woody-smelling air that's getting heavier by the second.

One of the vintage pocket doors to our left swings open, and a woman in business attire steps into the sitting area that looks over the balcony. Noticing us, she stops, switching the stack of papers she's holding from one arm to the other.

"Hello, James," she says with a tight smile as she looks over the rest of us. "Here for the Commander?"

Unable to help myself, I peek past her into the office she's stepped out of, only able to see half of a desk that's cluttered with binders and loose papers.

"Yeah," James says. "We have some newcomers who're meeting him."

"I'm not sure he's back yet." The woman glances at the gold watch dangling from her wrist. "He left earlier after a call from one of the guardsmen on the western border."

"You want me to have them wait here?"

The woman studies our group again, paying extra attention to Liam and me. My chest tightens at the thought of how much she and the other people here know about us. It reminds me of when I first arrived at the Everetts' and how they knew every little detail about my life. Only this time, it isn't as simple as knowing my clothing size and where I grew up.

"No," the woman says after a long pause. "Send them up. I'll let him know they're here as soon as I see him."

"Those for him?" James asks, motioning toward the papers in the crook of her arm.

"Oh, yes. Would you mind?"

James takes the papers from her. "No problem."

"Thanks—I'm swamped with paperwork right now. Can I get any of you anything? Something to eat or drink?"

Nixon speaks for us. "No, thank you, I think we're good."

"Let me know if you change your mind," the woman says. "It shouldn't be long." She returns to her office, keeping the door partially open.

"Commander's assistant," James explains as we climb the next flight of stairs.

"Resistance?" Nixon asks.

"Not technically. Her focus is on the government side of things around here."

"So there's a full government," I say.

"More or less," James says. "Nothing like the Enlightened Society, but still an entity to keep order."

I've learned next to nothing about this place, but the few crumbs of information are nothing like what I would've guessed. If I'm being completely honest, I expected this place to be more like the settlement we were held at—people barely scraping by while staying off the Society's radar. Just from what I've seen, it seems as though the Society should be completely aware of their presence. Are they?

We pass several identical closed doors on the third floor and make a couple of turns down what seem like endless hallways. Finally, we stop at a set of double pocket doors, and James slides them open. Hesitantly, we trail behind him.

A crystal chandelier hangs from the ceiling, but most of the light pours in through the massive windows behind the U-shaped executive desk. The rest of the walls boast endless mahogany cabinets, drawers, and shelves that are packed with books. The first thing I think of is Carson Everett's office.

Frustration simmers in the back of my mind again. This is just one small piece of the camp, but seeing such elegance feeds my anger toward the Commander. I haven't met the man, yet I want to scream at him for leaving all those people outside this city to struggle. Innocent people are going without a reliable source of food or shelter while he's here, protected and seemingly oblivious to what's going on beyond his borders. How is he any different from the Society?

James drops the papers onto the desk beside a coffee mug with a thump. "This is it," he says, turning to us with arms spread. "Make yourselves comfortable. I'll be waiting downstairs for you."

"You're not staying?" Liam asks.

"This isn't my meeting," James says, strolling toward the exit. "And honestly, these kinds of meetings bore me. Don't tell him I said that, though." Flashing us a smile, he pulls the doors shut, and we're sealed inside.

We stand in silence for a few seconds, looking around the office and at each other. My anxiety peaks, coursing through my veins like icy water. I'm hyper-aware of every inhalation and every beat of my heart, and I cross my arms to hide my trembling hands.

"Well, this is fun," Seb says, plopping down in one of the plush leather chairs across from the desk.

"Seb," Liam hisses, "stand *up*."

"Excuse you, *sir*," Seb says sarcastically, removing a rubber band from his wrist and tying his black curls in a bun, "in case you forgot, I was shot the other day. I think I have an excuse to sit."

"How are you feeling, by the way?" Nixon asks. He walks along one of the mahogany walls, inspecting the collection of books.

"Not too bad," Seb says. "So, how do you guys think this place got here?"

"It's from the Old World, obviously," Liam says.

Seb rolls his eyes and leans his head back, staring up at the vaulted ceiling. "I know *that*."

"Seems like they've been working on it for a while," I comment, unfreezing from my spot behind the two leather chairs and wandering the room aimlessly. "How long has the resistance been around?"

I assumed they assembled after the rise of the Enlightened Society, but I never thought to actually ask. If that's the case, and they found this city in the early days of the Northern Unity, this camp has been around for over forty years.

"Longer than any of us," Seb says.

"And the current Commander has always been the one in charge?" I ask.

"No," Nixon says. "He stepped up about twelve years ago."

I run a finger along a row of books, all their titles relating to the United States of America but nothing like the ones we had in school. These ones are missing the Northern Unity's symbol on their worn spines. "What happened to the last one?"

"From what I understand," Nixon says, "the resistance wasn't as organized before him."

"I don't even think they had a solid chain of command or broke their groups up into squads," Seb says. "The way some of the older members talk, it sounds like everything was pretty random."

"Yeah," Liam says, crossing his arms and leaning against the chair beside Seb. "A lot ended up in re-education, and some just disappeared."

They probably became victims of the Elite Auction or were executed. The Society may be unpredictable—at least to me—but those are two things they're consistent with.

Tightening my arms around myself, I round the massive desk, eyeing its contents—a nearly full coffee mug, the papers James left, a basic table lamp, a phone, a communication radio, and a yellow orchid in a vase at the corner. I stop at the windows that look out over a small botanical garden and the wooded area beyond it.

"How much shit do you think we're gonna get for this mission?" Liam asks.

"I don't know," Nixon says, "but it won't fall on you two. You were following my orders."

"You shouldn't get in trouble at all," I say, turning around. "This is what the resistance is meant for, right?"

"Still have to obey our superiors," Liam says.

"Seems like your superior isn't really doing what he promises."

"Technically, Nixon's my superior, so…"

"You know what I mean, asshole."

"What's with the sudden hostility toward the Commander?" Nixon asks, joining Seb and Liam.

"I'm not hostile," I say, "but even you said this is all weird."

Nixon raises an eyebrow. "It is, but not in a way that makes me not trust him."

But *why* does he trust him? Because they share the same hatred toward the Society? Because he gave Nixon some sense of purpose after he lost his parents?

"Well, I have no reason to trust him," I say, though it's not entirely true. He's giving us a place to stay. Even before the auction, he was going to offer me refuge here.

"But you can trust us," Liam says, unfolding his arms.

"Do you honestly believe we're safe here? That the Society will never find us, especially with two high-profile fugitives on the loose?"

Liam shrugs and shoves his hands in his pockets. "It's better than the alternative."

For now. Sooner or later, though, the Society *will* find this place—they have to realize that—and I don't want to be around when that happens. This may be an organized resistance, but that's not enough to stop a full military of brainwashed people who are hungry for blood.

Footsteps approach the door. Seb stands, and everyone's heads turn. The icy feeling in my body twists into my stomach like a knife. I step away from the windows, stopping by the leather chair behind the desk, and wait. The soft thudding sound draws closer, and I mentally prepare myself for the barrage of questions I know will come.

The footsteps pause. We stand completely still, rigid with tension. My mouth runs dry, and I push back the overwhelming urge to bite my already too-short nails.

One of the doors slides open, and all the oxygen is sucked from my lungs.

He steps into the office, shutting the door behind him, and Liam staggers backward. The air is so brittle it could snap. No one speaks.

Deep brown eyes I grew up both fearing and admiring, now surrounded by shallow wrinkles, travel over the four of us. His blond hair that was always kept trimmed and orderly is shaggy, parted down the middle and concealing his ears. When his eyes lock on me, a sad smile finds its way to his stubbly face, and I don't know if I want to yell or cry or run away.

The Commander. Chief Benjamin Clearson.

For the first time in a while, my mind is silent. All thoughts have completely vanished, and I'm left grappling for something to say.

"I'm so happy to see you two," our father says, looking between me and Liam but keeping his distance. He runs a hand through his hair, and his smile widens. "God, look at you. You're both so grown up now." Turning to his left, he extends his hand. "And you must be Nixon."

"Uh, yes—yes, sir," Nixon says, returning the brief handshake.

"It's good to finally meet you." He steps forward, shaking Seb's hand. "And you are?"

"Sebastien, sir," Seb says. "Green Zone, Squad One scout."

"Nice to meet you, Sebastien," he says. "Thank you for coming out here."

Liam glances at me, eyes wide and jaw clenched. For a fraction of a second, I wonder if he knew all along, though his expression tells me otherwise. But Nixon must've known. How the hell could he not? Why else would he have been so certain our father wasn't dead? He's worked directly under the man; he has to have known *something*.

The anger takes over. This man abandoned us. No goodbyes, no calls, nothing. We woke up one morning and he was gone.

"I'm sure you have a lot of questions," my father says, "and I promise I'll answer everything soon, but I have some business to take care of first." He turns to Nixon again, who looks just as stunned as Liam, and starts asking questions about our journey here—the settlement, if we came across any soldiers, if we were seen in the tunnels. With each passing second, my thundering heart drowns out their words.

Liam doesn't say anything. Pressed against the chair, his fingers curl at his side. The muscle in his jaw feathers as he grinds his teeth. He looks at me again, his eyes a mix of anger and hurt. He's spent all this time looking for our father, only for him to be his commanding officer.

The Commander—a man put up on a pedestal by Nixon, Liam, and every other resistance member I've spoken to. A man who's supposed to help people, to protect people from the Society. A part of me even feared him because of how highly everyone spoke of him. Now I'm just disgusted.

He knew. The entire time I was in the Red Zone, he knew and did nothing. He's been here, tending to other matters that were clearly more important than his own daughter. Meanwhile, his son was in the Green Zone alone—no mother, no sister, no leader. Liam lost everyone he was close to, with the exception of Addison, and our father still did nothing.

Why?

Why did we not matter enough? Why were we not worthy of his help when everything went to shit? Why did the resistance matter more than his children?

Rage explodes from my chest, its fiery presence scorching my nerves.

"What the *fuck* is wrong with you?" I spit.

Everyone's eyes dart to me—I can feel them—but I can only focus on his. Everything else around me fades, and I'm zeroed in on the man who was meant to protect me—the single person who was always supposed to be there.

"You abandoned us," I say. "You left without saying anything, and we never heard from you again."

"V, I can explain."

That nickname he gave me as a kid, one Mom and Liam adopted after he left, always made me smile. Now it makes my stomach churn.

"Shut up!" Dropping my arms, I dig my nails into my palms. "You don't get to 'explain'. You *left* us, your family, so you could play Commander."

"They needed me," he says, keeping his voice level, but I pick up on the tinge of hurt—a part of him pleading for me to listen to whatever he has to say.

"*We* needed you!" I slam my fist on his desk, the sound resonating throughout the room. The stack of papers collapses, and coffee sloshes over the rim of the mug. "Liam and I searched for you for three years! The only reason he even joined the resistance was for Nixon's help to find you! Jesus fucking Christ, you *talked* to him when we were in the Blue Zone, and you couldn't be bothered to tell him who you were. You wanted to hide behind this elaborate title and life you've created for yourself. Without us. Why is that?"

With trembling legs, I march from behind the desk and brush past Liam, stopping a couple of feet from my father. Regret flashes across his face.

"Was it because you were too afraid to face him after you deserted us?" I yell. "Or that you were hoping you'd never have to see us again—that this position was the perfect escape from your mundane family?" Pressure builds in my head and my eyes burn, but I don't let myself cry. He's not worth wasting tears over. "Or maybe it's because you, the almighty Commander, are just a fucking coward."

He bows his head and hooks his thumbs in his belt loops. "I was trying to protect you."

I laugh bitterly. "*Protect* us? The Society interrogated us for months after you left! They watched our every move. Your wife *sold* me—your own fucking daughter! Where were you then? Where were you when I was beaten and raped by an Elite I was being forced to marry?!"

He shakes his head, and for a moment I think I see tears in his eyes. "I didn't know any of that was going to happen. Believe me, I wanted you with me, but—"

"My interrogator told me you were dead. Said they found your body. I refused to believe it, but now I'm thinking maybe it'd be better if you were."

"Ivy," Nixon interjects.

My glare snaps to him. His brows are pulled together, mouth twisted into a half frown.

"You knew, didn't you?"

"No," Nixon says.

"Bullshit! You've worked with him this entire time!" I start toward him, but my father stops me by placing a hand on my shoulder. I jerk away as if his touch is deadly. "Don't touch me!"

"He didn't know," my father says. "Just Eli and a few others from his group." He exhales, pressing his hands together in front of his chin. "Let me explain. I didn't want to leave you behind. I just thought it'd be safer if I didn't drag you into all this."

I shake my head. "Fuck you."

"Sweetheart—"

"No. No, you don't get to do this. You don't get to put us through hell and then act like you're some savior." My vision blurs as the flames of my rage curl in the pit of my stomach, burning up to my chest and crawling through my veins. "Have fun with your little group here. I'd rather take my chances in the Northern Unity."

I shove past him and storm out of the room.

"Ivy!" he calls, but doesn't follow.

I hear the others' voices as I stalk down the hall, but their words are lost in the roaring of the blood in my ears and the frantic breaths I'm reminding myself to take. I blindly navigate the maze of hallways, finding my way down to the second floor. My father's assistant peeks out of her office when I pass by. She doesn't say anything, and I don't pay her any attention. She knew who I was to him already; it's clear now why she kept staring at me and Liam. Everyone here probably knows, including Adam and Lacey, and no one thought to tell me. As far as I'm concerned, I can't trust anyone here.

"Ivy?" James says, standing from the couch in the living room.

"Leave me alone," I mutter as I storm past him.

Throwing open the front door, I take the front stairs two at a time until I'm on the path toward James's parked car. Then I slow my steps and breathe deeply, unsure of where to go from here. My chest aches. It feels as though my heart has been clawed out by relentless, greedy hands and tossed aside, smashed and splintered.

This is his fault. All of it. If he'd just stayed, at least until Liam and I were both eighteen, this wouldn't have happened. Liam never would've joined the resistance. I wouldn't have been sold. Nixon wouldn't have been captured.

There's still so much work to be done within the Northern Unity, but my father fled. He sought refuge outside the walls with his armed guardsmen while leaving the members inside to do what he was too afraid to.

I want to turn back just so I can scream at him again. So I can watch his reaction as my words drive into his heart like a stake, so I can see him experiencing a fraction of the pain I have. But I know if I do, I'll only end up crying, and he doesn't deserve that. He doesn't deserve to see what he's done to me or a chance to comfort me. Because the second he attempts to, I know I'll collapse into his arms and sob against his chest like I did when I was younger. I'll search for that magical power he always had to make everything okay. Whether it's still there or not, I don't want it. I want to hate him.

I reach the end of the flagstone path when I hear, "Ivy!"

I turn around. Seb jogs toward me, and I roll my eyes, walking out onto the driveway. "What do you want?"

I half-expected Liam, or even Nixon, to chase after me, but definitely not Seb. I want to be alone. I'm not sure where I plan to go or what to do, but I need to get away from here.

"Damn," Seb says, trailing behind me, "you've come a long way from the girl I guarded at TCG."

That girl is dead, burned, and the ashes scattered, along with everything else from my old life.

"What do you want?" I repeat, allowing venom to seep back into my words.

"Came to check on you."

"Why you?"

"Thought you could use an unbiased person to talk to."

I glance back at him. "What do you mean, 'unbiased'?"

"Well, Liam's your brother, and with Nixon being the leader, and you two… you know."

Coming to a halt, I spin around and search his face for some hint of humor, but there isn't even a trace of a smile. "What are you talking about?"

Only now does he smirk. "I figured there was something, since you seemed a bit jealous about him and Elizabeth, and… I may have seen you guys outside last night."

I swallow hard but keep my face straight. "He needed someone to talk to."

"I've known Nixon for a while; he doesn't 'talk' to just anyone." There's a long pause, and I'm not sure if he's waiting for me to deny it. Finally, he continues, "But let's pretend that's not the case. He's still a leader and is expected to follow the Commander, who you clearly don't want to speak to right now, so you're left with me. Let's talk."

"There's nothing to talk about."

"Ivy," he says in a stern tone when I turn my back to him again, "I'll follow you if I have to, but keep in mind I'm injured."

I drop my shoulders and suppress a groan. He's really pulling that card, knowing that it'll make me feel guilty? It works, though. Walking to the scattered trees dotting the side of the driveway, I kick away fallen twigs and slump against the trunk. Seb takes a seat on the ground in front of me, wincing and leaning back with his palms pressed into the dirt.

We sit in silence, save for the knocking of branches when the wind sweeps through. I have nothing to say to him. I'm not sure I can form any coherent sentences that even scratch the surface of what I'm feeling.

I hug my knees to my chest and stare up at the sky, watching the clouds drifting overhead through the branches. Liam's still inside, and I wonder if he's taking the opportunity to lash out like I did or if he's being level-headed enough to hear what our father has to say. Aside from in arguments with our mom, Liam's normally been the one to internalize everything in the moment. He doesn't tend to act until he's had a chance to absorb everything.

"I probably would've reacted the same way," Seb says. "That can't have been easy."

"You have no idea," I mumble.

"Nixon seriously didn't know—none of us did."

"And to think I accused him of *killing* my dad!"

God, how could I have been so stupid? How did I really let myself entertain an idea that the Society put into my head? Nixon has been on my side from the beginning, even if I didn't realize it.

"Nixon may be a dick sometimes," Seb says, "but he's pretty understanding. I don't think he's going to take it personally."

"You probably think I'm crazy."

He chuckles. "No, not at all. I agree it was fucked up for your dad to do that to you and Liam, and you have every right to be angry, but I think you should hear him out."

I shake my head, my hair catching on the tree bark. "I don't want to hear excuses."

"As bad as it is, he probably had a good reason. At the very least, don't you want closure?"

I *have* closure. He left, just like I originally thought. I just didn't expect him to be the head of the entire resistance, especially since he was the Police Chief. For most of my life, he wasn't who I thought he was. He had a completely separate life from his family, and he chose it over us.

"If he hadn't left," I say, "none of this would've happened."

"And you likely never would've met Nixon," Seb says. When I look at him, he smiles and adds, "And me, of course, because we're all aware of how amazing I am." His grin widens, which forces a small smile from me in return. "But seriously, hear him out. After that, you can scream at him as much as you want, and we can go from there."

"We?"

"Me and Nixon. We've got your and Liam's backs. Resistance member or not, you're one of us."

"What happened to obeying your superior?"

"Technically, I answer to Nixon, and I guarantee he'll do everything in his power to make sure you're okay, even if that means disobeying the Commander again."

I run a hand over the dirt, the soft sprouting grass tickling my palm. "I didn't know about that until yesterday. Him going against orders to save me, I mean."

Seb nods and turns his head, looking toward the front yard. "He was pretty adamant—even had me and another member interrogate an Elite bodyguard to get information on you. I can guarantee he wouldn't have left his entire group behind for anyone else."

"I thought you said he didn't want to leave."

"He didn't, but he didn't want to be separated from you either. And with everything he's gone through, he needs someone like you who can get him to open up."

I pluck a twig from the ground and roll it between my fingers. "He told me about the incident during your training session."

Seb looks at me. "Yeah?"

I nod. "He feels like shit for it. Like it makes him less of a leader."

"Is it because of his captivity?"

I nod again, breaking the twig and tossing it aside. "He said when you grabbed him all he could think about was being back in the Red Zone. And he just snapped."

"That's what I figured." He sighs. "Nixon's a good guy and a good leader, and I can't imagine what he's dealing with right now—which is why he needs you. And I assume it's safe to say you need him, too." When I give him a questioning look, he says, "Liam told me about the panic attack and how Nixon was able to calm you down."

I hold back a smile. "Yeah, he has a way of doing that. Have you told—?"

"I haven't said anything to anyone. Your secret's safe with me." He winks, climbing to his feet. "So, think you can deal with facing your dad again?"

I groan, dropping my head back against the tree. While my rage has dulled, it's still very much present; the thought of looking at him again is nauseating. But I at least need to be in there for Liam. Like Seb said, we can get this over with and go from there.

"Maybe I can convince Nixon to go out to a bar afterward," Seb adds with another smile.

"Aren't you on pain meds?"

"I'll stop taking them just for the occasion. We can drown our sorrows in alcohol without worrying about being arrested."

I laugh, the tension in my body melting away. "I could definitely use a distraction after today."

"Is that a yes then?"

I hesitate, glancing back at the house. Whatever my father has to say won't make up for what he did, and I can't promise I'll keep my mouth shut for the remainder of this meeting. But I am curious about the story behind this city… and I'd rather hear it from the source, regardless of my feelings toward him. Despite what he did to our family, I have to admit that what he's done here is impressive.

I stand, brushing the dirt off the back of my pants. "Fine."

34. Trials

Nixon

"I don't know if I can do this," Liam says in a low voice.

We left the office soon after Seb followed Ivy. Despite the Commander's attempt to talk to him, Liam stormed out too, and I hesitated before going after him. He's pacing the hallway with his hands clasped behind his head.

My mind is still reeling over the Commander's identity. He was running the resistance from the Green Zone while I was there. Liam and I became friends when his dad was still around, and I had to inform him when Liam was inquiring about joining. Knowing the risks that come with what we do, why would he allow his son to join? Why would he insist I let him in, even after I originally refused?

Now I'm in a difficult spot, wanting to comfort my best friend and his sister while also expected to be a soldier.

"Ivy's right," Liam continues. "He abandoned us for the resistance. He talked to me on the radio and didn't say anything. How am I supposed to continue working under him?"

"He's still your commander," I say, leaning back against the wall with my arms folded. "As hard as all this is, that's still the case."

"How could you not know?"

"I'd never met him, and he keeps his identity a secret. How was I supposed to?"

It's amazing how he was able to tuck away an entirely different half of his life for so long. Chief Clearson stepped up as Commander twelve years ago, meaning he was doing this for most of his kids' lives, all while being the Police Chief. He worked the auction and met Elites without anyone ever knowing what he was really doing.

"You were the leader of our zone while he was still there," Liam says. "Fuck, you and I met six months before he left. He knew we were friends."

"He kept his identity a secret," I repeat, "in order to protect himself from the wrong people. Guess we know why now."

"But Eli knew. We were in his house and he didn't tell us."

"Probably because he was under strict orders not to." I glance out the full-length window beside me that looks over the front yard. Seb and Ivy are walking up the flagstone path together. "What do you want to do?"

Liam drags his hands down his face and leans against the wall beside me. "Finish this meeting? I don't know."

"If you don't want to, he'll understand—I'll understand. This is a lot to process."

A beat of silence passes between us, filled only by the pop of Liam's knuckles as he pulls at each finger.

"I'm sorry," I say. "I wish I'd known. But I'm here for you. We can put this on hold if you want, and go back to the hotel."

"I'm going to wait for Ivy," he says. "I should be with her. You go back in."

"He may be my boss, but you're my friend."

"I'll be in when they get back up here. Go."

I push myself away from the wall. "If either one of you wants to stop at any point, you let me know. I don't want you guys in there if you're uncomfortable."

"Yeah, got it."

I walk down the hall and knock on the door. The Commander calls me in from the other side, and I glance back at Liam. With his nod of approval, I enter.

The Commander stands behind his desk, reorganizing the papers Ivy knocked over during her outburst. Sliding the door shut, I take a few more steps inside and hesitate. I was anxious enough about meeting him, but this is all more than I expected, and being in here without my squad makes it worse.

He looks up at me, although it feels more like he's looking *through* me, as if he already knows everything about me and my most recent mission with his daughter. An uncomfortable sensation creeps up my neck.

"Seb and Ivy are heading back in," I say. "Liam wants to wait for her."

"We'll begin once they return, then," he says. He opens one of the drawers and stores the papers, leaving a few on the desk. "Eli mentioned you have some documents for me from the Everetts."

Shit. Liam and I risked our lives to get those back from the scavengers, and I somehow forgot to bring them.

"They're at the hotel," I say. "I'm sorry, I—"

"You've been through enough these past few days. I'll have James grab them." The drawer closes and he sits in the executive chair, turning his full attention to me. "I want to thank you for getting Ivy here safely. I'm eternally grateful. However"—he folds his hands on the desk—"that doesn't excuse your disobedience."

A weight settles in my chest. "No, sir, it doesn't."

"The six and a half years you've been in the resistance, you've been a phenomenal scout, and an excellent leader for the past three. You put your members above yourself and have always been compliant in anything I've asked of you. However, as much as I appreciate what you've done, you deliberately went against my orders and left your group behind to carry out an unapproved mission. Correct?"

I keep my hands at my sides, resisting the urge to bury them in my pockets. "Yes, sir."

"Why?"

When I spoke with him over the radio before leaving the Green Zone, I insisted I owed it to Liam to get his sister back, and that was partially true—but it's obvious now that he doesn't believe it. What am I supposed to tell him? That I wanted his daughter back because, for some reason, I feel like I need her in my life?

I could argue that this is what the resistance does—protect people from the Enlightened Society—but that would only raise more questions, like why I've never attempted this with any other victims of the auction.

I clear my throat and make sure not to break eye contact. "You were right when we spoke before this—I have some guilt over the outcome of the original mission." The Commander studies me, his dark eyes boring into me, brewing with suspicion. "But that's no reason to disobey your orders. I'm sorry."

"You left your group behind," he emphasizes again, "and risked the lives of one of your top scouts *and* your second-in-command by bringing them along with you, all of which is completely out of character for you." He pauses, allowing his words to linger in the tense silence. "I respect you as one of my leaders and recognize all that you've achieved, but this isn't something I can overlook. I'm going to go over the details with Eli, and he and I will decide your punishment."

"I understand," I say, although there's a piece of me that wants to argue. I brought his children to him. I took it upon myself to bring Ivy to safety, which left Eli's group more prepared for whatever's happening in the Red Zone following Wyatt's murder. That should count for something. Yes, I left my group behind, but I gave them strict orders to lie low until I returned, which I had every intention of doing.

That was before I knew Ivy had escaped and was destined to leave the Northern Unity, though. The second I saw her, I wasn't sure anymore, and the past twenty-four hours have made me more uncertain.

I *want* to go back to my group. I need to be there to protect them. But I also feel this overwhelming obligation to protect Ivy, and

I know for a fact she won't be sent back inside those walls. At this point, I'm not sure any of us will be. I'm a fugitive, and Seb's superiors at TCG have definitely noticed his absence by now. Liam's the only one with an alibi, but his family is here. Even if he's pissed at his dad, he still has his sister.

There's a knock on the door, and the tension crumbles.

"Come in," the Commander calls without looking away from me.

Seb enters with Liam and Ivy close behind, and only when the door shuts does the Commander's gaze break from mine. Seb and Liam take their places on either side of me, but Ivy remains by the door with her arms folded and a glare that could make even the most stoic soldier squirm.

The Commander opens his mouth to speak, but Ivy cuts him off by saying, "Save whatever bullshit sob story you have and just tell us what the hell is going on here."

I catch Seb attempting to hold back a smirk, and I internally cringe. She doesn't have to respect him the same way we do, and she has every right to be upset, but her attitude is only going to make things worse for me. I don't say anything to her, though; I've learned by now that when she's like this, she doesn't care to follow orders.

The Commander doesn't react to her spiteful words. Instead, he lets them linger before saying, "I can imagine what all of you are wondering. Yes, this city is safe, but that doesn't mean we're immune from all outside threats. There are, on occasion, instances of attempted breaches of the gates, but the perpetrators are always dealt with before they ever make it in. The city is still a work in progress, and we've been working on restoring it for over a decade."

"So what Nixon said is true," Ivy says. "You stepped up as the Commander twelve years ago."

"Yes," he says, "two years after I was promoted to Police Chief. The resistance existed before that but lacked structure. Eli was the only one at the time who had a semblance of a real group, and after my first year of working with him in the Red Zone, we came up with a new vision for the resistance—one that was methodical and encompassed each cell in the Northern Unity. We wanted everyone to operate together rather than independently."

"Why?" Ivy asks. "You told us you joined the police force when you were eighteen; why did you suddenly care about the resistance, aside from shipping them to re-education?"

"Ivy," I say, "let him speak."

The Commander holds up a hand. "It's okay, Nixon. This is an open discussion; I want to answer all of your questions." He stands, tucking his chair under the desk, and looks directly at me when he says, "I'm sure you discovered I played a role in the Elite Auction when you were looking into my disappearance."

"Yes, sir," I say. That's as far as I got, though. My group was never able to figure out for certain what he did.

"Three months after my promotion," he says, addressing all of us now, "one of the President's aides contacted me about an opportunity in the Red Zone, claiming they needed assistance with a covert method in eliminating 'terrorists.' As a new Chief and someone who was dedicated to seeing our country prosper, I accepted, especially since another pay raise was involved that would help our family." He eyes Liam and Ivy. "Essentially, I was an escort. It started with me transporting the victims from TCR to the facility where you two were kept"—he looks at me and Ivy—"and stayed that way for the first year.

"Then, once I earned the Enlightened Society's trust, I was put in charge of the Transitional Adaptation unit, where I would 'reprogram' the victims in the days leading up to the auction and escort them to the auditorium." He presses his lips together and turns his face toward the wall of shelves. "That's where I met Eli, and he more or less informed me of what the Society was actually doing."

"But you stayed," Liam says.

"I did. Much longer than I wanted to, and what made it worse was coming home to you two after those trips, wondering what I would do if one of you were taken to that place. But I had the advantage of working on the inside to benefit the resistance. I still didn't have the clearance to know everything that went on behind the scenes, but it was a start. For the next eight years, it stayed like that—Eli and I slowly rebuilt the resistance while collecting intel."

"And this city," Liam says, "how did you find it?"

The Commander opens a drawer and sifts through it, retrieving a map that he unfolds and smooths out across the mahogany. Rotating it toward us, he motions us over, and Seb, Liam, and I huddle around the marked-up map of the former United States of America. The northeastern states are bordered with different colors of ink, signifying the four zones of the Northern Unity. In the state just below the bottom of the Red Zone, the city of Asheville is circled in black marker.

"Not all of my trips away from home were for work," the Commander says. "Over the years, I made countless journeys outside the walls in search of a place that could be a refuge for those fleeing the Society, as well as a resistance headquarters. With the help of Eli and a few other dedicated members, we settled on Asheville." He taps a finger above the black circle.

"How did you convince the resistance to trust you?" Liam asks. "Since you were such a high-ranking officer?"

"They didn't—not at first. I owe a lot to Eli and his group. People trusted him, so they took his word when he assured them I was on their side. Even today, there are people here who know what I did and don't fully trust me, but I make it a constant goal to prove myself to them."

"How does the Society not know about this place?" Ivy asks, finally joining us in front of the desk. She stops beside Seb, peering at the map.

"They do know about it," the Commander says, and all of us look up at him.

They know this place exists, that resistance members reside here, and it's still standing? Why have they not bombed the place or at least infiltrated it with their military?

"Then how exactly is it safe?" Liam asks. "Especially for two of their top fugitives."

"We're nestled between two mountain ranges," the Commander says, sliding a finger down either side of the city's name. "The rough terrain was one reason we chose it. We also have these." He points to two red Xs—one in the state west of the camp, and another farther south. "A nuclear weapons lab and nuclear bomber base. The

Society has their own warheads, but they're well aware of ours and know we'll retaliate."

"A stalemate," Seb says.

"Exactly."

"And that's enough to prevent them from infiltrating?" Liam asks. "Why wouldn't they just reclaim the bases and wipe out the camp?"

"I didn't come here alone when I left," the Commander says. He folds the map, returns it to the drawer, and it closes with a hollow thud. He watches all four of us, waiting for us to catch on to what he's saying.

Micah mentioned that three years ago the Commander needed help outside the walls, so he brought Micah's father, the Green Zone's former leader, along. But that wouldn't help keep this camp safe. They'd need something—or someone—valuable to the Enlightened Society.

"You have a POW," I say.

The Commander nods. "A member of one of the thirteen families whom I got close to when working the auction. As long as my negotiator can confirm their man is alive, we're safe."

It has to be someone fairly high up if the entire Society has agreed not to retaliate. With that, combined with the nukes and the alliances with Canada and Mexico, he's been able to create a safe haven. But no paradise lasts forever. With time, this place will crumble, regardless of how dedicated he is to holding it together.

"But if they know you're here," Ivy says, "wouldn't they storm the place anyway?"

"They may have their suspicions," the Commander says, "but they don't have any evidence of my whereabouts, and aside from a select few members and the Special Ops, no one knows my identity."

The Society doesn't work off suspicion; they need solid proof.

"How does having a POW make you any better than the Society?" Ivy asks, the sharpness returning to her voice.

"We treat him well," the Commander says. "No torture, and his basic needs are met."

"And what about all of the people between here and the Northern Unity? If you're *so* concerned about helping people, why not do something for them?"

The Commander's stern face softens. "I would help every single person out there if I could, but we simply don't have the manpower to pull it off. We have about two thousand here, and not everyone is part of the actual resistance. A lot *are* people we've helped from outside the walls; others are simply loved ones of resistance members who needed a safe place to go. And as you've already witnessed, not everyone outside the walls wants to be saved. There are unfortunately groups who trade with the Society and don't think twice about it."

Ivy shakes her head and backs away from the desk. "People are *starving* out there! They're being abducted for the auction, the very thing you're fighting against, and you can't do anything about it?"

"We can't save everyone."

That's an unfortunate truth that even I've struggled to accept, although I know he's right.

"What if that was me or Liam?" Ivy says. "Would you use that same excuse, or would you do something about it? Oh, wait, I *was* like them—sold in the auction and had everything taken away from me. And you did nothing."

The Commander presses his palms against the top of the desk. "I tried, Ivy, but there was no way for me to find out where you were until you approached Ember, and we couldn't just break into an Elite's home and take you. There's a process to all this." Closing his eyes, he hangs his head and lets out a long exhale. "I never thought your mother… *Evalynn* would do that. She adored you. Yes, she always dreamed of being one of the Elites, but that's all I thought it was—a dream. I never thought she would go to the lengths she did."

"It was my fault," Liam says, turning to his sister. "I should've called Mom sooner to get the name and location."

"No," the Commander says. "None of this is your fault—or any of yours." His eyes drift over all of us, settling on me before he continues. "It was out of the Green Zone's hands. Involving you has only made things more complicated, and you're lucky you got out as easily as you did."

The regret doesn't leave Liam's eyes, though, and I empathize with him. Aside from Seb, we're all carrying some sort of guilt for what happened.

"These three are the only reason I was able to get out," Ivy argues. "It was Nixon's mission originally. *You* approved of that. Captured or not, he was going to be the reason I got here anyway."

"And I'm grateful you're here," the Commander says, "but Red's group was putting together a squad to escort you. Regardless, you were going to make it out of there."

"So you were going to leave Liam inside the walls? You expected me to stay here without my brother?"

"I'm still part of the resistance," Liam tells her.

"What does that have to do with anything?" Her voice rises again, but this time, it's with hurt rather than anger. I look back at her. Her nostrils are flared and her glare is just as stony, but the moisture coating her eyes is hard to miss. "You plan to leave me here?"

Liam shifts his weight beside me and takes a deep breath. "I have an alibi. If any of us were to go back to the Northern Unity, it'd be me."

"Are you fucking serious?" She clenches her fists. "You planned to go back the whole time? To *leave* me?"

"Nothing's set in stone," the Commander says. "For now, all that matters is the four of you are safe."

"That's not all that matters!" Ivy exclaims. "I am *not* staying here if you're just going to throw them back out there and get them killed!"

"I think that's enough for today," Liam says.

He walks toward Ivy and slips an arm over her shoulders, but she shakes him off. With a final glare at her father, she throws the door open and marches out of the office, Liam following.

Strained silence settles over the room again, and I feel obligated to apologize for Ivy's second outburst as if she's one of my members. I remind myself she's not, and that her reaction is deeper than anything to do with the resistance. It's not my place to get involved.

"You two can head out," the Commander says, straightening up. "We'll meet again once things settle, unless either of you have any other questions for me."

Seb looks at me. I know he probably has thousands of questions burning inside him—I do, too—but it doesn't feel right discussing anything more without the others. Or at the very least, Liam.

But there is one thing I need to speak with the Commander about. The sooner, the better. Considering my recent disobedience, he may not listen, but it's worth a shot. I made a promise on the way here that I need to keep.

"Go with the others," I tell Seb. "I'll be out in a minute."

35. Break Your Knees

Ivy

The anger has fizzled out.

I'm hollow—cold and empty and utterly alone, despite being surrounded by others. I try to drill into the trenches of my mind for something to cling to that will fill the void in my chest. Rage, sorrow, it doesn't matter—just something that will cut through the blanket of numbness that suffocates me.

I fold a cheese-saturated tortilla chip over a piece of grilled chicken in the aluminum container in front of me. After eating a third of my food, my stomach protests at the thought of consuming any more. If I don't at least act like I'm eating, though, Liam will make a big deal out of it, and I don't have the energy to argue with him, so I periodically shuffle the food around with the plastic fork and force myself to take a small bite every few minutes.

There's been no talk of the Commander or anything really resistance-related since I stormed out of the office the second time. Liam attempted to comfort me, insisting he's always here for me and, like our father said, nothing's set in stone, but his words didn't help. He was right when he pointed out he's still part of the resistance; his work doesn't stop because I'm here. I knew that, but him confirming those unspoken thoughts made them harder to accept.

"What do you think, Ivy?" Seb asks, pulling me out of my head.

I look up at him across the suite's dining table. "What?"

"Dragging Nixon to a bar with us."

"I told you I can't," Nixon says from beside me. "I have a meeting with the Commander in the morning."

Annoyance prickles my skin. He already spoke with my father privately after the three of us left. What else is there to discuss? And why just him? I may not be part of the resistance, but anything concerning this mission should involve me, as well as Seb and Liam.

Seb rolls his eyes, shoving a forkful of rice in his mouth. "Come *on*. You don't have to get wasted, just have some fun for once."

"Another time," Nixon says. "I need at least a few days to prepare myself for when you black out again."

"That's only happened twice."

"Three times," Liam says to my right. "You remember how fucked up you got two weeks ago, right? *I* was the one who had to babysit you."

"And you were horrible at it," Seb says.

Liam stabs a piece of chicken. "You're a whiny drunk."

"I was gone for a few weeks and you spent that time getting wasted?" Nixon asks with a trace of humor.

"It was a way to fill the void you left in my heart," Seb jokes, holding a hand to his chest. Facing me again, he jabs his fork in the air. "What about you? Up for a few drinks?"

When he originally brought it up, the idea sounded appealing. Now... not so much. Just the thought of being packed into a bar, bumping against strangers in a place I'm not even sure I want to be, makes me claustrophobic. I'd rather sift through today's events in peace.

"Next time," I say, forcing a smile. "Kinda overwhelmed after today."

Seb groans dramatically. "You guys are *lame*."

"Would she even be allowed to drink?" Liam asks. "The drinking age in the Old World was, what, twenty-one?"

"What're they gonna do—ID her?"

"Well, considering her connection to the Commander…" Nixon says.

"What's he going to do—ground me?" I say, taking a bite out of an avocado slice when Liam glances at me. "What do you have to meet with him for anyway?"

"Resistance stuff," Nixon says without looking at me.

"Then that would include them too, right?"

"Not exactly."

"Did you already get an assignment?" Liam asks.

"No," Nixon says, "not really." He pops the plastic lid back on his half-eaten dinner and leans back, wiping his napkin over his mouth. "Just some loose ends regarding this mission."

"Loose ends?" Seb asks. "We made it here and James took him the documents. What else is there?"

"Can't talk about it right now," Nixon says. "Although I'm pretty sure part of it will have to do with my punishment for launching this mission."

"Shit, that's right," Seb says.

"Did he say anything about it earlier?" Liam asks.

Nixon shakes his head. "Just that he's going to get all of the details from Eli before discussing it further."

"You shouldn't be in trouble at all," I mutter.

"I went against orders and left my group," Nixon says.

"So? You did exactly what the resistance is meant for, didn't you?"

"There's still a chain of command that needs to be respected."

Fuck the 'chain of command.' Nixon did more than anyone else could. With a bounty on his head and countless injuries, he still found a way to make it to the Red Zone and get me out of the Northern Unity. Liam and Seb came with him, too. I understand that *he's* the leader, but all the blame shouldn't fall on him. And it's not like Liam would've stayed behind anyway.

Or would he? He wasn't exactly unnerved at the thought of going back to that country. It was like he'd been planning on it the whole time. Why wouldn't he? He has Addison to go back to—the potential for a real, normal life.

The pit in my stomach deepens at the thought of being separated from him again. Seb and Nixon will eventually follow.

"What makes him so worthy of your respect?" I stab one of the soggy chips harder than I mean to, and one of the prongs of the plastic fork snaps. "For someone who doesn't trust easily, I'm surprised you're so willing to bend to his every whim."

"Ivy, chill," Liam says. "How you feel about our dad doesn't matter when it comes to this stuff."

"How *I* feel?" I fling my fork into the takeout container. "So, what, you're okay with what he did?"

"Of course not, but—"

"But what? He's still your Commander? You owe him your life when he clearly couldn't give a shit about yours?"

"Ivy," Nixon says. He shifts in his chair beside me, his knee brushing against mine. His voice is stern, but his face is gentle. "Being part of the resistance means setting aside our personal issues to get the job done."

I slump back, dropping my hands in my lap. "That doesn't mean you should be punished."

Hopefully what Lacey said is true—that his dedication says more about him than his disobedience.

"I'm only trying to do what's right," Liam tells me, seamlessly shifting the focus back to the topic of him remaining in the resistance.

I roll my eyes. "How are you so sure this is what's right?"

"I'm not, but I hate the Society for what they did to you—and what they're doing to others—and if I can play even a small role in stopping it, I'm willing to do it."

My face burns, and I stare out the glass door behind Seb. I forgot about admitting what Wyatt did to me when we were in our dad's office. It just came out; I wasn't thinking. Now that Liam and Seb know more about it, I want to shut myself away and avoid their burning gazes.

"I want to protect you," Liam continues, "like I should've before, and if that means going back inside those walls, I'll do it. Whatever it takes."

I chuckle bitterly. "I don't need you to 'protect' me."

"When that asshole comes looking for you—"

"He won't." I tear my eyes from the orange-streaked sky and suck in a deep breath before letting them drift to Liam. "He's dead."

Liam's eyes narrow. "What do you mean?"

I swallow hard, pushing my food away. I didn't want him to ever know, because I know he'll see me differently. He'll see I've changed and that I'm not the same person I was a few months ago, but I guess he's already figured that out by now. Still, I have this irrational thought that if at least one person doesn't know the entire truth, a part of who I was can live on, even if it's just in someone's mind.

While Seb and Liam's eyes are on me, Nixon slips his hand under the table and rests it on my knee. The subtle touch reminds me of when he did something similar the night after Liam and Addison showed up in the Blue Zone—only then it was all in fun. This time, it's a form of support. He gives a light squeeze, as if to say he's here for me, and for a split second, the void in my chest feels a bit less frigid.

Looking Liam directly in the eyes, I say, "I killed him. I killed Wyatt."

Liam's eyes widen and he covers his mouth.

"Holy shit," Seb says under his breath, but I don't look at him.

"The morning of the wedding," I continue, "I cut out my tracker and slit his throat when he caught me."

There should be tears. I should be crying at the recollection of taking someone's life. But nothing comes. The warring emotions are still there; the guilt still lurks in the depths of my mind, waiting to curl its fingers around the final shreds of my sanity—but right now, I'm numb. It's finally setting in that I'm free from him and he won't be able to hurt anyone else. It was a choice I didn't want to make, but it was the right one. Freedom comes at a cost.

"V, I'm so sorry," Liam says. He reaches for me, but I pull back.

"Don't be," I say. "It wasn't your fault."

"How are you dealing with it?"

I run a finger along the stitches on my arm, the thread tugging at my skin. "I honestly don't know. As best as I can, I guess."

The lightness of the mood has plummeted, but it's not tense or awkward or anxiety-driven. It's heavy, but with a depth to it—a new sense of trust and vulnerability.

"You could've told me," Liam says, running his fingers through his beard.

"I didn't want you to be upset."

He shakes his head. "I hate that you had to do that, but I wouldn't have been upset. And I understand." He looks from me to Nixon and back. "I killed someone a couple days ago. At the settlement, when we split up."

So that's why he was so distant that night, and must've been what he and Nixon talked about at the outpost. I remember Nixon telling me Liam had never killed anyone before, and he never wanted him to be put in that position. It must've been serious if that was their only way out.

"What happened?" I ask.

"He saved my life," Nixon says.

From the way Liam averts his eyes, though, I know he doesn't see it that way. He views it the same way I do with Wyatt: He murdered someone.

"Are you okay?" I ask.

"I will be," Liam says.

"You guys have us," Seb says, motioning to Nixon and himself. "We've been there. It's not easy, but we can help you through it."

"And it will get better," Nixon adds. "Even if it doesn't feel like it right now."

"What about you, Nixon?" Seb asks, looking at his leader. "Anything *you* want to share while we're all bonding?" He says it like he's joking, but I catch on to the underlying seriousness in his words.

Nixon's hand tenses on my knee, and I brush my fingers against the back of it. He shifts in the chair again, propping one leg over the other, and lets the question linger.

"I've been having flashbacks to my captivity," he finally says nonchalantly. His cool tone is nothing like when he talked about it last night. "That's why I snapped and held the knife to your throat." He looks at Liam. "And why I froze at the settlement when we were going to retrieve the documents."

I didn't know about the last part. What he's been through isn't only affecting him during training and in his dreams; it's impacting his real-life missions.

"There's no shame in that," Liam says. "You went through hell."

"Maybe this will be good for you," Seb says. "New place, taking some time off. You deserve a break."

Nixon removes his hand from my knee and drums his fingers against the table. "Yeah, maybe." Uncertainty coats his voice, though, and I know he's thinking about his group.

"What about you, Seb?" I ask. "What deep, dark secrets do you have?"

Seb blows air out of his cheeks and pushes aside his empty takeout container. "Let's see... A year into the resistance, I killed my stepdad." Remorse flashes in his eyes, almost undetectable when he conceals it with a nervous chuckle. "Dude was a dick anyway."

I look at Nixon and Liam, who stare at him, looking as shocked as I probably do.

"You never told me that," Nixon says.

Seb shrugs. "You weren't around then; didn't see the point in bringing it up."

"Why?" I ask.

"Why'd I kill him? He found my gun. My mom and brothers weren't home, and I walked into him going through all my shit... and there it was in his hand." Seb removes the rubber band from his hair and slips it around his wrist, shaking his curls free. "All I remember is him yelling, saying he always knew I was a terrorist. When he pulled out his phone to call the cops, I panicked and grabbed him and slammed his head into the corner of the nightstand. Over and over and over."

My stomach twists into a thousand knots. He shakes his head and lets out another nervous laugh. I know he's killed people before—I watched him slit that scavenger's throat in the cabin—but it wasn't like this. But instead of fearing him, I hurt for him.

"Jesus, man," Liam says.

"Yeah," Seb says. "So I ended up calling the cops. They came out and questioned me and I said the gun was his, that he was threatening me and I acted in self-defense. Our neighbors had called in a couple times before about concerns for our safety after hearing him and my mom fight and seeing bruises on me and my brothers, so the cops bought it."

My dad still being the Police Chief probably helped, too.

"I lived with my dad after that until I turned eighteen," Seb says, "and it wasn't brought up again."

"Was that the first time you killed someone?" Nixon asks.

Seb nods. "All to protect myself." Guilt creeps into his voice.

"And your group," Nixon says. "What you did kept them from getting caught."

Silence blankets the room. Months ago, I would've been terrified—angry, even—after hearing something like that. I would've fought my way out of the room and immediately found someone to report him to. At the time, I genuinely believed they were terrorists, and even after learning bits of the truth, I was still afraid of them.

Now, I'm like them to a certain degree. Seb, Nixon, Liam, me… we're all broken in a way—plagued by what we've had to do and in a continuous cycle of trying to rebuild ourselves. To make ourselves better than we were before.

The Society did this to us. They gutted us of who we were and left mangled carcasses in their wake. After unmasking the monster that hides behind the lies, we had no choice but to fight back.

"Guess we're all a bit fucked up," Liam says.

Seb laughs. "Which is why we make a great team."

I open my eyes to the orangish light filtering in through the semi-sheer white curtains. On my stomach, I turn to see Liam on the other side of the king-sized bed, his back to me and his face half-covered by the comforter. Blinking, I push myself up with my hands. I never heard him come in. I went to sleep before the others, having to convince them nothing was wrong and I was just tired. Which was true.

The comforter slides down my back as I sit up on my knees, combing my fingers through my hair. The neon green numbers of the bedside clock show it's nearing midnight. Not knowing what exactly made me wake up, I'm tempted to lie back down and curl up under the warm blankets, but a thought pops into my mind.

This was normally when I'd wander the city back home, something I haven't been able to do in a long time. I glance at the window again, and the yearning to aimlessly walk the streets burrows itself in my mind. This place isn't home—not even close—but to have even a sliver of normalcy might make it more bearable.

I slide off the bed and grab my discarded jeans and boots off the floor before shutting myself in the bathroom. I squint when the automatic, bright white light flicks on. Dots float into my vision as my eyes adjust, and I shiver when my feet meet the cold tiles. Yanking my shorts off, I slide back into the jeans and lace up my boots, fumbling with them as my mind claws its way through the grogginess.

Inching the door open, I slide through the small space, thankful Liam's back is still turned as the light streams into the bedroom. Arms outstretched, I feel my way through the dark, no longer acclimated to the lack of light. My hip bumps the edge of the dresser, and I hold back a whimper and pause, listening for any movement from Liam. I slide my hand along the smooth wood, finding the sleeve of my jacket I tossed aside earlier. Draping it over my arm, I secure the door handle and slip out into the hall.

The light from the living room illuminates my path, and I freeze at the sound of Seb's usual carefree voice.

"Okay," he says, "but do you remember that new recruit a couple years back—Jake, I think?"

Nixon groans. "God, he was such a little shit."

Seb laughs. "He wanted to join so bad but refused to listen to literally anything you said. I'd never seen you as pissed off as when we were training and he just left. Like, ten minutes in."

"And had the audacity to show up that night for a meeting."

I tiptoe away from the bedroom door, sticking close to the wall as they continue their conversation. The opening to the living room gets closer, and I pray that neither of them will notice me. It's not like I'm doing anything wrong, but I don't want either of them to question me or assume I'm trying to escape after the day we've had.

It's just for a few minutes—a half-hour at the most. A way to ground myself and clear my head, just like when I was in the Green Zone.

A couple of feet from the living room, though, I remember the keycards are on the dining table, and if they happen to go to bed while I'm still out, I'll be locked out of the suite.

Shit.

Letting out a frustrated breath, I walk through the living room, avoiding looking at them, and swipe one of the keycards from the table.

"Hey," Seb says. The cushions brush against his clothes as he shifts on the couch. "Did we wake you?"

"Nope." Shrugging on my jacket, I slip the card in the pocket and turn for the exit.

"You okay?" Seb asks.

I finally look at them. Seb's lounging on the longer side of the sectional, and Nixon's pressed against the armrest on the opposite end.

"Yeah," I say. "I was just gonna go out for a bit—walk around, see the city. Something I used to do back home."

Saying the word 'home' out loud feels wrong. In my head, the Green Zone is my home. It's where I spent my whole life. It's where my dad worked and where my mom and I ran the flower shop together. But a place like that shouldn't be home. Not to me or anyone else.

"Does Liam know?" Nixon asks.

"Does Liam have to know everything I do?" I zip up my jacket. "It's safe here, right? Nothing to worry about."

Seb looks between the two of us before swinging his legs off the couch and stretching his arms above his head, wincing immediately afterward. "Well, I'm going to bed. Night, guys." When he passes by me, he squeezes my shoulder and says, "Be safe."

The door to his and Nixon's room clicks shut. I linger between the dining table and the couch, unsure if Nixon's going to try to stop me from leaving. After a moment of awkward silence, I start toward the hall again and exit the suite.

The corridor is quiet, and although my footsteps are muffled by the carpet, they echo in my head. I walk quickly toward the elevator at the other end, desperate to breathe open air and be alone with my thoughts in a place that isn't sealed.

A door shuts and feet jog toward me.

"Ivy, wait," Nixon calls.

I stop with my finger hovering over the elevator button.

He slows his pace and pulls on his jacket as he approaches. "I'm coming with you."

We take the elevator down to the lobby, where two different employees stand behind the desk, sipping coffee and chatting amongst themselves. Nixon holds open one of the glass doors at the front, and we step out into the chilly night.

I wordlessly start toward the left, and Nixon follows. The pulsing music from a nightclub up ahead twists into my ears and muffles all thoughts, rattling in my chest as we near it. Patrons are gathered outside, smoking cigarettes, laughing, and drinking from plastic cups that splash liquid onto the sidewalk with every dramatic motion. The stench of smoke burns my nose as we pass by, and I hold my breath until we've cleared the area.

Music, chatter, and laughter mingle together in the air. No matter how much I try to block it out, I can't. In the Northern Unity, the streets were dead silent at this time. It was eerie yet peaceful, despite the looming threat of re-education had I been caught.

Except I *was* caught once; I just didn't face the consequences I expected.

If it hadn't been for my stubborn need to wander outside after curfew, Wyatt never would've seen me. I never would've watched him kill Elizabeth, and he wouldn't have decided on me as his wife. My mother had already inquired about selling me, but nothing was finalized yet. Even if I had ended up still being sold, I could've ended up with another Society member. Maybe someone who would've just used me as a maid.

Or, maybe, I could've been the woman in Nolan's house.

"What do you think of this place?" Nixon asks.

"Too loud," I say.

We pause at the edge of the sidewalk and wait for our signal to cross the intersection.

"Too loud?"

I nod. "The Green Zone was always quiet at night. I miss it. The silence, I mean."

The crosswalk signal changes, and we make our way to the other side, the music slowly fading behind us.

"What do *you* think of this place?" I ask. "You haven't said anything about it since we got here."

Nixon shrugs. "Not really my place to have an opinion. It's not the Northern Unity, so I'll take it."

"Do you actually think it's safe?"

"For now. Nowhere is ever completely safe."

It stings, but he's right. Everything is temporary, especially for people on the run like us. It's a miracle we've lasted even this long without Black Hats hauling us back to that perverse country.

"And what are we supposed to do when it's no longer safe?" I ask.

"We go somewhere else, I guess."

"In other words, we just live on the run."

"No matter what, I won't let anything happen to you. You have me, Liam, and Seb."

He can't promise that, though. None of them can. Because sooner or later, they'll get hurt in the process. It was pure luck that Nixon and I escaped our fates, and that didn't come without a cost. I don't want that to happen again, and I refuse to see it happen to Liam and Seb. And I don't want to be this helpless victim who always needs protection from someone else.

In a quieter section of the downtown area, we pass darkened storefronts, all closed until morning. Lamp posts light our path, reflecting from the windows of the cars parked on the side of the road.

"Do you think Liam's going to be sent back to the Northern Unity?" I ask.

Nixon's quiet for a few seconds. "I don't know," he finally says. "He does have a cover story, and our group needs at least one of us there."

"I don't want either one of you to go back. Can't you just appoint someone else to run your group?"

"It's not that simple."

I stop, spinning to face him. "Why isn't it?"

"We're still part of the resistance, Ivy."

"But why does one of you have to go back? Why can't you just work here?"

Placing a hand on my back, he guides me forward. "It's up to the Commander, and we don't know anything yet. Don't worry about that right now, okay?"

"Kinda hard not to."

"Just try." He glances at me as we walk, his hand still on my back. "That part of you hasn't changed—your constant worrying."

That line reopens the void in my chest, and I shiver, balling my hands in my pockets. I know I've changed. As desperately as I try to cling to life from before, I know there's no going back. All I can do now is rebuild and hope to leave the mess of broken pieces behind. But hearing that he's noticed my change, too, is different. The original image of me that he had is shattered, and until now, I hadn't realized how much I desperately wanted to maintain that.

"Is that a bad thing?" I ask. "That I've changed?"

Noticing the uncertainty in my voice, Nixon stops walking. "What? No. No, change is good."

"But I'm not the same person as before."

Facing me, he places his hands on my biceps and inhales deep, letting his gaze wander before settling on me. "At your core, you're still the same you. We've been through some shit, and neither of us will ever be exactly the same again. You're stronger now—braver—but you're still the same kind, gentle person. I could tell when you let that scavenger go."

"You were pissed about that."

He smirks. "In the moment, yeah, but… I understand. You didn't want to see someone hurt. You wanted to help; that's who you are." The orange streetlights cast a fire in his bright eyes. Their tenderness has returned, thawing the ice in my chest.

I drop my eyes to our feet. "When I killed… *him*… there was a part of me that wanted to save him. Like, stop the bleeding or get help." I shake my head. "I felt guilty for what I did, but almost more guilty for entertaining the thought of saving him."

"See?" His hands move down to mine, holding them tight. "You're still you, and you'll feel more like yourself once things settle down."

I doubt it, but if he can see that, maybe there is a fragment of the real me left. Buried under the ashes of my torched life, but there. One day, I'll dig it up and hold on to it, cherish it. Wyatt took almost everything from me; I won't let him take that, too.

I stare at mine and Nixon's hands between us, taking comfort in the feel of his callused palms and admiring the tiny scars that decorate the tops of his knuckles. He runs a thumb over the back of my hand, sending a wave of warmth throughout me that makes me forget about the sting of the cold on my face.

"Do you still feel the same?" I ask. "About us?"

My heart skips as soon as the words come out, and anxiety twists deeper in my stomach with each seemingly endless second that passes. We'll never go back to how we were—I know that—but I need to know if there's anything left, anything that can be salvaged. The few times we've spent alone have whittled away at the wedge between us, but I need to hear him say it. I need to know if this is for real.

"Yes," Nixon says. "It never went away."

I look up at him. "What do we do about it?"

"I want to be with you," he says in a gentle voice. That mask of his falls away, showing me all of him—his fears, his strengths, his insecurities. "I care about you. But if you're not ready—"

"I am." I step closer, leaving only a couple of inches between us. "I know it's technically 'wrong,' but I care about you, too."

He smiles—a genuine one. It's beautiful and warm and comforting, and I can't contain my own.

"You know," he says, leaning closer and resting his forehead against mine, "I'm going to get in a lot more trouble for this."

"We don't have to tell anyone."

His earthy scent envelops me. Heat radiates from him, seeping into me and latching onto my heart, tugging me closer.

"Hiding it will only make it worse." One of his fingers trails up my arm and over my collarbone, and my breath catches in my throat. "We'll tell someone soon—once we're all settled in."

Nixon loops an arm around my waist, pressing our bodies together. His heart drums against my chest, and the beat of my own picks up. He closes his eyes and hesitates for a moment, as if questioning whether we should do this.

For a moment, I'm teleported back to the Red Zone with Wyatt—his hands on me, his lips devouring every inch they could, the menacing words he'd whisper in my ear. My skin crawls at the reminder, and I'm tempted to recoil.

"Are you okay?" Nixon asks, pulling his head back slightly.

"Yeah," I say, though he doesn't look convinced.

I focus completely on him, telling myself he isn't the same as Wyatt. He's never hurt me. He's someone I can trust.

The safety his presence brings resurfaces from the trench it was buried in. It fights back the thoughts of Wyatt and Nolan and the Red Zone. It silences my fears and doubts, and wraps me in a blanket of peace.

"I want this," I whisper, draping my arms over his shoulders.

A small smile pulls at his lips before they find mine. It's gentle at first—a soft brush that makes my stomach flip and immerses me in a wave of euphoria. Our mouths move against one another with ease, and I savor everything from his taste to the warmth that radiates from him.

Heat courses through my body. One of his hands caresses my face, and my heart races, thumping heavily against my chest. Even through my shirt and his jacket, I know he must feel it, too.

Everything else dissolves. All of my worries melt, and I can't help smiling against his lips.

"I've wanted to do that since we were at Eli's," he murmurs, pulling back.

A couple walks past us, hand in hand, without paying us much attention. The man's speech is slightly slurred as he asks his stumbling partner if she wants to get something to eat. I ignore them, not caring about anyone else at this moment. Nixon's concentration is broken, though. He turns his head and watches until they round the strip of buildings and their voices fade. I squeeze his hand, and his attention turns back to me.

"I have to tell you something," he says, tucking a strand of hair behind my ear.

"What is it?"

His eyes search mine for a moment. "Remember that girl Seb and I followed? The one whose dad gave me that picture of his missing wife and son?"

I nod, the woman's face threatening to reappear in my mind.

"My meeting tomorrow has to do with that. The Commander's putting together a squad for me. We're going to find that man Seb and I saw and tell him about his wife."

"You're leaving? When?"

"Day after tomorrow."

"No." I draw back. "No. You can't."

"Ivy, I have to."

"We just got here! Why would he even approve of that?"

"I promised the guy I would do whatever I can to help. He knows I'm with the resistance, and if I went back on that, it wouldn't look good."

"That's what you care about? Making the resistance 'look good'?"

I expected him to have to leave again, but not this soon. Not when things are just calming down and we're starting to trust each other again.

"He deserves to know what happened to his wife," Nixon says. "You and I both know what it's like to lose someone and live without knowing exactly what happened to them."

He's right, as usual, but that doesn't make me okay with this. That doesn't mean it's safe for him. We weren't very far from the wall when we saw that girl. It was in an area infested with soldiers and re-education camps, not to mention the scavengers. Those were only the threats we encountered, too. There could be more.

"And the Commander wants me to bring him and his daughter back here," Nixon says, "where they'll be safe."

If they even make it back. I shake my head, erasing the thought. "Do Liam and Seb know?"

"No. I wanted to tell you first."

The thought of never seeing him again, of never hearing his voice or feeling his arms around me, makes my chest sink in and my lungs shrivel.

"Please don't go," I say, my voice shaky. I swallow the lump in my throat, not wanting to cry in front of him. "I don't want to lose you again."

He reaches for my hand and pulls me toward him again. "I'll be safe. I'll have two scouts and a medic with me." He rubs my back in wide, gentle motions, as if trying to draw all of the anxiety out of me. "I'd much rather stay here with you, but I have to do this."

"I know," I whisper, and I hate it and admire it all at once. "I want to come with you."

"No."

"Nixon—"

"You're going to stay here where it's safe. If something were to happen out there, I don't know that I could protect you—especially with two other refugees."

"I don't need you to protect me."

He smiles. "You're still incredibly stubborn. But you're not trained. Bringing you will only put you in danger." Tightening his arm around me, he molds me into him and presses his lips to my forehead. "It's only a couple days. I'll be back; I promise."

36. Change on the Rise

Ivy

I wake up two days later to voices—Seb's first, followed by Nixon's. Curled up in the center of the bed, I turn to find that Liam's gone, and his clothes from last night are thrown in the corner by the window. The morning's low light finds its way into the room, reaching across the wood floor.

Sleep lingers at the edges of my mind. Turning on my other side, I pull the covers tighter around me, tempted to slip back into unconsciousness and relive the other night over and over. The kiss we shared replays in my head, and I smile to myself. But what Nixon told me afterward interrupts it, and I squint at the digital clock. 8:07.

He leaves today.

I kick the blankets off and stumble to the dresser across the room. Pulling open the top drawer, I sift through the clothes I got yesterday and settle on the first pair of pants and long-sleeved shirt I find. As I get dressed, dread crawls over me like an icy chill. Once Nixon leaves this camp, anything can happen to him. I know he's strong and has been on countless missions before, but that was before he was a wanted man.

Although we didn't have any time alone together yesterday, he reassured me—and the others—that he'd be fine and this is something he has to do. No matter how many times he says it, though, it doesn't make a difference. It's dangerous out there, and no amount of training or confidence changes that.

I exit the room and find the other three in the living room.

"Oh, hey," Liam says from the couch. "I was about to come wake you."

"For what?" I ask, crossing the room and pushing aside the decorative pillow on the club chair before sitting.

"Our… Commander wants to see us—all of us."

"Why?" I look from him to Nixon, who's reclining in the matching chair on the other side of the end table. He's wearing the same all-black outfit as when we left Eli's, and his hair is twisted into a neat bun. "This mission doesn't involve us."

"Don't know," Liam says.

I sink back into the leather and roll my eyes. I'm not ready to see him again. Aside from Nixon, none of us had to meet with him yesterday, which I was grateful for—but less than forty-eight hours is nowhere near enough time to gather my thoughts and be in the same room as him again. I'm fairly confident, though, that it won't be some long-winded bullshit apology, since Seb's going to be there.

"Maybe we'll finally get an assignment," Seb says beside Liam.

"You won't be getting an assignment for a while," Liam says. "And if that were the case, Ivy wouldn't be there."

"Who knows? Maybe the Commander sees the same potential in her as I do." Seb winks at me, and I laugh.

"You realize you're talking about the same girl who had a mental breakdown at TCG, right?" I say.

Seb waves a hand in the air. "The past is the past. You're a badass now, and I still vote for you being in the resistance."

"Don't count on that," I say.

"You should think about it," Liam says. "At the very least, it could be a way to release all that pent-up aggression."

"Shut up, Liam." I toss the pillow at him.

He smacks it away before it hits him, and it tumbles to the floor. "See?"

"What do you think, Nixon?" Seb asks, plucking the pillow from the floor and stuffing it under his head, stretching his legs out.

I look at Nixon, realizing he hasn't spoken since I came out here. After his meeting yesterday, he was quieter than normal, and he became more reserved as the day stretched on. With his departure almost here, I think it's finally setting in just how dangerous this mission is.

Resting his fingertips against his temple, he shrugs. "Depends on what the future of our group looks like."

"Oh, yeah," Seb says. "You're on probation."

"Yup." Nixon sighs and drops his hand. "And with Piper's recent demotion, the resistance is stretched even thinner." He turns to me and offers a half-smile. "Either way, though, we can find a place for you."

I'm pissed he's on probation. He's still technically the Green Zone's leader, but he has to be supervised in everything he does relating to the resistance—either by Liam, the Commander himself, or someone appointed to him. Thankfully, that's as severe as his punishment gets, but the probation won't be lifted until he can 'prove' himself again.

Piper, on the other hand, got it much worse. Not only was she demoted and barred from all leadership positions, but she's not allowed to carry out any missions or be involved in anything resistance-related for the next thirty days. On top of that, she has scouts trailing her, watching her every move.

From the corner of my eye, I catch Liam watching us, his relaxed expression from just moments ago now hardened.

"What's with the sudden change of heart?" he asks. "Just a few days ago, you completely shut down the idea."

"I let the mission get the best of me," Nixon says nonchalantly. "We were all tired and irritable."

"Really?" Liam asks. His mouth dips into a frown. "Because you couldn't stand being near each other until I saw you both in the bunker."

My body tenses with panic. What happened in the bunker can easily be brushed off as Nixon helping me through a panic attack—and that's true from what Liam saw—but what about the time we've spent together since then? I rode with Nixon from the outpost and went with him to see Lacey. Liam wasn't too happy about either of those, but he let it go. He could've seen us on the terrace, too, though. Or maybe he noticed I left the other night and just never brought it up.

"We've talked things out," Nixon says. "No hard feelings."

"Just like that?" Liam asks, leaning forward. "I know you—you don't forgive easily."

I shoot Seb a pleading look for him to diffuse the situation like he normally does. The last thing I want brought up is the relationship between me and my brother's leader, especially today. There will be plenty of time for the arguing I know will follow once Nixon's back.

Seb takes the cue, sitting up. "We should get ready to head out," he says. "James should be here soon."

Liam doesn't move, though, and his gaze remains fixed on Nixon. "I don't want my sister getting hurt."

Is he referring to me joining the resistance as one of Nixon's subordinates, or something else?

"No one will let that happen," Nixon says.

"One of us will always be out there with her if that time comes," Seb adds.

"I never said I was joining." Standing, I swallow back the paranoia that's begun bubbling inside of me and take on a more light-hearted tone when I add, "And there's no way in hell I'd ever take orders from you, Liam."

We climb the grand staircase without James this time. Unlike when we first came here, the building is buzzing with activity. Men and women in their crisp business clothes pass by with papers and folders, offering us a subtle nod or ignoring us completely. Chatter drifts from open offices—two men discussing guard shifts, a woman on the phone talking about refugee placement. The normality of it all makes my head spin, and I struggle to comprehend how all of this is possible.

Walking up the next set of stairs, I watch Nixon in front of me, still wishing there was some way I could go with him. It doesn't matter how long he's gone; all I'm going to be able to think about is whether or not he's okay—just like in the Red Zone—and I hate it. I wish I could go back to hating him, or at least feeling indifferent, so I wouldn't have to make myself sick worrying.

We make it to the third floor and navigate the maze of endless halls once more. The double pocket doors come into view as we round a corner, and anxiety twists up my spine. This feels like the auction all over again, even though this is Nixon's choice. I understand his reasoning and admire his willingness to help people, but that doesn't make it any easier. It doesn't keep the nausea from swirling in my stomach or his potential death from playing in my mind like the nightmares I had for six weeks.

"Wait out here," Nixon tells us, pausing near the full-length window at the beginning of the final hall. "He'll talk with you guys once my squad's finished." Without waiting for any of us to respond, he walks briskly toward the double doors and knocks. A moment later, he disappears inside.

Seb slides down the wall beside the window until he's seated on the floor and winces, wrapping an arm around his abdomen.

"How're you feeling?" I ask, sitting beside him.

"Great," he lies. Probably noticing my disbelief, he laughs and says, "Could be worse. At least the dick who shot me had horrible aim."

"That doesn't mean you're ready for missions," Liam says. "Honestly, Nixon isn't either."

"Yeah, well, you know how he is," Seb says, stretching his legs out. "Once his mind's made up, there's no talking him out of it."

Liam shoves his hands in his pockets and props a shoulder against the wall, facing us. "I'm worried about him being out there alone."

"He has a squad," I say.

"But no one he knows," Liam says. "Normally that wouldn't matter, but after everything that's happened…"

Nixon's going to struggle. He's already had a hard enough time readjusting. If he's not careful, the same thing that happened with Seb could happen on this mission, and Liam won't be there to help.

I pick at my nails in my lap and glance at the double doors down the hall. The Commander doesn't know what Nixon's going through or how this mission could play out. I'm tempted to barge in and beg him to call it off, to send another person in place of Nixon, but force myself to remain seated. All that would do is piss Nixon off and make him appear incapable of doing his job when he's trying to prove the exact opposite. But who's he trying to prove that to—us or himself?

"He's strong," I say, "and he knows he has people back here who are safe and care about him." Liam's eyebrows go up and I quickly add, "You guys, Adam, Lacey…"

"As long as they don't run into any trouble," Seb says, "he'll be fine. And they'll be close to the outpost in case anything does happen."

"And if they get close to the walls?"

"They shouldn't. I can't see the Commander allowing anyone to get too close besides smuggling people in and out."

"I wonder what's going on in the Northern Unity right now," Liam says. He gazes out the window over his shoulder, gnawing on the inside of his cheek.

Seb shrugs and tilts his head back. "If it wasn't for all of the innocent people there, I'd say I'd like to see it go up in flames. Fuck that place."

That's not what Liam's worried about, though. Of course he cares about what happens to the innocent civilians and, more importantly, his group, but I know that's not what's on his mind.

"Addison's okay," I say. "I miss her, too."

I never really realized that until now. These past few days, I haven't thought about her at all—not since she drove us to the border. So much has happened, and I've been overwhelmed with everything from our exodus to reliving what happened in the Red Zone. The people I've traveled with have been my main concern, and I feel guilty.

Now, my chest aches with how much I miss my best friend. Had she been able to come with us, all of this would've been a lot more bearable. She could always make the blow of any devastating event softer and distract me from the chaos that surrounded me. We could tell what was wrong with one another without having to say anything, and even when there weren't words to take away the other's pain, just being in each other's presence helped. It's been that way since we were kids, and over the years, that effect has extended to Liam, too, long before they started dating.

"That's why you want to go back," I say—mostly to myself, but Liam hears it.

"I wish I could be with her," he admits, "and you. The three of us, like it used to be."

"It'll never be like it used to."

He turns away from the window but doesn't look at me. "I know that."

"You never know," Seb says. "Maybe we can bring her out here."

"She's the daughter of the Police Chief," I say, "who used to be best friends with our dad. Dragging her out here would put her and the camp in danger." Liam shifts his weight. "I'm not saying it's impossible to see her again, just not out here."

"I know," Liam says, and forces a smile. "Only thing I'm not looking forward to when seeing her again is how much she'll talk about you."

"Or how we'll both completely ignore you when we're together?"

His smile widens into a more authentic one. "Yeah, that too."

"Damn," Seb says, "you make the poor dude the third wheel of his own relationship?"

I laugh. "He's been the third wheel since we were kids. It's not my fault he decided to go after my best friend—which is still so gross to think about."

"So don't think about it," Liam says. "Who knows? Maybe she'll be your sister-in-law one day."

"Aside from the fact that she'd be marrying *you*, I'd love that."

A door at the end of the hall slides open, and we go quiet, all of us looking toward it as three people file out. Two women and a man, all wearing the same all-black outfit, complete with tactical belts. They walk at a brisk pace with their heads held high and shoulders squared as if they're about to go to war, which they may as well be. As they pass us, I spot the resistance tattoo on the man's inner wrist.

"Is there a system behind your tattoos?" I ask once the group disappears from view. The door is still open, but Nixon hasn't come out.

"Yeah," Seb says. "Scouts, like me and Nixon, have it beneath the inner left ankle. Logistics, behind the left ear; medics, inner right wrist; hackers, below the right collarbone."

"Helps us know occupations and who's safe," Liam adds. "Although members can be cross-trained. Like Eli—medic is his main occupation, but he was trained as a scout, too."

"What about you guys?" I ask. "Have either of you been cross-trained?"

"Nah," Seb says. "I haven't had an interest, and Liam is only good at being a nerd."

Liam chuckles. "I'd rather be a nerd than a punching bag. But we're trained in basic stuff from other fields. Like, basic first-aid, shooting, self-defense—that kind of stuff."

"Why the sudden interest?" Seb asks with a hint of eagerness. "Still thinking of joining?"

I shake my head. "Just something I've noticed."

Nixon finally emerges and strides toward us, folding the map in his hands and tucking it into his back pocket. I push myself to my feet, and Liam and I each hold a hand out to Seb, helping him up. He winces as he straightens up and secures his arm around his torso again.

"He's ready for you," Nixon says as he nears us. His expression is blank, but underneath it, I sense the same anxiety the rest of us feel. "My squad and I are heading out."

My stomach drops. This is it.

"You sure you're up for this?" Seb asks.

"I've done worse," Nixon says. That's not the point, though, and he knows that. After a short pause, he adds, "It's a Special Ops team. We'll be fine."

A strained silence pulses between the four of us, weighed down by the same collective thought between Seb, Liam, and me. We're worried about him. My reason may be different from theirs, but that doesn't change the fact that we're all aware he isn't ready for this yet, no matter how much he tries to convince us otherwise.

"Good luck out there," Liam says, giving Nixon a hug and a couple of pats on the back. "Be careful."

Seb steps forward next, doing the same thing while being mindful of his injury. "Love you, man. Don't die."

Nixon smirks. "You're not getting rid of me that easily."

He hesitates in front of me, and I catch Liam watching us. That same scrutinizing look as when Nixon asked me to go with him to see Lacey returns, and my paranoia resurfaces.

Nixon holds out his hand, and I step into his one-armed embrace, wishing it could be more but knowing that's not possible right now. In the half second with his arm around me, I take comfort in his hand on my back and the warmth of his body against mine. Once he steps back, it vanishes.

"Take care of each other," Nixon says to all of us. "Listen to whatever the Commander tells you, and take your jobs seriously."

"We're getting jobs?" Seb asks. "Like what?"

Nixon shrugs. "You'll find out from him. No missions though, Seb. And don't give Liam a hard time with all of your whining."

"Just because you said that, I'm going to make his life hell."

"I'll lock your ass outside," Liam says.

"And Ivy," Nixon says, "remember what we said about following orders?"

"Pretty sure you just said I had to follow *your* orders," I say.

"Just try to keep your outbursts to a minimum, okay?"

I roll my eyes but smile. "No promises."

Nixon smiles, too. It's faint, but there, and just like at the auction, I etch his face into my mind, paying extra attention to the way the incline of his mouth makes the scar along his jaw lift and his eyes brighter.

He cocks his head toward the Commander's office. "Head in for your meeting. I'll see you guys in a couple days."

He turns before we can say anything else and heads down the adjacent hall. I watch him, resisting the urge to run after him and wrap my arms around him, to beg him to stay. Every footfall makes my heart sink deeper. Even with the thick carpet and the growing distance between us, I swear I can feel each of his steps reverberating through me and echoing in my head. When he disappears from view, I remain frozen, as if expecting him to come back.

"Let's go," Seb says, tapping my elbow as he passes me and leads the way to the open office.

I reluctantly follow with Liam behind me, forcing myself not to look back. I try to tell myself Nixon will be okay, that he's strong and knows what he's doing, but that doesn't ease my electrified nerves or the roiling of my stomach. Maybe if Seb were able to go with him, I'd feel a bit better. At least then I'd know he was with a scout he knew and trusted.

Or, if I were trained, I'd go.

That's why Nixon said I couldn't go. It's the same reason he said Liam's original plan for us escaping the Northern Unity wouldn't work, when we were in the Blue Zone. If I was trained, not only could I go with him, Seb, or Liam on missions, but I could protect myself. I wouldn't be someone they'd always have to worry about saving.

Liam shuts the office door behind us, and our father turns, pulling a black binder down from one of the bookshelves.

"There you are," he says. "I hope you three are settling in okay."

"Nixon said you have jobs for us," I say, taking on the same bitter tone as the last time we saw him.

"I do." He drops the binder on his desk with a thunk and opens it, thumbing through the laminated pages. "I'm also working on your housing arrangements, which should be solidified by the time he gets back. Until then, you'll remain at the hotel."

Seb sinks into one of the chairs across from the desk. "Will we be together?"

"Two and two, more than likely," my father says.

"You do that for everyone who comes here?" Liam asks.

"We do, but that doesn't mean it's permanent." He pulls three papers from one of the laminate cases and passes the first one to Seb. "Sebastien?"

"Yes, sir," Seb says.

"You'll be one of our watchtower guardsmen on the northeast border. Dr. Reed informed me of your injury, so I'm starting you off with five-hour shifts—four days a week. You'll be paired with another guard until you're cleared, and we'll accommodate you as you heal. Any questions?"

"No, sir."

"Good. If you need to cut back your hours at all, come to me directly." He holds a second paper out toward Liam, who pauses by the second chair and takes it. "Liam, you'll work with our group of hackers at the library. The second floor is blocked off and reserved specifically for the five of you."

"How will hacking be useful here?" Liam asks, glancing over the paper in his hand. From where I'm standing beside the door, I can make out his name scrawled across the top and the address for the library. "I can't get past the Society's firewall."

"Have you met Nadia?" my father asks.

"Not directly, but I know who she is."

"She works as a journalist in the Yellow Zone and hosts a pro-Society blog."

I cringe at that thought, but understand having to play the part of a loyal citizen in order to survive.

"Your job," he continues, "is to decrypt hidden messages in the source code as well as any files we receive. Anything that can't be relayed to me over the radio will be found there."

"Sounds easy enough," Liam says.

"These positions are temporary," my father says, making eye contact with Liam, then Seb. "While they're useful to the resistance, I won't hesitate to put you back out in the field if necessary." He looks up at me, extending the final paper.

"You want me to work for you?" I ask, crossing my arms over my chest.

"You won't answer to me." For a split second, that remorseful look flashes over his face again. His brown eyes are soft, holding all the apologies I won't allow him to say. "The committee and I talked it over, and we thought it'd be best to pair you with Lacey, since you know her. You'll be helping her in the agricultural department. Nothing too extreme—just whatever she needs help with."

Agriculture? That's the best he could find for me? I adore Lacey, but nothing about the assignment sounds the least bit appealing. I want to do *more*. Maybe not something resistance-related, but something that has more of an impact. Something that's actually useful and in some way goes against the Society.

"No," I say.

My father's eyebrows furrow, making the newly acquired wrinkles in his forehead deepen. "No?"

"Ivy," Liam groans, looking back at me.

"I want to be part of the change like them." I gesture to Liam and Seb. "Not just watch it unfold."

"Sweetheart—" my father starts, but clears his throat and corrects himself. "Ivy, you're not part of the resistance. Without any training or proper—"

"I don't care." I finally move away from the door, fueled by a sudden burst of confidence. "My life was ripped apart by the Society. I spent six weeks with the Elites. If anyone's going to play a role in all of this, it should be me."

My father studies me, his expression reverting back to that of a Commander. It's unnerving how quick and flawless the switch is, as if he's a totally different person. As if the man I always looked up to isn't there and I'm staring into the face of a stranger. The only thing that reminds me of who he was is the slightly crooked smile that finds its way to his lips.

He returns the paper to its place in the binder and flips through it again. "I have one other job that might suit you. It's at one of our intake centers."

"What's that?" I ask.

"Think of it like the transport centers in the Northern Unity, where refugees wanting to be part of the camp are held until they're cleared. You'd conduct interviews with them, get their backgrounds, reasons for wanting to seek refuge, help them adjust… Sound like something you'd like?"

"Yes." It's a start. At least I'd be helping the people out there in some way.

My father slips a page out of the binder and circles his desk, retrieving a pen from one of the drawers. He writes my name across the top of the page and signs his at the bottom before holding it out. "It's done then." I reach for it, but he pulls it back just as my fingers brush against it. "Under one condition."

Rolling my eyes, I drop my hand to the desk. "What?"

"Try to work with me. I understand this is difficult, but I'm trying my best and need you to meet me halfway."

He *understands*? *He's* the reason for all this. Everything was preventable; all he had to do was stay.

I snatch the paper from his hand and step back. "Fine."

"Whenever you two are ready," he says, focusing on Liam and me, "I want to talk about everything. I don't expect anything to go back to normal, but I'd at least like us to come to an understanding."

From the corner of my eye, I see Liam glance at me as if expecting me to blow up again. *I* expect myself to blow up. But my anger has diminished over the past couple of days. It's still lurking at the back of my mind, but there are more important things to worry about right now, and I've just been given a new job. Father or not, he holds the power to reassign me to my original position. It's best not to push him too much.

"I think we need a little more time," Liam says coolly, "but soon."

A rapid knock on the door breaks my focus. Before my father can speak, the door slides open and his assistant steps inside, clutching a manila folder to her chest.

"This better be urgent, Cora," my father says, not masking his impatience. "I'm in the middle of something."

"It is, sir," Cora says. Her high heels click against the wood floor with urgency, and she holds out the folder with a subtle tremor in her hand. "The alpha outpost has been attacked."

Seb sits up in the chair beside me, his expression morphing from relaxed to alert.

My stomach twists into a knot. Alpha outpost? How many do they have? And which one were we at? Worse, which one is Nixon heading toward?

My father swipes the folder from her, eyes wide. Dropping it on the desk, he flips it open and braces his palms against the wood, scanning the first page—what looks like a transcript.

"Jackson just relayed it to me," Cora continues. "Luckily, it happened as the new team was relieving the current. They had more manpower, but—"

"One KIA," my father mutters. His shoulders slump forward.

"The attackers retreated," Cora offers, clasping her hands together in front of her.

"Which outpost is that?" I ask. My voice is soft and squeaky, the panic constricting my throat.

My father shakes his head and flips to the next page. "This was all done by scavengers?"

My legs begin to tremble and I take an unconscious step back, keeping a hand on the back of Seb's chair for support.

"Yes, sir," Cora says. "The scouts claimed their weapons looked brand new, with plenty of ammo, as if recently provided for them."

"By the Society, no doubt." My father runs a hand through his shaggy blond hair. "Damn it." He stands tall, jaw tight. "Have Jackson send backup for the squad that just left and tell them to change routes. And call for an emergency committee meeting."

The room spins. The constricted feeling grows, immersing me in the surge of panic. I focus on my breathing, but the icy-hot sensation flooding my veins fights for control.

It is the same outpost. The same one Adam is at and Nixon is heading toward.

With a curt nod, Cora scurries out of the office.

"Call off the mission," I force out through clenched teeth.

"You three are dismissed," my father says.

"Call off the fucking mission!"

A gentle hand rests on my back. Liam stands beside me with the same enraged eyes as my father.

"The scavengers have retreated." Closing the folder, my father picks it up along with a second one from one of his drawers. "The additional squad will provide them backup if needed, and they'll be able to gather intel while they're out there."

"You're going to get them killed," I argue. I wish I could yell or at the very least keep my voice from shaking.

My father sighs. "It's a Special Ops group; they know what they're doing." He picks up the binder and slides it into the crook of his arm with the folders. "Nixon will be fine. The backup squad will notify him of the attack and they'll change course."

"But—"

"If it will make you feel better, pay Jackson a visit. He's head of communications for the outposts. Cora can direct you to his office." He hastily strides from behind his desk. Seb stands, and we follow him out of the office. "I need to get to this meeting. In the meantime, James will put together transportation arrangements for your assignments."

With a final glance over his shoulder at us, he picks up his pace down the hall, each step full of purpose and each passing second full of uncertainty. He disappears from view, and I stop only a few yards outside his office.

I knew it was dangerous. I knew Nixon shouldn't have gone. But attacking the *outpost?* The scouts there told us the scavengers never bothered them. That was before we were abducted and arranged to be traded back to the Society, though. The soldiers at the nearest re-education camps were aware of our location, and the scavengers must've told them about the gunfight.

If the outpost is compromised, what does that mean for the camp?

"Hey," Liam says, stepping into my line of vision, "everything's going to be okay."

"He's your best friend," I say. "How are you not worried?"

"I am, but I've seen what Nixon can do. He's going to make it back."

Seb stops a few paces ahead and turns back to us. "Gotta trust your comrades. If Nixon feels it's unsafe once he's notified, he'll call it off."

I don't want to wait for that to happen. The scavengers may have retreated, but that doesn't mean they're not out there watching, waiting for their next chance to attack. Especially if the Society is pulling the strings. And if Nixon learns a member was killed, he won't want to call off the mission. It'll only fuel him to push forward.

"I don't necessarily think the Society is behind it," Seb says, like that's supposed to take the edge off.

"Why not?" I ask. "This is exactly the kind of thing they'd do."

He shrugs. "Using people outside the walls to do their dirty work? Sure. But they wouldn't just give those people high-end weapons."

"We already know they trade people for supplies."

"And they get the lower-end shit—the Society's leftovers."

"Especially if they're heightening their security inside the walls," Liam adds. "They'd stockpile as much as possible for the military in case of an uprising. And I don't see the President approving of something like this without any certainty of the outcome."

"Right," Seb says. "So unless there's someone who would just hand out firearms in hopes of taking over a heavily armed outpost, I don't see it. It's possible, but not very likely."

There *is* potentially someone like that, though. An armament manufacturing executive would have plenty of firearms at their disposal, especially with that same person being part of the Enlightened Society.

I shake my head, pushing the thought to the back of my mind. That would be stupid, especially with, like Liam said, the outcome being uncertain. Still, it's plausible, and people do stupid things when seeking vengeance.

Liam reiterates what Seb said about trusting our comrades as well as the Commander, and goes on to say something about how Eli will be keeping tabs on the outpost, too. But no reassuring words or promises of safety will take away the anxiety that continues to course through me. Nothing changes the fact that Nixon's out there and I'm here, guarded within the city.

How long until Liam is sent outside this camp for a similar mission? Or Seb? I haven't known him long, but he's quickly become someone I care about and don't want to see hurt… again.

The reminder that the Society has the power to rip away what little I have left picks at my mind. Up until now, I've lived with those lurking thoughts, believing there's nothing I can do about it. Maybe I can't offer as much as Nixon or Liam or Seb, but I can do something. The Society may have destroyed the life I had in the Northern Unity, but out here, I'm free.

I have control over what happens from here on. Not them. I need to prove that.

"I want you guys to train me," I blurt out.

Seb and Liam stop the conversation that I wasn't paying attention to, and their attention clicks to me.

"Train you in what, exactly?" Liam asks with eyebrows raised.

I look between the two of them, searching for an answer to give. Train me to shoot? Basic first aid? Hand-to-hand combat? I don't know what I'm capable of doing or what they can teach me, but whatever it is, I don't care. As long as I can do something worthwhile.

"Anything," I say. The shakiness has left my voice. "I want to fight back."

37. Hit the Floor

Nixon

"A little over a mile," I say into the walkie-talkie. "There's a gas station ahead we'll park at. My squad approaches the home; you guys fan out and watch the perimeter."

"Copy that," one of the men from our backup team responds.

I glance over the map in my lap with the new markings of our alternate route. Learning about the ambush of the alpha outpost almost made me call this mission off. Almost. Remembering that little girl and her father out here kept me from doing it, though. They're in danger and have already been tormented by the Society. I may not be able to save everyone, but I want to do what I can. I made a promise I can't go back on, not when that girl's frightened eyes and bruised face push their way to the center of my thoughts.

"Why exactly are we doing this?" the scout beside me asks without taking her eyes off the road. Since piling into the Humvee she's had a permanent scowl, and every sentence that's left her mouth has been short and edged with irritability.

"We help people, don't we?" I say, looking up at the windshield and watching for the gas station.

"Not randoms outside the walls."

"Commander's orders, Nat," the medic says from the backseat.

"I don't like *insiders* coming to our city thinking they can run shit," Nat spits back. She peers at me through narrowed eyes, reminding me of Piper. "What the hell makes you so special?"

"I'm not," I say. "But I *am* the head of this squad, so it's not your place to question me or the mission."

She scoffs. "What makes you qualified to lead a squad, let alone a Special Ops team?"

I suppress a groan and fold the map, tucking it into one of the compartments of my plated vest. "I'm the Green Zone's leader." *For now, at least.* Nat's fingers tighten around the steering wheel, but she doesn't say anything else.

The abandoned gas station comes into view, and a pit of uncertainty opens in my stomach. I didn't tell this group—or the Commander—that the likelihood of this man still being in the area is slim. I left out how I told him to leave a note with details of his next destination. I knew not having an exact location would've prevented the Commander from approving this mission. He would've told me it's too dangerous to aimlessly wander the wasteland, even for Special Ops. Maybe it is, but I couldn't go back on my word, and those people deserve answers and safety. I just hope they're not too far and we can find them before someone else does.

Nat pulls into the gas station and parks behind the tattered building. She unbuckles her seatbelt and shoots her hand out toward me. "Zoe and I will clear the building."

I pass over the gun I've been holding on to for her. "We're heading out as soon as the other squad gets here."

Without a response, she grabs the gun and hops out of the ve-hicle, and Zoe exits from behind me. As soon as the back door shuts, I let out a long exhalation and ready my own weapon. Our backup left not long after us. They should be here any minute.

"Don't let her get to you," Derek, the medic, says. "She's like that with all newbies."

"I don't care as long as she follows orders," I say.

If she were one of my members, though, I would've already put her in her place. I don't have the time or patience to deal with people who can't be bothered to have a shred of respect, but I unfortunately didn't have the opportunity to pick this squad. Thankfully, this is a one-time thing. I don't know what's going to happen once I get back to the camp, but at least I'll be with Liam and Seb. They don't question every little thing I say.

"She's not from the Northern Unity?" I ask.

"No, she is," Derek says. "She just has a superiority complex, like most people from the Yellow Zone."

I scan the treeline outside the windshield. "I wouldn't know—haven't met anyone there except their leader."

"Nadia, yeah, she's the exception—for the most part."

"What about you and Zoe?"

"I'm from the Canadian branch; we help where we can. If I re-member correctly, Zoe came from a settlement further south a year or so ago."

"So she's pretty new."

In the side-view mirror, I see the two women round the side of the building as a second Humvee pulls up behind us.

"Yeah," Derek says, "but she's good. And unlike Nat, she won't give you any problems."

"Let's hope Nat learns her place soon," I say, clipping the walkie-talkie to my vest.

I throw the door open and hop out of the Humvee.

Apprehension washes over me as soon as my boots meet the cracked asphalt. The scavengers shouldn't have come this far out, but that doesn't mean soldiers aren't lurking out here.

Derek joins me on the other side of the vehicle, shouldering his backpack and adjusting his weapon on its sling.

"What's the plan?" Nat asks as she and Zoe approach us, tightening her long ponytail with one hand. The four backup members follow—three men and a woman, all at least a decade older than me.

"The house is in a clearing on the other side of this treeline," I say. "You three are with me"—I gesture toward my squad—"the rest of you let me know when you're in position. You see anything, you notify me."

Our backup immediately breaks off, expressions firm and weapons ready. Two move left into the trees while the other two go right. I walk straight ahead with my squad following close behind. With my gun positioned in front of me, I study the ground as we move forward, just as I did when I was out here with Seb.

Like last time, there are impressions in the dirt—small footprints, unmistakably belonging to a child. Grass has been trampled over, beaten into the soil and dead leaves. Everything is quiet, exactly how we left it a few days ago.

Still, a knot of wariness clenches in my stomach and a prickly sensation crawls up my spine. Maybe it's because of what happened at the outpost a couple of hours ago, but something doesn't feel right. We took an alternate route out here, so we should be fine. Ambush or not, the outpost is still intact, and only ten miles away in case we run into any problems.

The small footsteps become more spaced out and take several sharp turns, weaving between the trees. She was running from something.

Quickening my pace, I survey our surroundings as I follow the tracks. Several more appear in the dirt. Larger, some fresher than others. After a few yards, the smaller prints loop around a trunk and continue for about five more feet—backward—before disappearing. The larger impressions continue ahead, overlapping with one another.

The knot twists in my gut. I tighten my fingers around the handle of my gun and click off the safety, letting my finger dip closer to the trigger. I listen for any noises other than our footsteps, but there's nothing except for the gentle breeze and chirping birds.

The clearing comes into view, and I slow down. In the center of the overgrown yard sits the house—shingles scattered across the property and rotting wood on the verge of collapsing. It's exactly the same as last time, save for the new prints. A part of me hopes they belong to the girl's father, but I know that's not the case. Not with how many there were and their different sizes.

Pausing, I hold a hand up, and my squad stops behind me. Crouching behind one of the trees, I peer at the front porch and then the door. I told the man to tie something to the handle and leave a note to let me know they'd left. There's nothing there. Not even marks in the soil leaving the house.

"You guys in position?" I say into the walkie-talkie on my chest.

"Yes, sir," one of the scouts responds.

"Affirmative. All clear," another one says seconds later.

Standing, I start toward the house, waving my squad forward. Each cautious step fuels the unease that trickles through my veins. It's quiet, which is good, but almost too quiet. Like the wind has stopped whistling and the birds have stopped singing. And maybe I'm imagining it, but the air is colder, too. Even with long sleeves and the vest trapping all my heat, I feel goosebumps pop up on my arms.

Nearing the porch, I notice prints on the steps. Their muddy outlines have crusted onto the mildew-covered wood. The blank door looms in front of me, its frame splintered and worn. No note or any indication he and his daughter left.

"I want every side of this building covered," I say, trying to keep the alarm from seeping into my words. "Get a window view if you can."

Giving a stiff nod, Derek, Nat, and Zoe split up, leaving me in front of the wooden steps. I turn and scan the yard and dense trees, the prickling of my skin intensifying. No soldiers. No Black Hats. No scavengers. Just the dried mud leading up to the door.

I wait a few more seconds, allowing my team to take their places; with a deep breath, I start up the stairs. The stench of mold and stagnant water assaults my nose. Pressure builds in my head as I hold in a cough.

A board creaks under my weight at the top, and I tense, easing my foot off it. Closing in on the exit, I strain to listen for any voices or movement. At first it's silent. Then there's the man's raspy voice and the girl's giggling. Faint, innocent, and chilling.

They shouldn't be here.

A fit of coughing interrupts the girl's laughter, and I cringe with the moan of pain that follows.

Lowering the volume of my walkie-talkie, I secure my fingers around the handle. My heart slams against my ribs, and the door squeals as I pull it open. The man shushes his daughter. An eerie silence settles over the house.

The first room I step into is vacant. Cobwebs cling to the corners and a thick layer of dust coats the plywood subfloor. The empty staircase at the back is missing half of its railing, and what's left of it is warped and decaying. I stick to the walls, examining every inch of the room with my gun poised.

A soft orange glow from the next room stretches across the floor, illuminating a dotted brown trail that tapers off near the doorway.

Blood.

Gunshots pierce the air outside. They're distant—maybe a hundred yards or so away. There's shuffling in one of the rooms above. Dread engulfs me. Adrenaline kicks in, surging through my body.

Uneven footsteps move toward me. I stop beside the entrance to the next room with my back pressed against the wall. Holding my breath, I tighten my grip on my gun and pivot around the corner, the muzzle stopping just inches from the man's chest.

His hollow eyes widen, and he stumbles backward with both hands raised. I scan the room behind him—a demolished kitchen with broken cabinets, busted countertops, and the ceiling sagging at the far end. Beneath one of the broken windows, the girl is huddled against the side of a counter, her face buried in her arms.

"You're here," the man says. His words drip with disbelief, and he cranes his neck to look around me. He lowers his hands, but I keep my gun on him.

He's not wearing the same clothes as the last time I saw him. Neither is his daughter. Both of their outfits look almost new, free of mud and dirt and not hanging from their frail bodies. His limp is still apparent, though, as well as a handful of new scrapes and bruises decorating his arms, face, and neck.

"So are you," I say, keeping my voice low and even. The girl peeks up, her brown eyes brightening when she sees me. A gash cuts through her right temple. It's begun to scab, but the skin around it is pink and swollen. Dried blood streaks the side of her face. "Decided not to go?"

The man shakes his head. "I'm sorry... I didn't..." He glances back at his daughter, who hides her face again. "They surrounded us, interrogated us... I didn't want them to take—"

"Where are they?"

"Upstairs. Three of them."

"Any outside?"

"I'm not sure. They followed my girl. Dragged her back here and asked questions about you and the group you were with." He shakes his head, eyes brimming with tears. "I'm sorry."

The movement I heard on the second floor is right above us. The chirp of a radio cuts through the air, followed by a man's muffled voice and footsteps.

"What did you say?" I ask, not bothering to lower my voice anymore. They already know I'm here.

"You gave us food," the man says. "And I identified you in a picture, but that's all. I don't know anything."

The boots beat against the stairs, reverberating in my head. Gunshots continue to pop outside, drawing closer.

"I found out what happened to your wife," I say. His eyebrows shoot up, and his daughter looks at us. The hope that fills their eyes slashes at my heart. "I'm sorry. One of my members saw her inside the walls, and—"

"Nixon Reed," a voice booms from behind me, "turn around and put your weapons on the ground."

The terror of being recaptured emerges once more, warring with the rational side of my brain. I knew this was a possibility, but that doesn't slow the erratic beat of my heart or fend off the flashbacks that threaten to take control.

"Weapons down!" the soldier barks.

I inhale deeply, fighting back the haunting reminders of the Red Zone. That won't happen again. I prepared for this. My squad prepared for this. I have to trust that they have my back like I have theirs.

Lifting my hands, I turn around and smirk at the three soldiers with their guns on me. "You found me."

"Weapons," one man snarls—a staff sergeant, judging by the insignia on his chest.

Bending over with one hand still raised, I set my gun on the floor and nudge it toward them with my foot before crouching. Unlatching my walkie-talkie, I press the button on the side as the clip snaps against the back and use my other hand to pull each item from my vest. I set the pistol, combat knife, and each magazine down one at a time, still holding down the push-to-talk button.

"Hurry up, asshole," the staff sergeant says, "or I'll shoot you right here."

Once he speaks, I set the walkie-talkie down and stand, glancing at the back door near the stairs where one of my other members should be positioned. The staff sergeant snatches the device up and jerks me forward by my arm.

"Who's on the other end?" he asks, dangling it in front of me.

"No one," I say, which he obviously doesn't believe. "Grabbed it out of habit."

"Any of your friends out there are more than likely dead. No one's coming to save you this time."

The other two men push past us. One shoves the father forward by the shoulder. He winces, grabbing his leg, but doesn't protest. The other yanks the girl up by her wrist, and she cries out as she's dragged toward us.

"What are you doing with them?" I ask.

The man digging his fingers into my bicep ignores the question. Instead, he presses the button of his own radio and says, "We've got him, Mr. Astor."

Astor. I know that name.

The radio chirps, and a young man's voice cuts through. "What about the girl?"

"No sign of her."

"Find her and bring them both to me."

"Yes, sir." Shifting his attention back to me, he says, "Where is she?"

"Like I'd tell you," I say, keeping my eyes on him but watching the front door from my peripheral vision. My team should be closer now after hearing him speak.

The soldier jabs me with his elbow, and pain radiates up my injured side. Grunting, I double over, clutching my ribs. I'm jerked up by my hair, and his knee slams into my stomach. The air is knocked from my lungs. My eyes water, and I let out a combination of a strangled yell and cough.

"Stop!" the girl cries.

The staff sergeant grabs my neck and steadies my face in front of his. "We know she was with you."

Pulling in a couple of ragged breaths, I manage to chuckle. "Fuck off."

Unfazed, he looks past me toward his comrades and their hostages. "Kill them."

"What?" the father says. "No. No, we did everything you said."

"You conspired with a domestic terrorist against the Enlightened Society," the staff sergeant says.

I spin around as the two other men force the father and daughter to their knees in the doorway of the kitchen.

"Don't!" I shout. "You have me. Just take me and leave them alone." Where the hell is my squad?

I survey the room. A gun is held to the back of each hostage's head. Their captors have their full focus on their leader behind me. The man trembles, reaching for his sobbing daughter's hand. I don't stand a chance against these three alone.

"Just take me," I repeat through gritted teeth.

"What's the location of Olivia Clearson?" the staff sergeant behind me asks. "The Commander's camp? Another outpost?"

Without thinking, I lunge toward them, only to be wrenched back. The staff sergeant's arm is secured around my neck, applying pressure to my throat.

"You're going to watch them die," he growls into my ear, "then we're going to hunt down your whore."

I fight against him, struggling to breathe through my constricted airway and the pain in my abdomen. He tightens his grip. The muzzle of my gun is shoved against my temple. The girl's sobs grow louder. Her father drapes an arm over her shoulders, his own face streaked with tears.

The two soldiers move their fingers to their triggers, watching for their leader's signal with flat expressions.

"One more chance, and you might be able to save them," my captor says. "Where is Olivia Clearson?"

I can't let these people die, but I can't let them find Ivy either.

My lips part. No sound comes out. Blood roars in my ears. Panic scratches at the edges of my thoughts.

"I'll—I'll take you," I choke out, hoping that can at least give me back a little more control of the situation. "I'll take you to her."

Saying it makes my stomach roil, but if I can just get their attention off the father and daughter and lead them outside where the scouts are…

The hold on my throat loosens, and the two men in front of me position their weapons down toward the floor.

"Kill the man," the staff sergeant says. "Load the girl up."

"*No!*" I yell when the gun returns to the back of the man's head.

A metal cylinder flies through the broken window behind the gunmen. It ricochets off one of the walls and thuds to the floor, rolling toward us. Everyone's heads whip in the direction of the object, right before it detonates.

Gunfire explodes inside the house. The girl screams. Soldiers yell. A deafening blast throws me off balance. And everything is consumed by blinding white.

End of Book Two

The Few: Book 3
Coming 2022

Acknowledgments

To my phenomenal beta readers, Josh Langlois, Lucie Ataya, Riley Powers, and Jordanna Hanson: This book wouldn't exist with you guys. Each of you helped me shape this story and the characters into what they are now. Thank you for reading over my messy drafts with love and care, letting me rant about writer's block, the long phone calls/voice messages/emails working out plot holes, and for continuously building me up and encouraging me. I'm so thankful to know all of you.

To my editor, Emma O'Connell: You, ma'am, are just simply amazing. Words cannot possibly describe how blessed I am to have you as an editor and friend. Thank you for everything you've done for my books, for being hard on me and not letting me settle for publishing a half-baked book. Chatting with you and reading your snarky comments has literally become my most favorite part of the publishing process.

To my best friend, Callie Gregory: I love you so much and am beyond grateful for our fifteen years of friendship. You're one of the few people who never gave up on me and supported my writing from the very beginning. The nights in middle school when we'd stay up on the phone, writing together and reading our stories out loud (after 9 p.m. because free minutes :P), helped me become the author I am today. Thank you for always believing in me, loving me, and being there for me no matter what.

To my husband, Martin Scurlock: You've stuck with me for seven years so far and pushed me to pursue writing. Almost two years into this author thing, and your undying support keeps me going. You're the best alpha reader, cheerleader, formatter, cover artist, and I.T. guy. Thank you for putting up with my chaotic mind, bringing me coffee and snacks during my long writing sessions, training me with knives so I can accurately write it, and staying up well into the night talking about sporadic pieces of my plot. I love you more than anything and am happy to have you by my side with everything.